WATCHING ROSE

Long past one A.M., lamplight still spills from the first-floor windows at 48 Shorewood Lane. He wonders whether Rose has fallen asleep on the couch in front of the television again, like she did last night. Or maybe she's awake, folding laundry, as she was when he peeked through the window late one night last week.

His boots make a squeaky, crunching sound in the snow as he crosses the small patch of side yard, boldly leaving footprints. At first, he was so careful not to disturb anything, never to leave a sign that he'd been lurking.

Not anymore.

By now, she must have received his first gift. By now, she's puzzled . . . perhaps even wary.

He smiles, imagining what she'll think in the morning when she notices footprints around the house.

Standing on the tips of his toes, he is able to peer through the ground-level window into the house. Through a veil of ivory lace, he plainly sees her sitting on the couch, writing something. Doesn't she know that anyone can see her inside?

Perhaps that's what she wants. Perhaps she knows he's here, watching her. Perhaps she's merely pretending not to be aware of his presence, inwardly taunting him, daring him to reveal himself. But he won't. Not yet. Not until it's time. And when it is, she'll be sorry. She'll beg for mercy.

And he'll laugh.

Just like before.

Just before he kills her

SHE LOVES ME NOT

Wendy Corsi Staub

PINNACLE BOOKS
Kensington Publishing Corp.

PINNACLE BOOKS are published by

Kensington Publishing Corp.
850 Third Avenue
New York, NY 10022

ISBN 0-7394-3254-0

Printed in the United States of America

For Stacey and Roman
on their second wedding anniversary
And for Brody and Mark, with love . . .
But most of all, for Morgan, who solved it.

ACKNOWLEDGMENTS

The author gratefully acknowledges the professional contributions of Ginny Baumgartner and Gena Massarone; the spark of an idea from Samantha Silag Stearns; the career strategizing and emergency child care from Richard Siegel; and the research guidance from Kimberly Omundson. Heartfelt thanks as well to Leslie Fox, Colleen Genett, Caitlin and Maureen Murphy, Wyatt Cadley, and Amy Handler for babysitting in a pinch (one at a time, that is . . . my kids aren't such a handful that they require a childcare team . . . *yet!*). Finally, deepest appreciation to my agent, Laura Blake Peterson, and her assistant, Kelly Going; my editor, John Scognamiglio; and everyone at Kensington, particularly Walter and Steve Zacharius, Laurie Parkin, Doug Mendini, Joan Schulhafer, and Janice Rossi Schaus.

On a personal note, I'd like to thank my family for bearing with my deadline panic; my friends for understanding why I fell off the face of the earth this summer; Eve Marx and Beverly Beaver for understanding what only fellow writers "get"; and the AOL SAHMs, for being there with laughs and support on a daily basis, especially Bethany, Tricia, and Big Grandma Honey, who provided celestial guidance!

Prologue

Her return to consciousness is a prolonged, painstaking process.

Each time she attempts to open her eyes, a blinding pain slices through her skull. When, after a few tries, she finally succeeds in keeping her lids open, she can see only blackness.

Blackness . . .

Again.

Dear God. Was it all a dream?

She turns her head slightly, teeth clenched against the excruciating effort. Now, backlit in a faint glow from some source of light, outlines of furniture begin to emerge around her.

No, it wasn't a dream.

A table . . .

You can see.

A couch . . .

You aren't blind.

A window, covered by a shade, a thin shaft of light seeping in through the crack at the bottom.

But the configuration is all wrong. This isn't her new apartment in Port Richmond. She isn't lying in her bed. She's on a cold, hard floor, splintery-rough wood against her cheek.

Where am I?

What happened?

Her eyelids flutter closed again, the ache in her skull intense. She wants to drift back to that far-off place . . .

But you can't, she tells herself with an urgency born of unadulterated instinct.

Something is wrong.

You have to think.

Images begin to flash back at her.

Leaving the office.

Walking across the parking lot through swirling snow.

Unlocking the car door.

Climbing nervously into the driver's seat, unaccustomed to driving on icy roads.

Suddenly sensing that she isn't alone.

A faint rustling in the back seat, then—

Explosive pain in her head.

And now . . .

This.

Where am I?

She forces her eyes open again. Agony. Throbbing. A wave of nausea washes over her. Swallowing acrid bile, she relinquishes control over her eyelids. But she can't allow herself to drift away. Not yet. First, she must make sense of what is happening.

Her other senses—senses upon which she instinctively relied for years, too many years—are stirring to attention.

The air smells musty—like the interior of a car with mildewed upholstery. Or the trunk in Aunt Lucinda's dining room, where she keeps the holiday table linens.

There are sounds. Hushed, rhythmic sounds. A clock ticking. Her own audible breathing. And a steady *thud, thud, thud,* punctuated by crackling, popping . . . a fire? Someone poking a burning log?

Steeling herself for renewed torture, she drags her eyelids open again; surveys her shadowy surroundings.

Couch . . .

Window . . .

Turn your head.

Oh, God, it hurts.

Farther.

The unmistakable orange flickering of firelight.

On a low table, in its glow, what looks like a snowglobe. The glass dome is swirling with white, as though somebody has just shaken it and set it back down.

Then she sees the silhouette of a human form, just beyond the table.

Panic grips her.

Somebody is sitting there, in front of the fire, only a few feet away.

Who is it?

What's happening?

The figure changes position, leans toward her, speaks. "Oh, good, you're awake. It's about time, Angela. I wouldn't want you to miss this."

The voice is chillingly familiar.

The name is not.

As the figure rises and walks across creaking floorboards toward her, her thoughts swirl as frantically as the artificial snow within the glass globe.

Angela . . .

The shadowy figure looms over her, brandishing a poker, its tip glowing red-hot.

One final coherent thought takes shape before giving way to sheer terror:

Who is Angela?

One

"Mommy!"

Rose Larrabee braces herself as her three-year-old rushes toward her across the toy-strewn floor of the day-care center. The place is nearly deserted, as it always is at this hour, with only Leo and one remaining adult on the premises.

She smiles as her son bounds toward her, a miniature Olympic runner executing hurtles: Tinker Toy skyscrapers and precariously stacked wooden blocks.

"Hi, sweetie." She winces as Leo throws himself into her arms with blunt force, slamming his wiry three-year-old body painfully against her rib cage. He greets her this way every afternoon when she arrives to pick him up from Toddler Tyme. The relief of having him safely in her arms again is well worth the impact against her fragile chest with its telltale scar.

Rose buries her face in Leo's light brown hair, inhaling the sweet smell of him—a hint of peanut butter mingling with the distinct scent of Play-Doh. She smiles when she strokes his head, her fingertips encountering a matted, straw-like clump. "Did you get grape jelly in your hair again at lunch time, Leo?"

"Nope." He tilts his head away from her and shakes it vehemently.

"Are you sure?" She strokes the sticky patch.

"Yup."

"He's sure that it wasn't *grape* jelly." Gregg Silva grins, coming up beside them. "It was strawberry."

Rose smiles at Toddler Tyme's newest employee. "He's quite the literal kid." She leans forward to set Leo on his feet.

"Aren't they all," Gregg chuckles. "We thought strawberry jam would be fitting since Valentine's Day is this week."

Valentine's Day. Oh, Lord. Rose forgot all about it—and it's tomorrow. She already bought both kids their boxes of cards to hand out at school, thank goodness. She gets a fifteen-percent employee discount on everything at the bookstore, including stationery.

Of course, Jenna grumbled about the generic cards Rose picked out for her, but Leo was perfectly content with the construction vehicle theme on his valentines. Bulldozers, dump trucks, cement mixers . . . these days, he's into anything that digs and or has anything to do with dirt.

Watching Gregg reach down to deftly fasten the top button on Leo's miniature navy and teal striped rugby shirt, Rose is struck by renewed surprise that this grown man—single, thirtyish, childless—has such a way with kids.

Gregg has only been employed as a day-care provider for a few weeks. Toddler Tyme's overly chatty director, Candy Adamski, told Rose that he recently moved here to eastern Long Island. He has a degree in elementary education, and he's going to be working here while he attends graduate school at Stony Brook in the evenings to finish his master's degree.

"I thought it would be nice to have a male staff member," Candy said, and added, with a meaningful expression, *"especially for boys like Leo."*

Rose cringed, though she didn't resent the implication. Yes, boys like Leo—boys without daddies—need positive masculine role models. And women like Rose—young, widowed mothers— should be grateful for any opportunity to expose their sons to men like Gregg Silva.

But that doesn't mean she will ever get used to the fact that her children are no longer part of a "normal" family. A two-parent family, all living under one roof.

All *living.*

Daddy, Mommy, Sis and Brother.

Perfect.

It was all so perfect.

How could she never have realized it then?

How could she have wasted so much time worrying about trivial things?

To think that she used to fret about paying five dollars extra each month for a premium cable channel, and the fact that Peking Panda refused to substitute hot and sour soup for won ton with the $4.95 luncheon special.

To think that she actually used to skip her usual workout at the gym whenever she had cramps from her period, or that she complained about the pain that lingered for weeks when she strained her back during kickboxing class.

To think that she yelled at Sam when he forgot to take off his muddy shoes at the back door, or ate Ben & Jerry's Chubby Hubby directly from the pint, or forgot to call and let her know if he was going to be late coming home.

Why didn't she thank God every single day that he *came* home?

Why didn't she appreciate every blessed day that she could get out of bed with pain that was merely a minor inconvenience and not a threat to her life?

Why didn't she revel in simple indulgences—take-out food, and movies on cable, and countless other everyday treats she could no longer afford?

"Mrs. Larrabee?" Gregg's voice intrudes, in the tone of one who has been trying to get her attention.

"Yes?" She hauls her thoughts back to the present.

Gregg's blue-gray eyes bear an expectant expression.

Rose can't help but notice how good-looking he is: tall, lean, and broad-shouldered beneath a corn-colored crew neck sweater. A shock of sun-streaked hair swoops above his handsome features, giving him a golden surfer-boy aura even now, in the dead of winter. He even looks as though he has a tan—perhaps from weekends spent on the ski slopes north or west of New York City. Sam used to have that ruddy appearance after a weekend spent playing outside with the kids right here on Long Island.

Oh, Sam. You were such a great daddy . . .

"The cupcakes?" Gregg is saying, as Leo tugs on her leg impatiently.

"Cupcakes?" she echoes, utterly blank, shoving the image of Sam's face from her mind.

"For tomorrow—the Valentine's Day party? At curriculum night in October, you signed up to bring cupcakes. I just wanted to remind you."

"Oh, that's right. Of course. The cupcakes. How many do I need to bring, again?"

"Thirty."

"That's right. Thirty." She flashes Gregg Silva a

tight smile, wondering what the hell she was thinking back in October, signing up to bring thirty
cupcakes tomorrow.

No—she *knows* what she was thinking. She was
thinking that she wanted to be the kind of mommy
who thinks nothing of bringing cupcakes for holiday parties. Homemade cupcakes, thirty of them,
preferably with pink frosting and heart-shaped
candy sprinkles . . .

"Mommy! My coat."

She absently grabs Leo's bright red parka from
a nearby hook and helps him put it on. It's a hand-
me-down from Jenna. Back when Rose's daughter
was an only child, everything she wore was pink,
or floral print. But once Leo came along, Rose
quickly figured out that little girls could be just as
cute in red, or hunter green, or even navy.

Luckily, Jenna hasn't turned out to be much of
a girly-girl. So far, she's been content to wear jeans
and sweaters that can easily be passed along to her
little brother. But Rose figures the time is coming
when her daughter will insist on picking out her
own clothes, and when that happens, she'll be in
trouble. There's no room in the household budget
for fashion.

After all, here she is wearing a camel-colored
dresscoat that's a decade old, and beneath it, an
unstructured maroon corduroy jumper that dou-
bled as a maternity outfit for the first six months
of her first pregnancy.

As she helps Leo with his hat, scarf, and mittens,
her thoughts march back to more pressing matters.

She didn't also promise to bring cupcakes to
Jenna's school, did she? Though riddled with uncertainty, she does, at least, recall that Jenna's

teacher, Mrs. Diamond, sent home a note at the beginning of the year stating that only wrapped, store-bought treats labeled with ingredients would be accepted. There was something about one of Jenna's classmates having some kind of food allergy . . .

Well, if Rose volunteered to bring a Valentine treat to the elementary school as well, Jenna will be sure to remind her. It'll be easy enough to pick up a bag of red lollipops at the A&P later. In fact, she can probably buy cupcakes at the supermarket's bakery, as well.

If they have any left.

And *if* she can scrape together enough pocket change to afford the nearly three dozen she'll need.

Money.

Always back to money.

Hard to believe there was a time when she had enough in the bank to put a down payment on the house, with enough leftover to have put both kids through college someday.

But she'd have traded that inheritance for another twenty years with her mother, who died far too young.

And anyway, the money is long gone, swallowed up by her vast medical expenses—and the last of it on Sam's funeral.

With a sigh, she zips Leo's jacket up to his chin, then remembers to check his pocket. He went through a kleptomaniac stage a few months ago, stealing not just small toys from school, but also candy from the supermarket and change from Rose's dresser top.

Both Candy Adamski and the pediatrician assured her that it's a normal phase for children Leo's age, but Jenna never went through it.

Then again, Jenna didn't lose her father until much later. Rose can't help but think that if Sam were still alive, Leo wouldn't be stealing.

If Sam were still alive . . .

Her own personal mantra.

Satisfied that Leo's pockets are empty, she reaches for his mitten-clad hand. "Come on, sweetie, let's get going home. Jenna's on her way."

"Jenna's Leo's big sister, right?" Gregg hands Rose several sheets of paper, some manila, some colored construction: Leo's latest artwork.

"Yes. She's six." Rose rolls the papers and tucks them under her arm.

"Does she go to Laurel Bay Elementary?"

"Yes, she's in first grade there. She has Brownies after school on Thursdays, and she should be getting out right about now," Rose informs him, checking her watch.

Gregg raises his eyebrows. "Does she walk home afterward by herself?"

"Of course not!" Rose's maternal defenses rise immediately. She reminds herself that he's just being friendly, just making casual conversation the way he does every day when she picks up Leo. He isn't implying that she's an unfit mother.

No, you're *the only one who thinks that,* Rose scolds herself.

She softens her tone, explaining, "Her friend's mom gives her a ride back to our house, and she'll be there any second, so we'd better run. See you tomorrow. Say goodbye to Mr. Silva, Leo."

"It's Mist-o Gwegg," Leo protests.

"Mr. Gregg, then."

"Goodbye, Mist-o Gwegg."

"See you tomorrow, kiddo," Gregg Silva calls after them.

"See you tomorrow." Rose wrestles her son out the door and into the snow-dusted twilight.

He finds himself gazing once again out the window at the wintry dusk, unaccustomed to the thick white coating on tree branches and rooftop. It's been a frustratingly mild January and February on eastern Long Island this year, but last night's storm dumped several inches on Laurel Bay.

According to the weather forecast, it's going to melt before the week is out.

Damn. What a waste.

He shakes his head at the irony: a rare snowfall on the very eve of Rose receiving his first gift.

A calculated presentation of the gifts is a necessary element to his plan. And so, of course, is snow.

But he has time. More than a month of winter lies ahead. There will be other storms.

In the meantime, he'll continue to keep busy working at the mundane job that has allowed him to blend into the small community. And making Rose gradually aware that he's watching her. And working on the scrapbook.

He bought it the day after Christmas, marked down a mere ten percent at a pricey little stationery shop in East Hampton. The angular blond saleswoman assured him it was an excellent choice; that the acid-free pages would keep his mementos safe through the years.

He smiled and thanked her.

"Is it a gift, sir?"

"No. It's for me," he told her.

Watching her carefully wrap his purchase in layers of pale blue tissue paper, he amused himself by imagining the look of terror that would cross her bland face if he told her his plans.

"You know, most of my customers are women," she said, handing him the package. *"It's nice to see a man who cares so much about preserving memories."*

Yes, he thinks now, with a self-satisfied grin. He cares very much about preserving certain memories.

As they walk down the steps of the day-care center, Rose counts each one aloud with Leo, reminding him to hold the railing. It's freezing out here, unusually cold for Long Island. A few inches of snow fell yesterday, much to the children's delight. If it sticks, she'll take them sledding over the weekend.

Leo pokes along. It would be faster to carry him, but those days are long gone.

Together, they trudge along the freshly shoveled path leading away from the low brick building, past the snow-covered playground toward the Chevy Blazer. The only other car in the parking lot is a dark green Nissan that must belong to Gregg Silva.

"Come on, Leo, climb in," Rose says, opening the door and helping him into his car seat.

"I'll do the stwaps," he protests as she pulls the harness around his shoulders.

"No, Leo, that takes too long. I'll do it."

"No! I can do it!"

Rose sighs and stands by, shivering in the chill as her son struggles with the straps of his seat. She's tempted to push his fumbling little hands aside and do it quickly herself, but Toddler Tyme's philosophy is to teach children autonomy. Most parents think that's a terrific thing. Rose does, too, ordinarily.

Tonight, she's too tired to stand here indefinitely while Leo figures out how to insert the metal buckles into the slots. She's about to do it for him when she hears a click and he looks up triumphantly.

"See? I did it!"

"You did do it, sweetie."

Relieved, she climbs into the car.

"Goodbye, Todd-wo Tyme," Leo chirps as they pull out of the parking lot.

Rose smiles, glad he's happy at the day care, which originated in the basement of Blessed Trinity Church a few blocks away. This new facility was built two years ago to accommodate Laurel Bay's burgeoning year-round population.

More and more working parents are willing to trade cramped, pricey city apartments and post-terrorism urban jitters for a long commute and the small-town serenity of eastern Long Island. In fact, the local school board has been holding meetings to address the influx of families and avoid overcrowding.

Driving along Center Street, Laurel Bay's commercial drag, Rose brakes for a stop sign and automatically glances at Bayview Books on the opposite side of the street. She can see her co-worker Bill Michaels standing by the register just beyond the brightly lit plate-glass window. His shift doesn't end until five o'clock. She admires the display of romance novels she arranged herself on a drape of red satin in honor of Valentine's Day. Perhaps, if the store's new owner doesn't already have a March display in mind, she can do the same thing for next month, with green satin fabric and books by Irish authors. Or perhaps just books with green covers . . .

But Luke Pfleuger, the store's new owner, will undoubtedly have his own ideas for the window display. He only allowed her creative control over the Valentine's Day window because he came down with bronchitis right after the holidays and was forced to take a few days off.

As Rose continues along Center Street, she notices that every one of the diagonal parking spots is taken, even at this late afternoon hour. People traipse along the sidewalks, popping in and out of the local businesses.

There was a time, as recently as when Jenna was born, when Rose recognized most pedestrians' faces, and most of the cars she passed when driving this route. Not anymore. Lately, the town seems filled with strangers.

Even the familiar businesses on Center Street are changing. It isn't just that the hundred-year-old hardware store, diner, and bait-and-tackle shop have received much-needed face-lifts.

Peking Panda has sprouted a kimono-clad hostess and a sushi bar. The new menu at Pizza Village is printed on leather-bound ivory parchment rather than laminated card stock, and includes Tuscan appetizers starting at $7.95. Belizzi's coffee shop has been replaced with an upscale cafe—albeit not a Starbucks. Not yet, anyway. But there isn't a doughnut to be found in the new place, much to Leo's chagrin. He isn't big on hazelnut biscotti.

She glances into the rearview mirror as she brakes to let a dog-walking stranger cross the street, doing her best to ignore her own haggard reflection: the off-center, crooked part in her long, bark-colored hair, the brown eyes free of makeup and underscored by dark hollows, the wide mouth that would benefit from a soothing layer of lip balm.

Gazing into the back seat in the mirror, she sees that her son is sound asleep in his car seat. Poor little guy. A full eight hours of day care is rough on him, especially when he hasn't been sleeping well at night.

Guilt seeps in, as always . . . along with weary rationale.

She has no choice about working full-time at the bookstore. Sam's meager insurance policy barely covers the essentials. Without her salary, she would have to sell the house.

They're driving toward the outskirts of town now. The speed limit has risen to forty-five miles an hour. She stops at the last traffic light in Laurel Bay. Almost home now.

Waiting for it to change, she tells herself, as she always does, that selling the house is out of the question.

Forty-eight Shorewood Lane is all she has left of Sam, and that fleeting, happy time.

No. That isn't true. You have the kids.

And after all they've been through, the kids need a safe harbor even more than she does.

Lifting her foot from the brake, Rose pulls the car forward, driving another half mile or so before slowing gradually. The roads are well salted, but lately this corner has been especially slick. Must be some kind of water leak someplace. Ice.

Her hands clench the steering wheel.

The tires grip the icy pavement as she makes the turn.

She's not sliding through the intersection.

But the thought that it could happen upsets her every time she drives through here when the temperature is below freezing.

The truth is, Rose knows it's not just the threat of a fender-bender that sends waves of trepidation through her in cold weather.

Ice makes her think of that night. Of Sam's death.

Filled with longing for spring, yet cognizant that even its arrival can't possibly banish the constant reminders of the freak accident that robbed her of her husband, Rose heads south down Shorewood Lane.

The block is lined with unremarkable Victorian-era homes, most of them shingled in brownish-red cedar, with white trim. The houses are small, some little more than cottages, others angled by recent, tacked-on additions whose much darker or much lighter shingles sharply contrast the mellow, salt-burnished tone of the original exteriors.

It's been nearly a decade since she and Sam bought the small Queen Anne style home on a quiet side street only block from the bay. They had such big plans for the place. Sam, after all, was a contractor. But business was booming; he was so busy with the city people renovating local homes that he never got around to much more than replacing the sagging front steps and starting the built-in floor-to-ceiling bookcases she always craved for the tiny nook off the living room.

The outer shells are there—eight-foot rectangular wooden alcoves standing against two walls. Sam promised he would get to Home Depot for the brackets and wood for the shelves that weekend . . .

That weekend.

It's been more than a year, and still, there are times when she can't quite grasp the finality of it.

They had a conversation about death the year before, when Rose was so sick. She told Sam that if anything happened to her, she wanted to be cremated. Sam shuddered.

"Don't ever do that to me, babe, he said. *When I die, I don't want to be shoved into an oven and burned. I want an open casket like my grandparents had, so that everyone can take one last look and give my hand a little goodbye pat before they stick me in the ground."*

That didn't happen. He wasn't cremated, but the burn marks on his face were so bad that the mortician advised a closed casket. She never got to touch his hand and wish him a safe journey.

It's all a blessed blur to her now, and was even as it unfolded. The crowded wake. The funeral at Blessed Trinity, where Sam was once an altar boy. The stirring eulogy by his oldest friend, Scott Hitchcock, who said Sam was the main reason he had moved back to eastern Long Island only a few months earlier, and who vowed to watch over his family. The burial, beneath a weeping gray sky, in the cemetery across town.

Rose hasn't visited his grave since last Father's Day, when she brought the children. The experience frightened them, and it saddened her.

She didn't feel Sam's presence there, anyway. She doesn't feel it anywhere, except in her heart. A heart that spent three decades beating in another woman's chest before finding a permanent home within Rose—only to be broken.

* * *

The pipes groan as Leslie Larrabee turns on the tap at the kitchen sink, but at least they aren't frozen. The first spurts of water are rusty brown. She leaves it to run, then walks through the chilly, eerily empty rooms to do the same thing in the hall bathroom, between the bedrooms that once belonged to her and to Sam.

As she runs water in the unfashionable gold porcelain tub, Leslie can almost hear her brother's fist banging on the door, and his newly masculine adolescent voice calling, "You're not going to take another one of those two-hour baths, are you Les? Because I'm late for practice . . ."

Oh, Sam. What I wouldn't give to go back in time and see you again . . .

She sighs and leaves the bathroom behind, the tub and the sink running freely. Dad said to open the taps for at least five minutes a day in cold weather. Mom, perpetually on the other extension during their twice-weekly long-distance phone calls, promptly told Leslie not to worry about it.

"She has other things to do, Doug," she scolded her husband. "She's working full-time at the gym now, and she's planning a wedding. She doesn't have time to go running over to the house to turn faucets on and off all winter."

"It's no problem, Mom, really. I don't mind," Leslie lied.

The truth is, she does mind. It isn't easy to return to the deserted ranch house, with its haunting memories and its unfamiliar scent of abandonment. She wouldn't tell her father, but there are cold days when she skips the visits altogether.

Today, she couldn't do that. She had to shovel the walks and the small rectangle of driveway in front of the attached garage, to make it look as though somebody were home when nobody has lived here in well over a year.

She wanders back to the living room, which is just the way they left it, complete with framed family photos on every spare inch of wall and table. There are Olan Mills baby pictures and yearly school portraits from Leslie and Sam's childhoods culminating in graduation caps and gowns, and a number of formal photographs from Sam and Rose's wedding. And of course, there are countless photos of Leo and Jenna, the cherished grandchildren. But none are more recent than the ones taken two summers ago—the last summer her parents spent at home.

Before that they spent only winters in Florida, ever since the year Sam was married. Leslie remembers that very clearly, because the wedding was in November, and her mother complained that they would be arriving in Boca at least a month after the other residents of the retirement complex. She wanted to drive down in October and fly back up for the wedding, but Dad said it would be a waste of money. He won, as usual, but Mom never let him hear the end of it.

"Please shoot me if I ever start to sound like her, Sam," Leslie once begged her big brother, who inherited their father's easygoing temperament and quiet strength.

Gladly, Les. Where's my shotgun?

Sam liked to tease her that she was just like their high-strung mother. Leslie has to admit, she does share a few of her more frustrating traits—like not always thinking before speaking, and assuming that everybody needs her help whether it's requested or not . . .

And yes, being prone to impulse buys, she acknowledges as her gaze falls on the piano crammed into one corner of the room, between the wall unit and Dad's recliner.

Out of the blue one day, Mom used two weeks' worth of grocery money to buy the upright monstrosity at a tag sale so that the kids could take lessons. Dad hit the ceiling, and Sam flat-out refused to lay a finger on it, saying piano lessons were for sissies. Leslie was forced to endure three years of lessons with Mrs. Helwig, the halitosis-plagued organist over at Blessed Trinity.

Now, she idly raises the lid and runs her hands over the keys. The piano is badly out of tune, but she manages to pick out the first few bars of Beethoven's *Fur Elise.* Maybe, if Mom and Dad decide to sell the house instead of leaving it in indefinite limbo, Rose can take the piano so that Jenna can learn to play.

Wouldn't that be nice, Sam?

Leslie finds herself picturing the imaginary piano recital her brother will never proudly attend, and tears fill her eyes.

She abruptly turns away from the piano and finds her way back to the streaming faucets, eager to leave the lonely house, with all its memories, behind once again.

Rose sighs heavily as she rounds the last corner onto Shorewood Lane. Their house, a cedar-shingled Victorian two doors down on the right, is dark against the purplish-black winter sky.

There's no sign of Brittany's mom's car in the driveway. Good. At least Rose beat Jenna home.

Last Thursday she got here five minutes after Brittany's mom did. Jenna was waiting in the car with Brittany, Brittany's younger brother, and Lori, their mom, who is pregnant and due in a few weeks.

Rose doesn't know Lori well—the family just moved out here from Huntington when the school year started. Jenna and Brittany bonded quickly. Lori seems nice enough, and she certainly didn't seem to mind Rose being late.

But Jenna minded.

And Rose minded, too. She wants to be here for Jenna. She wants her daughter to feel secure about that, at least.

She pulls into the driveway and turns off the engine. Leaning against the headrest, she closes her eyes and groans softly. Her entire body aches. What she wouldn't give to go inside, run a hot bubble bath, climb into it with a good book . . .

"And never come out," she says softly.

Instead, what lies ahead is the cupcake dilemma. Helping Jenna and Leo address, sign, and seal four dozen Valentines between them. Deciding what to do about dinner—which the kids will undoubtedly want immediately. Figuring out what, in the meager grocery stash, can be packed into lunch boxes for tomorrow. Helping Jenna with her inevitable homework, which Mrs. Diamond uses to encourage parents and children "some together-time" each evening.

Her eyes snapping open, Rose sits upright and groans again. Loudly this time.

Leo doesn't stir.

Rose opens her car door and swings her feet onto the snowy driveway, shooting a glance at the curbside mailbox.

Should she bring Leo inside before she runs back out to get the mail?

Should she get the mail now, before she gets Leo out of his car seat?

Just another daily domestic dilemma, complicated by sheer exhaustion.

The mail first, she concludes. Give Leo another minute to sleep—and stall the cloud of crankiness that will most certainly descend and linger until bedtime.

"Toddler PMS," Sam used to call it when Jenna was small and prone to late-day tantrums.

Sometimes, Rose and Sam actually laughed about it. Now, as a solo parent, Rose finds nothing amusing about the challenges that lie ahead tonight.

Breathing the pleasant scent of wood smoke wafting in the frigid air, she trudges to the foot of the driveway, the rubber soles of her ancient L.L. Bean duck boots making a squeaky crunching noise in the packed snow.

The sound always sends shivers down her spine.

Sam used to tease her about it—called it her "wince-able," in that unique way he had of coining phrases. The translation—wince-able: the everyday thing that makes you wince. According to Sam, most people—himself included—shared wince-ables. Like a fork scraping on a blackboard. Like Styrofoam squeaking.

Not snow crunching.

"Most people consider that a pleasant sound, Rose."

"I can't help it. It bugs me, Sam."

She stops in front of the domed plastic mailbox, noting that the black metal post is still wrapped in the red velvet ribbon Leslie insisted on twining around it the weekend after Thanksgiving. Sam's sister also brought over a boxwood wreath for Rose's front door. It, too, is still there, shriveled and browning at the leaf tips.

Rose really should take it down and get rid of the mailbox ribbon, too. But another day won't hurt. Besides, red velvet ribbon isn't just suitable for Christmas, she thinks wryly. Tomorrow is Valentine's Day.

And my valentine is gone. Forever.

A lump rises in her throat.

Oh, Sam . . .

She flips through the mail to distract herself. Pennysaver, telephone bill, credit card application, school board newsletter . . .

And a rectangular red envelope with a typewritten label addressed to her.

The kind of envelope that might contain an invitation, or a greeting card . . .

Or a Valentine.

Yeah, right.

Rose flips it over, looking for a return address label.

There is none.

Curiosity surging through her, she slips off her brown knit glove and slides her finger into the gap in the envelope flap. She rips it open, expecting to find a card.

There isn't one.

Frowning, Rose presses the outer edges of the envelope to peer inside.

At first, she doesn't see it. In the fading afternoon light, it blends in against the red paper envelope.

Then she spots it.

Pulls it out.

Unfolds it.

A red paper heart, creased down the middle.

That's all.

The kind of thing Jenna or Leo might make in school, with construction paper and safety scissors.

But this doesn't appear to be a child's handiwork. The edges are cut perfectly straight.

Who would send her a paper heart?

Rose turns it over and over again, and again and again, searching for a signature.

There is none.

A red paper heart.

A heart.

A chill slithers down Rose's spine—and this time, it has nothing to do with crunching snow.

Hearing a car door slam, Christine Kirkmayer rises from the couch and goes to part the drapes covering the wide bay window facing the street.

The little girl next door is home.

Jenna.

An oddly fragmentary name, in Christine's opinion. As though somebody were too lazy to complete it on the birth certificate.

Jennifer is much better. If Christine and Ben ever have a baby girl, maybe they'll name her Jennifer.

But hopefully, if they have a baby, it won't be a girl—at least, not one with her mother's unfortunate genes.

Christine sighs, watching Jenna Larrabee waving at the occupants of the car that just dropped her at the curb.

Then she notices Jenna's mother standing in the shadows over by her own car in the driveway.

She doesn't know Rose Larrabee well. In fact, she's only met her once and seen her a few times in passing since December, when she and Ben moved here from the city.

But anyone can see that something is wrong. There is tension in Rose's posture, in her rigid wave before the car at the curb pulls away, red taillights disappearing into the dusk.

As Rose goes to meet Jenna by the front steps, Christine notices that her expression is troubled—and that she's clutching something in her hand.

Papers, or . . . mail?

That's what it looks like from here.

Hmm. Maybe she got something disturbing in the mail.

Christine's imagination takes flight as she watches Rose hug her daughter and unlock the front door.

Maybe she just got a foreclosure notice from the bank. Or a letter from her late husband's mistress . . . not that Christine has any reason to suspect that her husband had a mistress. But wouldn't it be interesting if he did?

Both mother and daughter have disappeared inside the house. Just as Christine is about to turn away from the window, Rose steps back outside, without the mail.

She returns to the car, opens the back door and takes her younger child from his car seat.

The little boy is groggy. He doesn't want to walk to the house, but his mother coaxes him along.

Why doesn't she just pick him up?

Christine shakes her head, watching. If that were her child, she would carry him into the house, no matter how heavy he is.

She lets the beige curtain fall back into place, then glances back at the television set and the first of several New York evening newscasts. That's all there is to do at this time of day: watch the news. The five o'clock news, and then the five-thirty news. The six o'clock news, capped off by the national news at six-thirty. She probably knows more about current events than Tom Brokaw does.

If only Ben would let her get cable television. But he's too cheap—or thrifty, as he refers to himself— for that. He says cable TV is a waste of money, and more importantly, a waste of time. He says the same thing about the Internet, and won't spring for a DSL connection. As a result, the computer's modem is so slow that she rarely spends time surfing the Web, and that's fine with Ben. He wants her to spend her time doing other things. Reading, volunteering, maybe even taking a class or two at a local college.

That would cost money, of course, but Ben says it would be good for her, after all she's been through. He also says that if she wants, she can go back and get the teaching degree she never finished a decade ago, when her loan money and grants ran out and she left City College to take a secretarial job.

What Ben doesn't say is that if she became a teacher, she could go back to work and eventually bring in a good salary to supplement his.

Christine has no interest in a college degree or a teaching job. She wants only one thing.

A baby. *That* would be good for her.

The doctor says there's no physical reason she shouldn't be able to conceive, despite everything. *Just give it time and it'll happen. Just relax, and it'll happen.*

Well, they've been trying for almost a year now, and she's done nothing but relax in the two months since they moved to Laurel Bay. What else is there to do here?

Leaving expensive, crowded Manhattan was Ben's idea. They looked for houses closer to the city, in Nassau County. But everything was so expensive, and so small. Out here on the eastern end of the island, they could afford something decent—not that this two-story turn-of-the-century Victorian is Christine's dream house. But it does have charm, and the neighborhood is safe and family-friendly. It's so close to the water that gulls fly overhead and the dank scent of salt and seaweed hangs heavy in the air on warmer days.

Ben said he wouldn't mind the commute to his midtown accounting firm—two hours each way. And he doesn't seem to mind.

Christine is the one who minds.

She sighs. Another evening stretches ahead, long and lonely. Ben won't be home until almost nine. She's become a suburban housewife cliché. Nothing to do but watch the news, daydream about babies, and spy on the neighbors through a crack in the curtains.

"Mommy, can I lick the beaters?" Jenna asks, hovering at Rose's elbow as she turns on the mixer. Her long hair, precisely the glossy dark shade of the devil's food cake batter, hangs perilously close to the bowl.

Rose tucks the wayward silky-straight strands back over her daughter's shoulders, saying firmly, "No, you can't lick the beaters. There's raw egg in there."

"I like raw egg."

SHE LOVES ME NOT

"It's not good for you, Jenna. You can get sick from it." Rose checks the back of the Duncan Hines box to see how long she's supposed to mix the batter.

"You used to let me lick the beaters," Jenna grumbles.

"That was before I read that raw eggs aren't good for children." Oops. She was supposed to be mixing it on medium speed, not low. She hurriedly adjusts the dial.

Too high.

A chocolate shower spatters all over the tan Formica counters, the knotty pine cabinets, the green striped wallpaper.

"Mommy!" Jenna shrieks.

"Shh!" Rose hurriedly turns off the mixer. "You'll wake up—"

Leo's frightened cry drifts down from the second floor.

"—your brother," she finishes lamely.

Just what she needs.

It took her a half hour to get Leo down the first time. Now he'll want her to sit with him again until he drifts back to sleep. At this rate, she's not going to finish the cupcakes till midnight—at which point, she'll have to start writing out valentines for Leo's classmates, and praying he'll miraculously sleep through until morning.

He used to do that, but for the past few weeks, he stirs at every little sound. At first she thought he might be coming down with the flu that's been going around, but he's been healthy. And he's long past the teething stage.

"Wow, what a mess." Jenna's brown eyes are more enormous than usual as Rose surveys the kitchen in despair. "There's cake mix everywhere, Mommy—even up in the sky."

Rose looks up just as devil's food raindrops fall from the ceiling, landing in her eye.

It stings, and dammit, Leo is howling up there.

It's all Rose can do to keep from joining in.

"I'm going to go up and calm him down," she tells Jenna as she hurriedly splashes water in the sink, trying to flush her eye. "Don't you dare touch the mixer."

"But I can finish—"

"No!" Rose's tone is sharp. "You could get your fingers cut off in the beaters. It's dangerous."

"You think everything is dangerous," Jenna mutters, idly picking up Rose's electronic pager from the kitchen table.

"And don't touch my pager, either," Rose admonishes.

"It's Daddy's pager, not yours," Jenna snaps at her, tossing the pager back on the table.

Rose's breath catches in her throat. Jenna's right. It is Sam's pager. Rather, it *was*. But she's been using it ever since she started working again, carrying it just in case one of the kids' schools needs to reach her in an emergency. It's cheaper than buying a cell phone . . . and anyway, it makes her feel closer to Sam. He always had the pager hanging from his belt loop when he left the house.

She chooses to ignore Jenna's comment, saying only, "Did you finish your math worksheet?"

"Yup." Jenna is smug.

"Did you remember to put your name and the date on top?"

"I put my name. I didn't know the date."

"It's February thirteenth," Rose says over her

shoulder, making her way to the front of the house. "Which reminds me . . . if your homework is done, then go start writing out your valentines, Jenna."

"You said you'd help me."

"You know how to do it."

"It's not fun alone."

No. Nothing's fun alone.

Rose sighs. "Okay, wait here. I'll be back down as soon as your brother's back to sleep."

She grabs her coat and the kids' jackets, which are draped over the stairway bannister, and carries them up the stairs. The house is a true Victorian, with very little closet space upstairs and none on the first floor. Sam was going to turn an alcove off the living room into a coat closet someday.

Someday . . .

Rose climbs the stairs, pushing Sam from her thoughts only to have them taken over by the mysterious red envelope again.

Who sent the construction paper heart?

And why the typewritten address label?

Maybe she has a secret admirer. But if that's the case, wouldn't he have written something? Or at least, have sent a regular card, instead of a plain red heart?

It isn't necessarily scary.

Just . . .

Odd.

Rose doesn't have the patience or the energy for *odd*. She's doing all she can do to make it through each day as it is.

"Mama!" her youngest child wails.

"Coming, Leo." She trudges wearily up the stairs.

* * *

Fresh from a relaxing late-night bubble bath, Christine turns a critical eye on the full-length mirror on the back of the bathroom door.

Her blond hair looks good, at least. The baby-fine, hippie-straight hair that fell out with chemotherapy never grew back, and was replaced instead by thicker, bouncier tresses that air-dry in the kind of loose waves she used to futilely attempt with a curling iron.

Yup, all it took was life-threatening cancer and the ravages of chemo to give me the kind of hair I always coveted, she thinks dryly.

And anyway, she isn't thrilled with her image from the neck down. Maybe she should have taken one of her flannel nightgowns out of her drawer to wear tonight, instead of this skimpy negligee she got as a bachelorette party gift from the girls in her office. This old house is so drafty that her bare arms and legs are covered in goose bumps, and the nightgown doesn't fit right anymore, either. The slinky fabric strains across her midsection, and the bodice gaps where her cleavage used to be.

She turns away, knowing that if she continues to critique her reflection, she'll lose her nerve.

The tub faucet is dripping again. Ben tried to fix it last week, and whatever he did worked for a while. But now, when Christine bends to turn it off, no matter how tightly she twists the knob, there's a steady *plop, plop, plop* of water into the drain.

Her first thought is that she'll have to call the super.

Then she remembers that there *is* no super. Ah, the joy of being homeowners.

She'll just tell Ben they're going to have to spring for a plumber. The next-door neighbors must have a good one—and lousy pipes. She frequently spots a panel truck—*Hitchcock and Sons, Plumbing and Heating Contractors*—parked over there.

Christine leaves behind the dripping tub and thoughts of plumbers, hangs the bath mat over the shower curtain bar, turns off the light, and makes her way back across the hall to their bedroom.

The house is chilly. She contemplates running downstairs to adjust the thermostat, but knows what Ben will say about that. Oil is expensive. Sixty-two degrees is as high as he'll allow the temperature to go during the day; sixty at night.

She left her husband reading the latest issue of *Kiplinger's*. Now he's curled up on his side of the bed, snoring already, the magazine still clutched in his hands.

Disappointment steals over her.

She turns off the bedside lamp and slips between the cold sheets on her side.

"Ben?" she whispers, poking him. "Ben?"

He mumbles incoherently, his back to her.

Shivering, she stretches out beside his warm body, wrapping her arms around him, kissing his shoulder. "Ben?"

He grunts, rolls over. "Why did you turn off the light?"

"You were sleeping."

"I'm reading." He turns the lamp back on.

"You're not reading anymore." She kisses his neck.

He closes his eyes again, wearily as opposed to passionately.

"Ben. Warm me up, will you? It's freezing in here."

"Turn up the heat."

I'm trying, she thinks grimly, pushing the comforter and sheets back to expose her supposedly provocative self. Her teeth are practically chattering, and Ben's eyes are still closed.

"Ben . . . " She kisses his neck again. "Look at me. Please?"

He opens his eyes. If he's enraptured by the sight of her in her nightie, he's doing a hell of a job keeping his burning desire under wraps.

"No wonder you're cold," he says. "Go put on something with sleeves."

"Or I could take this off and not put anything on," she says, feeling slightly ridiculous. She isn't good at seduction. She never has been. Dammit, why won't Ben take the lead? She trails kisses along his collarbone.

He squirms. "Come on, Christine, cut it out. It's tax season. I need to get some sleep."

"You just said you were reading."

"Well, now I'm sleeping. I took cold medicine an hour ago and it knocked me out."

"Why? You're not sick."

"I think I'm coming down with the flu. Everyone at work's been getting it."

Terrific. Ben is prone to frequent moaning when he's ill. When they were newlyweds, she relished the chance to play Florence Nightingale, but that got old very quickly. Especially after she got seriously sick herself, and Ben's bedside manner left something to be desired.

"This is my fertile time, Ben," she points out. "How am I supposed to get pregnant if you have no interest in me whatsoever?"

"I didn't say I had no interest in you whatsoever, Christine, I just said I'm not in the mood tonight."

"You're never in the mood."

"I'm coming down with the flu, and I'm wiped

out after a fifteen-hour day. You try riding the train round trip for hours every morning and night and see how you feel."

"I'm not the one who wanted to move out here, Ben. You are." She rolls away from him and sits up, pulling the blankets to her chest, partly because she's shivering, partly because she's suddenly self-conscious about the plummeting neckline. "You know I would have been perfectly content to stay in the city."

"You were miserable in the city for the entire last year we were there. I thought a change of scenery would help."

"I went through hell last year, and it had nothing to do with where we lived. If you want to help me, you know that a baby would— Where are you going?"

He's out of bed, throwing a sweatshirt over his pajamas and heading for the door.

"Out for a walk."

"I thought you were so goddamned tired."

His reply is lost in the door's staccato slam.

She's left alone to cry into her pillow, shivering from the chill.

Long past one A.M., lamplight still spills from the first-floor windows at 48 Shorewood Lane.

He wonders whether Rose has fallen asleep on the couch in front of the television again, like she did last night. Or maybe she's awake, folding laundry, as she was when he peeked through the window late one night last week.

His boots make a squeaky, crunching sound in the snow as he crosses the small patch of side yard, boldly leaving footprints.

At first, he was so careful not to disturb anything, never to leave a sign that he's been lurking.

Yes, at first, he was content simply to win her trust by day, and watch her by night.

Not anymore.

By now, she must have received his first gift.

By now, she's puzzled . . . perhaps even wary.

He smiles, imagining what she'll think in the morning when she notices footprints around the house, so close to the spot where her husband died.

Will she think it's Sam's ghost, coming back to haunt her?

But ghosts don't leave footprints. Only human intruders do that.

Will she be frightened?

Will she realize how vulnerable she is, alone in the house with two small children?

In her perpetually distracted state, she may not notice the footprints at all. It will take something more conspicuous than the footprints, or the red paper heart, to get her attention.

All in due time . . .

He slips into the shadows alongside the house. Overgrown forsythia boughs and a wooden lattice laced with a tangle of bare wisteria vines screen him from the street, should anyone come by.

It isn't likely. At this time of night, all is quiet on Shorewood Lane in Laurel Bay. So different from the city—and in more ways than that.

In Manhattan, people pay little heed to new-comers. One can come and go without arousing undue attention.

Out here, it takes time to become integrated into the community, to become one of the locals. Time, and patience.

He's painstakingly lain the groundwork in Laurel Bay, same as before.

And now, at last, he's made his first move.

The rest will follow.

Standing on the tips of his toes, he is able to peer through the ground-level window into the house. Through a veil of ivory lace, he plainly sees her sitting on the couch, writing something.

When he first saw the sheer panels covering her windows, he was torn between amusement and anger.

Doesn't she realize how flimsy the curtains are? Doesn't she know that anyone can see her inside?

Perhaps that's what she wants.

Perhaps she knows he's here, watching her.

Perhaps she's merely pretending not to be aware of his presence, inwardly taunting him, daring him to reveal himself.

But he won't. Not yet. Not until it's time. And when it is, she'll be sorry. She'll beg for mercy, just like before.

And he'll laugh.

Just like before.

Just before he kills her . . .

Again.

Two

"Well, look at you!" Bill Michaels greets Rose from behind the register as she dashes through the door into Bayview Books the next morning at ten.

"Good morning, Bill." She's already shrugging out of her camel-colored coat, shivering in the twenty-degree windchill. After flipping the CLOSED sign in the window to OPEN, she strides toward the back room, with Bill falling into step beside her.

"You *look* like a rose today, Ms. Rose." His aquamarine eyes twinkle at her from behind trendy wire-rimmed glasses. "You should wear that color more often."

Sam used to say that, too. He always urged her to wear pastels instead of her usual monochromatic wardrobe: black, brown, gray, navy. In fact, he's the one who bought her this soft raspberry-colored cashmere sweater the last Christmas they had together. It was an extravagant gift, but as he pointed out, it wasn't just Christmas time. It was the one-year anniversary of her new lease on life.

Before now, she wore it only once, the week he gave it to her. She felt conspicuous in it even then, and it lay forgotten on her closet shelf for more than a year. It was just as well. Her somber-toned wardrobe suited a grief-stricken widow.

But this morning, as she tied pink ribbons into Jenna's hair and buttoned Leo's red cardigan, they asked her if she was going to wear something special for Valentine's Day, too.

So here she is, in the sweater that brings back memories of that cozy Christmas morning with Sam.

"Is Luke here yet?" she asks Bill, hanging her purse and coat on a hook in the stockroom.

"He was, but he went across the street to get coffee."

Good. That'll take awhile, especially if he lingers at Milligan's Cafe to chit-chat with the cluster of morning regulars.

Rose isn't in the mood to deal with her new boss just yet—not that he's technically *new* at this point. It's been a few months already since he bought the business from Netta Bradley. Sweet, elderly, *easygoing* Netta Bradley, who choose to run a bookstore because she had an affinity for literature and small-town folks. She'd no doubt have continued to manage Bayview Books until her dying day if she didn't fall from a stockroom ladder and break both hips, which led to a series of surgeries and her reluctant retirement.

Enter Luke Pfleuger, a former Madison Avenue executive. According to Netta, after being laid off from a large Manhattan advertising agency, Luke successfully sued his employer for age discrimination. He used his settlement to purchase the bookstore and a seaside cottage in East Hampton.

Unlike Netta, Luke is a stickler for punctuality. Rose is supposed to be here fifteen minutes before the store opens.

This morning, she had to cram a day's worth of

errands into the hour after she deposited the kids, along with dozens of cupcakes and valentines, at school and day care. Then it was on to the bank, the dry cleaner's, the post office, and the library with a stack of overdue books that racked up eleven dollars' worth of fines. At the pharmacy, she dropped off several orange plastic prescription bottles for expensive monthly refills. Even with insurance, her medication costs more than she can afford. But she has no choice. It keeps her alive.

"You have nasty dark circles under your eyes," Bill notes, peering closely at her face. "Late night again?"

"Don't ask. I think I made it to bed by two A.M., and then Leo was up from three to four."

"Why?"

She shrugs. "He's just been restless lately. Maybe it's nightmares. He used to sleep like a rock. I should probably take him to the doctor and see what they say about it. I should probably do a lot of things, but—" She breaks off to cover an enormous yawn with her hand.

"Don't be hard on yourself, Rose. You're juggling a lot, raising two kids on your own."

Yes, and he doesn't even know the whole story. There are some things she just isn't comfortable sharing with anyone—not even Bill, with whom she's forged a close friendship in the eight months they've been working together at the bookstore.

Aside from Leslie, her coworker has become her closest confidant these days. She had other friends before her illness, before Sam's death. There were mommies from Jenna's play group, women she'd met at Lamaze while pregnant with Leo, couples with whom she and Sam socialized occasionally.

They hovered around her worriedly for a few months when she was so sick, but Sam and his family took such good care of her she didn't need to lean on anyone else. Most of her old friends came around again to offer support when she was newly widowed, but by then, Rose was used to keeping her distance.

It's much simpler that way.

Now the only people she speaks to on a regular basis are Leslie and Bill.

Scott Hitchcock, too. But he was Sam's friend, never hers. He comes around to play with the kids and see if she has any leaky faucets that need checking. Sometimes they have coffee and chat, bound by shared grief and their separate memories of the man they both loved.

She knows Hitch misses Sam desperately. Leslie and his parents do, too. Hell, everybody does. Sometimes it seems that not a day goes by in Laurel Bay when she doesn't run into somebody who wants to reminisce about her husband.

But their lives have all gone on without him, while for Rose and the children, nothing will ever be the same.

Yes, their lives have resumed a comforting rhythm of daily rituals. But even on her brightest days, Rose is never quite able to shed the sensation that doom lurks like a serpent in the shadows, waiting to strike again when she least expects it.

Leslie flips through the CDs in the Rock section, wishing she knew what her fiancé does and doesn't have. She knows Peter likes Dave Matthews, and the Barenaked Ladies. But does he already own all of their CDs?

She has no idea—and she knows what her brother would say about that.

Oh, shut up, Sam. The fact that I have no idea what's in Peter's CD collection has nothing to do with whether I know him well enough to marry him, she silently retorts.

Leslie met Peter Lenhard when he took her yoga class back in October. He said his doctor recommended it for his chronic back pain. He made it through only one class, asked Leslie out on a date afterward, and they were engaged by Christmas. Unofficially, of course. They've gone ring-shopping a few times, and Peter says he's saving to buy her one.

They spend most of their time at her place. Peter rents a basement apartment in a private home in Mastic, and says that his elderly landlord warned him against having female guests on the premises, especially overnight ones. In Leslie's opinion, that was out of line, but Peter insists that the rent is so cheap that he's willing to put up with Mrs. Callahan's restrictions.

You'd like him, Sam, she tells her big brother now, as she flips through another stack of CDs. *He's a carpenter, like you were. And he takes care of me, like you did.*

Giving up on the music store, Leslie wanders back out into the mall. It's quiet at this hour on a weekday morning, the cavernous corridors populated by the occasional stroller-pushing young mother and a smattering of senior citizens walking in groups.

Mom and Dad would fit right in with them, Leslie thinks, eyeing a passing cluster of silver-haired mall-walkers wearing jogging suits. Her parents are making a conscious effort to stay fit—or so they say. Leslie suspects that Dad hasn't really given up red meat, that her mother's water aerobic class is weekly rather than daily, and that neither of them has shed a pound, let alone fifteen each. If Sam were around, he'd get a kick out of their parents' exaggerated fitness claims.

Oh, Sam.

Leslie misses him desperately, even after thirteen months. There are some things only a sibling understands.

Now she's an only child. There's no longer somebody with whom she can exchange an amused or knowing glance at family gatherings—not that there have been many of those since the funeral.

Mom and Dad couldn't bring themselves to return to Long Island this past summer as they usually do. They said it would be too painful to be in Laurel Bay without Sam. Now they're even talking about selling the house.

Grief does funny things to people. You'd think Mom and Dad would want to be here as much as possible, to help their widowed daughter-in-law and fatherless grandchildren. That duty, however, now rests squarely on Leslie's slim shoulders. Not that she's complaining. She adores her niece and nephew, and Rose is the sister she never had.

Okay, so maybe she never really *longed* for a sister. Life was pretty cushy, growing up in Sam's sheltering shadow. They were an unlikely team, the four years between them bridged by a shared interest in sports and an irreverent sense of humor. Sam looked out for her from the day she was born. Mom liked to tell stories about Sam forcing her to walk several yards behind as he pushed his baby sister's stroller along Center Street, so that everyone would think he was "Wes-wee's Daddy."

Now there's a gaping cavity in her life where her protective big brother used to be. Unaccustomed to this hollow vulnerability, Leslie knows it must be far more difficult for Rose, having survived a life-threatening illness and surgery only to find herself abandoned with two young children.

An only child, Rose lost her mother while she was still in college, shortly before she met Sam. Leslie met her sister-in-law's father only once, at their wedding. He was there with his second wife and Rose's three teenaged half sisters, all of them sun-kissed California blondes.

Leslie can recall just one occasion when Sam and Rose brought the kids to visit their maternal grandfather on the West Coast. And he's never returned to Long Island. Not even when Rose was so sick . . . or when Sam died.

Leslie can't help feeling that Rose needs somebody to look out for her. Somebody other than a shell-shocked sister-in-law who, in the wake of Sam's death, has been left feeling that the world is a perilous place.

Only lately, when she's with Peter, has Leslie felt remotely safeguarded. Her fiancé is quieter and more low-key than Sam, but carpentry isn't all the two men have in common. When Peter is around, Leslie is certain nothing bad can happen to her. And when he isn't with her, she finds herself increasingly fearful that something might happen to him.

More fallout from Sam's accident, she supposes. Life has seemed precarious ever since her stalwart big brother proved tragically mortal.

Realizing she's stopped walking and is staring into the window of a store filled with clothing suited for teenyboppers half her age, Leslie snaps out of it and checks her watch. Okay, she has exactly an hour and fifteen minutes before she has to meet one of her clients for a training session at the gym. She'd better get busy finding something for Peter.

She continues along the corridor, vetoing the bookstore—Peter doesn't read—as well as Brooks Brothers, the jeweler, the pet store . . .

Leslie finds herself backtracking a few steps, drawn to a little black puppy in the window. He's just sitting there with a big red bow around his neck, watching her with a wistful expression that clearly says *Please take me with you.*

Leslie's apartment building has a strict no pets policy, and she's certain Peter's rigid landlady wouldn't welcome a puppy.

"Sorry, fella," she tells the little puppy, pressing her hand against the glass. "I'd buy you if I could."

He looks even more forlorn.

Leslie forces herself to keep walking—then stops short.

She can't buy the puppy for herself or Peter.

But she's just been struck by an idea so brilliant she can't believe she never thought of it before.

Smiling, she makes a beeline back to the pet store.

Working quickly, Rose and Bill unpack several new cartons of books and load them onto carts, with only two interruptions to ring up sales. At this time of year the shop is quiet, drawing familiar local bookworms and an occasional browsing stranger who's just passing through.

"Something tells me this is going to be another long, slow day." Bill stacks several copies of Emeril Legasse's latest cookbook on the bottom shelf of the cart, then says, as Rose starts to lift a heavy stack of hardcovers. "Here, wait, I'll get that."

"Thanks, Bill." She wonders, as she often does, whether Netta told Bill about her surgery, or if he's simply the gallant type. He always seems to be hurrying to lift unwieldy boxes for her, as though he's concerned she might strain herself. Someday maybe she'll tell him about the illness that nearly ended her life—and the miraculous operation that saved it.

Maybe.

"A long, slow day is perfectly fine with me." She yawns. "I'm too tired to deal with people."

"Yeah, but time flies when we're busy. Remember what it was like when we first started working here?"

She nods. "We were lucky if we had time for a lunch break."

"Right, and if we did have time, it took forever to get waited on at the cafe, even for takeout."

While the town's year-round population is growing steadily, it's the hectic summer months that keep the small independent bookstore afloat. Laurel Bay lies squarely on the well-traveled route between New York City and the Hamptons. From Memorial Day to Labor Day, its streets are choked with traffic; its sidewalks invaded by upscale tourist types.

Sam resented the seasonal flood of strangers. He complained about the long lines at the drive-through ATM, about the litter, about the BMW convertibles arrogantly taking up two spaces in the supermarket parking lot.

Having grown up in a bustling Brooklyn neighborhood, Rose tends to take the summer commotion in stride. Sam's rants amused her, particularly since his carpentry business depended on a healthy local economy.

"If Laurel Bay was a ghost town, you'd be out of work," she used to tell him.

"Then we could spend every second together," he'd say, hugging her close.

"We'd probably get on each other's nerves."

"No, we wouldn't."

"We'd be flat broke."

"Why? You have plenty of money in the bank."

"For our future. And the kids' college. We can't touch that. We'd have nothing to live on."

Then he'd say, imitating Patricia Neal in the old movie *The Homecoming*, *"We'd live on love."*

And they'd laugh.

Now here she is, flat broke anyway, longing for Sam, living on *if onlys*.

She and Bill take their time shelving the new stock, chatting about their Valentine's Day plans. Rather, Bill's Valentine's Day plans, which are infinitely more exciting than Rose's quiet evening ahead. He tells her that his friend Jeffrey has arranged a blind date for him with a handsome Broadway dancer.

"I thought you didn't like creative types, Bill," Rose teases.

"I don't, but he's too good-looking to pass up. And he's got orchestra seats for the new Sondheim revival."

"So basically, you're using him."

"Basically, yes. But don't tell me you've never used a man, Rose. Something tells me you weren't always so sweet and innocent."

It strikes her as an odd accusation, considering her status. She met Sam ten years ago. Before him, there were a few boyfriends, but nobody serious. She was too busy putting herself through college and trying to make it on her own in New York to date much, let alone indulge in femme fatale behavior.

Bill, apparently unaware that her grin has faded, glances toward the plate-glass window. "Uh-oh. Here comes trouble. I'd better go get the other cart."

"And leave me up here alone with him?"

"Better you than me. At least he's civil to you. He just grunts at me and looks like he wishes I'd go back to Christopher Street, or wherever it is homophobics like him think I belong." Bill disappears into the back room as the street door opens, its brass bell tinkling on a gust of cold air.

"Good morning." Luke strides briskly into the store, wearing a long black cashmere overcoat and carrying a steaming paper cup of coffee in his leather-gloved hand.

"Good morning." Rose picks up the pricing gun and aims it at a paperback's cover.

"It's gorgeous out there today, isn't it?"

She looks up, surprised. It wasn't like Luke to make small talk.

"Cold, though," he adds.

Rose follows her boss's gaze to the wide, plate-glass window. Bare tree branches cast sharp shadows in bright winter sunlight. Across the street, beyond the row of storefronts, is a cloudless ice-blue sky.

"Yes, it's cold." Rose can't think of anything else to say, but he seems as though he expects more from her.

She clears her throat, wishing he'd move on. Instead, he pauses to straighten a nearby Valentine's Day display of romance novels and self-help relationship books. He works with precision, carefully aligning each book on the shelf.

Rose watches him out of the corner of her eye, wondering, as she often does, why he's not married. He's a good decade or more older than she is, and handsome: a graying Harrison Ford/Richard Gere hybrid. She knows he's single and childless, but has no idea whether he's divorced, or widowed, or has a girlfriend. It's not the kind of question she feels comfortable asking. In fact, she tends to feel awkward around him under any circumstances.

It doesn't help that she occasionally catches him looking at her with what strikes her as something more than professional employer-employee interest.

He must know about Sam. It's a small town; people talk. Yet Luke doesn't ask personal questions. In fact, today's inquiry about the weather is about as verbally casual as he gets.

Turning away from the display, Luke says, "When you finish stocking the shelves, Rose, you can get to work on the valentines cards."

"Straightening them?"

"No, putting them away."

"Already? Netta used to leave the seasonal cards up until a few days after the holiday, just in case—"

"You can put them away today," Luke repeats. "We have to make room for more Saint Patrick's Day stock, and the rest of the Easter and Passover cards should be coming in from the distributor any day now."

"Okay."

"Be sure to sort the cards as you put them away. Make sure each one has the right sized envelope."

She nods, resenting his explicit instructions. How difficult is it to put away greeting cards?

But Luke, in his characteristic micro-management style, goes on, "Stack any cards that don't have envelopes together with rubber bands. They seem to be walking away from the display this year."

"The cards?"

"No, the envelopes," he says over his shoulder, already heading toward the back of the store.

Envelopes.

Rose is reminded yet again of the strange Valentine she received yesterday.

The envelope was red. Not a small one you might get in a box of note cards, but the larger, rectangular kind that comes with a full-sized greeting card.

A ridiculous thought flits into her mind, and she shoves it promptly out again.

Of course Luke had nothing to do with it.

Why on earth would he anonymously send her a paper heart?

But then . . . why would anyone?

Hearts.

Hearts, flowers . . .

Christ, they're everywhere today, aren't they?

Hearts, flowers . . . reminders.

With a grimace, David Brookman turns abruptly away from the red and white stationery store window display, focusing instead on the intersection before him. A steady stream of traffic zips past the towering gray office buildings that line Lexington Avenue. David takes a step back as a yellow cab swerves to miss a pothole, spattering brown slush onto the pedestrian-congested curb. The air is wet with icy precipitation that can't seem to decide whether it wants to be rain or snow.

If there's a more dismal place in which to spend

the month of February, David can't imagine where it might be.

You don't have to stay here, he reminds himself. *It's your choice. You can go south, the way you used to.*

His father just called again last night to urge him to join him and David's stepmother on the balmy Gulf Coast.

David regularly escaped to his own condo there right after New Year's, staying at least through President's Day weekend. Hell, he'd have gone down for the whole winter, but *she* didn't want to spend the holidays in the South. Said it wouldn't seem like Christmas without cold weather, and snow.

She loved snow.

He closes his eyes briefly, pushing aside an unwanted memory.

When he opens them again, the orange DON'T WALK sign across the street has turned to a white WALK. He crosses the intersection, careful to side-step puddles in his black calfskin Ferragamo oxfords.

One of these days, he really should find a closer rental garage. Parking his Land Rover three blocks from home isn't practical on a day like this.

Halfway down the next block, he mounts the steps of a narrow brownstone, snaps his black umbrella closed, and turns his key in the lock.

Home.

Home again.

A new maid, whose name escapes him, scurries into the entry hall as he wipes his feet on the mat.

"Good morning, sir." She radiates polite detachment and a bit of uncertainty.

Soon, she'll take his frequent absences in stride, just as the others have.

He nods at her, depositing his dripping umbrella in the stand by the door and tossing his wet Burberry trench on the coat tree.

"Would you like a cup of tea?" the maid asks, as he flips through two days' worth of mail in its designated basket on the nearby table.

"No thank you." He picks up the customary stack of bills, financial statements and credit card offers, then strides toward the double glass doors leading to his study.

Stepping across the threshold into a dim, paneled haven, he inhales the familiar scent of leather, furniture polish and lingering pipe tobacco.

Here, with the maroon draperies drawn the silence punctuated only by the steady tick of the antique mantel clock, David is sheltered from the harsh city at his doorstep; from the harsher past with its haunting memories.

Sitting at his desk, he slips a finger beneath the flap of the first envelope on his pile of mail then curses.

Blood oozes from a paper cut. He sticks his finger in his mouth, wincing at the warm, salty taste, then opens the top drawer to find his letter opener.

He really should use the damn thing more often, if only for practical reasons. Never mind that it's an heirloom, custom-designed, engraved with the family coat of arms and monogrammed with David's initials. His grandfather gave it to him the day he returned to New York with his MBA and joined the family's real estate business. Well, empire would be a more accurate word, David thinks, rummaging through his drawer.

The letter opener doesn't seem to be here.

He frowns, trying to recall the last time he used it.

Truth be told, he *never* uses the letter opener.

Well then, when was the last time he saw it?

He has no idea. It's so easy to lose track of time these days, he thinks, glancing at his daily calendar.

Shaking his head, he tears off several pages: the eleventh, the twelfth, the thirteenth.

Today's date stares boldly up at him.

He toys with a sharpened pencil, rolling it back and forth in his fingers.

February fourteenth.

Valentine's Day.

So?

It's just another bleak day in another bleak month.

Just another holiday spent without her . . .

He clenches his jaw.

Without Angela.

As vulnerable in David's strong fingers as the fragile neckbone of a hapless fowl, the pencil splinters abruptly in half.

Turning onto Shorewood Lane late that afternoon with her children strapped into the back seat, Rose glimpses a familiar blue car parked in her own driveway.

"Hey, look, Aunt Leslie's here!" Jenna exclaims. "Do you think she can stay for dinner, Mom?"

"We'll ask her." Rose parks at the curb, not wanting to block Leslie in and have to come out again later to move the car. According to the WLIR meteorologist on the car radio just now, the freezing rain that's been falling over New Jersey and the city all day is moving slowly eastward, and may turn to snow before dark.

Rose intends to change into sweats and warm socks, light a fire, and stay indoors for the rest of the evening. She had planned to brood, as well, but that will be impossible with upbeat Leslie around.

"Hi, guys!" Dressed in her skintight black gym clothes beneath a yellow parka, Leslie bounds out of her car as soon as Rose turns off the ignition. "Happy Valentine's Day. Look what I brought!"

Yes, look what she brought. Rose doesn't know whether to laugh or cry.

It's a puppy. A little black puppy with an enormous red bow around his neck.

Jenna and Leo dash across the snowy yard, squealing with joy.

Rose follows more slowly, lugging the bag of orange prescription bottles, Jenna's backpack, the pink construction-paper-covered tissue box filled with her valentines, and a paste-smeared, heart-decorated white paper bag containing Leo's.

"Hey, Ro." Leslie flashes a broad white grin and twinkly green eyes, looking enough like her brother to create a fresh wave of aching loss in his widow. "The puppy's for the kids. I've got something for you in the car."

"Leslie—"

Jenna whirls on her with a pleading expression. "We can keep him, can't we, Mommy?"

Too befuddled to think clearly, she doesn't know what to say.

"Sam told me he was planning to get them a puppy that last Christmas, but that you wanted to wait till they were a little older." Leslie shrugs. "I figured, they're more than a year older now . . . and

I saw this little imp in the window of the pet store at the mall this morning. He was so adorable. It was like he was made for you guys. I would've called first to check with you, Rose, but I knew you were at work and I didn't want to bother you."

Of course you didn't. And a puppy is no bother at all.

Rose looks from Leslie to Jenna to Leo. Her son is giggling as the squirming puppy licks his face. She sighs. "Okay. We'll keep him."

What else can she do?

Leave it to Leslie to go and spring a dog on them when it's all Rose can do to singlehandedly feed and care for two children, not to mention maintain her own health and sanity.

"I'm so glad, Rose." Leslie looks relieved. "I've got to call Peter and tell him he was wrong."

"Wrong about what?" Rose asks.

"When I told him about the puppy, he said it was a bad idea. He said you don't go and buy someone a dog without asking them. But I told him to mind his own business, and that he doesn't know you well enough to say that."

Sometimes Rose wonders if Peter and Leslie even know each other well enough to be planning a future together. They certainly seem like complete opposites. Leslie is a vegan yoga instructor/personal trainer; Peter indulges a fierce nicotine and caffeine addiction. And Rose has never heard the reserved carpenter say more than a few words without being interrupted by bubbly Leslie. But then, he doesn't seem to mind.

Besides, just because Rose is the look-before-you-leap type doesn't mean a whirlwind courtship can't work for somebody else. Particularly somebody like Leslie, who wears her heart on her sleeve and lives her life guided by instinct alone. She's clearly head-over-heels for Peter. Rose just hopes he feels the same.

"Well? What are you going to name this little guy?" Leslie is asking the children.

"Cupid," Jenna says promptly.

"No! Jenna, I want to think of a name!" Leo says.

Okay, here we go. Puppy fight number one. Rose closes her eyes, exhausted just thinking of what lies ahead.

Leslie intervenes. "Hey, Leo, just think about it. Cupid is a pretty great name for a Valentine's puppy."

Miraculously, Leo's ominous pout transforms to a reluctant grin. "Yeah, Cupid is okay. But I get to feed him first."

"Then I get to walk him first," is Jenna's response.

"Come on . . . we can walk him now. All three of us." Leslie sets the puppy on the ground.

A sudden gust sways the bare branches overhead and tosses a tuft of Rose's long, loose hair across her eyes. Arms laden with the kids' belongings, she turns to face into the wind. As her hair blows back from her face, her gaze falls on the side yard.

She frowns. The white blanket of snow is marred by tracks of some sort.

"How are we going to walk him?" Jenna is asking. "Won't he run away?"

"Nah, I bought him a leash. We'll let Mommy go inside and get settled before we bring him in. Okay, Mommy?"

"Hmm?"

"We're going to walk the dog while you go inside. What do you say?"

Rose turns to flash her sister-in-law a tight smile. "Sounds good, Aunt Leslie."

Leslie looks more closely at her, lowering her voice as the kids romp at her feet with the puppy. "You okay, Ro?"

"Yeah . . . it was just a long day. And Leo was up in the middle of the night."

"Again?"

She nods. "Mr. Gregg said he was so exhausted that he fell asleep with his head on the table after snack this morning."

"Who's Mr. Gregg?"

"The new instructor at Toddler Tyme."

"A guy working in day care? That's unusual."

Rose shrugs. "He's great with the kids. Especially with Leo. And he had a good suggestion for getting him to sleep through the night again."

Leslie leans her willowy frame back against her open car door. "Yeah? What? Drug him?"

"Actually, he said I should get a sound machine. You know, the kind that creates white noise in the room. He said his mother has used one in her apartment in the city for years. It drowns out sirens and street noise."

"Well, there's no street noise out here." Leslie gestures at the quiet neighborhood around them.

Rose looks again at the side yard.

There appear to be footsteps in the snow there. Maybe an animal? Or kids cutting through the yard?

Or maybe it's just your imagination, because that's where Sam died. Maybe you want to think his ghost is hanging around there . . .

"Here, Ro—this is for you." Leslie takes a gold-wrapped box of Godiva truffles from the front seat of the car, along with a leash for the puppy.

"For me? Thanks, Leslie." Touched, Rose kisses her sister-in-law on the cheek, wishing she had thought to buy Leslie a valentine treat, or at least send her a card.

Sam always brought his sister flowers on Valentine's Day. His mother, too.

"They get carnations, but the roses are only for my Rose," he would say, as though he thought she minded his gifts to the other women in his life.

Of course she didn't. She always took pleasure in seeing how bighearted Sam touched the lives of everyone around him.

"Here . . . let me put this in Jenna's backpack for you," Leslie is saying. "You don't have a free hand."

"Thanks." Rose wrestles her thoughts away from Sam as his sister unzips the backpack on her shoulder.

"Oops," Leslie says, as a calculator drops out.

"My calculator!" Jenna shrieks. "Did it break? I need it for my homework!"

"Calm down, Jenna," Rose admonishes.

Leslie turns it on, commenting, "I can't believe you get to use a calculator for math homework these days. Back when I was a kid, you'd get into trouble if you did that. Don't worry, Jen, it works fine," she announces, pressing some buttons and handing the calculator to her niece. "Look. What numbers are those?"

"3-1-7-5-3-7," Jenna reads off.

"Now flip the calculator over and read it upside down."

Jenna does, and her face breaks into a broad grin. "It's your name! Leslie!"

Rose peers over Jenna's shoulder. Sure enough, it does say *Leslie.*

"Your dad taught me that when I was a little kid," Leslie says.

"Do my name!" Jenna commands.

"I can't, but I can do Leo. See?" She punches in 0-3-7 and flips it over.

"It says Le," Rose observes.

"Darn it. I forgot. The zero won't stick when you push it first. Oh, well. It's still pretty cool, huh, guys?" She tucks the calculator back into Jenna's backpack, zips it closed, and bends to attach the leash to the puppy's collar. "All right, let's go, everyone. We'll head down to the bay."

"Just don't let Leo get too close to the water," Rose calls after them as they set off down the block, pulled along by the scampering puppy.

She walks up onto the porch, unlocks the door, opens it, and deposits everything she's holding inside. Then she retreats down the steps, flinching at the sound the snow makes under her boots as she walks across the yard.

There are definitely footprints here.

Okay, this is no reason to worry. Don't let your imagination get carried away with you.

But it isn't her imagination.

Someone has been here, and it wasn't a ghost.

Judging by the prints in the snow, it was one person—and an adult, at that.

The footsteps lead from the street to a thatch of shrubs along the side of the house, just beneath the living room window.

Rose's heart begins to pound.

Has somebody been prowling around while she's gone during the day?

Or—even more unsettling—while she's here at night?

She stands on her tiptoes and examines the win-

dow for signs of a break-in. There are no pry marks.
The inside latch is securely locked.

The tracks make an about-face at the window, retreating toward the street again, yet Rose slowly
circles the house, checking every ground-floor window, making sure everything is secure.

Should she call the police?

And say . . . what? *I'm alone, and I'm afraid?*

But she has a reason to be frightened. Someone
has trespassed on her property. That's a crime . . .
isn't it?

Coming full circle to the living room window
again, Rose has every intention of going inside
and calling the police. Maybe they can send a patrol car around to keep an eye on things when
she's at work . . . and at night, too. After all, she
was in such a rush this morning, the footsteps
could very well have been here then, and she just
didn't notice—

Oh.

Her gaze falls on the silver-gray electric meter a
few feet from the window, almost obscured by a tangle of bare wisteria vines that climb the lattice
against the house.

That explains it.

The meter-reader must have been here while she
was out.

Case closed.

Relieved, Rose sighs and gazes skyward. Thick
black storm clouds are rolling in from the east. And
somewhere up there, Sam is probably laughing at
her.

See, babe? Nothing to be afraid of. Everything is fine.

No, it isn't, Sam. It's Valentine's Day, and you're not

*here to bring me roses that cost too much, and chocolates
with cream-filled centers that nobody likes.*

She tries to remember last Valentine's Day, her
first without him. It came only a few weeks after his
death. The day, like every day in that first month
without him, is a blur. Maybe Leslie was here. Probably. She does her best to cheer up Rose on difficult
occasions. On what would have been Rose and
Sam's eighth wedding anniversary in November,
Leslie came over with four tickets to see the Rock-
ettes at Radio City. She meant well, but she talked
about Peter the whole time, telling Rose that she
was sure he was The One. Caught up in her own
wedding day memories, Rose didn't pay much attention to Leslie's romantic rhapsodizing. In the
decade she's known her sister-in-law, Leslie has
been through at least four The Ones.

But Rose has to admit, this time it seems like the
real thing. Leslie doesn't have a diamond ring yet,
but she swears Peter is saving for one. And they
have a deposit on a wedding hall in Great Neck.

The wind gusts again. Rose turns toward the house
with a shiver. On her way toward the steps, she remembers the mail and heads to the box instead.

She can't help feeling a little uneasy as she opens
it today.

And when she spots several red rectangular envelopes inside, her stomach turns over. Pulling
them out gingerly, she turns one over . . .

And sees that it's addressed to Miss Jenna
Larrabee, in her mother-in-law's distinctive handwriting.

The second card is for Leo.

The third, for Rose herself.

Valentines, undoubtedly.

She smiles and goes into the house at last, unaware that she is being watched by two pairs of eyes.

Christine watches her neighbor disappear inside, puzzling over Rose's journey around the perimeter of the house. She seemed to be looking for something.

Maybe she dropped something, or one of the kids lost a mitten, or—

Or maybe you really need to get a life.

Maybe Ben is right. Maybe she should be volunteering at a senior citizens' home or something. When the highlight of her afternoon is the next-door neighbor's return, something is obviously missing in her life.

Well, no kidding. You know something is missing . . . and you know what it is.

A baby.

Christine stares vacantly into the snowy yard, reliving the confrontation she had with Ben late last night, before he went storming out of the house. She fell asleep and never heard him come home or back to bed. She stirred only when she heard Ben leave for the train as dawn's light filtered in through a crack in the bedroom drapes.

Apparently, he isn't too sick with the flu to commute to a grueling day at the office—only too sick to cuddle with his wife.

He called to check in from work just past noon, as he often does. She didn't pick up. He left a message on the answering machine: "Christine? Christine? Are you home? Where are you?"

Let him wonder.

Let him worry a little.

But he probably won't. Ben isn't a worrier. Even in the darkest days last year, he remained steadfastedly—almost irritatingly—optimistic. He went to work and he ate three square meals and he slept soundly through each night, while Christine's world was caving in all around her.

It must be nice, she thinks, gazing out the window. It must be nice not to—

A sudden flicker of movement catches the corner of her eye.

Startled, she turns her head toward the Larrabees' yard. Something is stirring in the dense evergreen shrubbery in the far corner.

A squirrel?

A bird?

No, something larger.

Christine swears she can see the silhouette of a human figure there amidst the branches.

Her heart begins to pound.

Are her eyes playing tricks on her in the fading afternoon light?

Why on earth would anybody be lurking in the neighbor's rhododendrons?

She closes her eyes, rubs them, and looks at the spot again.

This time, it's empty.

Good, Christine thinks, relieved—before she notices that the boughs are still swaying gently, and there's no breeze.

Three

Pulling into the parking lot of her Patchogue apartment complex at last, Leslie searches for Peter's red truck.

There it is, parked at the far end, which means he hasn't been waiting here long. The spots closest to the building entrance fill quickly, especially in lousy weather like this.

Sunrise Highway is slick tonight; what is normally a fifteen-minute drive back from Laurel Bay took her twice as long. Eager to see Peter, Leslie had to fight the urge to step on the gas and venture out into the passing lane to sail by the slow-moving traffic on the right. There was a time, not so long ago, when her big brother teasingly called her "Maria Andretti."

But since Sam's death, she finds herself skittish in icy weather. Especially on the highway. Especially now that her ancient blue Toyota has more than a hundred and fifty thousand miles on it. She's been saving for a new car for almost a year now.

After parking beside Peter's pickup, Leslie raises the hood on her down parka and grabs the Sears shopping bag from the seat beside her.

After rushing through the mall with the puppy in tow, on a futile search for the perfect Valentine's gift for her fiancé, she settled for a Craftsman tool belt to replace his worn one. Not exactly romantic, but Peter is more the practical type, anyway.

Wet snow pelts her as she makes a dash for the door. Then, safely inside the brightly lit, locked entryway, she checks her mailbox. Junk mail, junk mail, junk mail . . . and a red rectangular envelope that bears a familiar Florida return address.

Leslie smiles. Mom and Dad never forget her on Valentine's Day—or any other minor holiday, for that matter. Over at Rose's, she watched her niece, nephew, and sister-in-law open cards from her parents and discover letters, photographs, and cash tucked inside of each one.

Leslie slits open the envelope as she heads for the stairs. Her mother has sent her twenty-five dollars and instructions to "treat yourself to something fun," along with several pictures, most of them indistinct shots of a dark speck in a milky southern sky. Mom's handwriting on the back states that they're photographs of the most recent shuttle launch, taken from her parents' backyard a stone's throw from Cape Canaveral.

Dad bought her a good-quality camera when she retired from teaching, and she frequently sends pictures—mostly incomprehensible scenic snapshots, sometimes with a thumb blocking the lens, or out-of-focus. But as Sam used to say, at least Mom has a hobby to keep her out of Dad's hair—what's left of it, that is.

Stopping in front of her door at the far end of the second floor hall, Leslie smells coffee brewing. She smiles as she turns her key in the lock. It's a homey scent, and one she has come to associate with Peter. He drinks caffeine just about every waking moment.

The knob turns just as she reaches for it. The door opens, the doorway filled with Peter's broad-shouldered frame. He has on jeans and a moss-colored plaid work shirt that transforms his hazel eyes to a pale green. His dark curly hair is more unruly than usual, as though he just slept on it.

"Hey, babe." Peter pulls her against his soft flannel shirt. "I was worried about you. I just called Rose and she said you left awhile ago."

"The roads were icy."

"We've got to get you a better car, Les. I worry about you driving around in—"

"How about if we go to a few dealerships to look next Monday? It's a three-day weekend."

"That sounds good."

They smile at each other. She tilts her face up. He pushes back her parka hood, then kisses her. His five o'clock shadow scratches her cheeks and he tastes of coffee and cigarettes.

He doesn't smoke in her apartment, but the scent lingers on his breath and in his clothes. He says he has no intention of quitting—not even for her.

"Hey, I brought you something." Leslie holds up the shopping bag.

"For what?"

"It's a Valentine's Day present."

His smile fades. "I didn't know we were getting each other—"

"It's no big deal." She beams brightly to hide her disappointment. "It's just something I thought you needed."

"I feel like a clod."

"Don't. It's okay."

Not really.

She was hoping . . .

No, she was certain he would have an engagement ring for her tonight.

She puts the bag into his hand.

He stands holding it. "I meant to get you a card . . . and some flowers . . . but it was a crazy day."

A card . . .

Flowers . . .

What about a ring? she wants to ask, yet merely says, "I know."

"You're mad at me."

"I'm not mad."

Hurt, maybe.

Silently agreeing that he *is* a clod, yes.

But not mad.

He opens the bag and exclaims over the tool belt, but his forced enthusiasm robs her of any pleasure. For the first time since she met Peter, Leslie finds herself wishing she were alone in her apartment.

"I checked that knob that you said keeps falling off your dresser drawer," he says, refilling his coffee cup in the kitchen as she takes a bottle of Poland Spring from the fridge. "The screw is stripped. I'll pick up another one at the hardware store tomorrow."

"Thanks. That would be great." She tries to sound grateful. And she should be. Sam was always the one she turned to when something in the apartment needed fixing.

Now Peter does it.

But I have to ask him to do things, sometimes more than once.

Not Sam. There were times when she'd come home and find him puttering around her place.

"I let myself in to fix that shower rod that keeps falling down," he'd say.

Or, "I put a new dead bolt on the door, Les. I don't like you living alone with just that one flimsy lock."

Back in the living room, Leslie and Peter sit on the couch talking about his latest project, a bunga-low renovation in Bellport. Then he asks her how Rose and the children liked the puppy.

"The kids loved him. Rose seemed a little thrown by it, but I think it'll be good for her when she gets used to the idea. Plus, she needs a dog. It'll make her less nervous about being alone in the house with two children every night."

He looks up from his cup of coffee. "She's ner-vous about—"

"She doesn't *say* it, but she must be."

"Well, it's not like you got her a big German shepherd. You said he was a puppy."

"Puppies grow up. And they bark at intruders."

"Intruders? In Laurel Bay? Come on, Leslie, it's not as though she's living in some crime-ridden neighborhood in the city."

"She's a woman alone in a house every night. She needs some kind of protection, and if she's not going to even keep bullets in Sam's gun . . . "

"Sam had a gun?"

Leslie nods. "They were always arguing about it. Rose was worried one of the kids was going to find it and get hurt. They keep it in the drawer of their bedside table, but she made him lock the bullets away in the top of their closet."

"What good is a gun that's not loaded?"

Leslie shrugs. "That's why I think she should have the dog."

"Why? Do you think he can convince her to keep bullets in the gun?"

Irritated with his lame joke, and knowing it stems

mainly from the fact that he ignored their first Valentine's Day together and still hasn't bought her the promised engagement ring, Leslie changes the subject. "I was thinking that if my parents do decide to sell their house, Rose and the kids might want to move in there."

"Why would she want to? Isn't her place bigger?"

"Not much bigger . . . and it's so old. You know how Victorian houses are. There's no storage. They have to hang their coats upstairs in their bedrooms. Leo's room doesn't even have a closet. And every time I see the shells of those bookshelves Sam started to build for her . . . " She trails off, shaking her head over her brother's metaphoric unfinished project.

"Bookshelves?"

"In that teeny alcove off the living room, behind the French door. Sam used to tell Rose that when he finished, they could call it the library. And then he was going to install one of those protruding bay window-shelf things in the mud porch for her plants, and he said they could call that the conservatory." She smiles at the memory.

Peter looks thoughtful. "I can finish the shelves, Leslie."

"You'd do that?"

"Sure."

"That would be . . ." She touches his muscular forearm. "I'm sure Rose would appreciate it. But do you have time?"

"I'll make time. I know she's been through a lot."

"She has. And she gets tired so easily. I worry about her health." Early in their relationship, she confided in Peter about the cardiomyopathy that nearly claimed Rose's life two Christmas seasons ago.

"Maybe there's other stuff I can do for her while I'm there. It sounds like she can use a man around the house," he says gruffly, squirming a little, until she removes her hand.

Okay, so he's not the type to want a fuss over his noble gesture. But she can't help being touched by it. It's certainly not like him to volunteer for handyman jobs.

Maybe you've underestimated him, she thinks guiltily.

After all, Peter knows she's always worrying about Rose. He obviously wants to give her some peace of mind and share the burden of looking out for her brother's widow.

Aloud, she muses, "I almost wish Rose were the type to get married again someday."

"What, you don't think she will?"

Leslie shakes her head. "Sam was her soulmate, and there's no way she'd ever—"

"Soulmate?" He snorts a little, and Leslie is right back to being irritated by his unromantic soul.

"What, you don't believe in soulmates?"

She expects a flat-out no, but he surprises her. "I don't know . . . do you?"

"I *thought* I did."

"Come on, Leslie . . . don't be mad at—"

"Who says I'm mad?"

"You are. I can tell. You're mad about Valentine's Day. I just didn't think about it."

"How could you not have thought about it? You knew I was out shopping this morning. I told you I got the kids a puppy for Valentine's Day and you said it wasn't a good idea."

He shrugs. "I didn't think it was."

"That's not the point. The point is . . ."

The point is, he blew off Valentine's Day. Is he

showing his true colors? Will he ignore their wedding anniversaries, too, in years to come? Will he never bring her flowers, or buy her birthday gifts?

She looks at him and finds herself wondering who he is. Suddenly, he seems like a total stranger.

A stranger who has infiltrated her life and commandeered her future.

Stop it! You're being overly dramatic.

"What's the point, Leslie?" Peter asks.

"Hmm?"

"The point. You said 'the point is—' and then you stopped talking. You have this glazed look on your face."

"I do? I guess I'm just tired."

"Really? You should go to bed."

And you should leave.

No. She doesn't want to ask him to do that. It would open the door to something she isn't so sure she wants to confront right now.

Maybe she *is* just tired. Maybe things will feel right again in the morning.

"I'm going to stay up and watch the Knicks game." Peter reaches for the television remote.

She's grateful, for the first time, that all that coffee tends to keep him up long after she goes to bed. It isn't unusual for her to leave him on the couch with the television and lights on, but only after trying to lure him into bed with her—at least long enough to make love.

Tonight, that's the last thing she feels like doing. So much for the red lace teddy she planned to wear in honor of Valentine's Day.

"Hey, Les?" Peter says.

"Yeah?" Maybe he was going to apologize again. If he does—

"Let Rose know I'm going to stop by tomorrow after work and see what kind of lumber I need to get."

"I will." She plants a perfunctory kiss on his head and adds, "Thanks."

"For what?"

"For helping Rose with the shelves."

He shrugs. "She's family to me now, right?"

Not yet, she isn't.

Alone in her room, Leslie quickly undresses and puts on a pair of flannel pajamas. She turns out the lamp, parts the blinds, and peers out into the night.

Bare branches sway wildly in the wind. Grainy precipitation pelts the windowpane. What a miserable night.

She thinks of Rose, alone with two children in the old house by the bay.

Feeling uneasy for her sister-in-law, Leslie climbs into bed, once again glad that Peter is here with her. He may not be perfect, but at least she's not alone.

She hears an abrupt sound from the other room. Was that the apartment door closing behind Peter? Of course not. But . . .

"Peter? Are you still here?"

"Where else would I be?" he calls back. "I just dropped the remote on the floor."

Reassured, Leslie rolls over, closes her eyes, and drifts into a sound sleep.

The lights flicker ominously as he unlocks the bottom desk drawer.

Hand poised on the lock, he looks up, waiting to see whether he'll need the flashlights and candles he's had ready, just in case the storm knocks the power out.

It doesn't happen. Not this time. But he fears that sooner or later, the room will be plunged into darkness.

When he was a child, his father taunted him about his phobia of the dark. Daddy said night-lights were for cowards.

One might assume that all those years of being forced to sleep in a pitch-black room might have conditioned him to it in adulthood. On the contrary, he keeps both his overhead bedroom fixture and the bedside lamp burning brightly through the night.

Only when Angela stayed beside him in bed until morning did he willingly sleep in the dark, her mere presence seeming to banish the shadows.

He opens the drawer and pulls out the leather-bound scrapbook he's been working on.

The first page contains the front page from the *New York Post* with its December 25 dateline and its bold black two-inch type.

SNOW ANGEL CLINGS TO LIFE.

Accompanying the grim headline is a photograph of Angela, one he never saw before it was printed in the paper. It shows her tanned and smiling, wearing a skimpy, unfamiliar bikini and standing on white sand with aqua-colored water and palm trees in the background. Every time he opens the scrapbook and catches sight of that picture, he staves off a renewed flood of resentment.

Yes, she had another life before he came along . . .

But that isn't the trouble.

It's the other life she had while she was *with* him that stings like seawater on an open blister.

The photograph was undoubtedly taken within the last few months of her life. In it, her hair is shoulder-length and streaked with blond. She wore it long and dark until that final summer, when he talked her into the cut and highlights. He went to the beach with her a few times after she changed her hair . . . Long Island beaches, with nary a palm tree in sight.

The newspaper photo is evidence that at some point that summer or fall, she snuck away to a southern beach without telling him.

What else didn't she tell him?

Jaw clenched, fingernails digging into the palms of his hands, he glares into her smiling face, then turns the pages abruptly, past similar headlines and articles clipped from other newspapers. He pauses briefly another front page from the *Post.* December 27.

TRAGIC SNOW ANGEL HEAVENBOUND AT LAST.

He snorts at that; resumes flipping pages.

The last big headline devoted to Angela reads SNOW ANGEL'S PRECIOUS GIFTS. Beyond that, the type grows smaller, the articles fewer and farther between. And after funeral coverage—grainy snapshots of her grieving husband, father, friends, all in dark sunglasses—there is nothing more.

Not for a year.

Then . . .

STATEN ISLAND WOMAN MISSING SEVERAL DAYS.

And, months later, after the spring thaw . . .

POLICE BELIEVE BODY THAT OF MISSING STATEN ISLAND WOMAN.

But those accounts didn't make the front pages. The tabloids had more pressing stories to cover than the mysterious unsolved disappearance and murder of a young woman who was found by hunters in a shallow grave sixty miles from where she was last seen. The remains were presumably skeletal; there was no mention in the press that both her eyes had been burned out before she died.

Humming to himself, he takes more clippings from the envelope where he's been keeping them all. It doesn't take him long to paste them into the album following the others. These are one-paragraph articles clipped from various sources. Staten Island Woman's death, while brutal, lacked the glamour and poignancy, the exquisite *timing,* of the Snow Angel's tragic accident.

He takes the last clipping from the envelope, an article clipped from Newsday, the local Long Island paper. A photo accompanies it: a smiling man cradling a newborn.

LAUREL BAY DAD ELECTROCUTED.

He runs the glue stick over the album page, then presses the last clipping on, carefully smoothing the edges with his fingertips.

There. Done.

For now.

He leafs through the empty acid-free pages. Soon, there will be more headlines to paste here.

He smiles in anticipation, wondering how the papers will describe her.

WIDOWED MOM, most likely.

But WITHERED ROSE has a nice ring to it, too.

Perhaps, he thinks, she'll be legendary once again. As legendary as the lovely, noble Snow Angel.

But the press will never make the connection between Snow Angel and Withered Rose and Staten Island Woman.

Nor, he gloats, will the police.

Only he knows the truth.

Only he knows why she has to die.

Only he knows when that will be.

Giddy with power, he closes the book as the lights flicker again.

Fatigued, he swiftly locks the scrapbook safely in its drawer once again.

Then he goes to the next room and climbs into bed, taking the flashlight with him. He turns it on, just in case.

Just in case the lights go out in the night.

Only cowards are afraid of the dark.

He grins, remembering his father's face the last time he glimpsed it—beneath him, cowering in terror.

Who's a coward now, Dad? Who's a coward now?

Still smiling, he drifts contentedly off to sleep.

Four

A week later, Rose holds Leo's hand as they pick their way around the puddles in the Toddler Tyme parking lot. The morning sun beams brightly. Bare tree branches stir overhead in an unusually warm breeze for February. It feels more like April.

Rose glances up at the blue sky. It's hard to believe snow may be in the forecast for the holiday weekend ahead.

It's also hard to believe she's not engaged in a mad morning rush for once. She had to drop off Jenna fifteen minutes early today and help her set up her prehistoric diorama in the school gym. Rose promised she would come back to tour the first grade's annual dinosaur exhibit later—which means she'll have to ask Luke to let her leave work before her shift is officially over. She's not looking forward to that, but the day has begun so brightly that she refuses to dwell on potential cloudbursts.

Reaching the top step, Rose opens the door and ushers her son into the dim vestibule.

"Nobody's here yet, Mommy."

"I saw Miss Candy's car in the parking lot," Rose assures Leo, leading him into the hallway. The lower walls are lined with labeled cubbies and hooks; the upper with bright construction paper artwork.

"Did you see my howt, Mommy?" Leo points at a jagged red shape clumsily pasted to a white doily mounted on manilla paper.

"It's a beautiful heart, Leo." Rose smiles at him. Before the sight of the paper heart propels her thoughts back to last week's bizarre, anonymous Valentine, she hears a voice calling her name.

"Hello, Mrs. Larrabee. Hi, there, Leo!"

Candy Adamski coming toward them down the corridor. The director is wearing a denim jumper with a red and white striped turtleneck, tights, and ballerina flats. Her dark hair is pulled back into a ponytail tied with a red ribbon, and red plastic balls dangle from her earlobes. They look like tomatoes, or . . .

Cherries?

Yes, they're cherries.

It takes a moment for Rose to make the connection. Cherries . . . George Washington . . . Presidents' Day!

Congratulations, you have just advanced to the bonus round.

"You're looking cheerful this morning, Mrs. Larrabee."

Rose realizes she's grinning. "Oh . . . well, I guess that's because I'm not in a rush for a change. And Leo slept through the night, thanks to Mr. Silva's suggestion."

"Oh? What was that?"

"He told me I should buy one of those white-noise machines for Leo's room. I bought one the other day and ever since then, he's been sleeping much better. He likes it when I make it sound like ocean waves. It's soothing for him."

"I'll tell Gregg that it was a success."

"Tell me that what was a success?"

They turn at the sound of a male voice behind them. Gregg Silva is wiping his brown Timberlands on the mat just inside the door.

Leo makes a beeline for him. "Hi, Mist-o Gwegg!"

"Hey, buddy. How's it going?"

"He's got extra energy today, thanks to you." Rose tells him about the success with the sound machine as Candy turns on lights and takes out craft supplies.

"I'm glad it worked," Gregg says. "My mother swears by hers. And if my upstairs neighbors don't quiet down, I'm going to have to get one myself."

"I grew up in Brooklyn, in a building with hard-wood floors," Rose tells him as Leo hangs his coat and hat in his cubby. "I remember how loud footsteps overhead can sound."

"It's not the footsteps that are keeping me up at night." Gregg flashes a white-toothed grin. "My neighbors are newlyweds. It sounds like their bed-springs could stand to be oiled—and I'd swear the damn thing is on wheels and they're moving it around the room."

Rose can feel her cheeks grow hot. She can't think of a thing to say, other than, "That must be loud."

Luckily, children are trickling into the hallway ac-companied by harried working parents. Fumbling in her pockets for her gloves, then remembering it's too warm to need them, she says, "Well, I'll let you get to work."

Gregg smiles. "Have a great day."

"You, too." She quickly kisses Leo goodbye and beats a hasty retreat.

Outside again in the winter sunshine, Rose finds herself looking forward to the long weekend ahead. When Netta Bradley hired her at the store, it was with the stipulation that she wouldn't have to work evenings, weekends, or holidays. Netta knew about her cardiomyopathy and was concerned about her health. Luke, presumably unaware of all she'd been through, only grudgingly agreed to maintain that limited schedule.

With the kids off from school on Monday for Presidents' Day, there will be three lazy mornings without having to rush out the door. Three home-work- and hassle-free evenings. Three days to do whatever they feel like doing. If it really does snow, maybe she'll take the kids—and the never-used sleds Hitch bought them for Christmas—over to the hill behind the school.

Reaching her car in the rapidly filling parking lot, Rose opens the door and climbs inside. She's about to turn the key in the ignition when she sees the red package on the passenger's seat.

Slowly, she removes her hand from the key and reaches for the small, shrink-wrapped, heart-shaped box of chocolates.

Valentine chocolates—the inexpensive kind that are sold in every supermarket and drugstore in town.

What are they doing here, in her car?

She turns the box over, then searches the seat and the floor of the car.

There's no note.

Nothing but the chocolates.

A week after Valentine's Day.

She left the car unlocked. She always does. Anyone could have left the chocolates on the seat while she was inside the school.

But who would do it?

And why?

Maybe they were here before, she thinks suddenly. Maybe she just didn't notice them earlier. Maybe one of the kids put them there.

Leo.

Is he stealing again?

It's been awhile since he went through that phase, but it does make sense. He's crazy about chocolate. Maybe he saw the box of candy someplace and—

She gasps, hearing a sudden rap on the window beside her head.

Turning, she sees Gregg Silva standing beside the driver's side of the car. He pulls the door handle, opening it before she can protest.

Rose fights the urge to cry out.

"You dropped this," he says, smiling, and she realizes he's holding one of her brown knit gloves.

"Oh . . . thanks. It must have fallen from my pocket."

Can he hear her voice wavering? Can he tell how badly he frightened her, looming up beside her the way he did?

"No problem." His gaze falls on the box of candy in her hand. "It's a little late for Valentine's Day, don't you think?"

She shrugs and looks away, catching sight of a dark green Nissan parked in the next spot over, on her passenger side. That's Gregg Silva's car.

It would have been easy for him to get out of his car earlier, open her passenger door, and slip the chocolates onto her seat. It would have taken him a couple of seconds at most, and even if there were other parents in the lot, they would most likely be too distracted by their children to notice.

"Are you okay, Rose?"

She turns toward Gregg again, trying to imagine that he's secretly infatuated with her.

The notion is almost laughable. Even in her young, single days, she never attracted men who look like him. He probably has too many blond, skinny girlfriends to give this world-weary widow a passing thought.

"I'm fine," she tells him.

"Are you sure? You look upset."

"I'm just . . . I'm late for work. Thanks for the glove."

He grins and steps back from the door.

"You're welcome. Enjoy the chocolates."

He's just being friendly, she tells herself as she pulls the door closed. *He's not trying to hint that he left the candy for me.*

Troubled, Rose starts the ignition and drives slowly out of the parking lot, glancing into the rearview mirror.

She half expects to see Gregg Silva still standing there, watching her, but the spot where he was standing is empty.

Rose glances again at the heart-shaped box on the opposite seat. Then she reaches down with her left hand and pushes the button to lock the car doors.

Control.

It's all about control.

He reminds himself of this as he paces through

the living room. His watch reads two fifty-seven A.M., but he isn't sleepy. The lamps are brightly lit, the television is droning, he's fully dressed.

You have the upper hand, he reminds himself. *Just as long as you don't reveal that you know who she really is, you have the upper hand.*

But it's tempting. So tempting to taunt her, at least, with the truth. Now, in the dead of night, when she's lost in a sound sleep. Or perhaps she's awake, feeling vulnerable, pondering his little gifts.

His hand grips the cordless telephone receiver.

No. He can't let himself dial. He mustn't.

Yet it infuriates him that she dares to feign innocence, just as she did before. She acts as though she doesn't recognize him; she plays the part of the virtuous suburban mother, so certain nobody suspects.

And they don't seem to.

He is fairly certain that he alone is aware that the real Rose Larrabee died that day . . .

The day the Snow Angel supposedly saved her life.

By ten o'clock Saturday morning, Rose wonders why she ever found herself thinking a long weekend would be a good thing. While romping through the living room with the puppy, Leo toppled and shattered the Lenox vase Sam gave her on their last anniversary. He denied it—and a half hour later flatly denied squirting an entire bottle of liquid rose-scented soap down the sink drain, though he reeked of the stuff.

While trying to wash down the suds Rose realized that the lightbulb over the medicine cabinet is burned out and she doesn't have a spare one on hand. Then the puppy pooped on her bedroom carpet and Leo tracked it all over the upstairs. And of course, the kids have been bickering all morning.

She can't even get them out of the house. With the temperature hovering just above freezing, the promise of a snowfall has been transformed into the threat of sleet. In fact, a storm appears imminent as Rose glances at the western sky through the kitchen window above the sink.

"Mommy, I'm hung-wee," Leo whines from the doorway.

"Are you kidding me? I just spent the last half hour making the chocolate chip pancakes you begged me for, and watching you push them around on your plate before you fed them to the puppy under the table when you thought I wasn't looking." Rose rinses the remnants of batter from the bowl with the sprayer, then squirts liquid soap into it.

"I did not do that, Mommy! I ate them!"

She sighs. Terrific. First it was a stealing phase with him; now it's blatant lying. What's next? Sneaking cigarettes?

"Anyway," he grumbles, "I don't like that kind of choco-wat chip pancakes. I like the kind in the dye-no."

At the diner, a.k.a. Milligan's, there are no child portions on the menu and her kids refuse to share. She winds up paying more than ten dollars so that they can each take a few nibbles from two heaping platesful of chocolate chip pancakes with sides of bacon. Even Sam couldn't have polished off those portions.

"The diner is too expensive," Rose tells Leo. "Homemade food is much better."

"I hate homemade food."

Rose runs hot water into the soapy mixing bowl. "We don't say hate in this house."

"Jenna says it."

"Well, the next time you hear Jenna say it, you let me know."

"Jenna!" Leo shrieks. "Mommy told me you're not awowed to say hate anymore!"

In the living room, parked in front of a Scooby Doo cartoon, Jenna ignores him.

Leo resumes his mantra. "I'm hung-wee, Mama."

Rose sighs. He calls her Mama when he wants to play up the *poor little me* attitude—and it usually works.

"I'm hung-wee. Can I have something to eat?"

"Leo, you'll have to wait until—"

A shadow falls over the sink.

She gasps.

"What, Mommy? What happened?"

Somebody is looming outside the window.

A hand knocks on the glass.

"Oh . . ." Rose presses a hand at the base of her throat, relieved. "It's only Hitch."

She dries her hands and crosses to the back door to let him in, glad she got dressed between the pancakes and the kitchen cleanup. Granted, she's only wearing faded jeans and one of Sam's old sweatshirts, but it's more presentable than the flannel boxers and droopy T-shirt she's slept in for the past three nights.

"Hey, Jenna! Uncle Hitch is here!" Leo dances his way over to the door in his footed pajamas.

"Careful, Leo, don't slip." Rose steadies her teetering son by the shoulders as she opens the door.

Scott Hitchcock, who always says that front doors

are only for "real" company, steps into the kitchen. A taller, burlier version of Sam, he has a thick thatch of black hair and a crinkly-eyed grin. His clothes could have come out of Sam's closet: work boots, jeans, a flannel shirt, and a well-worn canvas barn coat.

"Hey, Rose. Hey, lion-boy."

Leo giggles. "My name isn't wion-boy."

"You sure about that? Because I seem to remember you roaring pretty loudly when you were a baby."

Rose has to smile at that. Home on leave from the army, Hitch once slept on their couch on a memorable weekend when Leo was a colicky newborn. Sam got a big kick out of his bachelor pal's aversion to the screaming baby. He kept insisting that Hitch hold him, plunking the red-faced, screaming Leo into his arms and cooing, "Here, go to Uncle Hitch. He'll sing you a lullaby."

"Don't let him fool you, Hitch," Rose says now. "He still knows how to roar pretty loudly."

"I'll bet. Where's her highness this morning?"

"Watching cartoons. Jenna! Come say hi to Uncle Hitch."

"Hi, Uncle Hitch! I'll be right there," comes the bellowed response.

"She'll be right here," Rose echoes dryly. "She has to get her cartoon fix on weekends because I don't let her turn on the TV on school mornings."

Hitch smiles. "No problem. I'm not in any hurry this morning. I've spent the last three hours under an old lady's sink. I need a nice long break."

Hitch moved back to the island a few years ago to take over his family's plumbing business. Though he learned the trade right out of high school, he left after a few years to join the military. His father optimistically continued to call the business Hitchcock and Son.

"Mark my words—he'll be back someday," Sam always said. *"You can take the boy out of Long Island but you can't take the Long Island out of the boy."*

Rose doubted that. She couldn't imagine a man like Hitch finding a reason to settle down alone in a such small town after living all over the world. But Sam was right.

She'll never forget the day Hitch called from somewhere in Saudi Arabia to say he was coming home for good. Sam's "Whoo-hoo" was so ear-shattering it set the neighborhood dogs barking.

"You want coffee, Hitch?" Rose offers, trying to sound cheerful.

"Only if it's made."

"I've been through one pot already, and I was just about to make another."

"Uh-oh. Rough night?" He looks more closely at her, making her wish she has on makeup to hide the dark circles that must underscore her eyes. Not that she needs to look good for Hitch. He's as no-frills a guy as Sam was, and Rose certainly isn't trying to impress him. Nor does she want to discuss her sleepless night, or the reason behind it—which has nothing to do with Leo. Her son has slept soundly through yet another night, thanks to the sound machine.

Even the shrill ring of the telephone at three A.M. didn't wake Leo. Nor did it wake Jenna.

Only Rose, who had finally drifted off to sleep less than an hour earlier, was disturbed by the unexpected call. She woke with her heart pounding, certain that something was terribly wrong.

After all, it was a wee-hour phone call to her dorm room that informed her of her mother's death years ago.

She pushes the grim memory from her mind and busies herself measuring coffee grounds into a clean filter.

"Guess what, Uncle Hitch? We're going swed-ding!" Leo announces.

"On the grass?"

"No, in the snow. Mommy said it's going to snow."

"Really, Mommy?" Hitch looks at her. "Do you have one of those snow-making machines stashed in the shed?"

"I wish. Leo, I said last night that the weatherman predicted snow, but this morning he changed the forecast. Now it's just going to be yucky and rainy. So we won't be able to go sledding after all."

Leo opens his mouth to protest, but Hitch cuts him off. "Maybe you can come with me today, Leo."

"I can? Mommy, Uncle Hitch said—"

"I heard him. Aren't you working?" Rose asks.

Hitch shrugs. "Nah. I'm done for the day." He swings Leo up into his arms and says, "I can take you to the movies and then we'll go get pizza."

"Can we go to the dye-no for choco-wat chip pan-cakes?"

Her back to them as she fills the coffee pot with cold water, Rose smiles.

"Whatever you want, Leo. Is that okay, Rose?"

Before she can reply, the puppy starts barking in the living room, the front door opens and a famil-iar voice calls, "Anyone home?"

"In here. That's Leslie," Rose tells Hitch.

"I figured." He looks uncomfortable.

A moment later, Leslie breezes into the kitchen. "Who's parked in the driveway? Peter needs to get the lumber out of the truck and he's going to—" She stops short, seeing her brother's old friend, whom she used to date. "Hey, Hitch. How's it going?"

"I've been pretty good," Hitch says. "How're you, Leslie?"

"Fine. What happened to your panel truck? Don't tell me you gave up on Hitchcock and Son already?"

"Nah, I just don't like to bring the truck out on days when the roads might ice over. The tires are almost bald, and I don't have a death wish . . ." He trails off into awkward silence.

Rose is certain that all of them—at least, everyone but Leo—are thinking about Sam.

He didn't have a death wish, either. He was simply worried about the ice coating the wires, not wanting them to lose power in the night with two small children in the house.

Rose barely stirred when he leaned over her in bed and said he was going out to knock off the ice. She murmured "Be careful" and went back to sleep.

Realizing that the silence in the kitchen has stretched beyond a moment, Rose—perhaps because she's grown accustomed to such rough conversational spots—gets past it first. "So what are you driving instead, Hitch?"

"My father's car. He can't see to drive anyway these days."

Leslie reaches down to give her nephew a hug. "Hey, I thought we'd go out and do something today, Leo. That way Mommy can have some time to herself for a change. What do you say?"

"I say I'm going to eat pancakes with Uncle Hitch."

"Oh. That's great," Leslie says brightly. She looks at Rose as Leo scampers into the next room. "Can I take Jenna?"

"Be my guest." Rose knows she should feel giddy at the prospect of an entire afternoon to herself, but she isn't necessarily looking forward to being alone in the house. Not after last night.

The phone call was probably just a wrong number, she tells herself.

And the chocolates on her car seat were obviously intended as a gift.

A gift that might very well have been placed there by Leo, though he denied it when she asked—or perhaps by whoever sent her that heart on Valentine's Day.

She threw the chocolates in the Dumpster behind the bookstore when she got to work and tried to put the incident out of her mind. Bill asked her a few times if anything was wrong, though. She was tempted to tell him, but it seemed silly to be bothered by something so innocuous.

At least, it seemed innocuous in the broad light of day, in a public place. Lying in bed in a darkened house at midnight, she couldn't help being frightened at the thought of an anonymous somebody sneaking around, perhaps even following her to leave those chocolates on the seat.

"Hitch, would you mind moving your car out of the driveway so that Peter can unload some stuff?" Leslie is asking.

"Sure." He jangles his keys. "Who's Peter?"

"My fiancé."

"That's great, Leslie. I'm happy for you."

"Thanks." She smiles awkwardly.

"Be right back," Hitch says.

As soon as he's gone, Leslie turns to Rose. "I didn't know he was going to be here."

"He stops by sometimes. He likes to see the kids."

"Are you sure it's not you he's coming to see?"

"What?"

Leslie shrugs. "Maybe he has a crush on you."

"That's ridiculous. He just pops in to check on us because he was Sam's friend."

"Really? He didn't come around very often when Sam was alive."

"Leslie, he was in the military until a few years ago, remember? He was living halfway across the world. He couldn't exactly drop by for coffee."

"Well, all I'm saying is that if he's doing that now, he might be coming to see you. But take it from me. If you do start dating him, don't trust him."

"Leslie! Shhh! And anyway . . . I'm not going to date him." Rose hesitates, then asks, "But why wouldn't I trust him if I did?"

"Because he cheats. We went out for a while, years ago. You knew that, right? Anyway, it turned out he was seeing someone else behind my back."

Yes. Denise. Rose knows all about her. According to Sam, she was the love of Hitch's life. They got engaged on his twenty-first birthday, and she broke it off a few weeks later. That was when he abruptly joined the army and left Laurel Bay.

"You can't blame him for something that happened when you were kids, Leslie." Even as she says it, Rose wonders why she's defending Hitch. After all, for as close as he was to Sam, and for as often as he pops in, it's not as though she knows him very well.

"I was sixteen. Didn't you have your heart broken

when you were sixteen, Ro? It's not the kind of thing you get over easily. And anyway—I'm not still angry at him. I'm just saying you shouldn't trust him."

Rose shrugs. She takes milk from the refrigerator and refills the sugar bowl from the canister. Hitch likes his coffee light and sweet.

Okay, so maybe she does know more about him than she even realized. Maybe, somewhere deep down inside, there's a part of her wishing that what Leslie said is true. That Hitch is coming here more to see her than the kids.

Now she can't help wondering whether Hitch could be the one who left the chocolates and sent her the unsigned Valentine.

Maybe she should be hoping that's the case. After all, having Sam's old friend as a secret admirer might be a little awkward, but it certainly isn't threatening.

What about the phone call last night?

It didn't seem like a routine wrong number.

Nobody spoke.

But whoever it was seemed to listen for a few moments before hanging up.

Hitch would never call her in the middle of the night. He'd know how that would frighten her, and that it might wake the kids.

Rose frowns, troubled once again.

And now Hitch is taking Leo, and Leslie is taking Jenna, and she's facing a day alone in the house.

Or is she?

"Leslie," she says suddenly, remembering. "Is Peter planning to stay here to work on the bookshelves today?"

Her sister-in-law nods. "He was. Why? Is that a problem?"

"No, not at all."

Of course it isn't. She'll feel safe with Peter around.

Not that you shouldn't feel safe anyway.

"Are you okay, Rose?" Leslie asks.

"I'm fine. It's just . . ." She finds herself spilling the whole story. About the heart, the chocolates—which she's still fairly certain were placed on the car seat by Leo—and the telephone hang-up.

"It sounds like you've got a secret admirer." Leslie grins. "And I'd be willing to bet that it's—"

"Who has a secret admirer?"

Startled, Rose turns to see both Hitch and Peter standing in the kitchen doorway. She was so caught up in unburdening herself on Leslie that she didn't even hear them come in the front door.

Leslie answers her fiancé's question. "Rose has a secret admirer." She shoots a meaningful glance at Hitch as she adds, "And it's scaring her."

"What's scaring her?" Hitch promptly appears concerned. "What's going on, Rose?"

Before she can answer, Leslie tells him, "He's been leaving her presents, and calling and hanging up."

"Maybe he thinks that's romantic."

"Oh, come on, Peter, there's nothing romantic about a coward."

"A coward?" Her fiancé frowns. "I don't think that's—"

"If a grown man is interested in somebody, he should speak right up and say so. Beating around the bush is just . . . well, it's so junior high."

"I'll keep that in mind, Les," Peter says dryly. "Listen, Rose, Hitch is going to help me unload the truck."

"That would be great. I guess you introduced yourselves, then."

Hitch nods, accepting the steaming cup of coffee Rose hands him. "We thought we'd stack the lumber around back and cover it with a tarp to keep it dry."

"That's fine," Rose murmurs, hoping Hitch didn't pick up on Leslie's implication that he's her secret admirer.

Maybe it isn't that far-fetched a theory. He *is* shy, and he might not feel comfortable having feelings for his best friend's widow. Maybe this is his way of approaching her, bizarre as it seems.

"Mommy!" Jenna hollers from the living room. "Leo's outside in his pajamas!"

"What?" Rose hurries into the next room, just in time to see her son guiltily scurry back up the front steps.

She opens the door and pulls him back into the house. "Leo, what are you doing? You know you're not allowed to—"

"I just wanted to check and see if it was snowing yet."

"Leo, I told you, it's not going to snow today." She shakes her head. "Don't you ever go outside on your own again, do you understand? Somebody could drive by and see a little boy out there and . . ."

She trails off, not wanting to scare him.

"And kidnap you," Jenna supplies, her eyes still on the television. "Right, Mommy?"

Rose sighs. "Just don't ever go outside without asking first. Either of you. Got it? Leo?"

He nods.

"Jenna?"

"What?" She's not even listening, focused on

Scooby and Shaggy chasing a headless ghost through an old mansion.

Rose exhales through puffed cheeks. It's so damned hard, doing this alone.

She leaves both children, duly warned, in front of the TV and retreats to the kitchen, where her three guests are discussing the bookshelves.

"Hey, Rose, mind if I grab some of that coffee?" Peter breaks off to ask.

"Oh, Peter, I'm sorry. Of course. I didn't even offer you any."

"That's okay. I'm family. I can help myself." He takes a mug from the cupboard.

Family.

Funny. She doesn't think of him that way.

But Leslie is Sam's sister. Peter is going to be the kids' uncle—and yes, Rose's brother-in-law—in a matter of months.

Rose watches him settle himself at the table across from Hitch, who's spooning sugar into his coffee. How *wrong* it seems, suddenly, to have these two men here, in her kitchen, where Sam hasn't been in over a year.

It would be different if he were here with them, sitting at the table in his Saturday flannel shirt, drinking coffee and joining the conversation about lumber or whatever it is they're discussing. But if Sam were here, perhaps Peter and Hitch wouldn't be. Maybe Leslie wouldn't be rushing into marriage to a man she's only known a few months.

And maybe Leslie's right about Hitch—maybe he wouldn't be popping in so often. Maybe he's here because he's interested in her. Hitch is a great guy, but . . .

But what?

Face the facts, Rose. Sam is gone.
You're not just alone; you're lonely.

"Will I be in your way if I stick around to work on the shelves this afternoon, Rose?"

"Not at all," she tells Peter, pushing aside her unsettling thoughts. "In fact, I may go out and get groceries while you're—"

"Groceries?" Leslie wrinkles her nose. "That doesn't sound like much fun. Why don't you indulge yourself for a change, Rose? Go get a manicure or something? Or come with me and Jenna to the mall?"

"Or you can come along with us to the movies if you want," Hitch speaks up.

"Are you kidding? If you guys had kids you'd know that grocery shopping without two of them underfoot *is* self-indulgent."

"In that case, knock yourself out." Leslie takes a glass from the cupboard and runs cold water at the sink. "But I can't promise you that Jenna and I won't be stopping for manicures during *our* self-indulgent afternoon."

"Oh, Leslie, I don't know. The last time you—"

"This time I swear I'll let her get pastel polish only," Leslie promises, joining the men at the table with her glass of water.

Peter raises an eyebrow. "Pastel polish? As opposed to . . . ?"

"Black."

"It wasn't black, Rose," Leslie protests. "More a silvery gray."

"It was black."

They laugh about it; the conversation meanders amiably.

But Rose is merely going through the motions.

Because when she glances toward the window at the gray sky, wondering if it might snow after all, she suddenly remembers something.

The footprints in the snow.

The footprints she was convinced belonged to the meter reader.

Now she isn't so sure.

Saturday nights are the most difficult, David Brookman concludes, staring moodily into his second glass of single malt scotch.

It was on a Saturday night that he met Angela, a Saturday night that he married her, and a Saturday night that he saw her with *him*.

He lifts his glass to his lips to sip the amber liquid but swallows too much: a gulp that burns his throat all the way down. He barely notices, focused on a recollection of the anguished moment when his suspicions were confirmed and he saw her coming out of a dive on St. Mark's Place with another man.

Yes, St. Mark's Place, of all places, and she looked every bit the Village bohemian, wearing jeans and sandals, her newly shorn, highlighted hair falling into her eyes as she laughed at something her companion was saying. David's veins were a simmering cauldron as he watched the other man reach out to brush her hair back at her temples. The casual intimacy of the gesture assured him that this was no first-time dalliance.

When he resorted to following her downtown that night, he was hoping against hope that she was meeting a female friend, or, when her cab ventured into the heart of the Village, perhaps one of the men she'd met through her AIDS charity work.

Later, he would try to convince himself that he knew all along what he would find; that it was no shattering surprise. That he never really trusted her from the moment he met her at that party in Quogue; the party to which she had never been invited. She liked to tease him that she was just a Jersey girl there to land a wealthy husband, and voila! David Brookman swept her off her feet, and vice versa.

But the truth was, he did trust her. And it went against everything he had learned, growing up in the dual Brookman households, one on Park Avenue and one on Fifth. He was the product of his mother's first marriage and his father's second. There were half-siblings and step-siblings; men he called "uncle" who eventually became stepfathers, shadowy mistresses who were transformed into stepmothers, but only for a while.

Maybe David should have seen Angela for what she was right from the start.

His parents certainly did. Neither of them liked her. They considered her beneath the Brookmans. They accused him of marrying her simply to spite them.

And maybe, in retrospect, that was true. Maybe Angela was his way of rebelling. After all, he did everything else properly. He wore the clothes they chose for him, he went to the schools they had attended, he socialized with the sons and dated the daughters of their friends . . .

Until Angela.

Maybe he should have been prepared to find her gazing into another man's eyes on St. Mark's Place on that warm May evening.

Maybe he should have confronted her right there on the sidewalk.

But he didn't.

Brookmans don't cause scenes.

In the end, he never came face-to-face with her lover. For all those months that he kept his discovery to himself, he fantasized about finding the guy and beating him to a pulp. But he never did.

Angela ended the affair—or so she claimed—in the weeks before her death. David never knew who he was. It occurred to him, after her funeral, that he might have been there, among the mourners, but at the time, David didn't have the presence of mind to scan the crowd. And anyway, why would he? Angela was gone.

But gradually, when his initial shock subsided, David came to realize that her lover was still out there, still anonymous, perhaps smugly believing that her husband never even knew; perhaps grief-stricken, consumed by his own intimate recollections of David's wife.

Somehow, all of that makes David's grief that much more bitter. He was cheated out of the chance to—

"David? David Brookman?"

He looks up from his scotch to see a complete stranger standing before him, clad in what Angela once referred to as "the uniform." Saturday night in this dimly lit club on the Upper East Side calls for khaki slacks, a chambray shirt with an open collar, and a navy Brooks Brothers blazer. Only the initials on his jacket's gold monogrammed buttons set David apart from the newcomer.

"I'm sorry . . . have we met?"

"Dennis Carrington. I was a year behind you at MIT."

"Oh, right. Dennis." He's drawing a blank. "How are you?"

"Good, good." The man rests an elbow on the bar and motions for the bartender to come over. David lifts the glass to his lips again.

"Listen, I was sorry to hear about your wife."

This time, he chokes on the acrid gulp of scotch.

Dennis Carrington looks flustered. "I'm sorry. I didn't mean to upset you. I just—I read about it in the papers when it happened, and . . ."

David nods. Of course. The papers.

The entire world read about the Snow Angel's death in the papers. By the time they finished with her, she was a heroine, an icon, a saint.

"It was wonderful, what you did," Dennis goes on awkwardly. "After you had her, uh . . ."

"Unplugged?" The word is brittle.

"Look, I didn't mean to—"

"It's okay." David rises from the bar stool and throws down some bills.

"Why don't you let me buy you a drink?"

"No, thank you. I have to get home. Good night."

He makes his way through a haze of pipe and cigar tobacco, past countless other scotch-drinking men in their Brooks Brothers blazers with monogrammed buttons. The few women in the mix are wearing silk and pearls, mutely sipping white wine and looking as though they'd rather be anywhere else.

Angela would have hated this place, David thinks, as he tips the coat-check girl, who greets him by name.

She'd have found it incredibly dull. But she wouldn't have admitted it. No, she'd have been here in her silk and pearls, sipping wine and hovering at his elbow, pretending to belong in this crowd, to be one of them.

And all the while, would she have been thinking of *him*? Of the man who brushed her hair back from her eyes? Hair that was all wrong on her, in David's opinion. With her dark brows and olive skin, she looked unnatural as a blonde.

How many times, since that Saturday night on St. Mark's Place, has he wondered if she cut and dyed her hair for her lover?

It was just another unexpected change amidst myriad more subtle ones that last summer and fall. She took to listening to pop music instead of the classical she claimed to enjoy when she met him. She stopped eating red meat; she bought a juicer and concocted strange-colored beverages; she took up Pilates at the gym.

For her March birthday, when he "kidnapped" her one morning and surprised her with an impromptu trip to Barbados on a weekend when he was supposed to be working, she faltered before feigning pleasure. And she excused herself to go to the ladies' room several times at the airport. He followed her and saw her duck into a private corner, dialing her cell phone.

David later realized she was trying to reach *him*, to cancel whatever plans they might have had.

Perhaps it was partly his own fault. If he hadn't spent so much time working; if he had been more attentive, less preoccupied . . .

She might not have fallen in love with somebody else.

But she'd still be dead.

So what, in the end, is the difference?

Either way, he'd still be alone, and miserable on this gloomy Saturday night in February.

The difference, he reminds himself grimly as he steps out onto Third Avenue, turning up his collar against the icy blast, is that she'd still belong to David. Even in death.

Five

On Sunday morning, Christine leaves Ben sleeping soundly in the bedroom—and the faucet dripping steadily in the bathroom tub—and goes out into the freezing rain to eight-thirty mass at Blessed Trinity church three blocks away. She can't help feeling guilty as she slips into a back pew. This is just the second time she's set foot in Blessed Trinity since they moved to town, and she's only here because she has a selfish prayer.

As the elderly priest drones on in an endless homily about forgiveness, Christine silently closes her eyes and begs God to send her a child.

A child will change everything. A child, she is certain, will bring joy to her lonely days; will transform her increasingly taciturn husband into a loving family man.

God answered her prayers once before. Last year, when she discovered the lump in her breast that proved to be a malignant tumor, she turned in desperation to the religion she relinquished when she married out of faith.

Guilty now that the return to her Catholic roots lasted just long enough for her to receive a clean bill of health, Christine closes her eyes and promises God that this time, she won't stray. If she is blessed with motherhood, she'll christen the baby and raise it Catholic. Surely Ben won't mind. He hasn't set foot in a synagogue since his bar mitzvah.

When Christine opens her eyes, she sees that a steady stream of parishioners fill the aisle to receive communion. Her gaze falls on a familiar face.

It's her neighbor, Rose Larrabee. Christine almost didn't recognize her here, with her dark shoulder-length hair pulled straight back from her face in a wide clip at the base of her neck. The severe style renders her features gaunt; her posture exudes a fragile weariness.

Glimpsed from a distance through a windowpane, Rose has always appeared healthier and younger than she does now. She must be around Christine's age—perhaps in her early thirties—but she looks like she's been through hell.

I should be a good neighbor and ask her if there's anything I can do for her, Christine decides, watching Rose disappear behind a pillar on the aisle.

Five minutes later, as the organist plays "Now Thank We All Our God," Christine buttons the long cashmere wool dress coat she hasn't worn since her working days in the city. She steps into the aisle. Her stomach flutters a bit at the sight of a drowsy infant resting on its mother's shoulder just in front of her.

Maybe next year at this time . . .

Please, God.

She smiles at the sleepy-eyed baby, who looks startled. Uh-oh. The child scrunches his face as though he's about to burst into tears.

Dismayed, Christine looks away and glimpses Rose Larrabee a few steps behind her. Her head is bent as she dips her fingers into a font of holy water and crosses herself.

Christine steps out into the cold February air and waits until Rose draws nearer. She notes the nubby spots on her neighbor's beige-colored coat and the faint scuff marks on the unfashionably rounded toes of her brown boots. Money must be tight in the Larrabee household.

"Rose . . . ?" Christine touches her arm.

The other woman looks blank for a moment, before the recognition dawns.

"Oh, hi. Christine, right? You live next door? I haven't seen much of you since you moved in."

"I've seen you coming and going with your kids, but it's been too cold for me to stick my head out and say hello."

Too cold to stick your head out? What kind of lame excuse is that?

"Maybe we can go grab a cup of coffee or something across the street at the diner," Christine adds hastily. "That is, if you don't have to run back home to the kids?"

"Actually, they spent the night with my sister-in-law. She insisted. She thought I needed some time to myself."

"I'll bet that was nice for you," Christine tells her, thinking that she would gladly trade away her own endless solitude. Ben spent last night complaining about how lousy he was feeling and working in his upstairs office while she repeatedly surfed the measly few local television channels in a futile search for something to watch.

Rose shrugs. "It was restful. I dozed off at eight o'clock watching television and slept straight through till this morning. It was good to catch up on sleep, but . . ."

"You miss the kids? Let me guess . . . can't live with 'em, can't live without 'em, right?"

"That's pretty much it."

The wind gusts off the bay, tinged with the dank smell of the sea. Christine tucks her hands into her pockets, wishing she had remembered her gloves. The rain has stopped but the salt air still feels raw and wet, colder than before.

"So do you want to get some coffee?" she asks Rose, who looks at her watch, then nods. "Sure. I have about an hour before Leslie is supposed to bring the kids back home. I usually don't make it to mass this early. It's impossible to get out the door with the two of them before noon on a weekend. Do you usually come alone?"

"I usually don't come at all, but . . ."

But I'm bargaining with God again.

"Okay, guys, what do you want for breakfast?" Leslie rests her elbows on the laminate breakfast bar, her chin in her hands, and regards the pint-sized siblings parked on the pulled-out couch in front of her television set.

Only Leo looks up, and only long enough to suggest, "Candy?" before refocusing his gaze on Cartoon Network.

"Candy," Leslie echoes, shaking her head. "I had to ask."

She yawns, wondering what Peter is doing. He rarely sleeps in when he's here, but maybe at home it's different. Maybe he's still in bed.

She glances at the clock. Hmm. At nine-thirty? No way.

She reaches for the phone. Maybe he can pick

up some bagels and come over. They left their plans for today up in the air when they parted last night.

Normally, Peter would sleep here and they would spend Sunday morning together.

When Leslie returned from her outing yesterday with Jenna, she found Rose wrestling with a wailing, miserable Leo. It seemed Hitch had brought him to a movie, pumped him full of candy, and dropped him off before rushing off to fix somebody's pipe that had sprung a leak—at which point Leo threw a tantrum and begged to stay with Hitch.

"It's snowing here," he yelled at Rose. *"You said we could go on our sweds."*

Glancing from her sister-in-law's fatigued expression to her red-faced nephew to her eye-rolling niece, Leslie spontaneously said, *"I have an idea. I'll take the kids to my place for a sleepover."*

Cheers erupted from the kids. Rose tried to protest, then quickly gave in. Peter wrapped up his work on the shelves for the evening, and took everyone out for pizza before dropping Leslie and the little ones at her place.

"Have fun." He kissed her briefly on the cheek. *"I'll miss you."*

"You're not staying?" she asked, dismayed.

He eyed Jenna and Leo. *"I don't think that would be right, do you? I mean . . . we're not married yet. And anyway, there's no room."*

Now, as the phone rings on the other end of the line, Leslie finds herself wishing she had insisted that Peter stay anyway. She isn't accustomed to waking without him beside her, and last night was oddly lonely despite the children sleeping on either side of her in her queen-sized bed.

There's no answer at his place. She tries Rose, but she's not home either. Or maybe she's still sleeping. Leslie hopes she's still sleeping. She debates paging her sister-in-law, knowing she wears Sam's old pager every time she leaves the house when the kids aren't with her, but decides to wait until later.

Instead, she dials Peter's cell phone. He answers on the third ring, in his truck.

"Are you on your way here, I hope? I can use some bagels and—" She peers into the fridge. Not much here besides condiments, a stick of butter, bottled water, and two cartons containing her skim milk and Peter's coffee creamer. "—and some cream cheese. And whole milk, too. Or at least, two percent."

"I was going to call and tell you I'd meet you over at Rose's," he says. "I have to pick up more nails at Home Depot."

"Rose isn't home."

"That's okay. She gave me the spare key yesterday."

"Really?" Leslie shuts the fridge. "I already have a key to her place."

"I know, but it was when you were gone and she was on her way out to go grocery shopping. I told her I might run out to the hardware store and she said she didn't want me to leave the house unlocked."

"I told you, that anonymous admirer of hers is freaking her out. And I'd be willing to bet that it's—"

Conscious, suddenly, of the children within earshot, she clamps her mouth shut. Leo, especially, adores Hitch. He talked about him all night.

It breaks Leslie's heart that her brother's son is so hungry for a male role model.

"You'd be willing to bet that it's what?" Peter prods in her ear.

"Nothing. So I'll meet you at Rose's. We'll get breakfast on the way. Do you want anything?"

"Nah, I ate earlier."

She smiles. "Earlier? How much earlier?"

"You know me. Around six-thirty."

"Well, tomorrow morning you'd better plan on sleeping a little later," Leslie says. "And don't forget we're going to go look at cars for me."

"Les, you're fading. Can you hear me?"

"I can hear you just fine."

"I'm losing you, babe. I'll see you at Rose's."

He hangs up.

"Aunt Wes-wee? Got any choco-wat?"

She looks down to see Leo standing there in his footie pajamas.

"How about if I make you some . . . uh, chocolate toast?"

His face lights up. "What's that? It sounds good. Is it good?"

I have no idea, she thinks, opening a cabinet. She pulls out some powdered chocolate drink mix Peter bought, and what's left of a slightly stale loaf of bread.

"How do you make it?" Leo asks.

She smiles, taking out the sugar bowl as an afterthought. "It's a secret recipe. Sort of like cinnamon toast."

"On-wee it's choco-watee."

"Right. It's chocolatey."

"Can we call Uncle Hitch and tell him to come over to have some?"

"Nah, not today," she says. "But Uncle Peter will be waiting for us at your house, okay?"

Leo ponders this. "Petah's my uncle, too?"

"Well, not yet. But he's going to be married to me so he's going to be your uncle very soon. Your real uncle."

"Gweat! That's one, two uncles."

"Well, Uncle Hitch isn't really your uncle, Leo. He was a very good friend of your daddy's when they were little boys."

"And when they were big men, too."

She considers this. Hitch more or less vanished from Laurel Bay for the decade he was in the army. Presumably, Sam kept in touch with him through-out those years, but he rarely mentioned him to Leslie. Or maybe he did, and she didn't pay much attention.

Now, she can't help a twinge of resentment as she considers the fact that Hitch might be interested in replacing her brother in Rose's life. Sam should be here. Nobody can take his place.

But you don't want Rose to spend the rest of her life alone.

Of course not. But this just . . . it feels too soon. And the unsigned valentine, the chocolates . . .

That's not romantic, and it's not what Rose needs right now.

"Aunt Wes-wee?"

She looks down at Leo's solemn little face.

"Yes, sweetie?"

"Can you tell me more stowies about my daddy when he was a witto boy?"

A lump rises in her throat. At bedtime last night, after she taught them several nursery rhymes she and Sam used to sing when they were little, she told them

Daddy stories in the dark until they fell asleep. Of course, she embellished a little, and Sam always came off heroically. But that's what he was to Leslie, and that's what he was to his children. A hero.

"Sure, Leo," she tells the little boy who looks so much like his father did at that age. Sandy hair, green eyes, freckles across the bridge of his nose. He's the picture of Sam. "I'll tell you Daddy stories while we make the toast."

"Tell the one about how he saves the puppy who got caught in the bwambwee bushes by the beach. I wish my daddy was still around in case Cupid ever gets stuck in bwambwee bushes. Do you think anjos can save dogs? And people?"

The unexpected question brings tears to her eyes. "Sure, Sam. Angels can save dogs and people."

"I'm Weo! Wememb-o? Not Sam. Sam was Daddy."

She ruffles his hair. "Sorry, kiddo. Of course you're Leo. Okay, it was a sunny summer day and your daddy and I were at the beach with Grandma . . ."

"More coffee, ladies?"

"I'd better not. I should get home," Rose regretfully tells Christine, seated across the booth from her.

"None for me either. Just the check," Christine tells the waitress, who nods and drifts back behind the counter with her half-full coffeepot.

Christine Kirkmayer has been a pleasant surprise, Rose thinks, spreading another bit of concord grape jelly on her last triangle of toast. She looks up at the pretty, round-faced blonde on the other side of the table. Christine reminds her of Jenna, somehow, though with her pale complexion, light blue eyes, wavy hair, and all-around chubbiness, she looks nothing like her. But she seems to exude a warm, little-girl enthusiasm that Rose finds especially appealing on this dreary Sunday morning.

"It was so nice to have the chance to chat with another adult without the kids underfoot," Rose tells her neighbor.

They've spent the last forty-five minutes in fluid conversation, mostly about Laurel Bay, and small-town life versus the city, and what the Kirkmayers should expect when the summer people arrive on eastern Long Island in a few months. Rose described to her how Bayview Books goes from being quiet and empty to jammed with out-of-towners seeking local maps and postcards, bestseller beach reads, the occasional obscure, intellectual title—and any number of things no year-rounder would expect to find in a small-town bookstore.

"Well, feel free to call me any time you're around," Christine says. "Like I said, I'm home most of the time."

"I wish I were."

"But you seem to like working at the store."

"I do. It's good for me to get out and see people, and I really like Bill—he's the guy who works with me."

"The cute one with the blue-green eyes? I've seen him when I've gone in there to browse."

"He's the one."

"He's so good-looking. He reminds me of the actor who plays Chandler on *Friends*. Is he married?"

"Uh-uh. He's gay."

"Too bad." Christine takes a last nibble of her toast. "And too bad your boss is such a pain in the—"

"Luke?" Oops. Did she make him sound that way? She'd better be careful about venting when she's in earshot of the locals. The last thing she wants is for it to get back to Luke that she was bad-mouthing him in the diner. "He means well, and he knows what he's doing. He's just . . . he's all business, you know?"

"I definitely know. I'm married to someone exactly like that."

Rose searches her memory for Christine's husband's name. She only met him once, on the day they moved in. Is it Brian? No . . .

No, Ben. That's it.

"Ben works in the city, right?" she asks Christine, who nods.

"He's an accountant, and it's tax season, so . . ."

"So you won't be seeing him until mid-April?"

"If then. He's always pretty busy."

"My husband was usually busiest in the summer," Rose tells her. "He was a contractor."

"I didn't know that."

Rose wonders what else Christine doesn't know. The other woman looks slightly uncomfortable.

"Did I tell you he was electrocuted?" Rose asks, knowing perfectly well that she didn't. But she feels the sudden need to explain—or maybe, just to talk about her loss for a change with somebody who doesn't share her grief. Somebody who will just listen.

"I didn't know that. I'm so sorry." Christine shakes her head. "Was he on a job?"

"No. He was in our own backyard."

"Oh, God. That's so . . . How long ago was it?"

Rose doesn't have to stop and think. She is perpetually aware of just how long it has been since the cozy walls her husband's love had built around her came crashing down. "Thirteen and a half months."

"I'm sorry," Christine repeats, as heartfelt as before. "I can't imagine what it must be like for you. It's hard enough to lose somebody, but that young, and so suddenly . . ."

"The thing was . . . I never expected it to be him." The words escape Rose before she realizes that she may have revealed more than she meant to.

It's too late to take them back.

Instant understanding radiates from Christine's Wedgwood eyes. "You thought it would be you? Were you with him when it happened?"

"No, it isn't that . . . he was out there alone. Not that I haven't thought a million times that if I had dragged myself out of bed and gone with him—or stopped him from going out in the first place—I could have changed things."

"You can't do that to yourself, Rose."

Yes, she can. She can, and she frequently does.

Ignoring Christine's comment, she takes a deep breath and says, "I was sick. A few years ago, right after I had Leo. It was my heart—hypertrophic cardiomyopathy. It's a genetic condition. My mother had it too."

And it killed Mommy, out of the blue, when she was only in her forties . . .

But that's too much information. She doesn't have to share that. She doesn't have to share any of it, really. Strange that she finds herself wanting to.

"Oh, Rose . . ." Christine reaches across the table to touch her trembling hand. "You've been through so much."

She nods. "It got so bad they didn't think I was

going to make it. Then I had a heart transplant, and . . . here I am."

As if it were that simple.

As if she never struggled through the dark, endless months of illness, waiting for the call that seemed as if it would never come . . .

Then, when it did come, the unexpected guilt that she was given this chance to live only because somebody had died. A woman her own age, tragically, unexpectedly. Rose never knew her name, only that she had been on life support after a Christmas Eve hit and run in Manhattan. Sam said they could easily find out who she was, but Rose didn't want to know. Somehow, that would make it harder.

She still vividly recalls that day, the one that started out so normally and ended in a flurry of preparations. It was dusk when Sam rushed her to the hospital; the city's skyline a stark silhouette against a surprisingly bright winter sunset. Sitting silently in the passenger seat, Rose stared at the fading light, wondering if she would ever see another sunset. The day, the month, the year itself were drawing to a close; perhaps her life was, too.

She still gets a lump in her throat when she remembers the traumatic goodbyes at the hospital, just in case . . .

Then, the surgery.

The recovery.

The realization that she was going to be okay. That she and Sam were going to get their happy ending after all.

Or so she naively believed.

It was Sam's idea for her to write to the donor's family. He thought the woman's husband would want to know about her.

It was the hardest letter Rose ever had to write. She labored over it for days.

In the end, she kept it simple.

She thanked the donor's family, and promised that she'd take good care of her heart.

She never received a reply.

And after she lost Sam, and experienced paralyzing grief first-hand, she understood why.

Even after a year, it's all she can do to make it through each day.

"A heart transplant?" Christine is gaping at her. "You went through a heart transplant, with two small children? That's incredible."

"It was a few years ago." As if that makes it any less extraordinary.

But you get used to it. You get used to anything.

Rose shrugs, unwilling to accept Christine's admiration, or worse, her pity. "I'm fine now. I just get tired sometimes, and I have to be careful. You know, physically."

"And emotionally. Because if you let yourself, you'll be afraid every second that it's going to happen again." Christine meets Rose's gaze with unexpected empathy. "You never really get past that threat, do you?"

"You sound as though you're talking from experience."

"I've been there. I'm still there, actually. Mentally, if not physically. It was breast cancer. Stage two, an aggressive form, with nodes involved. But I'm clear now. Nothing left but a jagged scar across my chest to remind me every day of how lucky I am to be alive."

"Oh my God." Rose gapes back at her, at this kindred spirit who's been right under her nose for months.

"So you see, I get it," Christine says. "I know where you're coming from. I don't have kids—and I do have my husband—but I know what it feels like to be . . . well, a survivor. That's what they call it, right? At least with cancer."

Rose nods. "That's what they call it. And that's how it is with me, too."

Whenever she sees a tragedy on the news—some global disaster: an earthquake, a terrorist attack, a plane crash—she relates to the bruised, bleeding people who stagger, dazed, from rubble and smoking ruins. Survivors. Shaken, battered, but so damn lucky to be alive.

"I had no idea you'd been through so much," Christine tells her.

"Same here. I guess we have a lot in common."

The waitress silently drops the check as she passes.

Christine picks it up. "If you ever need to talk . . ."

"You, too," Rose says, sensing that it's time to leave. She pulls out her wallet, grabs some bills.

"No," Christine says. "It's my treat. You get it next time."

Rose smiles. Next time. That would be good. She could use a friend. A friend who understands.

"Thank you, Christine."

"No problem. I think I'm going to wait and get Ben a coffee and a bacon and egg sandwich to go. But don't tell my mother-in-law. According to her, he should be watching his cholesterol and eating kosher. But I always say, let the poor guy live a little. He's getting over the flu and he's probably hungry."

Rose smiles. "What a nice wife." She used to do things like that for Sam. Bring home a little something for him after she'd been out, or pick up his favorite ice cream as a treat . . .

"Yeah, well, he doesn't deserve it considering how cranky he was while he was sick," Christine says. "But there's nothing in the house for breakfast anyway, and I shop on Mondays so that I can clip the coupons from Sunday's paper . . . oh, here I go again. I've got to let you go. Can you tell I don't get out much? I'm talking your ear off."

"It's okay. I know how it is. And I'm just glad I got my grocery shopping over with yesterday." Yes, along with piles of laundry and some dusting and vacuuming.

Rose realizes that the whole blessedly unconstrained day stretches ahead of her. Tomorrow, too.

"Enjoy the rest of the weekend, Christine."

"You, too, Rose. And you know, I always see you dragging your kids into the car to run errands— like I said, I'm around every day, and it gets lonely with Ben working so much. I can babysit anytime."

"Oh, I wouldn't ask you to do that."

"Why not? It would give me something fun to do. I love children, and yours seem very well behaved."

Christine's smile seems a shade wistful.

"Well, thank you. You never know, I just might take you up on that offer someday," Rose says. With a wave, she makes her way out of the diner, past a line of churchgoers waiting for tables.

She gets into the car and turns the key in the ignition.

"—and you're listening to *Sunday Morning Oldies* on WLIR," a DJ's voice greets her. Driving the few blocks back to Shorewood Lane, she finds herself singing along with an old Neal Sedaka song.

A few thin rays of winter sunshine stream down through a fracture in the clouds.

"Dum dooby doo dum du-um . . ."

Leslie and the kids aren't here yet. Good. She'll have time to change into some comfortable jeans before they arrive, and maybe even read a chunk of the thick Sunday *Newsday*.

Feeling almost carefree, she pulls into the driveway and bounds up the front steps, still humming. She can hear Cupid barking from somewhere inside as she turns her key in the lock.

"It's okay, buddy, I'm home. I'll take you for a walk," she calls, wondering why he isn't scampering to the door to greet her as he's been doing since they got him last week.

She steps over the threshold. As she wipes her boots hastily on the mat, she realizes that Cupid's barks sound oddly muffled.

Then, as she closes the door behind her, she becomes aware of another sound.

A deafening sound that sends a cascade of arctic chills down her spine.

The entire house reverberates with the steady, unmistakable rhythm of a beating heart.

You never know how busy a Sunday morning at Millpond Realty is going to be. At least, not at this time of year.

In warm-weather months, hordes of young Manhattan couples are guaranteed to venture to northern Westchester County on weekend mornings with real estate ads and paper gourmet coffee cups in hand, pushing toddlers down the leafy suburban streets in Peg Perago strollers. More often than not, the wife is pregnant and has just realized, in a panic, that there is no way to fit another child with all the trimmings into a Junior Four on the Upper East Side.

Isabel Van Nuys was once that woman, about two decades—a lifetime—ago.

Now she's the one seated behind a desk in the realty office in the heart of Woodbury Hills, discussing new and potential listings with the other agents between occasional phone calls.

Her hair, once a long, mousy brown, is frosted ash-blond and styled in a simple pageboy. A recent Botox treatment helped to smooth the tiny wrinkles around her mouth and her hazel eyes. She wears a smart navy suit, medium-heeled pumps, and simple silver studs at her ears, looking every bit the classic Westchester matron she never thought she'd want to be.

"Did you hear that Jason Hollander is getting his place ready to sell?" asks the similarly coifed, similarly attired Mary Mitchell, taking a sip from her black coffee, which is the only thing Isabel has ever seen her ingest in the four years they've been working together.

"Jason Hollander? The record producer?" Cameron Josephson, twentysomething and having just passed her brokerage exam, looks up from the phone she was dialing. "Where does he live?"

"Out on Pond Ridge Road," Isabel informs her, as Mary rolls her eyes to suggest that anyone in their business should be well aware of this fact. "He has a fifty-acre estate out there. I hear there's a recording studio in the main house and a mini amphitheater on the grounds."

"Wow. I'd love to see it."

"Well if he lists the place, you most likely will."

Isabel smiles at Cameron's slightly star-struck expression. She's just a kid, really—not long out of Bryn Mawr, living back home with her parents over in Bedford, half-heartedly dabbling in a relatively cushy career while attempting to land a husband before the biological clock starts ticking.

There are dozens of young women like her around here; Isabel supposes that after next year—her last at Vassar—her oldest daughter will join the ranks.

Andrea won't be able to afford a place of her own—certainly not in the city, and not even here. Her father sure as hell can't be counted upon to give her money once he's fulfilled his tuition obligation.

These days, Ted is financially focused on the Mc-Mansion he's having built down in Armonk, and on the toddler sons he has with his second wife. Formerly the "other woman" in Isabel's doomed marriage, Shelby is a living cliché: blond, slender, and apparently oblivious to the fact that she's got a few good years at most before her husband strays—if he hasn't already begun to.

Oh, well. Ted's infidelity is no longer Isabel's problem, thank goodness. He belongs in the past, along with her low self-esteem, her money problems, and her life-threatening illness.

These days, she's fit and healthy, feeling good about herself and her single lifestyle at last. She may not be wealthy by Westchester County standards, but she just deposited a nice fat commission check in her savings account and a slightly smaller one in her checking account, enough to cover the in-ground pool she plans to install this summer.

And unbeknownst to her coworkers, she's already

laid the groundwork to snag the Jason Hollander list-ing when he puts his estate on the market next month. She's the listing agent for Hollander's good friend and Pond Ridge Road neighbor Hesper Cantwell III, who is asking and will probably get 2.5 million dollars for his sprawling Victorian mansion on ten acres. Hess, as he prefers to be called, intro-duced her to Jason Hollander last weekend.

There was something slimy about the way the record producer looked her up and down appre-ciatively before she removed her sunglasses and he apparently realized she was almost old enough to be his mother. Still, she gave him her card, and he said—

"Isabel?" Amy, the high school student who helps out with the phones on weekends, interrupts her thoughts. "I'm forwarding a call to your desk."

Well, speak of the devil. At least, Isabel hopes it's Jason Hollander. Wouldn't that be a nice way to top off the weekend?

Seeing Cameron's wistful expression as she sits beside her silent phone, Amy adds, "He specifically asked to speak to Isabel."

Meaning, he isn't a random caller willing to be transferred to any available agent.

"Thanks, Amy." Isabel lifts the receiver as it rings. "This is Isabel Van Nuys. How can I help you?"

A male voice clears its throat. Then an unfamil-iar voice says, "Hi. I'm interested in relocating to Westchester County, and I was wondering if you'd be able to show me some properties."

"Of course. We specialize in relocations, actually, so . . ." She picks up a pen and holds it poised over her notepad. "Is this a corporate relocation?"

"No."

Too bad. When an employer is helping to foot the moving costs, people tend to spend a little more on the house itself.

"Do you have any idea what you're looking for, Mr.—?"

"Gabriel."

"All right, Mr. Gabriel, why don't you give me your price range, number of bedrooms, desired location, when you're moving, that sort of thing?"

There's a pause.

She can hear a radio playing in the background. Sounds like an old Billy Joel song.

"Something medium sized, I guess," he says. "In the, uh, five to six hundred thousand dollar range."

"Mmm hmm . . ." She makes note of that. "And is it just for you, or . . . ?" She trails off tactfully.

He takes her cue. "I have a wife, and . . . and a baby. And we want to have more kids, so I guess we'll need, uh, at least three bedrooms. Four would be better."

He seems vaguely nervous. She doesn't blame him. He's about to spend a helluva lot of money on less house than he would get for half a million anywhere else in the country.

"Well, I have to assure you that Woodbury Hills is a wonderful place to raise a family." Wonderful and outrageously expensive.

"That's what I hear."

It occurs to her to ask him how he did hear, and how he happened to specifically request to speak to her. She opens her mouth but he speaks first.

"It sounds like you're speaking from experience. Do you live there in town?"

"Right outside of town," she tells him. "Now, let's

see, Mr. Gabriel, do you like old houses, or are you looking for something more modern?"

"Either, I guess."

She scribbles the word *flexible,* and beside it, *27 Gilder Road?*

That particular property has been on the market for at least six weeks, which is unusual in Woodbury Hills. Isabel isn't surprised it's been such a difficult sell so far. For one thing, it's in a rather remote location as opposed to the widely desired family-friendly neighborhood within walking distance to town and the commuter line to the city. For another, the contemporary split level with a boxy stucco exterior doesn't appeal to most buyers, who tend to favor classic clapboard houses with shutters, windowpanes, and red brick chimneys.

Isabel realizes that Mr. Gabriel has fallen silent again.

"*. . . the sinners are much more fun . . .*" Billy Joel sings in the background on the other end of the line.

"I'll put together some listings, Mr. Gabriel, and I'll FedEx them to you so that you can go through them with your wife and decide which ones you want to see. Then you can let me know when you'll be in town so that—"

"Oh, you don't have to send them to me first. I'll just come up and you can show me whichever houses you think I'd like."

"Are you sure? Sometimes it's possible to weed out homes just based on the listing. It could save you—" *And me*—"a lot of time."

"No, thank you. I don't have time to see listings first. I'm, uh, actually going to be there tomorrow."

"Tomorrow?" she repeats. "Well, that's sooner than I'd expected."

"Is that all right?"

"Of course. Of course it's all right." There goes her plan to drive up to Poughkeepsie and spend the day with Andrea. "I'll get some listings together for you and we can meet here in my office in the morning. I'll give you directions. Which airport are you coming from?"

"Oh, I'll be driving down from Boston," he says unexpectedly.

Boston? For some reason, she assumed he was relocating from someplace down South. What made her think that? It wasn't an accent—he doesn't have the slightest trace of one.

She gives him directions, arranges to meet him at nine-thirty, then hangs up to find nosy Mary looming over her desk.

"You've been pretty busy lately, Isabel."

"Yup." Smiling, she opens a manilla folder and hunts through it for the listing for 27 Gilder Road as the Billy Joel song continues to play in her head.

"Excuse me, Miss, did you want butter on that egg and bacon sandwich?"

"No," Christine says automatically, her thoughts on the leaky faucet back home. She forgot all about asking Rose about her plumber.

Belatedly, it occurs to her that Ben would probably like a little butter on his sandwich. She opens her mouth to call the waitress back to the counter, but she's already disappeared into the busy kitchen at the back of the diner.

Oh, well. Ben can always put butter on it at home if he wants it. For all she knows, he still hasn't regained his appetite. Maybe a container of chicken soup would have been a better thing to bring him.

She eyes the desserts in the rotating glass case by the register as she waits for the sandwich. The carrot cake blanketed in cream cheese icing looks especially good, but she can't indulge. Not today. Not for a while.

She can't help wondering whether, if she takes off the extra twenty pounds or so she's gained since marriage, Ben will find her more attractive.

If he finds her more attractive, he'll be more inclined to make love to her during her next fertile period. Which means she has a little over two weeks to lose a few pounds.

She used to be skinny. Not as skinny as Rose Larrabee, but nobody would have called her chubby a few years ago.

These days, every time she looks in the mirror, the word *chubby* is what comes to mind—along with *frumpy*.

Not that Ben is currently the spitting image of his youthful self, either. For one thing, he had a hell of a lot more hair when they met, and it was less conservatively cut. He wore contacts instead of glasses, and his wardrobe wasn't quite as—well, stodgy as it is now.

Of course, she looked different back then, too: a size eight when she met Ben, and wore tailored skirts and heels to work daily as an executive secretary just across Forty-second Street from his office. She used to see him almost every morning in Grand Central Station: a dark-haired, wedding-ring-free stranger who invariably rode up the escalator reading a hardcover novel in a transparent glossy cover. She was intrigued by this; not just by the fact that he read something other than the newspapers, but that he clearly got his books from a library.

So she knew right away that they had something in common. Christine was quite fond of the New York library branch near her Queens apartment. She never saw eligible-looking men during her weekly browsing visits there, just senior citizens, students, and the occasional story-hour-bound dad with toddlers in tow.

Now, looking back, she is amused that it never occurred to her that Ben might be using the library because he was too poor—or too cheap—to buy books.

She was too busy with her investigation, figuring there was a good chance that the library-book-toting commuter lived in Queens, as she had seen him exiting the number 7 train a few times. She hoped she might bump into him in the library stacks some day, as she couldn't seem to work up the nerve to speak to him in the midst of rush-hour chaos.

Nor did it ever occur to Christine that Ben was noticing her as well. He seemed perpetually engrossed in his reading. Thus, she was utterly caught off-guard when Ben looked up from his Tom Wolfe novel one morning out of the blue and made eye contact with her as she was riding up the escalator two steps behind him.

She remembers what he said, and exactly how he said it. *"How's it going?"* he asked, his voice cracking a little on the *go* syllable.

She has no idea how she responded. But the next thing she knew, he was asking her out for coffee. As it turned out, he didn't live in Queens, but on Long

Island—he transferred from the Long Island Railroad to the number 7 train each morning.

They started meeting regularly for lunch at Houlihan's near their respective offices, moved into a Tudor City studio apartment together a year later, and were married two years after that. They were about to start trying to have a baby when she found the lump.

She sighs as the waitress comes out of the kitchen with a foil-wrapped sandwich and a steaming take-out cup full of coffee. The coffee smells wonderful—far more appealing than the cup of decaf she had with Rose. She doesn't dare indulge in caffeine, just in case she might be pregnant.

She doesn't want to get her hopes up, but her period was due yesterday. She doesn't feel as though she's premenstrual, but you never know.

"You want cream and sugar?"

"That's okay. He'll put it in at home." Fumbling in her wallet for money, Christine comes up short. Oh, right. She put a twenty into the collection basket at mass earlier—a shameful attempt to bribe God into answering her prayers.

"Do you take credit cards?" she asks, fishing for her Visa.

"Credit cards, and checks, too, if you're local."

"I'm local, and that's good to know. But I'll use my Visa today."

Christine doubts that any diner in Manhattan would take a check. That's the nice thing about living in a small town. People get to know you. Especially in a place like this. Looking around, she decides that half the population of Laurel Bay seems to be waiting for a booth here, most dressed in their Sunday best, others in their comfy Sunday sweats or jeans. She even sees a few familiar faces, including a middle-aged woman who walks a German shepherd by the house every morning, and the guy who pumps gas at the full serve down the block, now wearing a suitcoat and carrying a little girl in a pink dress.

The waitress takes her card and runs it through the machine, then hands the slip to Christine, along with a pen that's inscribed with the name of the restaurant. It says Milligan's Cafe On the Bay, but she's lived here long enough to know that nobody ever calls it that. It's just "the diner." Christine adds a tip, signs the receipt, and hands everything back.

"Keep the pen," the woman says. "We have millions of 'em. They're giveaways."

"Oh, thanks." Christine tucks it back into her purse, grabs Ben's breakfast, and heads out the door, hoping she'll find her husband in a decent mood for a change.

" . . . *You had a nice white dress and a party on your confirmation,*" Leslie sings along with the radio as she turns off the main road toward Shorewood Lane.

"Aunt Leslie? What's a confirmation? Is it like a wedding?" Jenna asks from the back seat.

"Sort of. More like a first communion, though."

"I'm going to make my communion next year," Jenna proudly informs her. "And I'm going to get a beautiful white dress with a veil. Mommy said so."

"So am I."

"Leo! You are not!"

"I am too."

Jenna sighs with the exaggerated exasperation of a seven-year-old sister. "Aunt Leslie, tell him he's not."

"Leo, you'll make your first communion in a few years."

"And you won't have a white dress with a veil," Jenna adds.

"I will too."

And here we go again.

Spending time with her niece and nephew has been mostly a pleasure, but their constant bickering is really starting to get on Leslie's nerves. At McDonald's, where they stopped for breakfast after the kids decided the chocolate toast had just been a pre-breakfast snack, they argued over everything, from who got to sit on the same side of the booth with Aunt Leslie to whether Chicken McNuggets can be construed as a healthy breakfast.

Before they left, Jenna started crying because the Barbie doll she'd brought with her was missing. Leslie combed the car, the parking lot and the restaurant before spying a tuft of blond nylon hair sticking out of Leo's coat pocket. Naturally, he said the doll got in there by accident.

"It did not!" Jenna shrieked so loudly that everyone in McDonald's turned to stare. *"You're always stealing things! I heard Mommy say so."*

Leslie will be glad to hand them over to their mother again. How the heck does Rose do it? She always seems so patient. Maybe she just tunes them out.

Leslie tries to do just that now, turning up the volume and singing along with the radio, but the song is just about over.

The DJ announces, "That was Levittown native

Billy Joel with 'Only the Good Die Young,' and you're listening to *Sunday Morning Oldies* on WLIR. Next, here's Petula Clark with—"

"Later, Petula," Leslie mutters, pulling into the driveway behind Rose's car and turning off the radio. Hmm. Peter isn't here yet. He must have gotten hung up at the—

"Hey, what's Mommy doing?" Leo sounds concerned.

"Uh-oh. She looks mad," Jenna adds.

Leslie glances up to see Rose out on the front porch in her dress coat. She doesn't appear to be coming or going, just . . . standing.

And she doesn't look mad. She looks upset. Terribly upset.

Leslie's stomach twitches. Has there been bad news?

Peter.

Oh, God.

Did something happen to Peter?

She opens her car door and hurries toward her sister-in-law as Leo hollers, "Wait, Aunt Wes-wee, get me out!"

"Rose? Is something wrong?"

Rose nods, her arms wrapped around herself as she turns haunted, frightened eyes up to meet Leslie's expectant gaze.

"Someone's been here," she says in a low voice. "In the house. While I was gone."

"Oh, Rose . . ." Leslie exhales in relief. "That was probably just Peter. He said he was coming over and that he had the key. He probably just ran back out to get a cup of cof—"

"No, Leslie, not Peter. Somebody else. Somebody who's trying to scare the hell out of me."

"What do you mean?"

"Mommy!" Jenna calls from the car. "I can't unstrap Leo. Help!"

"I'll be right there," Rose calls as she reaches behind her for the knob and pushes the door open a crack. She whispers to Leslie, "Listen."

Leslie leans in. Startled by the loud, pulsating sound, she looks at Rose. "What the heck is *that?*"

"It took me a few seconds to figure it out. . . . It's Leo's new sound machine. It has a heartbeat setting and somebody must have—"

She breaks off abruptly at the sound of gravel crunching and tires splashing along the wet road.

Leslie turns to see Peter's truck pulling up at the curb.

"Mommy!" Now both Jenna and Leo are hollering from the back seat of her car.

"I'll get them," she tells Rose. "You just . . . wait here."

"I don't want the kids to hear it," Rose protests. "They might be scared."

"Of the sound machine? Do you want to run in and turn it off so that—"

"No! Leslie, I'm afraid to go into the house. Somebody's been in there."

Peter's car door slams. "Hi, guys," he calls jovially.

"Hi, honey. Maybe . . ." Lowering her voice, Leslie searches for something reassuring to tell Rose. "Maybe the sound machine's on some sort of timer and it went on by itself?"

"It doesn't have a timer. And we keep it on the mountain stream setting, and never this loud."

"Well, maybe Leo changed the setting and the volume," she suggests, seeing Peter take a hardware store bag from the back of the truck.

"Yes, but Leo has been gone. The house has been empty since I left for church two hours ago, Leslie. I'm telling you, somebody came in. And it's a *heartbeat*, Leslie."

"So you think somebody is . . . I don't know, teasing you? About the heart surgery?"

"Mommy!"

"Coming!" Rose shouts impatiently, then asks Leslie, "What do you think?"

"I think it's your secret admirer trying to tell you he's in love with you. I think that's what the heartbeat means. And I think that the secret admirer is—"

"Hitch," Rose says flatly. "I know you do. But Leslie, Hitch wouldn't do something like this. He knows it would scare me to think that somebody's been in the house when I'm not here. And in my car. And he would never call me in the middle of the night, either."

"Well, you don't know that that has anything to do with this. It was probably just a wrong number," Leslie points out, watching Peter walk over to the truck where her niece and nephew are waiting restlessly. He reaches in to release Leo's seat restraints.

"I didn't feel like it was a wrong number. I know it sounds like I'm losing it here, but . . . Leslie, I can't help being freaked out. Somebody was in my house."

"What are you talking about?" Peter asks, coming up beside the porch, the kids trailing behind him. "Somebody was in your house? Who?"

"Shh . . ." Leslie raises a finger to her lips and shoots a meaningful glance at the children.

"Thanks for getting them out of the car." Rose hurries down the steps and past him to hug Jenna and Leo, who are bickering about who gets to feed Cupid.

"Oh . . . the dog," Rose turns toward Leslie and Peter. "She's in the house. She was barking when I opened the door. I ran back out again when I heard—"

She breaks off, conscious of the children listening.

"Heard what?" Peter asks, looking from Rose to Leslie.

"Hey, guys, we forgot to get your overnight bags out of my trunk," Leslie says brightly, taking her niece and nephew by the hand and leading them back to the car.

Behind her, she sees Peter and Rose talking quietly for a moment. Then Peter pats her sister-in-law briefly on the arm before going up the steps and into the house.

"Be careful, Peter," Leslie calls after him, frowning.

"Why does he have to be careful? Is he going to use his hammer?" Leo wants to know.

"No, it's just . . ." *Just what, Les? That there was an intruder in the house while Mommy was gone?* "Um, power tools," she amends. "He's going to use his power tools and I always tell him to be careful with them."

"Can I go watch?"

"Not right now."

She stares up at the house. Rose is hovering nervously on the porch. The children race each other down to the sidewalk and back, with Jenna contradicting Leo's repeated shouts of "I win!"

Leslie wants to believe that Rose is overreacting to this sound machine incident, and the phone call, and the anonymous gifts. But what if she isn't? What if somebody other than harmless Hitch is actually behind this?

"Excuse me . . . is everything okay over there?"

She looks up, startled, to see an unfamiliar man poking his head through the open front door of the house next door. Leslie recalls Rose saying that a couple moved in there a few months ago, but this is the first time she's seen anybody over there.

Rose appears to be at a loss for words, distracted by the children and by Peter inside the house, so Leslie crosses the patch of grass to speak to the neighbor.

"Hi, I'm Rose's sister-in-law, Leslie," she tells the man, who has now stepped out onto the small porch.

"Ben Kirkmayer." He reaches down over the railing to shake her hand. The gesture seems oddly formal, considering that he's wearing flannel pajamas and slippers. She senses tension in his handshake and in the dark eyes regarding her from behind thick horn-rimmed glasses. He's probably self-conscious about what he's wearing, and looks like he'd be far more comfortable in a suit and tie, carrying a briefcase instead of the terry cloth dishtowel in his hand.

"Rose just got home and she thinks there might have been an intruder in the house," Leslie tells him. "You didn't see anything strange over there, did you?"

"No, but then, I'm not the type to spy on my neighbors through the windows," he says, sounding almost defensive.

"I didn't mean—I just thought you might have glanced out and seen somebody prowling around."

"If I had, I would have called the police," he informs her. "What makes her think there was an intruder in the house. Are there signs of a break-in?"

"No, it's not that, it's . . ." Leslie eyes the man,

uncertain how much she should reveal. He is, after all, a stranger. Besides, you never know. What if . . . ?

Nah. She dismisses that theory as quickly as it flits into her head. There's no way this uptight married man is concealing a flaming infatuation for Rose. In fact, it's difficult to imagine him being passionate about anything.

At the sound of wild barking, both Leslie and Ben Kirkmayer turn back toward the house next door. Peter has emerged onto the porch, the puppy wriggling in his arms.

"Ow! He bit me!" He lets go of the dog abruptly and he drops the few feet to the ground.

"You dropped our dog!" Jenna shouts as the puppy releases an accusatory yelp. Trailed by Leo, she scampers after her pet across the brittle, muddy lawn.

Leslie abandons the neighbor on his porch and hurries toward Peter, who has thrust his knuckle into his mouth, wincing with pain.

"Are you okay, Peter?"

He removes his hand from his mouth and examines it. "He barely broke the skin. I thought you said he was friendly, Leslie."

"He is. I don't know why he'd—"

"Where did you find him?" Rose interrupts.

"He was shut in that small room where I'm working on the shelves. And he crapped in the toolbox I left there yesterday."

"But . . . he was upstairs when I left." Her uneasiness now verges on alarm. "You're saying the French door was closed and he was trapped in there?"

Peter nods, his knuckle back in his mouth.

"What about the sound machine?" Leslie asks.

"It was on," he says with a shrug. "The volume was all the way up. I unplugged it. Maybe there's an electrical short in one of the wires."

Electrical short. Wires.

The disturbing memory of Sam's freak electrocution bursts into Leslie's thoughts.

But that wasn't a short in a wire. That was high-voltage cables coming down in a storm.

"Was there . . . was there anything else?" Rose asks, her eyes shadowed with trepidation.

He meets her gaze and shakes his head. "I checked the whole house. It doesn't look like anything was ransacked, and there were no broken windows or anything like that. I'm not sure how anybody could have broken in. Maybe it was just a short in the wire, like I said."

"Then . . . what about the dog?" Rose's voice rises, shrill with barely contained hysteria.

They turn their gazes to the children romping on the grass with the barking puppy.

"Maybe he got himself trapped in there on his own."

"How? By turning the doorknob with his paw?"

"Rose, try to calm down," Leslie says, pushing aside her own worry and resting a hand on her sister-in-law's coat sleeve.

"You never know. Puppies are capable of all kinds of mischief, Rose," Peter says.

You never know.

Just what Leslie thought moments earlier about Rose's taciturn neighbor. She glances over at the porch next door, intending to give him a wave to show him that everything is okay, whether it is or not.

But the porch is empty; the front door closed.

"I'm calling the police," Rose says.

Leslie turns her attention back to the matter at hand. "That's a good idea."

"But won't the kids get scared if the police show up? You said Leo's been having trouble sleeping as it is," Peter says.

Rose looks torn. "Leslie, can you take the kids out for—I don't know, for ice cream, or something? If somebody has been in the house, I need to report it."

"Sure."

"I'll come, too," Peter says.

"Maybe you should stay here to talk to the police with Rose," Leslie tells him. "You know, so you can tell them what you found."

"Oh . . . right. Okay."

As she loads the kids—and Cupid, whom they refuse to leave behind—into her car, Leslie glances again at the house next door.

It almost looks as though a figure is standing in a window on the side of the house facing Rose's.

She blinks, and the figure—if it was ever really there in the first place—is gone.

Hmm . . .

You never know.

"Are you hungry?" Christine asks Ben, sticking her head into his office.

He jumps, his hand knocking the coffee cup beside the computer. It sloshes over onto some papers.

"Dammit!"

"Sorry." She hurries across the hall to the bathroom and returns with a wad of paper towels. "Here. I didn't mean to scare you."

"I told you never to sneak up on me when I'm working."

"I wasn't *sneaking*, Ben." She sighs inwardly. *Here we go again.* "I was just trying to be nice, and now we're about to have yet another argument? Maybe I should just stay away from you altogether."

"What are you talking about?" He mops his desk furiously.

"Are you kidding me? Have you forgotten all about the blowup because I didn't get butter on your sandwich from the diner?"

"All I said was, 'oh, no butter?' and you blew up at me," he retorts, tossing the sodden paper towels into his wastebasket and shoving his fingers through what remains of his hair.

"I didn't blow up."

"Yes, you did. And then you went on and on about how there was some intruder next door—"

"On and on? All I did was tell you about it, and you acted as though you couldn't care less. I'm alone here all day, every day, and it doesn't even seem to have occurred to you that something could happen to me."

"This doesn't have anything to do with you, Christine. It was the neighbors who had the prowler, if there even was a prowler in the first place. It's really none of our business."

"Of course it's our business. We're right next door."

"Well, what the hell do you want me to do? Grab a torch and lead a posse through the streets?"

She glares at him. "That was so uncalled for. For your information, I thought I saw someone lurking in their bushes the other day."

"You *thought* you saw . . . ?"

"I'm pretty sure of it. I was thinking maybe I should go to the police and tell them."

He shakes his head. "Tell them what? That you were spying on the neighbors? They'll think you're the one who's prowling around the house. I say stay out of it, Christine."

"We're not in the city anymore, Ben. You're the one who wanted to move to a small town. This is what it's like in a small town. You help your neighbors. You look out for each other. In fact, I was just telling Rose next door that I'd be happy to babysit for her kids if she needs me."

He brightens. "That's a good idea."

"Really?" She's surprised by his reaction. "Because they're such sweet kids, from what I've seen, and I thought it would be fun."

"Yeah, and that's a good way for you to bring in some extra money."

Horrified, she blurts, "Ben, I wasn't going to charge her for it!"

"Not charge her? Why would you babysit, then? You're not running a day care over here. She has a lot of nerve to ask—"

"She didn't ask. I *offered.*"

He shrugs and mutters something she doesn't catch, and doesn't want to.

With a sigh, she asks, "Did you want anything for dinner? Because we're pretty much out of everything. But I could order a pizza—there's a coupon from a new place in town."

She's thinking that is sure to get him. Ben likes her to use coupons. He expects it—just like he expects her to buy the generic brand of everything, to save money.

"You get a small cheese pizza free if you buy a

large with one topping," she goes on. "And I was thinking we could put the small pizza right into the freezer and save it for one of those nights when you come home late from—"

She breaks off, realizing that his gaze has drifted down to the pile of papers on his desk. "You're not even listening to me, are you?"

"I'm just really busy, Christine," he says, sounding exasperated.

"Well, you heard what I said about the free babysitting. And about the break-in next door, and that I'm almost positive I saw—"

"Come on, Christine, stop making a big deal out of nothing."

"A break-in is not nothing. And I didn't even tell Rose that I thought I'd seen someone there, in her yard."

"Well, don't."

"Why not? What if I was witness to somebody casing the . . . the . . ."

"Joint?" he asks dryly.

Actually, she was looking for a word other than "joint." The last thing she wants to do is sound like she's spewing dialogue from an old gangster film— or admit to Ben, or anyone else, that she spends quite a bit of time looking at the neighbors' house through the curtains. She doesn't want to be seen as some kind of nosy recluse . . . but maybe that's exactly what she's become.

She turns and walks toward the door.

"Where are you going?" Ben asks.

"Downstairs to find something to eat and watch *60 Minutes.* I'm sorry I bothered you."

"It's okay. And Christine?"

She hesitates in the hallway, hoping he'll tell her

he's going to quit working for the night, that he'll say to order the pizza and he'll come downstairs and watch TV with her. If he does, maybe she'll tell him that her period is already more than twenty-four hours late, and she doesn't feel as though it's coming on.

"Yes?" she asks, holding her breath.

"Can you please close the door so I can concentrate?"

The house is silent, aside from the faint pattering of rain on the roof. According to the eleven o'clock news, it's snowing north and west of eastern Long Island, but out here in Suffolk County, it's still just an icy downpour and isn't expected to change over at all.

Propped on several pillows in the queen-sized bed she used to share with Sam, Rose turns another page in the romance novel she's been trying to read all night. Leslie gave it to her, claiming it would take her mind off everything, but she hasn't gotten past the first chapter since she climbed into bed with it hours ago, at around midnight.

She stares at the page, reading the same passage over and over, wondering if she should go check the kids again.

Poor Leo cried himself to sleep earlier, distraught when she told him he couldn't have his sound machine in his room tonight.

"But Misto-Gwegg said it would help me!"

"I know, sweetie. We'll get you a new one. That one was broken."

Nothing seemed to calm him down, not even

Rose leaving the lamp on for him so that he wouldn't be alone in the dark.

"You're a big brave boy, Leo. You don't have to be afraid of the dark."

"Mist-o Gwegg is a big bwave man, and he said he sometimes he's afwaid of the dowk, too. He said he used to think the bogeyman wivved behind his bookcase."

Terrific. Rose knows Mr. Gregg is only trying to help by relating to Leo's fears, but he didn't need a new one to worry about.

As for the sound machine . . .

She threw it into the garbage right after the police officer left, hoping he was right about it having a short. That might explain how it could have turned on by itself.

But it doesn't explain how Cupid got locked in the sunroom.

Both Peter and Leslie seemed inclined to agree with the police officer's assessment that the puppy somehow managed to get himself shut inside.

Rose supposes she can't blame any of them for wanting to believe that. It makes a hell of a lot more sense than the theory that somebody got into the house with nary a sign of a break-in, ostensibly only to turn on a sound machine. Nothing has been ransacked; nothing is missing.

The nice young police officer—whom Rose has seen crossing kids over at the elementary school when the regular crossing guard is absent—was patient, thorough, and sympathetic as he took her report. She even felt temporarily reassured, and actually managed to relax as she and Leslie played several rounds of Candyland with the kids while Peter worked on the bookshelves.

But tonight, alone in the house after Peter and Leslie went home, she has found herself on edge all over again.

Sleep is out of the question. It would mean turning off the light, and she's afraid to be alone in the dark.

Isn't that silly, Sam? I'm a grown woman, and I'm afraid of the dark, just like Jenna and Leo.

Yes, it's silly. About as silly as not putting bullets in that gun in the bedside table. It's not going to do you any good if it's not loaded, Rose.

But it can't hurt the kids if it's not loaded, either.

She left the hallway light on for Jenna and Leo as always, and their doors ajar. She's been in to check them several times already, reassured to gaze at them tucked cozily into their beds and to hear their hushed, even breathing.

She has also reached a decision. She'll have to somehow scrape together enough money to get an alarm system installed, as the police officer suggested on his way back to his patrol car. It will be worth it, for peace of mind.

A loaded gun wouldn't give her peace of mind. Hell, she doesn't even know how to shoot a gun.

Sam learned.

Hitch taught him. Apparently, Mr. Military is big on weapons. Sam told her once that Hitch even carries a gun in his truck. His plumbing supplier is in a rough neighborhood in the Bronx, and he's convinced he might need it for protection.

Belatedly, Rose realizes she should have asked Hitch about that before she let Leo go off with him the other day. Hitch was driving his father's car, but for all she knows he keeps a loaded gun in there, too.

She makes a mental note to discuss it with him, and decides she should check on the kids again.

Swinging her feet over the edge of the mattress, Rose sets the book aside on the bedside table. She means to lie it down in an open position so she won't lose her page, but it topples to the floor. Oh, well. She should probably start all over again with the prologue anyway—or scrap the whole thing and try to fall asle—

The telephone rings.

Rose gasps.

Her gaze flies to the phone, and then to the digital clock beside it on the nightstand. It's three-thirteen A.M.

It rings again.

If only she had an answering machine that could pick up and intercept the call. But theirs broke right before Sam died, and she never did scrape together the money to replace it.

Outwardly, Rose is motionless, her feet rooted to the floor, her hand pressed against her mouth as if to stifle her terror. Inside, however, chaos reigns: her thoughts careen wildly, her heart thrashes about her rib cage, her stomach quakes with fear.

Another ring.

Don't answer it.

But what if it's important? What if something's happened to somebody?

Ring.

The children are safe. Sam is gone. Mommy, too.

But there are other people. Leslie. Dad and his new family in California . . .

An image of Christine Kirkmayer's face comes to mind. What if it's her neighbor calling? Christine pulled into her own driveway when the police car was here earlier, and rushed right over to make sure everything was okay. She seemed concerned that there was potentially a prowler in the neighborhood and promised to keep an eye on things when Rose isn't around.

Ring.

Maybe Christine got up in the middle of the night, happened to look out the window, and saw somebody prowling around the property. Maybe she's calling to warn Rose that somebody is trying to break in.

She lunges abruptly for the receiver. "Hello?"

Nothing.

"Hello?"

Still nothing.

Her blood runs cold . . .

And then she hears it.

Piano music.

Chords she remembers vaguely from her childhood; a duet she used to play with her father, back when he was still living at home, before Mommy got sick and he left.

She tried to teach it to Sam on his parents' piano when they first started dating, but gave up when he couldn't learn the treble melody or the chords. She remembers his mother laughing about it, saying she recalled him telling her once that only sissies played the piano.

"Who is this?" Rose's voice wavers; she struggles to keep it low, not wanting to wake the children.

No answer.

Just the piano music.

"Who is this?"

Nothing.

Rose slams the phone down, her heart pounding.

She sinks onto the bed, her knees pulled up to her chest, her arms wrapped tightly around them as if to somehow shield herself from the anonymous caller, whoever—and wherever—he is.

The song was a stroke of genius. He is quite pleased with himself as he hangs up the phone, then presses the stop button and sets aside the tape recorder. Pure genius.

After all, if he's going to keep making these middle-of-the-night phone calls, he might as well let her know he means business, lest she assume he's just a random wrong number.

Now that he's on a roll, maybe he should also call—

No. Not yet.

He should never even have crept out of the shadows to announce himself to her. She didn't seem suspicious of him, but that's beside the point. It isn't her turn. Not until he's finished with Rose.

One at a time—that's how he planned it.

First Olivia—a.k.a. Staten Island Woman, he thinks, his lips curling into a smile.

Then Rose.

Then . . .

Stop! Don't even think about her. You're supposed to be focusing on Rose, and only Rose.

Too late for that now. It's already begun again. He's already complicated things.

He clenches his fists in anger, pacing the room, squeezing his eyes shut whenever the stern voice in his head makes him cringe with remorse.

What's the matter with you? Have you no patience?

*Why did you have to jump into the next one already?
You were supposed to wait until Rose was taken care of before moving on. Just like you did before. That was the
plan. The plan was about control. The plan depends on
control, dammit!*

Roiling in self-fury, he impulsively snatches a
water-filled glass and lifts it, prepared to hurtle it
against the wall.

No! Stop! Get hold of yourself.

*Somebody will hear the glass breaking, think it's a
break-in, and call the police.*

He sets the glass gently on the table again and
takes several deep breaths.

Maybe he's being too hard on himself.

So he got a little too eager to meet his next challenge. So he slipped up. So what? He can't undo
that now.

What he can do is take his time from here on in,
savor the process, relish every moment.

After all, when it's over, she'll be gone for good.

*And that's what you wanted. You wanted to make her
pay for what she did. You wanted to make sure she could
never betray you again.*

*She thought she was so clever. She thought she had you
fooled. She still does. Won't she be surprised to learn that
you've had the upper hand all along?*

Grinning, he looks across the lamplit room at his
bed, and then at the clock. Earlier, before he made
the call, he felt fatigued. Now his body is fired with
an adrenaline rush sparked by the sound of Rose
Larrabee's terrorized voice.

He won't sleep now—nor does he want to. He
should begin getting ready for the big day ahead of
him. And after it's over, he'll focus only on Rose
once again. She deserves his full attention.

He walks swiftly and quietly down the short hall to the bathroom, where he stands in front of the mirror and lathers his face with shaving cream. The eyes that stare back are naked, almost unfamiliar without the colored contact lenses to which he's grown accustomed.

Perhaps they aren't necessary. Chances are, nobody would ever think to connect him to the Snow Angel or Staten Island Woman. Still, the slight disguise—colored contacts, a different hair color and style—helps to keep him in character. So does the wardrobe that fits his current identity perfectly, but is a far cry from anything he'd have worn in the old days, in his real life.

And what is your real life going to be now?

He finds himself wondering, as he sets aside the can of shaving cream and reaches for his razor, where he'll go from here.

After it's over, all of it. After Angela is gone for good . . .

Thoughtful, he raises the razor to his face.

He originally thought the completion of this project would have to wait until next winter. But now that he's impulsively taken the first step, there's no real reason he can't accelerate the plan a bit without sacrificing his enjoyment.

Yes . . . and then what?

Then he'll have to start building a whole new life for himself. A life without—

"Ow! Dammit!"

He hurtles the razor across the room in fury.

In the mirror, he glimpses the trickle of crimson now winding along the white foam on his cheek.

Just like Angela's blood in the snow.

Just like Olivia's blood in the snow.

Just like Rose's blood will look on the snow, any day now . . . just as soon as the weather cooperates.

He dabs at the cut on his cheek, then gingerly finishes shaving his face, crooning a Christmas carol. Ironic, isn't it? Angela once told him that it was her favorite.

"Let it snow, let it snow, let it snow . . ."

Six

Monday morning, Rose is awakened from a dead sleep by the piercing ring of the telephone.

She impulsively fumbles for it on the bedside table, remembering only as she lifts the receiver what happened earlier, in the middle of the night.

Braced for silence, or that eerily familiar piano music again, she clears her throat and manages a tentative, "Hello?"

"Rose?"

A strange male voice is on the other end of the line.

She grips the receiver. "Yes?"

"It's Luke."

Luke? It takes her a moment to place the name. Then, realizing she's speaking with her boss, she sits straight up in bed. Luke rarely calls her at home.

"Oh . . . good morning." She rubs the sleep from her eyes.

"I'm sorry to bother you so early on a holiday . . ."

Her eyes go automatically to the clock on the nightstand. Eight-twenty-six.

" . . . but I'm in a bind. Bill says he has the flu"—Luke's tone indicates he doesn't believe it—"and I have to be out of town today so I can't be at the store to cover for him. Would you mind opening this morning and staying until Emily gets there at two?"

Emily is the college student who works three jobs to pay her tuition. Rose opens her mouth to protest.

"I'll pay you double-time and a half since it's a holiday," Luke adds hastily, as though he read her mind.

Double-time and a half?

"I don't know, Luke. I promised my kids that I'd—"

"Triple-time," he interrupts, sounding as though he's trying to quell his impatience, tempering his brusque offer with, "I know you aren't required to work holidays, but I'm really in a bind, Rose."

Triple-time. She'll be able to put that directly toward the alarm system.

And in truth, she didn't promise the kids anything special for today, other than yet another a game of Candyland.

"All right," she decides, "I'll come in, as long as I can get somebody to watch Jenna and Leo for the day."

"Terrific. Thanks, Rose."

After she hangs up, she hesitates, still grasping the phone. Normally, she'd call Leslie to take the kids. But is that fair? Her sister-in-law has been with them all weekend. She never seems to mind, but . . .

What about Hitch?

He's always offering to help. And he mentioned, when he dropped off Leo on Saturday afternoon, that he'd be puttering around the rest of the weekend if she needed him.

I need you, Hitch, she concludes, dialing his number.

But the phone on the other end only rings. And rings. And then an answering machine picks up.

"Hitch, it's Rose. I was calling to see if—well, nevermind. You're probably out for the day. Um, I'll talk to you soon. Bye."

She presses the Talk button to disconnect the call. Belatedly, she thinks she should have left him Sam's pager number. He probably doesn't know she carries it with her. As far as she can recall, only Leslie and the kids' schools have that number.

But asking Hitch to page her when he gets the message won't solve her babysitting problem. She has to get her butt to work, and she has to find somebody to take the kids now.

It'll have to be Leslie again, poor thing. No matter what she and Peter were going to do today, she'll offer to change their plans. Rose wonders if Leslie's fiancé is beginning to get sick of sharing her with a needy single mom and a pair of kids who are terrific, but, in high enough doses, would manage to drive a saint to a loony bin.

And Peter seems to take his uncle role in stride, but you never know. Rose wouldn't blame him if he would prefer to spend the day alone with his fiancé for a change.

Who else is there, though?

Christine?

Her babysitting offer certainly seemed genuine. Even enthusiastic.

Rose pads over to the bedroom window and parts the blinds to peek down into the driveway next door.

Only Christine's Volvo station wagon is parked in front of the detached garage. And though it's a holiday, the Chevy Christine's husband drives to the commuter train station on weekdays is gone.

Well, she did say this is his busy season and that he's been working constantly.

But maybe he just ran out to get a newspaper and coffee or something. Chances are, if he's going to be home, he won't be thrilled to spend Presidents' Day babysitting for a couple of kids he's never met.

With a sigh, Rose reluctantly begins dialing Leslie's number after all.

Isabel pulls the Mercedes out of the two-car garage of her two-story colonial and finds herself in a gray world covered in an inch or so of slushy wet snow—with more on the way, according to the weather forecast on the car radio.

"Folks north and west of New York City are expecting a good six inches before dark," the weather reporter says, sounding gleeful. Maybe he's a skier.

Isabel, who most certainly is not a skier, moans loudly as she steers carefully down the curved, slippery driveway, knowing it will be plowed and salted before she gets home. The man who does her landscaping in the summer clears her driveway in winter, but he doesn't shovel.

Six inches of snow means she'll have to find somebody to come shovel the steps and walkway. She can't do it herself anymore—at least, she's not supposed to. Doctor's orders.

But sometimes doctor's orders aren't very practical. Especially for a woman who lives alone for nine months of the school year.

Driving carefully along a slick stretch of winding, woodsy Route 22 on the way to her office, she turns

up the radio to sing along with an old Jimmy Buffet
song. Ostensibly chosen by the DJ to conjure images of summer on this blustery day, the tune
reminds Isabel of last winter's vacation to Key West
with Rob.

"Wastin' away again in Margaritaville . . ."

Yup, that pretty much describes it. She smiles, remembering the long, lazy days in the sunshine
sipping the frozen drinks, eating conch fritters and
key lime pie. They had been dating almost a year by
then.

Isabel's smile fades with the song's last notes, as
she recalls how Rob left shortly after their return.
An investment banker, he was abruptly transferred
to his firm's London office. Of course, she couldn't
possibly have gone with him. She has two daughters
to think about.

And anyway, he didn't ask.

"It's a good thing rush-hour traffic is nonexistent
on this holiday Monday," the DJ cuts into her
thoughts, "because a tractor-trailer that jackknifed
several hours ago across three lanes west of Hartford on Interstate 84 *still* has westbound traffic
backed up for miles."

Uh-oh. Chances are, Mr. Gabriel is caught in the
mess. She told him 84 was the most direct route
down to Westchester from Boston.

Well, she can catch up on paperwork while she
waits for him. There's always plenty to do.

As Isabel turns onto Route 35, the tires hit an icy
patch on the pavement.

She feels them lose traction, feels the car sliding
toward a towering oak tree at the edge of the road.

Panic rises within her as she turns the wheel,
fighting her instinctive urge to slam on the brake.

At the last instant, with the tree looming closer, she regains control of the car and swerves to miss it.

"You're okay," she whispers, shaken, pulling onto the shoulder.

Well, of course she's okay.

Dr. Henry's calm, reassuring voice echoes back to Isabel as she takes a deep breath and steers onto the highway again.

Just remember that the odds for survival are with you, Isabel.

Yes, but Dr. Henry wasn't talking about the odds of surviving a car wreck.

He was referring to the fact that more than half of those suffering from primary pulmonary hypertension make it to the three-year mark after surgery.

"If you make it that far, Isabel, Dr. Henry promised, *then there's an excellent chance you'll be around to dance at your daughters' weddings."*

But it hasn't been three years yet, she reminds herself. She has ten more months to go until that milestone.

She smiles, thinking about the best Christmas present she ever received—a pair of healthy lungs that came from a total stranger she'll tragically never be able to thank.

"Hey, what are you doing here today?" asks Camille, the receptionist, as Leslie steps into Fit 'N' Fabulous. "It's a holiday. No classes, no personal training sessions. Remember?"

"I know, but I felt like I needed a workout." Leslie unzips her parka and steps behind the counter to hang it in the closet beside Camille's jacket.

"Uh-oh—let me guess. Too many slices of cherry

pie to celebrate George Washington's birthday and now you need to work off the extra calories?"

More like one big fight with Peter, and now she needs to work off the tension. But she isn't about to tell Camille her personal business. Next thing she knows, it'll be all over the gym.

"Something like that." She flashes the receptionist a cheerful smile and slings her gym bag over her shoulder once again.

In the locker room, she trades her boots for a pair of sneakers, then sheds her sweatshirt and hangs it in a locker with her gym bag. A woman steps out of the shower room clad in only a towel, and rubbing another one over her wet hair.

"Hey, Leslie, what are you doing in here?" Renee, a fellow trainer, asks before Leslie can duck out unseen.

"Oh, I'm just working out, for a change."

Willowy, frosted-blonde Renee is by far Leslie's least favorite person at Fit 'N' Fabulous. She's always bragging about her perfect husband and their three perfect children and their perfect house. Her husband is a successful bond trader so she doesn't even have to work. She calls training her hobby and frequently giggles about how her paychecks pile up because she always forgets to cash them. Not exactly hilarious to someone like Leslie, who is doing her best to make ends meet and save up for her summer wedding.

"I thought you said on Friday that you and Peter were going to go look at cars today," Renee comments. She naturally has a perfect memory to go along with her perfect everything else.

"Yeah, we changed our minds."

In truth, Peter changed his mind.

Rather, Peter *forgot*.

Leslie wasn't surprised when he rolled out of bed before dawn this morning and took a long shower. But when she staggered into the kitchen thinking it would be nice if she joined him for breakfast, she didn't expect to find him dressed in his steel-toed work boots and pouring his coffee into a travel mug.

"So what are you guys doing instead today?" Renee asks, opening a locker and pulling out her gym bag.

Leslie averts her eyes, and not just because Renee has dropped her towel with no sense of modesty. She admits, "Peter's working."

"Working? But it's a holiday!"

Apparently, not for Peter, who claims he had told her all along he wasn't taking today off. *"How can I take off, Les? I need this job. Arty's one of the busiest contractors around, he pays better than anyone else. There are plenty of carpenters who'd be glad to take my place."*

"What about Rose and her shelves?"

"I'll finish them as soon as I can," he growled. *"She's not pushing me . . . why are you?"*

"Oh, I forgot," Renee says, pulling on her black lace bra. "He's a construction worker. I guess they don't get paid holidays."

"He's actually a carpenter, and he's in the middle of an important job over in Bellport."

Or so he says.

"You must be so disappointed." Shaking her head in sympathy as she steps into her matching panties, Renee is acting as though Peter's just left Leslie standing at the altar.

"Actually, it's no big deal at all." Leslie can't believe she's defending him when just a few hours ago they were at each other's throats.

"Really? If you don't have plans for today, why don't you come home with me? I've been wanting to show you my new granite countertops. They're much brighter than the old ones." The ones she had ripped out a few months after they were installed, because she didn't love the color—which she, of course, had spent months picking out.

"I'd love to come over, Renee, but I have a few other things I have to do today," Leslie lies, slamming her locker door shut and heading toward the exit to the fitness floor.

"Well if you change your mind—"

She lets the door close on the remainder of Renee's offer.

Hopping onto a vacant elliptical trainer, she sets the display for a forty minute workout and begins pumping her legs furiously.

Damn Peter.

The fight was about so much more than the fact that he neglected to tell her he has to work today.

"But what about looking for a new car?" she asked. *"When are we supposed to do that?"*

"You can still do it. You don't need me there."

"But you said you'd come. And anyway, we're going to be getting married. Shouldn't we be deciding on big purchases together?"

"I'll help you pay for it, if that's what you—"

"It's not about the money, Peter! It's about the decision. I thought this was a joint project."

"It's going to be your car, not mine. I already have the truck."

All she could think was that Sam gladly helped her pick out the Toyota five years ago, traipsing from one used car lot to another for days on end, with Rose's blessing.

When she started crying, Peter seemed to shut down instantly. The more emotional she became, the more he withdrew.

"Why the heck are you crying?" he asked, sounding disgusted.

Because he let her down. And because he ignored Valentine's Day. And because . . .

Well, because she misses her big brother desperately.

By the time she opened her mouth to tell him that—all of it—he was checking his watch and striding toward the door with his coffee mug in hand.

"I'll call you later," he said, and was gone.

It was the first time he ever left her without a kiss goodbye.

So here she is, at the gym bright and early, with the whole stupid lonely day stretching ahead of her.

She wonders what Rose is doing.

She might as well swing by there after she's done at the gym.

But she's not about to tell Rose about her fight with Peter. She gets the feeling her sister-in-law doesn't approve of Peter—or maybe, it's just their whirlwind engagement she frowns upon. When Leslie first told her she and Peter had set a summer wedding date, Rose hugged her and said, *"I'm really happy for you . . . but isn't it a little soon? Maybe you should wait until you know each other better—you know, so that you can make sure this is what you both want."*

At the time, Leslie assured her that it was.

But now . . .

Well, she can't help wondering if Rose was right.

* * *

Arriving at the office precisely at nine-thirty, Isabel leaves her silver Mercedes in a half-hour parking spot right out front, reluctant to walk the slushy block from the municipal parking lot. If Mr. Gabriel is late, as she expects he will be, she'll have to move the car. Crime is so low in this part of Westchester that the cops have little else to do but hand out parking tickets.

There's no sign of her client as she steps into the warm, coffee-scented office. Mary is chattering on the phone at her desk, and Amy is watering the philodendron by the Poland Spring cooler.

"Hi, Isabel. I thought you were going to see Cassandra today at school," says Amy, who was a year behind Isabel's youngest daughter in school. Cassandra is a freshman at NYU this year, but isn't nearly as tolerant of visits from Mom as her older sister is. Cassandra has always been a daddy's girl. She somehow blames Isabel for the divorce, and Isabel can't bring herself to tell her daughter about Ted's adultery—which might not make much of a difference. Cassandra would probably blame her for that, too.

"Actually," she tells Amy, "it was Andrea I was going to see, and I've got a potential buyer coming in so I had to postpone that."

"Not a great day to be on the road anyway," Amy says, mopping up a drip from the plant she just watered.

Isabel hangs her black cashmere coat on a hanger in the small closet and wonders if she has time to grab a quick cup of coffee before Mr. Gabriel arrives. She didn't have time to make any at home; just grabbed a quick cup of microwaved tea to sip while she got ready.

"Amy, I'm going back to the kitchenette to get some coffee, so if—"

She breaks off abruptly as the street door opens and a man steps into the office. He's bundled into a down parka, the lower half of his head obscured by a scarf and the upper half by a knit ski cap pulled down low. All she can see of his face is piercing dark eyes.

He stamps his boots on the doormat and asks, "Are you Ms. Van Nuys?" His voice is muffled by the scarf.

"Yes. Please call me Isabel. And you're Mr. Gabriel?"

He nods, pulling the scarf down to reveal a polite smile that fails to reach his eyes.

Terrific. Isabel can tell already that spending the day with this guy is going to be a barrel of laughs. Ten years in the real estate business have made her proficient at pegging those who will make easy conversation in the long hours of house hunting, and those who will transform the air-freshener-scented, climate-controlled confines of the Mercedes into a claustrophobic dungeon.

Mr. Gabriel, she is certain, belongs to the latter group.

"Did you find our office all right?" she asks.

"Yes, it was no problem. Your directions were easy to follow."

"So you came down 84 from the Mass Pike?" she asks, surprised when he nods.

"It was very easy," he says. "Traffic was light since it's a holiday, so I had smooth sailing all the way."

"Really? I thought you might have gotten caught up in that traffic jam past Hartford."

He hesitates slightly. "Oh . . . yes, I forgot about that. It wasn't that bad."

She opens her mouth to tell him about the radio traffic report, and that they must have exaggerated the situation.

Either that . . . or he's lying, she finds herself thinking. *Maybe he didn't come down from Boston after all.*

Something he said yesterday on the phone made her think he was coming from someplace south of here. And now this . . .

But why would he lie about Boston? That doesn't make sense. Unless he's a local who, for whatever reason, wants to feign being a newcomer to the area. Maybe it's a shrewd business tactic. Maybe he's a New Yorker who wants her to think he's naive about the real estate market around here . . .

"Are you ready to go, Ms. Van Nuys?" he asks, switching his black canvas shoulder bag from one arm to the other.

"Oh, you can call me Isabel."

She expects him to respond in kind, but he doesn't. She has no idea what his first name is, and can't think of a polite way to ask.

Isabel regards him uneasily, noting that he seems eager to get out of the office. Well, most house hunters are enthusiastic, but . . .

"Are you ready?" he asks again.

All right, is he overly impatient, or is her imagination suddenly getting the best of her? Maybe she's seen too many woman-in-jeopardy movies on Lifetime.

She glances toward the window, where the world beyond is suddenly swirling with large white flakes.

"Oh my goodness. . . . Looks like it's starting to snow pretty hard out there."

"Oh, that's quite all right with me, Isabel. I don't mind snow. In fact, I've always rather enjoyed being out in it."

For the first time, his smile is genuine.

Isabel returns it, quickly shedding her misgivings about him. "Then I'll just get my listings and we'll be off."

"Good morn—" With a glance at her watch, where both hands are easing past the 12, Rose alters it to, "Good afternoon, Bayview Books."

"Rose! What are you doing there?"

"Bill? How's your flu?" She puts down her pricing gun and leans against the counter, glancing out at the drizzly street beyond the plate-glass window.

"A little better, thanks. Luke wanted me to call him this afternoon to tell him whether I'll be in tomorrow but how the hell am I supposed to know? I'm not a goddamned psychic."

She grins, feigning dictation. "Not . . . a. . . . goddamned . . . psychic. Okay, I wrote down your message for him."

"What, he's not there?"

"No. He said he had to be out of town today."

Bill snorts. He can't stand Luke. He thinks he's homophobic, and a snob.

"He's probably got a taste for creme brulee and decided to jet to Paris for lunch," Bill says cattily. "So why did you agree to come in on a holiday? Did you forget that we aren't getting our paychecks till Tuesday this week?"

"Luke called me in," she says simply.

"Because I'm sick. Rose, I didn't mean to stick you with working today. I figured Luke would be here anyway so he could cover for me."

She opens her mouth to tell him about the triple overtime, but thinks better of it. Bill is one of her dearest friends, but he's still a coworker. It's probably not a good idea to discuss her pay with him. She's fairly certain he would've received three times his hourly wage if he'd been well enough to work his shift today.

"Oh, it's not a big deal. I felt like I had to get out of the house—the kids have been miserable because I 'promised' them we'd go sledding this weekend and all it's done is rain."

"Well, I heard on the forecast that we're supposed to get a big snowstorm before the week is out. So don't put the sleds away yet."

"Yeah, right. I'll believe that when I see it. Hey, did you go out with that Broadway dancer again the other night?"

"Yup, third date and I think I'm head over heels."

Rose laughs. "Already? It seems to me that you fall in love with everyone you date, Bill."

"Nothing wrong with a little romance. Maybe he has a straight friend for you, Rose, and we can double-date."

"Those days are over for me," she says with a pang.

The bell on top of the door tinkles as an elderly couple steps into the store. Rather than heading back to browse, they march straight up to the counter.

"I've got customers, Bill," Rose says. "I'll see you tomorrow. Feel better."

"Thanks, sweetie."

She hangs up, then spends the next half hour trying to help the couple locate a novel whose title and author have escaped them. But they do know that the main character's name is Henrietta—rather, the wife is certain of that. The husband is convinced her name is Helga. They agree that the setting is somewhere in Canada, and that the book was a *New York Times* paperback bestseller all last summer.

"You know, the title is right at the edge of my consciousness," the elderly woman tells Rose. "It keeps flitting in and then right back out again before I can grasp it. Has that ever happened to you?"

"Yes," Rose says simply.

The piano duet she used to play with her father has been running through her mind all day. For the life of her, she can't remember what it's called, but the tune is still so clear she's certain she could still play all the chords.

"I think the title has the word 'fungus' in it," the old man tells his wife.

"Fungus?" Rose repeats, her mind on the bizarre wee-hour phone call.

"Don't listen to him." The old woman dismisses her husband with a wave of her blue-veined hand. "He doesn't know what he's talking about."

By the time Rose locates the book—a non-bestselling hardcover entitled *They Broke the Mold*, set in England, with a heroine named Hermione—her customers decide they'll wait for it to come out in paperback.

Alone in the store once again, Rose decides to call home to see how Christine is doing with the kids. When she couldn't get hold of Leslie this morning, she had no choice but to ask Christine if she could possibly babysit for a few hours today. Christine was thrilled. Or at least, she managed to sound thrilled.

"But what about your husband?" Rose asked guiltily.

"Oh, he left for work early this morning, and he won't be home until late. I'll stay with the kids all day if you need me."

Now, as she dials her home number, Rose decides that if it sounds as though Christine has everything under control, she'll tell her she's going to stop off at the hardware store down the block on her way home. The owner, Joe, was a good friend of Sam's. He'll probably be able to recommend somebody to install the alarm system, and he might even know how much it will cost. She has no idea whether it's hundreds of dollars or thousands. Either way, she's determined to get one.

Rose straightens the shelf of special orders behind the counter as the phone rings once, twice, three times on the other end of the line.

By the fourth ring, she has gone absolutely still, clutching the receiver against her ear as dread creeps over her.

Five rings . . .

Six . . .

Seven . . .

Where the hell are they? Why isn't Christine answering?

Rose's eyes dart to the window again. Sheets of wind-driven rain are pouring down. There's no way they're outside walking the dog or playing in the yard.

Maybe Christine brought the kids over to her house. Rose hangs up mid-eighth-ring and frantically flips through the local phone book. There's no listing for Kirkmayer, Ben—nor for any Kirkmayer at all. They're too new in town.

She dials information, praying that the number will be listed.

It is.

But there's no answer at the Kirkmayers' home, either. Only an answering machine with Christine's cheerful voice telling her to please leave a message at the beep.

"Christine? Christine, it's Rose Larrabee, and I'm very concerned . . . where are you? Are the kids okay? Please call my pager as soon as you get this message."

Rose slams down the phone, heart pounding.

She's left her children with a complete stranger, and now she's trapped alone in this store with no way to check on them.

Calm down, she tries telling herself. *They're probably fine. Of course they are.*

But what if they're not? What if whoever keeps calling in the middle of the night is a crazed, psychotic killer? What if—

You're being ridiculous, Rose. This is real life, not a horror movie.

There are no crazed, psychotic killers prowling the streets of Laurel Bay. Crank callers, maybe. Secret admirers, perhaps. But not cold-blooded killers who prey on widowed mothers and their children.

You've got to go home and check on them, the frantic inner voice protests. *Just in case.*

But how can she leave the store? She can't just lock up and take off . . . can she?

If Luke happened to call or come by while she was gone . . .

Luke is out of town.

But what if he just said that because—well, because he didn't feel like coming in to cover for Bill
today? Or what if he changed his plans?

Rose can't just leave. If she does, she might not
have a job to come back to. There's no other—

Bill.

He said he's feeling better, and he only lives ten
minutes away. Maybe he'll rush over here so that she
can run home to check on Christine and the kids.

First, she tries home again. Then Christine's
house again.

Then, realizing she has no other choice, she calls
Bill.

She doesn't even have to look up his number, dialing it quickly from memory and holding her
breath as it rings.

There's a click—and then Bill's recorded voice.
It's gone directly to voice mail. Dammit. Is he on
the phone? Or did he go out somewhere?

Rose doesn't bother to leave a message. She
slams down the phone, grabs her keys, and heads
for the door.

Rose's SUV isn't parked in the driveway, and
there's a vaguely familiar car at the curb in front
of her house.

Normally Leslie would walk right in the front
door, but today, she knocks. When there's no reply,
she tries the knob.

To her surprise, it's unlocked.

"Rose? Hello? Anybody home?" Leslie calls.

Silence.

Frowning, Leslie pushes the door open and steps

into the house, wondering why Rose would leave it unlocked after yester—

A figure suddenly looms in front of her in the hall.

She lets out a bloodcurdling shriek.

It takes her a moment for her to realize that it's a man—and he's no stranger.

"Where are Rose and the kids?" she demands of the unsmiling Scott Hitchcock. "And what are you doing here?"

Isabel reaches home shortly after one o'clock to find that her driveway hasn't been plowed after all. The landscaped half-acre surrounding her gray-shingled, green-shuttered colonial is draped in a pristine blanket of white, marred only by the barely visible indentations left by this morning's tire tracks.

Scowling, Isabel pulls the Mercedes as far off the road as she can without sliding down into the snowy ditch. She steps out the driver's side door and her leather pumps vanish promptly beneath a frigid drift.

"Dammit," she mutters under her breath. She has no idea what she did with the plow guy's phone number. She never has to call him—he just comes when it snows. Except today, she thinks grimly. Today, when it's snowed more in the last five or six hours than it has since Christmas.

It just figures. It's just been that kind of day.

She already had to drive all over creation on slick, winding roads with Mr. No Personality sitting silently beside her, vetoing just about every house she showed him based on the curbside view alone. The few he agreed to go into were so disparate in architecture, size and cost that she still has little sense of what it is that he's looking for.

When she suggested that they break for lunch, Mr. Gabriel abruptly told her he had to get on the road back to Boston before the weather got any worse. He promised to call her by midweek to discuss the properties they looked at.

Maybe he will, and maybe she'll never hear from him again. The latter might be preferable, even if it means losing a potential commission. All she wants to do right now is curl up on the couch with a cup of hot coffee and the remote control, and stay there for the rest of the afternoon. The rest of the week, maybe, if this crummy weather keeps up.

She spent all her days on the couch watching daytime television during the bleak winter months when she was recovering from her surgery. Though she'd never admit it at the office, or even to her daughters, she kind of misses Judge Judy, the soaps, and QVC.

Leaning into the back seat to retrieve her leather briefcase, Isabel sees Mr. Gabriel's black canvas shoulder bag on the floor beside it.

Terrific. She may be hearing from him sooner than she wants to.

She takes his bag with her as she wades up the snowy driveway to the house, her feet already numb and her shoes most likely ruined. Dammit again. Turning the key in the side door deadbolt, she decides that the first thing she'll do—after she changes into a pair of warm slippers—is find the phone number for the plow guy.

No, she amends, as she sets her briefcase and Mr. Gabriel's bag on the bench inside the mudroom, the first thing she'll do is call his house in Boston to see if his wife can track him down. He left over an hour ago, but maybe he stopped for lunch and hasn't gone very far. If he doesn't want to turn around and come back for his bag, she can always FedEx it tomorrow.

Isabel kicks off her wet shoes and wiggles her frozen toes on the slate tile floor, then opens her briefcase to find the client sheet she wrote up for Mr. Gabriel earlier. She uses her cell phone to dial the long-distance number, sitting on the bench to peel off her soaked stockings as it rings on the other end.

"Service," a male voice says abruptly in her ear.

She hesitates. Service? What the heck?

"Is this the Gabriel residence?" she asks.

"This is Frank's Auto Parts. You got the wrong—"

"This isn't 617-555-3987?"

"Right number, wrong place." He hangs up.

Isabel looks more closely at the phone number to see if there's an eight she might have mistaken for a three, or a seven that might really be a one . . .

Nope. She wrote it very carefully.

Now what?

She glances at his bag, hoping there isn't anything important inside of it. It certainly isn't very heavy. In fact, it almost feels empty.

Well, maybe there's some contact information inside. Something like an office telephone number, or a cell phone number.

Should she look?

It wouldn't be snooping. She's simply trying to figure out how to contact the man.

Holding the bag gingerly on her lap, Isabel slowly slides the zipper tab toward the opposite strap. If the contact information isn't handy—say, on a business card stuck in a plastic compartment inside—she won't go through his things. She'll just wait for him to call her.

You could do that anyway, she reminds herself.

But the bag is already unzipped, and she can't deny that she's dying to look inside to see what she can find out about the enigmatic Mr. Gabriel.

Isabel pulls the bag open, peers into it . . . and gasps.

When Rose turns the corner onto Shorewood Lane, the first thing she notices is Leslie's car parked in front of the house. Driving closer, she sees that Hitch's truck is right in front of it.

The front door of the house is ajar.

She pulls up at the curb and, leaving the keys in the car, rushes up the porch steps, glancing over at Christine's driveway as she goes. It's empty.

Rose bursts into the house, hoping against hope that she'll find Leo and Jenna waiting to greet her.

Only Cupid dashes into the hall, barking wildly, tail wagging excitedly. Rose brushes past him, her heart pounding.

"Rose?" Leslie emerges from the kitchen, cordless phone in hand. "I was just trying to page you."

Hitch is right on her heels. "I got your message from this morning. Rose, is everything okay? Where are the kids?"

"I don't know," Rose wails as a fresh wave of panic washes over her. "I left them here with my neighbor when I got called into work."

"Not that creepy guy next door?"

"What creepy guy next door?" Hitch asks Leslie.

"The one who came out yesterday when the police were here, to see what was going on. There was something about him that I didn't—"

"The police were here yesterday?" Hitch interrupts. "Why? Rose, what the heck is going on?"

"It's a long story . . ." Her mind is whirling. She leans against the wall for support. What should she do next? Where can they be?

Calm down. Maybe Christine just took them out for a little while. Maybe they'll be back any second.

Rose takes a deep breath. If it weren't for the strange things that have happened around here in the last few days, she'd never suspect that anything might be amiss. But right now, she can't shake the terrible suspicion that Christine Kirkmayer has kidnaped her children.

That's ridiculous. She's a good person. You wouldn't trust just anybody with the children.

Well, what if somebody abducted Christine *and* the kids?

But why would anybody do that?

Then again, why would anybody make prank calls in the middle of the night, and break in here to leave the sound machine on at full blast?

"Which neighbor had the kids, Rose?" Leslie is asking. "Please say it's not that guy."

"It's his wife, Les. She was so sweet, and she offered to babysit, and—"

"Why didn't you call me?"

"I did! I called both of you but when nobody was home I called Christine."

"Dad has the flu—I had to bring him to the doctor first thing this morning," Hitch says apologetically. "The second I got the message that you needed a favor, I tried to call you back, and when I didn't get you, I came over. I got here about a half hour ago, and the front door was unlocked."

The knot of fear tightens in Rose's gut. She looks from Hitch's concerned gaze to Leslie's frightened one and asks, "What should I do?"

"Call the police," her sister-in-law says promptly. "Or the FBI. Kidnapping is a federal offense."

"Wait a minute, we shouldn't jump to conclusions." Hitch lays a gentle hand on Rose's arm. "Maybe your neighbor just took the kids out to eat."

"And maybe she's a psychotic killer. Her husband sure as hell acted like one."

Dazed, Rose asks Leslie, "What are you talking about?"

"Maybe I'm jumping to conclusions, but Rose, I'm telling you, that guy gives me the creeps." Leslie has tears in her eyes. "If he did anything to Jenna and Leo I'll—"

"Cut it out, Leslie!" Hitch says harshly. "Rose said she didn't leave the kids with him, and it isn't helping to stand here speculating about worst-case scenarios."

Leslie clamps her mouth shut, but glares at him, sniffling and wiping at her eyes. She goes into the kitchen, phone in hand, dialing.

"Who are you calling?" Rose asks.

"The police."

Rose nods. A strangled sob escapes her.

"Look, it's going to be okay, Rose." Hitch puts his arm around her trembling shoulders. "Trust me."

She finds herself leaning against him, grateful for his rock-solid bulk beside her. It's how she used to feel with Sam at her side.

She looks up at Hitch. "You really think it's going to be okay?"

"I know it is."

Rose wants more than anything to believe him.

Duct tape.

Why the hell would he need duct tape?

Isabel drops it back into the bag and tosses the bag on the mudroom bench, recoiling as though she's just found it filled with live roaches.

As the bag lands, something falls out of the side pocket and clatters on the tile floor.

It's only a pen.

Good.

There's nothing ominous about a pen.

There shouldn't be anything ominous about duct tape, either. Plenty of people use it. Electricians, plumbers, mechanics . . .

Serial killers.

She laughs aloud, albeit nervously, at the ridiculous thought. It's a strange, hollow sound in the empty house.

What she needs is to make some tea, turn on the television, and forget about the unnerving Mr. Gabriel. She never should have looked into his bag in the first place. She deserves to have her imagination run away from her.

Isabel bends to retrieve the blue and white plastic pen from beneath the bench. About to tuck it back into the bag, she catches sight of the inscription on the side.

Milligan's Cafe On the Bay.

There's a phone number, too. One that has a 631 area code.

She's certain she's dialed it before. It must be a new one for a section of Massachusetts, but she doesn't know anyone there, really.

Frowning, she tosses the pen into the bag, leaves the bag in the mudroom, and heads for the front hall.

She's halfway up the stairs when it strikes her.

The 631 area code doesn't belong to Boston.

It's Long Island.

So?

Isabel is doing her best to remain rational, but after the duct tape discovery, it isn't easy.

Maybe he's visited someone on the Island, or been there on vacation.

Or maybe her fleeting suspicion yesterday was correct, and he lied about coming from Boston in the first place.

But why?

One thing is certain. Potential commission or not, Isabel is through with Mr. Gabriel.

Seven

"Can I have more M&Ms, Chwistine?" Leo asks from the back seat.

"Sure, sweetie." She takes the open bag from the console and reaches behind her to hand it to him without taking her eyes off the road. It's still raining like crazy and she's out on Sunrise Highway.

"I don't know if he should have more," Jenna says worriedly, strapped in beside him. "Mom says you get a tummy ache if you eat too much chocolate."

"She does not," Leo protests, his mouth crammed full of candy.

"Yes, she does! You're lying! Christine, he's lying!" Jenna says as urgently as if Leo were teetering on the rail of the Triborough Bridge.

Now what? What does she say to that? How does she respond without taking sides?

She has definitely gained new respect for Rose—in fact, for all mothers, including her own. She figured this babysitting experience would be a good opportunity to find out what it's like to have children, and she still wants some of her own, desperately. But she has to admit, after a few hours of nonstop chatter with frequent eruptions, blatant sibling rivalry, crumbs, spills, and stains, she's looking forward to turning the kids back over to their mom.

Christine is spared having to conjure an appropriate response to the lying accusation, as the kids have seamlessly moved on to an argument about who got the better toy in their fast food kid's meal. From what Christine could tell, they both consisted of pieces of colored plastic that were ostensibly meant to be saved, and more pieces collected so that an actual toy could be assembled.

"Can we stop for ice cweam on the way home?" Leo interrupts the toy argument to ask, as they pass the Carvel shop.

"Maybe later," Christine says, pushing back a twinge of guilt. A glance at the dashboard clock tells her their mother should be arriving home shortly.

"Please, Christine? Just one quick sundae?" Jenna begs.

"Not right now, sweetie. We need to get back before Mommy does."

Christine wonders belatedly if maybe she should have paged Rose, or even called her at the bookstore to tell her she was taking the kids out for lunch and to rent some videos at Blockbuster. She made the decision impulsively, when she found herself on the verge of having to play yet another game of Candyland. At the time, anything seemed preferable. Even lugging two children from place to place in a drenching downpour.

She figured they'd be back long before now, having underestimated the amount of time they'd spend deciding where to eat, what to order, where to sit, which movies to rent, and which snacks to get from the bulk candy bins, not to mention tracking down public rest rooms everywhere they went.

In one of them, Christine discovered that she got her period after all.

Late, but unmistakably here.

Now all she wants to do is go home and cry, as she does every month when this happens. She really let herself think that this time, there might have been a chance.

Pushing the bitter disappointment from her mind, she turns the Volvo onto Shorewood Lane, saying, "When we get inside we'll clean up the mess you guys made in the—"

"Look, the police are back!" Jenna calls out abruptly.

"Yay! The powice!" Leo chimes in. "Maybe the powice guy will wet me sit in his car again."

Christine stares in dread at the patrol car parked in front of the Larrabee residence, along with three other vehicles, one of which belongs to Rose.

The fried chicken sandwich and onion rings she swallowed earlier begin to churn in her stomach as she instinctively slows the car.

"Did something happen to Mommy?" Jenna asks fearfully.

"Of course not," Christine says with a certainty she doesn't feel. "Mommy's fine."

"Uncle Hitch is here," Jenna says as Christine passes the house and turns into her own driveway. "And Aunt Leslie, too."

"They-o's Mommy!" Leo shouts as Rose bolts out onto the porch next door.

Christine exhales in relief. Thank goodness. Thank goodness nothing has happened to Rose. For a moment she was certain—

"She's crying!" Jenna fumbles with her seat belt.

Numb, Christine sits with her hands frozen on

the wheel, watching Rose dash across the muddy grass toward her car.

"Thank God!" she sobs, throwing the back door open. "Thank God you two are all right!"

"Who, us?" Leo's innocent question is swallowed by his mother's fierce embrace.

"Rose, was there another break-in?" Christine asks as Rose hauls Jenna toward her across the seat to hug her, too. "What's going on?"

"What's going on?" Rose turns on her, her voice trembling. "You disappear with my children and you ask what's going on? Where the hell were you?"

Christine is stunned. The greasy contents of her stomach pitch and roll. The police are here because of *her?*

"Hell is a bad word," Jenna informs her mother.

Rose ignores her, glaring at Christine. "How could you have taken off with my children? I didn't give you permission to drive them anywhere, in your car, without their booster seats—"

"I thought—I didn't think—I mean . . . my car has built-in booster seats," Christine says lamely, on the verge of tears. "I would never drive them someplace without booster seats."

"Where were you?" Rose's voice is shrill.

The children are silent, watching their mother with enormous eyes.

"I just took them out to lunch and to get a movie. I'm so sorry, Rose. I didn't—"

"You left the door unlocked. After everything that happened yesterday, you left the door unlocked. Anyone could have walked in."

"I couldn't lock it. I didn't have a key, and—"

"I didn't have a spare key to give you. And anyway, this isn't about the door. It's about you taking my children."

How the hell could you have been so stupid? She's right. You just went without thinking.

She repeats, "I'm so sorry, Rose. I didn't mean to scare you. And I never thought about yesterday when I left the door unlocked. I figured it's a safe neighborhood, and we weren't going to be gone long, and . . . I screwed up. I know."

"Everything okay, Mrs. Larrabee?" a male voice calls from the porch next door.

Christine looks up to see a uniformed police officer keeping a watchful eye on them.

"They're fine," Rose calls back. She pulls both children out of the car. "Come on. Let's go home."

"My toy!" Leo protests. "I want my toy!"

Rose ignores his plea, trudging across the lawn with him squirming in her arms. Jenna trails along beside her, the bag of videos dangling from her hand. The little girl shoots a last wary glance at Christine over her shoulder as they walk up the porch steps.

Rose doesn't even look back.

"That cop thinks I'm an idiot," Rose tells Hitch, who has sat with her at the kitchen table since the police officer finished taking his report and left twenty minutes ago.

"He does not," Hitch says, but he doesn't sound very convincing.

The officer—the same one who was here yesterday when she found the sound machine blasting—seemed almost amused when the children came into the house utterly unscathed, arguing about which video they were going to watch first. He questioned them about what went on while they were out with Christine, and actually laughed when Jenna accused Leo of stealing her Barbie doll in McDonald's.

"I have kids, too," he told Rose, in parting. "I know how it is. My wife freaks out over every little thing."

Freaks out.

Every little thing.

"He definitely thinks I'm an idiot," she tells Hitch again. "I swear, it's going to take an armed robbery at the store for me to ever call the Laurel Bay Police Department again."

A shadow passes over his face. "Don't even say that. And anyway, you did what any mother would do. Just be glad the kids are all right."

They sure are. They each ate a big bowl of ice cream before going out to walk Cupid with Leslie, who has promised to stay with them until Rose gets home again.

"I have to go back to work," she says reluctantly, rubbing her aching neck.

"Why don't you just call and tell them you can't come back today?" Hitch asks.

"There's no one to call. I was in the store alone today. I just locked the door and rushed out of there. I left the lights on, and the money drawer in the register—if Luke finds out, he'll be livid."

"Luke is your boss?"

She nods and wraps her hands around the still-warm cup of tea he made for her, saying it would calm her nerves. It hasn't. At this point, she can't imagine what will.

"Just tell him what happened, Rose. If he's human, he'll understand."

"I doubt it. He might be human, but he isn't a parent. He can't possibly—"

"I'm not a parent, and I understand." Hitch reaches out and touches her arm.

She looks up at him, surprised—especially when she sees the expression in his eyes. Mingling with his compassion is something else, a sweet tenderness that she's never glimpsed there before.

"Rose, you've got so much to deal with. I wish you'd ask me for help. I wish you understood how much I really . . . I want to be here for you."

"Hitch, you are here for us. Just like you said at Sam's funer—"

"Not just for all of you. I mean . . . for *you*." His fingers tighten slightly on her arm.

The teacup shakes in her hand, sloshing warm liquid over her fingers.

She pulls away from him, reaching for a napkin, nervously wiping the spill.

"I'm sorry," he says softly. "I shouldn't have said anything."

You didn't *say anything*, she thinks, rising to toss the soggy napkin into the garbage beneath the sink. *At least, not what I wanted to hear.*

Wanted to hear?

Does she want Hitch to be interested in her?

Confusion whirls through her, stirring long forgotten needs along with a wave of caution.

Was it her imagination, or was Hitch implying that he's interested in her? It's been so long since she tried to read between the lines when talking to a man.

Sam was never good with words. After years of marriage, she knew how to interpret him, knew how he felt about her.

It was like this in the beginning, though, she reminds herself, turning on the faucet at the sink, reluctant to again face the man sitting silently at her table. *Sam was like Hitch. He would say things, things that would make my heart skip a beat, things that would make me wonder.*

She absently squirts liquid soap onto her hands and holds them beneath the warm stream of water, pondering her own reaction to what she believes—or maybe *wants* to believe—Hitch was trying to convey. To her surprise, she can't deny, try as she might, that his cryptic words have sparked a familiar warmth somewhere inside of her, in a place left cold and vacant with Sam's death.

If I turn toward him again, will that look in his eyes be gone?

Slowly, she turns off the water and dries her hands on a dish towel, then turns to face Hitch again.

Her breath catches in her throat.

He's still looking at her that way. As though . . .

As though he cares about her. As though he longs to offer her more than friendship.

She catches her lower lip beneath her teeth, uncertain what to say, what to do, but knowing the next move is hers.

Go for it, a voice commands her.

Sam's voice, she realizes.

Sam would want this. If I was going to give any man a chance to live up to Sam, he'd want it to be Hitch.

She crosses to the table and takes a deep breath. "Hitch—"

The back door bangs open.

The puppy scampers in, trailed by Jenna and

Leo, with Leslie behind them calling, "Wait! You guys are all muddy! Rose, sorry, I told them to wipe their feet."

Surrounded by chaos, Rose looks at Hitch. He's grinning at something Leo is saying as he climbs onto his lap.

The moment has passed.

And now that it has, Rose isn't at all sure she wants it to come again.

With tapering snow flurries dusting the windshield of his car, David pulls up to the cabin. He turns off the ignition and opens the door, taking a moment to breathe in the pure mountain air and absorb the absolute silence.

There. That's better. Much better.

His boots make a pleasant crunching sound in the snow as he walks up onto the porch. He stands on his toes to remove a loose plug from a knothole high in the wall beside the door. After fishing the key from its hiding spot, he unlocks the door, then replaces the key in the knothole.

One of these days, he thinks, as he has countless times before, he should probably take it with him instead of leaving it here.

Then he asks himself, as he always does, why bother? His family has used that hiding place for the key for a good fifty years, and nobody has ever stumbled across it before. Even if somebody did, there's nothing of tremendous value in the cabin that anybody would bother stealing.

That was part of the reason Angela never really liked this retreat in the Catskills. Roughing it held little appeal to a girl who'd grown up in a shabby two-bedroom, one-bath ranch on the wrong side of the tracks in Jersey. Plus, she claimed the two-hour drive up here from the city made her nauseous, and that the cabin smelled like mildew.

Maybe it does smell like mildew, he acknowledges, as he opens the wooden door and steps over the threshold, but he's never minded.

The scent reminds him of childhood summers spent here with his grandfather, the family patriarch, a man who owned fabulous, professionally decorated mansions filled with exquisite antiques in Manhattan, Palm Beach, and Monaco. But Pop preferred this old log cabin he'd built himself, in his youth. When he died, he left David the cabin, along with an equal share of the vast family wealth—split among all twelve grandchildren, of course.

The Brookman money has granted David a successful, respected lifestyle, but it's the cabin that has saved him. Saved his sanity, saved his marriage, and after he lost Angela anyway, saved his soul.

He closes the door behind him, shutting out the frosty air, then wipes his boots on the mat in front of the door.

The place looks the same as it did last week; the same as it has for the last fifty years, he'd be willing to bet.

He wanders the main room with its two-story vaulted ceiling, rustic wooden furniture, and braided rugs. On the wall are framed photos of various family members posing on the front step of the cabin—mostly Brookman men, as Angela pointed out the last time they were here together.

"That proves it. I knew I couldn't possibly be the first woman in the family who isn't crazy about this place," she said with a grin.

He laughed. *"At least you're willing to come up here with me. My mother was here once before the divorce, saw a snake in the yard, and never came back."*

"Oh, I've seen snakes," Angela told him. *"I'm a country girl, remember?"*

Yes, he remembered. She was a country girl when he met her—if you considered western New Jersey the country—but it didn't take her long to become an uptown girl. Uptown, downtown, all around the goddamned town.

He was so crazy about her that he refused to wonder whether she married him because she loved him, or because she loved his lifestyle. He so didn't want their marriage to be that cliché . . .

But it was exactly what they became, on the spring evening when he saw her in the Village with another man.

David sighs. The old oak floorboards creak beneath his feet as he walks across the floor to the fireplace.

He lays a fire the way Pop taught him, with patience and precision, then ignites the kindling. As he waits for it to burn, his thoughts drift back to that weekend, the one after Thanksgiving. The one that saved his marriage.

He brought her up here because he couldn't stand it anymore. He could no longer pretend he didn't know what she was doing behind his back, and he could no longer bear the thought of her in another man's arms.

He brought her up here to confront her, to give her the option of leaving him, or staying—on the condition that she give up her lover.

He expected—maybe he even wanted—her to deny the affair.

That she didn't filled him with resignation. So it was irrevocably true.

He expected her to walk out the door.

That she didn't gave him hope.

She cried. She apologized. She begged him to forgive her.

David jabs at a red-hot log with a poker; sparks fly dangerously close to the rug beyond the open hearth. He ignores them.

"Who is he?" David asked her, at one point that weekend.

"Just someone I met. Just . . . nobody. Nobody who matters. I promise I'll never see him again, David. Never."

He believed her.

David tosses the poker aside and turns abruptly away from the fireplace. His gaze falls on a nearby table.

He crosses to it and picks up Angela's snow globe, remembering . . .

At one point that Thanksgiving weekend, they left the cabin to go into the nearest town for food and other supplies.

There's a ski resort nearby; naturally, gift shops have sprung up around it. Angela insisted on stopping at a few. He remembers how he teased her about how she could find a way to indulge her shopping habit even up here, in the middle of nowhere.

In the corner of one country store, he found her shaking a snow globe with childish fascination. In that moment, he felt as though a tremendous weight had been lifted from his shoulders. Things were back to normal at last. Angela was herself again—not the furtive, distant creature who always seemed on guard around him.

"Look, David . . . it's an angel," she said, holding it up to show him.

Sure enough, as the artificial white flakes settled at the bottom of the dome, the figure of a cherub emerged.

He bought it for her.

And when they emerged from the little country store, the winter's first snow was coming down.

He picks up the snow globe now and shakes it, watching the fat, lazy flakes dancing behind the glass.

That last day here with her, on the very spot where he's standing, before a roaring blaze, he made passionate love to his wife. Then they made plans to get away from it all, to go to the islands for a few days, where they could have a fresh start.

They returned to New York on Monday and flew right to Barbados, just as they had for Angela's March birthday. This time, she never once slipped away from David in the airport to make a mysterious phone call. She seemed focused entirely on him, on renewing their relationship. He allowed himself to believe that the nightmare was over.

Less than a month later, she was dead.

What a waste. What a goddamned waste.

He looks down at the snow globe in his hand.

The flakes have settled once again.

The angel gazes at him with a frozen smile from behind the glass.

David curses and raises the globe, prepared to hurtle it into the fire.

No! Don't. Don't destroy it. It's all you have left of her. At least, here, in the cabin. It's the only thing that proves Angela was ever here.

He lowers his arm and sets the snow globe gently

back on the table. Sinking into a nearby chair, he stares into the crackling fire.

"Your wife can live on, Mr. Brookman," the woman at the hospital told him. *"If you make a gift of her organs, she will live on through others. You'll be saving lives."*

It took him a long time to make that decision.

He made it, not because he was certain it was what she would have wanted, or because it was the noble thing to do, but simply because it was the easiest thing to do. They kept asking, gently but persistently; they kept reminding him that she was already gone, that only the machines were keeping her heart beating.

In the end, blinded by grief, wanting it to be over, he simply signed the papers.

They told him, later, what happened.

Angela's eyes went to a young blind woman from Staten Island.

Her lungs went to a middle-aged woman in Westchester.

And her heart went to a mother of two on Long Island.

Yes, David thinks dully, Angela lives on in three strangers.

All of them wrote him letters that were forwarded to him through the donor agency. The first arrived just as spring tulips were obscenely bursting into bloom on the Park Avenue island; the other two around Christmas and the one-year anniversary of Angela's death. He never bothered to open any of them, just tossed them into a desk drawer. They're still there somewhere, he supposes.

Until now, he's never felt the need to open them.

But maybe, when he gets home, he'll consider it.

Maybe that will bring him the closure he so desperately needs.

When Rose pulls up in front of Bayview Books, Emily is on the sidewalk in front of the bookstore, huddled under the narrow awning in her too-short, too-thin leather jacket. She's leaning with one leg bent and her foot braced against the redbrick wall, her shorn, maroon-tinted hair looking damp and more unkempt than usual.

Now, as Rose hurries toward the store, sidestepping puddles on the sidewalk, she glances at her watch. Emily must have arrived here at least fifteen minutes ago. She doesn't seem to be perplexed, though, or harried. She simply looks resigned, almost as though she's been waiting patiently for Rose to return.

"Rose! There you are!" Emily pushes her foot off the wall to stand up straight, her eyes narrowing beneath her multipierced brows. "Where were you?"

"I had an emergency at home with the kids." Rose fumbles with her keys, jabbing the wrong one into the lock and nearly breaking it off trying to turn it. "I couldn't get hold of anyone to watch the store so I locked up while I ran home."

"Is everything all right now?"

She nods, unlocking the door, holding it open so that Emily can step past her.

Yes, everything is all right, except that she acted like a lunatic, practically accusing her neighbor of kidnapping her children.

"She can't possibly blame you for that, Rose," Leslie said, once Hitch had gone and the kids were settled

in front of a cartoon and Rose had pulled herself together.

Leslie shook her head. *"She had no right to take them someplace without telling you. You did what any worried mom would have done."*

"I don't know. Maybe I overreacted. She was doing me a favor by taking the kids. And I never said not to go anywhere with them."

"It's common sense that she'd ask first. I always call you or page you to check, and I'm their aunt, for Pete's sake."

Maybe I'll call Christine later and apologize, Rose decides. Now, with her children safe at home in Leslie's capable hands, and she's resolved to put the unnerving episode with Hitch behind her, it's easier to think clearly. And with clarity comes a twinge of guilt.

"Hey, I'll call Luke and tell him you're back." Emily's voice intrudes upon her thoughts.

"Luke?" Rose jerks her gaze toward her coworker, who has shed her jacket to reveal a purple velvet catsuit that clashes with her hair. "Luke knows I was gone?"

"I called him on his cell when I got here and found the store locked. I didn't know what else to do."

"Was he angry?"

"He'll get over it." Emily is maddeningly casual, flipping open a compact and reapplying her rust-colored lipstick.

"So he was angry?"

Emily shrugs and puts the compact back into her leopard-print bag, which she tosses on a shelf beneath the cash register.

"You should put that in the back room," Rose advises. "Somebody can steal it from up here."

"They can have it. There's nothing in it."

Nothing, Rose suspects, but her cigarettes and lighter. Bill is convinced that Emily keeps her purse under the register so that she can sneak smokes when business is slow and she's alone in the store.

Rose changes the subject, asking, "What did Luke say when you told him I wasn't here?"

"He said he'd be right over."

"I thought he was out of town."

"Well, he can't be far if he's on his way over. Hey, there's his car now, isn't it?"

Rose looks at the store window in time to see a silver Jaguar pulling into a diagonal spot across the street.

Emily promptly heads to the stock room with her jacket as Rose checks her watch again. Her shift is technically over, and she told Leslie she'd be home shortly.

Luke is stepping out into the street and putting up an umbrella.

Should she stand here in her coat with her keys in her hand? Or should she hurriedly stash her stuff in a locker and make it look as though she's busily working?

Dammit.

He's striding across the street toward the store, and he doesn't look as though he's in a pleasant mood.

Rose lifts her chin and stands her ground, figuring she might as well face him head-on. If he fires her, he fires her.

"Rose! Where were you?" he demands, blowing into the store on a gust of wet wind.

"I had to run home. There was an emergency with my children."

"What kind of emergency?"

She hesitates. "They were missing."

"Missing!"

"But they've been located."

"Good." His tone, while still gruff, is laced with concern. "You must have been pretty worried."

"I was," Rose admits, startled that he's human after all. "I'm really sorry that I left the store untended. I didn't know what else to do. I couldn't reach Bill, and—"

"You could have tried me."

"I thought you were going out of town."

"I was in the city this morning but I've been back almost an hour. And I always carry my cell phone with me."

"I'm sorry," she murmurs again.

He surprises her, flashing an understanding smile. "Luckily, it's a slow day. So no real damage was done. But next time you have to find it necessary to run out of here, at least call and let me know what's going on."

"Hopefully there won't be a next time."

"Hopefully not. Where's Emily?"

"In back. And my shift is over, so . . . can I leave? I never got a chance to eat lunch, and—"

"Neither have I. Come on across the street to Milligan's with me. I'm going to go get one of those wrap sandwiches and some coffee."

"Oh . . . no, thank you." Taken aback by his invitation—one that was worded more like an order—Rose does her best to sound casual. "I'm kind of anxious to get home and hug my kids again."

"I can imagine. Well, another time, then."

She forces a smile. "Sure."

Another time?

Does Luke want to *date* her?

First Hitch, and now Luke. It's too much. Too much, too soon after Sam.

"I'm going to go back to talk to Emily before I leave," he says. "Have a nice afternoon with your kids, Rose. And drive home carefully. Weather like this can be deadly when you're out . . ."

He trails off.

She looks down at the scuffed toes of her boots. "I'll be careful."

"Oh, God, I'm sorry, Rose. I forgot . . . about your husband."

"It's okay. He didn't die on an icy road."

"I know, but . . ." He shrugs, looking helpless.

He *knows?*

"It's okay. " She wonders who told him about Sam. Netta? Bill? Someone sitting on the next stool at the counter in the diner?

"I just didn't mean to remind you of anything sad."

"I know." She wants to tell him that there are reminders every moment of every day. That nothing he says can possibly make it any harder for her.

But she only says, "I have to go. I'll see you tomorrow," before hurrying out into the rain.

"Ben Kirkmayer."

"You're there!" Christine is surprised to hear his voice on the other end of the telephone.

"Of course I'm here. Where else would I be?"

"I tried to call you earlier, a few times. I kept getting your voice mail."

"I was working down the hall in the conference room. Why didn't you leave me a message?"

"It wasn't important."

"Oh. Well . . . how are things going? Did you alphabetize the CDs like you were going to?"

"No, I . . . I didn't have time."

No, she only had time to cry. And brood. And wonder how she's managed to create a lifelong enemy out of their next-door neighbor less than twenty-four hours after befriending her.

"Is it snowing out there?" Ben asks. She hears paper rustling on his end.

Christine glances out the kitchen window at the soggy, dismal dusk. "No. Just raining. Why? Is it snowing in the city?"

"It was. Not anymore. Listen, I've got a lot to do before I can get out of here, so . . ."

"I'll let you go," she says, because she knows he expects it, not because she wants to.

"Okay. I'll call and let you know what train I'm taking. They're running on a holiday schedule, so . . ."

"Ben?"

"Yeah?" He sounds distracted. She hears the tapping of a keyboard.

"I got my period."

Silence.

Then, "Oh. That's too bad, babe." He says it in the same tone he'd use if she told him she just poured a bowl of Cheerios, then realized they're out of milk. He adds, "Maybe next month."

"Maybe."

Silence again.

Then the keyboard resumes its tapping.

"Bye, Ben." Christine hangs up and stares bleakly into space.

* * *

Caught up in *Love Story,* munching microwave popcorn, Isabel is dismayed when the phone rings.

Granted, she's seen Ally McGraw's lingering death scene so many times she can recite the lines by heart. Still, she resents the interruption of what has thus far been a relaxing evening spent curled up beneath the ugly but warm afghan Cassandra made years ago when Ted's mother taught her how to crochet.

At the second ring, Isabel reaches absently for the cordless phone on the table beside the couch. Screening the call doesn't even enter her mind. In her line of work, you pick up the phone whenever and wherever it rings.

"Hello?" Her eyes are on Ryan O'Neal, wearing an awful seventies brown plaid blazer and trying to stave off grief for his beloved Jenny, who looks astonishingly robust for somebody who is moments away from death.

"Is this Isabel?"

The instant she hears the voice, she knows who it is. In a rush, everything that happened earlier today comes back to her, and *Love Story* is forgotten.

"Yes, this is Isabel." She wedges the receiver between her shoulder and ear and reaches a trembling hand toward the television remote to press Mute.

"This is Mr. Gabriel. I don't suppose you happened to notice whether I left my bag in your back seat earlier?"

"I . . . No, I didn't notice."

The moment the words are out of her mouth, she regrets them.

There's a moment of silence on the other end of the phone.

He knows. He knows I'm lying.

But if he does, he refuses to let on, merely saying, "I'm sure I left it there. If you wouldn't mind keeping it for me, I'll come back to town to get it in a day or two . . ."

"I can leave it at the office for you, in case I'm not—"

". . . and I'd like to bring my wife along and take a look at one of those houses again."

"You would?" Startled, she tries to recall whether he showed more than a passing interest in any of the properties she showed him earlier. "Which house is it?"

"The contemporary with the large wooded lot."

"Twenty-seven Gilder Road?" Of all the houses they saw, that one was by far the least likely to attract a buyer. Then again, it's twice reduced and one of the more affordable listings; it's also vacant so that a new resident can move in right away.

"That's a wonderful home, Mr. Gabriel," Isabel says with false enthusiasm. "And I think the owner is ready to accept a reasonable offer. When would you and your wife like to see it?"

"Would tomorrow afternoon be too soon?"

"Not at all."

"Wonderful. We'll take the shuttle down from Logan and rent a car. We can meet you in the office at three so that we can drive right over before it gets dark. I want my wife to see the grounds. She's an avid gardener and when I showed her the listing and all the details about the perennial flowerbeds she was excited."

Isabel opens her mouth to remind him that the

property will still be snow-covered tomorrow, but he's already saying briskly, "So we'll see you then?"

"Yes, I'll see you then."

Only when she hears a click, followed by the dial tone, does it occur to Isabel that she still doesn't have his correct phone number. Damn. She should have asked him for it before he hung up.

Perhaps, she thinks, the wrong number was inadvertent.

That doesn't explain the duct tape.

But maybe there's a logical explanation for that, too. She had no business snooping through his bag—and she has no business suspecting him of anything more than wanting to buy a house.

Selling 27 Gilder Road would be a coup, considering how long it's been on the market and how many agents have unsuccessfully shown the property. She could certainly use the sale as additional leverage to land the Jason Hollander listing. That particular property is going to sell itself, probably in a matter of days, and the commission will enable her to give Andrea a spectacular graduation gift in May. A car, or a month abroad . . .

Feeling better already, Isabel picks up the remote and turns up the television volume again.

For the first time ever, as she watches the tearjerker wind to a close, her eyes are dry. They're focused on the screen, but her thoughts are on Mr. Gabriel.

She still thinks he's odd, to say the least. Yet she can't help being reassured by the knowledge that he's bringing his wife along tomorrow, and they're meeting at the office.

If Isabel feels the least bit uncertain about the

situation, she'll simply come up with some excuse to back out.

And lose the opportunity to sell 27 Gilder Road?

That's not going to happen, she reassures herself. *Everything will be fine, so stop dwelling on it.*

She turns up the television volume another notch, just in time to hear the dying Jenny Cavilleri say, "It doesn't hurt, Ollie, really . . . it's like falling off a cliff in slow motion."

The words never fail to send a chill through her—now, more than ever.

Was death like that for the woman who was struck down in that Christmas Eve hit and run?

If it weren't for that stranger's tragic fate, Isabel would undoubtedly have already discovered whether Jenny's eloquent description rang true.

A familiar wave of guilt washes over her. Survivor's guilt.

She was meant to die, because I was meant to live.

Isabel has to believe that. It's the only way she can come to terms with what happened.

With a shudder, she wraps the afghan more closely around her shoulders.

Stupid.

Stupid, stupid, stupid!

How could he have left his bag in the back of her car?

She was lying when she said she didn't open it. He's certain of that. Does she think he's gullible enough to believe her?

Well, what did you expect from her?

She's always been a liar. You knew that.

She said she wanted to be with you forever, that she

didn't love him. That you were the one she loved. The only one.

She said she would spend Christmas with you.

Then, when she told you that she couldn't, she said it was because her mother was sick.

Did she think you weren't aware that she didn't give a shit about her mother? That you weren't aware that she hadn't visited her mother since the wedding? That you didn't know she only wanted to forget every part of her life as Angela Marie Patino from South Jersey?

A sick mother.

He shakes his head.

Even her excuse was a cliché.

He still remembers how badly he wanted to believe it, though. So badly that he tailed her around the city for hours on that blustery Christmas Eve, in and out of shops and department stores. A few things she bought would have been suitable for a sick mother—or so he wanted to believe. Just as he wanted to believe a limousine would arrive to take her out to Jersey to visit her mother.

It wasn't easy, keeping her in sight that busy afternoon. Snow was falling over Manhattan—snow on Christmas Eve, for the first time in decades. It seemed that the entire population of the metropolitan area was out in it.

The merry crowds clogging the sidewalks and the department store aisles made it somewhat difficult to keep Angela in sight, but it was all the easier for him to find camouflage in the throng. He had on jeans and a big hooded parka—slumming it, Angela would have called it. She always got a kick out of dressing down when they were together.

"Look at us! Nobody would ever guess that we're multi-millionaires," she would say gleefully.

It used to amuse him, how readily she counted herself among the elite, when her own status was earned merely by virtue of marriage, while his was . . .

All right, it wasn't exactly *earned*. But . . .

"But that doesn't mean you don't deserve it," Angela told him once. "I like to think that we all get what we deserve."

Her way of justifying her own gold-digging past, no doubt.

It infuriated yet fascinated him, watching her drop thousands of Brookman dollars on lavish gifts that Christmas Eve. Gradually, his hopes began to rise, as he watched her pick out an extravagant men's cashmere sweater and an imported Italian silk tie that would be just right with his newest custom-made suit.

Could she possibly be shopping for him?

Had she changed her mind about not spending Christmas together?

Was she planning to surprise him with piles of presents?

If she was, he would give her the one he bought for her. The custom-designed heart-shaped, diamond-encrusted gold pendant engraved with her name. When she told him she wouldn't spend Christmas with him, his first thought was that he should walk over to the river and throw it in. Something had stopped him from doing that, and now he's glad.

Angela's last stop, as the snowy December sky turned dark, was Tiffany's.

He feared he might run into somebody he knew among the last-minute shoppers, or that an acquaintance would call out his name, and Angela might hear it.

Luck was with him, and he went unrecognized.

He stood behind a tall vase filled with Christmas greens as she spoke with a clerk, who assured her that her special purchase was ready for her, just as promised.

"Thank you for putting a rush on it," he heard Angela say. *"Next year I'll get my holiday shopping started earlier."*

"I'll show you the engraving so that you can check the spelling, Mrs. Brookman," the clerk said, and added with a laugh, *"Although if it's wrong now, you'll have to rely on Santa Claus to leave something under the tree for your husband."*

He boldly peered from behind the boxwood boughs to see Angela holding up an expensive gold watch. She was only a few feet away—too far for him to see what was engraved on the back of it.

But he heard her clearly reading the letters aloud, spelling out a name that wasn't his own.

That was when he knew what he had to do. He didn't know how he would go about it, or even when, other than that it had to be soon. If he couldn't have her, nobody would.

He followed her when she left the store, clutching her light blue shopping bag with the pile of others in her gloved hand.

He watched her pause to tuck a folded bill into a charity Santa's hand, and throw several dollars into a supposedly blind beggar's cup.

She must have been in a good mood. Usually, she had disdain for street people, as she did for anyone she considered beneath her. For all her high-profile charity work, Angela had little interest in helping anyone other than herself.

Swamped in rage, he stalked her at a distance as she made her way uptown and east, heading toward home from the crowded sidewalks of Fifth and Madison. The storm was growing worse, and people were retreating to the cozy comfort of their homes and churches this Christmas Eve dusk.

In the east sixties, Angela turned up a quiet side street dotted with brownstones and luxury apartment buildings. The block was all but deserted.

He followed her, wondering how he could do it and make it look like an accident, just as he did with his father . . .

A random mugging turned violent, perhaps? But if he attacked her on the street she would start screaming. Knowing Angela, she would put up a tremendous fight to protect her precious jewelry and cash.

Maybe it won't be tonight, he decided—just as he spotted a yellow cab pulling up in front of the awning in front of an upscale high-rise up ahead. A uniformed doorman came out to greet the fur-coat-draped female passenger as the cabbie opened the trunk. It took both men to unload the piles of paper shopping bags and parcels. The cabbie seemed reluctant to help carry them inside, but changed his mind the moment the woman flashed him a large tip. He left the motor running.

In the split second it took for the doorman, the cabbie, and the woman to step through the glass entrance to the building, he slipped behind the wheel of the running cab.

Shifting it into Drive, he pulled the car forward, barreling toward the sidewalk, and Angela.

Her body made a dull thud as she was struck by the bumper. She flew up into the air and landed on the snowy curb, deathly still.

It took only a moment for him to put the cab into reverse and back it up the few yards to where it had originally been parked.

He left the motor running and the door open.

The cabbie would be none the wiser.

He strode down the quiet street, fighting the urge to stop when he reached Angela.

He glanced at her as he passed by. She lay face-down in the snow, red blood pooling in the white drift beneath a crack in her skull. He smiled when he realized that it reminded him of the raspberry snow cone he bought her at Coney Island last summer, long before she betrayed him.

His only regret was that she never knew what hit her.

He glimpsed the cabbie getting into his taxi and driving off, oblivious to the dent on the fender or the broken body lying in the shadow of several garbage cans.

His heart light and his steps jaunty, he walked around the corner, leaving her there to die without a backward glance.

By the time a passing businesswoman discovered her and called an ambulance, he was several blocks away. He smiled when he saw the sirens racing down slippery Second Avenue, sensing where they were going, and that they were too late.

You liked to think we all get what we deserve, Angela, he reminded her silently as he continued toward home through the falling snow. *And you certainly did.*

* * *

Hearing keys in the door, Leslie looks up from the issue of *Self* magazine she's been trying to read for the last hour. She spent most of that time wondering if Peter is going to show up here after work. Now that she has her answer, she wonders whether he's going to pretend this morning's fight never happened.

The door opens.

She remains on the couch. *Be casual. As though it never occurred to you that he might go home tonight instead of coming here.*

"Hi, babe. Man, it's crummy out there." He wipes his boots on the mat inside the door, then drapes his wet coat over a hanger.

"Don't put that back into the closet," Leslie tells him, seeing that he's about to. "If it's wet, just hang it on the doorknob."

He does, then comes over and plants a kiss on the top of her head. He smells of rain and cigarettes.

"What'd you do today?" he asks, sitting beside her and reaching down to unlace his boots.

"Worked out. Went to Rose's. Stopped at my parents' house to check the pipes." She decides not to tell him about her temporarily missing niece and nephew. While the drama was unfolding it seemed important that she share it with him. She tried a few times to reach him on his cell phone and hung up on his voice mail.

Now that it's all over and the kids are safely home, she isn't in the mood to tell Peter. At least, not at the moment. She'd rather resolve this morning's argument so that she can put aside her nagging doubts about marrying him.

"Did you eat dinner?" Peter asks, removing his left boot.

"I stopped to pick up some Chinese on the way home." She won't tell him that she has no appetite and wound up putting the cartons into the fridge, untouched.

"Really? That sounds good," he says, bending to unlace his other boot. "What'd you get?"

"Broccoli with garlic sauce and vegetable lo mein."

He looks disappointed. "No moo shoo pork or spareribs for me?"

She shrugs. "I didn't know you were coming."

"Where'd you think I'd go?"

"I don't know . . . home to your place?"

He pauses, about to remove his right boot. "Why did you think that?"

"Because you were so pissy to me when you left," she says. "You didn't even kiss me goodbye."

"I was late."

"You said you'd call me, and you didn't."

"I couldn't. My cell battery was dead."

She wants to tell him that's no excuse. That he could have found a pay phone, or borrowed one of his coworkers' cells.

All she says is, "Oh." Then, seeing him lacing his right boot again, she asks, "What are you doing?"

"Putting my boots back on."

"Why?"

"Because I'm going home. You obviously don't want me around."

"Of course I want you around."

"You aren't acting like it." He quickly ties the lace and shoves his left foot into the boot.

If he leaves now, this will become huge. If he stays, they can get back to normal. She *needs* normal right now. She needs him.

"Don't go, Peter," she says, looking at him. "I don't want to fight with you."

He pauses, his hands poised on the boot laces. "I don't want to fight with you, either, Les. I'm beat, and it's been a crappy day, and I'm soaked to the bone."

She touches his arm. "Then stay. Go take a hot shower. I'll heat up the Chinese. I'll even order you some moo shoo pork if you want. Just . . . stay."

She waits for him to hug her. To tell her that everything's okay. To say he's sorry for this morning, that he'll never break another promise to her, that he'll never leave her that way, not ever again.

But he simply says, "Okay."

Disappointment ripples through her. She pushes it aside; reminds herself that he's not the articulate type. He doesn't like to talk things out. He doesn't feel comfortable displaying emotion, nor dealing with hers.

He quickly pulls his boots off again and heads for the bathroom, unbuttoning his work shirt as he goes. "I won't be long. Oh, and babe?"

"Hmm?"

"Why don't you order some ribs to go with that moo shoo?"

He disappears into the bathroom. A moment later, Leslie hears water running.

She sighs and heads toward the phone.

* * *

Don't answer it.

Rose sits straight up in bed and stares at the ringing telephone on her bedside table, illuminated in
the shaft of light filtering in from the hall.

Just let it ring.

She tries.

And it does.

It rings, and rings, and rings.

Ten times.

Twenty.

Thirty.

She counts the rings automatically, the way she
counts the day care center steps with Leo. Downstairs, Cupid's toenails are scampering across the
floor to the foot of the stairs. He lets out a few short
barks, as though to make sure she hears the telephone ringing.

Thirty-one . . .

Thirty-two . . .

Thirty-three . . .

Silence.

Rose exhales shakily.

It's over.

She waits a moment, just to make sure, then
slowly sinks back against the pillows.

Maybe now, she can get some sleep. She dozed
off initially when she climbed into bed at midnight,
but it wasn't long before Leo awakened. After she
soothed him back to sleep, she found herself lying
awake for hours, not tossing and turning restlessly,
but tense, poised, not just mulling over all that happened today, but waiting for the inevitable.

Now that it's happened, sheer exhaustion takes
over. Rose allows her rigid limbs to relax into the
mattress, her thoughts moving ahead to morning.

The alarm will be ringing in less than three hours, and it will be time for the weekday whirlwind to begin. Finding something to wear to work that she hasn't worn in the past week, wiping out the globs of toothpaste clumping in the drain, brushing the knots out of Jenna's hair, and the toast crumbs off Leo's chin, and—

The shrill ringing of the telephone shatters the night again.

Oh, God. Please. Please make it stop.

There's only one way to do that.

She snatches up the receiver, fury bubbling inside of her.

"Who the hell are you?" she demands.

No reply.

Nothing but music.

Jaunty piano chords and a staccato treble melody . . .

That familiar duet. The one every kid learns. The one Daddy taught Rose, and Rose taught Sam . . .

"Leave me alone! Stop calling here!"

She disconnects the call, then hurriedly lifts her finger from the button. A dial tone hums reassuringly in her ear.

She takes a deep breath; another. Her heart is racing painfully.

Calm down. You have to calm down. Nobody can call back if the phone is off the hook.

She sets the receiver on the empty pillow beside hers—Sam's pillow. The dial tone gives way first to a low-pitched beeping, then to an operator's recorded voice. At last, there is blessed silence.

Gradually, Rose breathes a little more easily.

Finally, she drifts off to a sound sleep.

So sound that she never hears the puppy's star-

tled barks somewhere below, nor his abruptly cur-
tailed howl of pain.

Nor the creaking on the stairs . . .

Nor the stealthy footsteps crossing to the bed.

Eight

On Tuesday morning, as she's pouring herself a glass of grapefruit juice in her sun-splashed kitchen, Isabel receives a phone call from Jason Hollander's personal assistant.

"Mr. Hollander would like you to come over today for an appraisal," the young man informs her. "Can you be here at one-thirty?"

Her thoughts fly to her appointment with Mr. Gabriel and his wife. Surely she can track down a phone number for him somehow, and postpone their meeting at Gilder Road.

"I'm afraid I have a three o'clock showing," she says, "But I can try to—"

"Then how about eleven-thirty?" the assistant says efficiently. "Mr. Hollander is home all day, and he wants to speak with you himself."

Pleasantly surprised, Isabel says, "Eleven-thirty would be fine."

She hangs up the phone and looks around for her briefcase, which contains her appointment book. Remembering that it's still in the mudroom, she heads in there. Not that she's likely to forget a meeting with Jason Hollander, but she takes a certain satisfaction in writing it, in crisp blue ink, on the page for Tuesday.

As she closes the book and puts it away, her gaze falls on Mr. Gabriel's bag again. She has no reason to look inside of it. No reason at all.

Yet she finds herself bending to pick it up. Toying with the zipper.

It's wrong to snoop.

And look what happened when you did yesterday. Your imagination got carried away.

For all she knows, there wasn't even duct tape in there at all.

Yeah, right. Maybe it was really a gray elephant.

Shaking her head, Isabel puts the bag down on the mudroom bench and steps back.

Why go looking for trouble? The sun is shining, the driveway was plowed first thing this morning, and she has an appointment with Jason Hollander himself later. This is shaping up to be a good day, and the last thing she wants to do is cast a dark cloud over it.

"Would you like more coffee, Mr. Brookman?" the maid asks as David sets his half-full china cup on his linen place mat beside a matching plate containing an untouched bagel and pale orange heap of nova lox garnished with capers and dill.

"No, thank you." He pushes back his chair and tucks the unread *Wall Street Journal* under his arm, ignoring the maid's obvious disapproval. Where she comes from, it's a sin to waste food. In his world, everything is wasted. Food, money . . . lives.

David strides into the hall and deposits the newspaper into his briefcase. Maybe he'll read it later, at the office. And maybe he won't. Today, he has found little comfort in the usual rituals. Nothing seems very important.

Nothing but what he's about to do.

He thought about it all night, so restless that his imported Egyptian cotton sheets began to feel like clammy tentacles gripping him.

You're trapped, he tells himself now, walking briskly toward the door to his study.

With every day that has passed since Angela's death, he's become more ensnared in crippling grief. Until now, he had no idea how he could possibly come to terms with it.

Sliding into the chair behind his desk, David pulls open the bottom drawer—the one that holds his personal files. It doesn't take him long to locate the folder he needs. He pulls it out and sets it on the desk, then stares at it.

The antique clock on the mantel ticks loudly.

Maybe he's wrong.

Maybe this won't help him at all. Maybe nothing will.

Maybe he's doomed to spend the rest of his life mired in sorrow.

"No," he says aloud flatly.

He's a Brookman. Brookmans don't give up.

He opens the folder.

He expected the envelopes to be right on top, but they aren't. Frowning, he pushes aside papers, most of them legal documents, wondering whether he was mistaken about where he filed—

No.

No, he wasn't mistaken at all. Three envelopes are tucked among the contents of the file, all of them sent to him, care of the donor agency. They're here, just as he knew they were.

He takes a deep breath.

Are you ready to open them? Are you ready to confront this at last?

Yes.

It's time.

The letter opener.

It would certainly be appropriate to use it on such a momentous occasion. He opens his top drawer, certain he overlooked it the last time he tried to find it. But it doesn't seem to be here.

He rummages for a few moments, then loses his patience and gets back to the task at hand. He'll worry about the missing opener later.

After setting two envelopes aside, David turns over the remaining one.

His breath catches in his throat, then, and he stares down in disbelief.

What the hell . . . ?

"Mommy! The tooth fairy came!"

"Hmm?" Rose burrows deeper beneath the quilt. It can't possibly be morning already. The alarm hasn't even rung yet.

"I didn't know you lost a tooth."

It's Jenna's voice, close to her head. She can feel her daughter's weight beside her on the bed. Desperate for a few more precious moments of sleep, Rose drifts back toward that serene oblivion. . . .

"Which tooth did you lose, Mommy? Can I see?"

Jenna's cold fingers are poking at her mouth.

Rose reluctantly opens her heavy eyelids to see her daughter leaning over her, dark eyes curious.

"I didn't lose a tooth, Jenna," she croaks, wondering what time it is. Her head feels so heavy on the pillow she's not sure she can manage to turn it to look at the clock.

She hears Leo's footsteps racing along the hall. He bursts into the room. "Mommy? When is it going to snow? I checked outside and it *still* isn't snowing. I want to use my new swed from Uncle Hitch."

"Hey, Leo, look!" Jenna is saying to her brother, who ignores her.

"I'm hung-wee! Mama, can I have bweakfast?"

Rose groans. "In a few min—"

The alarm rings shrilly.

So much for catching another few winks of sleep. Rose fumbles for the snooze button on the nightstand.

"Leo, look!" Jenna repeats. "The tooth fairy came to Mommy's room in the night! Why doesn't she bring you dollars, Mommy?"

"Wouldn't that be nice? I wish somebody would bring me dollars," she tells Jenna wryly around a yawn, as Leo bounds onto the bed. His foot slams painfully into her ribs, and she winces.

"I'd rather have presents," Jenna declares. "What do you think it is?"

"Leo, please stop bouncing." Rose reaches a weary arm from beneath the quilt to drape around her son's shoulders.

She tries to pull him close but he squirms out of her grasp, shouting, "I wike to bounce! *Boing, boing, boing . . .*"

"Mommy! Aren't you going to open the present?"

"Jenna, I have no idea what—"

Rose stops short as, in her confusion, she follows her daughter's gaze.

Her blood runs cold.

For there, precisely in the center of the vacant pillow that once belonged to Sam, sits a small gift-wrapped box.

Leslie comes awake slowly, stretching her yoga-toned body, reluctant to open her eyes and begin the day. When at last she does, she's pleasantly surprised on two counts: the sun is shining through the cracks in the blinds, and Peter is still lying next to her, asleep.

She turns her head to look at the clock. It's past seven. He never stays in bed this late.

The hurt and anger she felt toward him yesterday seem to have evaporated in the hours since she left him on the couch munching barbecued spareribs, absorbed in one of those stupid reality television shows he likes so much. Now, watching his chest rise and fall with his slow, even breathing, Leslie is seized by a wave of tenderness.

He's a good man, and she loves him.

No, he's not perfect. But what man is?

Sam, she finds herself thinking. *Sam was perfect.*

Okay, that's not true. Her big brother had his faults . . .

So why can't you think of any?

Maybe that's her problem. Lots of people can-onize their loved ones after death. But Leslie realizes, with an unexpected burst of perception, that she did so while Sam was still alive.

In her eyes, he could do no wrong.

Is she unfairly comparing Peter to the beatific image she keeps of her brother?

Maybe.

Okay, yes. She is. She can't seem to help it.

Sam helped her buy her car. Sam fixed things around her apartment without being asked. Sam brought her flowers every Valentine's Day.

And he proposed to Rose the right way, down on one knee, with a diamond ring.

But you shouldn't expect Peter to automatically do those things, she tells herself. *And it could be that he just doesn't know how much they'd mean to you.*

Maybe she should tell him.

Maybe she will, the first chance she gets.

More content than she's been in days, Leslie snuggles against his back, wrapping her arms around his strong chest, feeling his breathing gradually quicken.

"Hey . . . are you awake?" she croons in his ear.

"Mmm hmm."

"You decided to sleep in, huh? You must have stayed up pretty late."

He rolls toward her and opens his eyes. "I did," he says sleepily. "Too much moo shoo. It gave me indigestion."

"Yeah? I know a good cure for that." She traces his stubbly jaw with her fingertip.

"What's that?" he asks, grinning as she presses herself against him.

"Here . . . I'll show you."

Christine's fingers tremble as she dials Ben's cell phone number. He's probably still on the train, she thinks, glancing at the clock on the microwave.

Or maybe he's already in the office. She knows he left early this morning. Even earlier, it seemed, than usual.

Alone in their king-sized bed, she soaked her pillow with tears.

Now, a few hours later, she's managed to get up, showered, and dressed. But she can't help feeling more depressed than ever.

This can't go on, she thinks, sinking into a wooden kitchen chair as the phone rings once, twice, three times.

She needs help.

She needs Ben.

"Hello?" his voice crackles in her ear.

"Ben! You're there! Thank God."

"Christine? What's wrong?"

What *isn't* wrong? Where does she even begin?

All she wanted, as she lay there in bed, sobbing, was to talk to him. Now that she has him on the phone, she has no idea what to say.

"Christine? I think the connection is breaking up."

"No, Ben, I think I need—"

"What?" he asks, as though he can't hear a thing. "Speak up, Christine. I can't hear you."

She raises her voice, practically shouts, "I need help!"

"Help? You need help? With what? What's going on?"

He sounds harried, dammit. As though he's out of breath. He's probably walking across town from Penn Station to his office on Forty-second Street. He has no time or patience for her.

"I'm really upset," she manages to say, before her voice breaks.

"Are you *crying?*"

"Yes," she wails. "I'm crying. I've never been so miserable in my life. I need you to come home, Ben. Please."

"But . . . why? What's going on?"

"I'm just . . . sad. And I need you."

"Christine, you've got to pull yourself together. I can't just turn around and come home because you're sad. I've got to work, and it's tax—"

"I know it's tax season, dammit!" she shrieks. "You tell me every chance you get. It's tax season. It's tax season. It's tax season. What about me? What about your wife? I need you, Ben."

There's silence on the other end of the line.

"Ben? Talk to me, dammit. Please."

Nothing.

"Ben?"

She realizes the connection—deliberately or not—has been broken.

The envelope has been slit open.

What the hell . . . ?

David examines the top fold. The edges are sliced so precisely that the cut is barely visible just by looking at it.

Somebody undoubtedly used his missing letter opener to do it.

Who would do something like that?

He flips the envelope over to look at the front, as though he expects to find some kind of clue there.

It merely says *Donor Family,* with a case number and the donor agency's address.

There's a return address label: *I. Van Nuys, 20 Colonial Drive, Woodbury Hills, NY 10534.*

No canceled stamp, though. This envelope, like both of the others, was forwarded in a larger one from the donor agency, along with a letter stating that it was from one of the organ recipients. He distinctly remembers discarding both the outer envelope and the agency's letter, and filing this one away, still sealed.

Frowning, David picks up the other two letters. He's positive he did the same with them.

Yet both are now open, their top edges sliced as neatly as the first.

One bears a Staten Island return address; the other is from a place called Laurel Bay, NY. That's on Long Island, he recalls vaguely. The agency woman told him.

David stares numbly at the three envelopes, turning them over and over in his hands.

Somebody opened his private mail.

Who?

One of the maids?

But why?

Maintaining his privacy among the household staff has never been a problem before. He always finds his mail unopened in a basket in the hall. True, he keeps his desk drawers unlocked, but there's never been evidence of anyone snooping among his private papers . . . let alone outright stealing something. But the letter opener is definitely missing, and these envelopes have been slit open.

He taps the tampered envelopes thoughtfully against his chin, astounded that somebody has apparently read these letters before he ever had a chance to. Somebody knows more about the three women who received Angela's organs than he does.

As he ponders the blatant invasion of his personal property, curiosity seeps in to merge with his fury.

The first order of the day, he decides, will be to fire the entire household staff. A snoop and a thief lurks among them, and he hasn't the time or the patience to find out who it is.

No.

That will be the *second* order of the day.

The first is to read the three letters at last.

"Open it, Mommy!" Jenna says again, as Rose stares at the box on Sam's pillow.

"It's a va-wentime," Leo observes solemnly, having stopped his bouncing.

Rose looks sharply at her son. "How do you know?"

"I just know. Maybe it's fwum Daddy. You cwied because Daddy didn't give you a va-wentime this year."

A fresh wave of grief melds with Rose's trepidation.

"It's not from Daddy, Leo. Daddy is in heaven," she reminds him gently.

"Well, he's an anjo. Maybe anjos can leave va-wentimes. Aunt Wes-wee says—"

"Well, it's not a valentine," Jenna says in big-sister exasperation. "It's from the tooth fairy."

"No. See? Howts." Leo points at the red-and-white heart-dotted paper.

"Mommy, tell him—"

"Jenna, stop!" Rose blurts out, burying her face in her hands. She rubs her forehead, hoping that when she looks up again, the box will be gone and the kids will be back in their beds, asleep, and this will all part of some bizarre nightmare.

But she can hear a wounded Jenna sniffling pitifully, and Leo is bouncing on the bed again, and when she opens her eyes, the goddamned box is still there.

* * *

"I have a great idea," Leslie says, lazily running her fingertips down Peter's bare chest.

"Uh-oh." He groans. "I don't think I have the energy for another one of your great ideas, Les."

She grins. "Not *that* kind of idea. I was thinking we could play hooky today. We could stay right here—right in bed, even—all warm and cozy. What do you say?"

"I'd love to, but I've got to get to work."

Disappointed, she says, "Come on, Peter. You're already late for the job. Why don't you call Arty and tell him you're sick?"

"Because I'm not sick."

"You said your stomach was bothering you."

"It was heartburn, and it's fine now." He stretches and gently pushes her off his chest, sitting up. "I've got to get ready to go, Les."

She turns away from him, toward the window. Her instinct is to pout.

But you're not a little girl anymore, and Peter isn't your big brother, there at your beck and call.

"I guess you're right," she says. "I've got a double training session first thing this morning with two new members, anyway."

"And I've got to finish Sheetrocking the kitchen on the job because the cabinets are already in."

"Did you remember to charge the battery on your cell phone?"

He slaps his temple. "Damn. I knew I forgot something last night."

"Maybe you can find a place to plug it in on the job," Leslie suggests. "I don't like feeling like I can't get a hold of you if I need to."

"I'll try," he says. "But the electrician was there

yesterday, and he had the power turned off for most of the afternoon."

He's out of bed, now, walking naked across the bedroom carpet to open the blinds. Sunlight splashes into the room.

"It's a beautiful day," Peter says, looking out, and then over his shoulder at her. "Good to see the sun again, especially after all that rain and wind yesterday, you know?"

Leslie nods, thinking, *the calm after the storm.*

Only when Peter is in the bathroom, whistling and turning on the water for his shower, does she remember that she got the old saying backward.

It's the *calm* before *the storm,* she recalls, and pushes aside an inexplicable little twinge of apprehension.

Christine is still seated at the kitchen table, numbly clutching the cordless phone in her hand, when it rings.

Ben. It has to be.

She would give anything to have caller ID, just to be sure. But he vetoed that, along with call-waiting, cable television, and just about everything else that might make her life a little bit more pleasant.

It rings again.

It has to be Ben, calling back to apologize for hanging up on her . . .

Or to blame that on his cell phone's weak signal.

Her finger poised on the Talk button, about to push it down, Christine realizes that she doesn't want to hear what he has to say.

When she called him a few minutes ago, there

was nothing she wanted more than to speak to her husband.

Now, he's the last person she wants to talk—or listen—to.

She removes her finger from the button and looks down at the phone as it rings again.

And again.

"Go to hell," she mutters, tossing the phone onto the kitchen table so ferociously that the plastic battery cover pops off.

She grabs her coat, her keys, her purse and heads out the door without the faintest idea where she's going.

Olivia.

Her name is Olivia McGlinchie, and she was born blind, suffering from a genetic condition called ocular albinism. When she started kindergarten, children made fun of her, so her parents scraped together enough money to send her away to a special school for blind children. She grew up surrounded by others who shared her disability, but longing for some kind of miracle cure.

Hope built when, in her twenties, she found herself on the transplant waiting list. It waned when a potential donor's family changed their minds at the last minute.

At last, her prayers were answered . . .

Just as mine were being ignored, David thinks bleakly, putting aside the letter and leaning back in his chair.

He's read it through so many times he practically knows it by heart.

Because of Angela's death, a young woman

named Olivia McGlinchie is able to see. She looked into her parents' eyes for the first time; she experienced her first glorious sunrise over the Atlantic; her first art gallery; her first movie. She was able to move out of her parents' house and into an apartment of her own at last.

She was even learning to drive, back when she wrote the letter that spring, and said she hoped to have her driver's license by summer.

For all David knows, he's passed her tooling along on the West Side Highway, never sensing her presence . . . or Angela's.

What would it be like to look into her eyes again . . . in somebody else's face?

He shudders.

It's too soon.

Too soon to even consider meeting one of the recipients. Too soon, even, to read the other two letters. They can wait, he decides, tucking them back into the folder, then returning it to his desk drawer.

He stands and looks at his watch. He really should get to the office. But first, he has to fire the staff, and call the employment agency for temporary and permanent replacements.

It's going to be a long day, David concludes, walking briskly toward the door.

Only as an afterthought does he return to the desk. Fishing a keyring from his pocket, he makes several attempts to fit a key into the slot in the bottom drawer lot.

Finally, he finds the right one and gives it a satisfied turn.

There.

Locked.

Just in case.

*** * ***

"Leo," Rose says, her eyes still glued to the gift box on the pillow, "did you put that present there for Mommy?"

"Nope." He shakes his head vehemently.

"Are you sure?"

He nods.

"Then who could have done it?"

"My daddy. He's an anjo."

Jenna is exasperated. "It wasn't an angel. It was the tooth fairy. Why won't anyone lis—"

"Jenna, why don't you and Leo go downstairs and decide which cereal you want for breakfast?" Rose cuts in, her nerves rapidly fraying. She's obviously not going to get a straight answer out of her son about the box.

Her thoughts are racing, and so is her heart.

Leo had to be the one who put it there. He probably thought it would make her feel better about not getting a valentine from Sam this year. He must have stolen it from somewhere.

"I don't want ce-wee-al," Leo protests. "I want choco-wat toast."

"Do you have Aunt Leslie's recipe for chocolate toast?" Jenna asks.

"No. Yes. I don't know. I'll ask her when I see her," Rose says absently. "Go downstairs. You can turn on the television. Just . . . go."

Thrilled at the prospect of forbidden weekday morning cartoons, Jenna bolts from the room, with Leo trailing along behind her.

"Leo?" Rose calls after him.

He pauses. "What?"

"I know you put the box here. And it was very

sweet of you to try to make Mommy happy. But stealing is wrong."

"I didn't stee-o, Mommy!"

"Lying is wrong, too."

"I'm not wying!" He sounds on the verge of tears.

"We'll talk about this later."

Left alone in her bed, Rose exhales shakily.

Could Leo be telling the truth? But if he didn't leave the box . . .

Then somebody else was here, in her room, while she was asleep.

Could it possibly have been Hitch? Is this his twisted idea of a romantic surprise? The notion doesn't seem quite as far-fetched as it might have before their stilted conversation yesterday in the kitchen.

Ire builds within her as she reaches for the box and tears at the wrapping paper, thinking that it's far easier to assume it was harmless Hitch—or even Leo—than to consider the alternative and address the fear that accompanies it.

What about the other day? The sound machine, and the dog being locked into the side room?

It wasn't a break-in. Even the police officer didn't think so. You're letting your imagination run away with you again, just like it did yesterday when you thought Christine had kidnapped the kids.

Tossing the crumpled wad of paper aside, Rose finds herself holding a black velvet jeweler's box with a curved top.

Her fear begins to evaporate, and with it, her anger.

Okay. So if it was Hitch, he was just trying to be sweet.

And if it wasn't Hitch, it was Leo.

And if it wasn't Leo . . .

No. It was one or the other.

Her mind sprints ahead with the Hitch theory. Knowing Sam, he gave Hitch keys to the house and neither of them ever remembered to mention it to Rose.

But wouldn't Hitch realize it would scare the hell out of her to think that someone was in her room while she was sleeping?

And what about the phone calls?

Maybe they're not related to the gifts, she decides. Maybe it's just kids, fooling around, thinking it's funny to call strangers in the middle of the night . . .

"Cupid! Where are you!" she hears Leo's voice calling downstairs. "Time for bweakfast!"

"No! Don't feed him, Leo," she calls, hurriedly running her nails along the crack beneath the lid of the box to pry it open. "I'll be down in a minute to do it."

Last time Leo tried to feed the puppy on his own, he cut his finger on the sharp edge of the dog food can.

Rose snaps the box open. Her jaw drops.

Inside the box is an exquisite heart-shaped, diamond-encrusted gold pendant.

"Mommy!" Leo calls.

"Hang on! I'm coming!"

Carefully not to tangle the delicate chain, Rose examines the pendant, then flips it over. Something is engraved on the back.

The necklace trembles in her hands. Her suddenly rapid breathing seems to thunder through the quiet room.

Now, at last, perhaps she'll know if Hitch—

Running footsteps pound across the hardwood floor below.

"Mom!" Jenna bellows as Rose holds the pendant up and angles it toward the window, tilting it so that the sun catches the small, scrolled lettering etched in the glinting gold surface.

"Mommy!" Leo shrieks.

He's crying. They both are, hysterically, Rose realizes with an incredulous jolt, in the split second before she makes out the single word engraved on the back of the locket.

Angela.

The shovel makes a dull, scraping sound as he plunges it into the sandy soil one last time.

There.

That's deep enough.

After tossing the shovel aside, he walks the few yards across a spongy bed of dead leaves to his car, parked in the limited seclusion offered by a stand of trees. It isn't likely that anybody will venture to this deserted, remote corner of the seaside park just past dawn on a cold winter morning. But you never know.

He wearily rubs the aching spot between his shoulder blades as he walks. It always burns there when he's exhausted. He'd like nothing more than to go home after he takes care of this, and sleep for hours. Days, maybe.

He can't.

With a sigh, he thinks about the day ahead, and Isabel.

At least there's still snow on the ground up in northern Westchester.

But he wanted it to be different, with her.

He wanted to take his time, to play with her as he had the others.

He wanted her to be his grand finale—though not for any reason other than the timing.

With Rose, Valentine's Day worked so beautifully. Even the pendant—the one he could never bring himself to throw into the river after all—fit his carefully planned theme.

His plan was to take care of Rose, then move on to Isabel.

Then Isabel made him angry, lying about looking in his bag.

She knows too much already. She's too suspicious. You'll never be able to slip into her day-to-day life and toy with her the way you have the others.

It would have been such a pleasure, though . . .

No. It's too late to go back to the original plan. Just accelerate everything. Do what you have to do.

Isabel will be next; Rose, his grand finale.

Then he'll go back to his real life, to his original appearance, to . . .

To what?

There are times when he can't even remember what his life was like before Angela. But one thing is certain: it was lonely.

Well, maybe you'll meet somebody once you've settled in back home, he tells himself. Somebody who won't betray you, the way Angela did.

After unlocking the car trunk, he casts a furtive glance over both shoulders to be absolutely certain he's alone.

Yes. Good.

This will only take a moment. After he's finished, he'll drive over to the mall to get everything he'll need: more duct tape, a pillow, and something to use as a tarp. A couple of vinyl shower curtains, he thinks, his lips curling into a grin. Maybe he can find something lavender and pretty for her. Lavender was Angela's favorite color.

When he used her house keys to sneak into David Brookman's brownstone last winter in search of the organ recipients' names, he detoured into her walk-in closet. Her wardrobe was still intact, and he helped himself to her favorite lavender sweater and a filmy lavender-sprigged scarf. Souvenirs, along with the monogrammed letter opener.

He reaches into the trunk and removes a small bundle wrapped in the navy wool pea coat he was wearing a few hours ago, when he left Rose's bedroom. Now, unfortunately, it's soaked in blood.

He didn't like the coat much when he bought it last fall—it really isn't his style. But it's grown on him.

Oh, well. You wouldn't have been taking it with you when you move on, anyway, he reminds himself. And if the weather cooperates, he'll be leaving in a matter of days.

The forecasters are promising snow on the island before the week is out.

With a grimace, he holds the stiff bundle at arm's length and carries it back to the waiting hole.

He bends to drop it in.

"Sorry, little guy. I let you go once, but this time, you got in my way."

It's a shame. A real shame. He's always liked dogs.

Shaking his head, he begins to shovel dirt over the little black puppy's lifeless body.

Nine

"Thank you. Have a nice day," Rose tells a departing customer, Mrs. Abernathy, who just bought the complete set of Little House books for her granddaughter at Rose's suggestion.

Too bad I'm not working on commission, she thinks ruefully, tucking the Visa receipt into the register drawer just as Luke comes out of the stock room, wearing a belted trench coat she's never seen before

"I'm going to lunch, and then I have to do some errands," he tells her. "I may not be back until after you leave, but I told Emily Bill is still out sick and she promised to get here an hour early so that you'll be on time to pick up your children. Have a good—"

"What about my paycheck?" she cuts in, dismayed. It's already coming a day later than usual because of yesterday's holiday, and this is the shortest month of the year. The mortgage payment is looming and her American Express bill is overdue.

"Oh, right." He looks uncomfortable. "I was going to stop at the payroll accountant's to pick up the checks later."

She sighs. She'll have to drag the kids back to the store after dinner and homework to get her paycheck. It's the last thing she wants to face at the end of this draining day, but she has no choice. She has to deposit it as soon as the bank opens in the morning.

Rose gloomily watches Luke pause to straighten a pile of paperbacks on a display table, lining up the bindings with precision.

What a crappy day, all around.

First the odd gift on Sam's pillow, with its cryptic inscription. *Angela?*

Who is Angela?

Leo must have stolen it from somewhere. It's the only explanation that makes sense.

What doesn't make sense is to call the police about it—though the thought has crossed her mind throughout the day. She's undoubtedly already the laughingstock of the Laurel Bay police force. She wouldn't feel comfortable at this point calling them if somebody stole a necklace from her, let alone calling because somebody left her one.

Another thing that doesn't make sense, no matter which scenario she conjures, is that Cupid is missing.

"Maybe he climbed out the window when the tooth fairy flew in last night," Jenna suggested, when her hysterical tears had finally subsided.

"I doubt that. Leo, you didn't let the puppy out, did you?" Rose asked her son.

Naturally, he denied it.

"When you came into my room this morning you said you checked outside and it wasn't snowing. Did you open the door to check?"

"No. I just wooked out my window."

"Are you sure?"

"Yup."

But how can she believe him? He lied about

breaking the Lenox vase, about the liquid soap, and probably about leaving the chocolates in her car and the *Angela* necklace on her pillow. And it wouldn't be the first time he went outside in his pajamas to check for snow. The puppy could have followed him out.

But if Leo's telling the truth and he had nothing to do with anything . . .

"I'll drop the check at your house for you later if you want," Luke offers unexpectedly, turning away from the pile of books and breaking into Rose's troublesome thoughts.

"You will? That would be . . ." Grateful, she says, "You don't know how much I'd appreciate it."

"It's no problem. I go that way on my way home every night."

"You know where I live?"

He nods. "Shorewood Lane, right? What's the number?"

"Forty-eight," she murmurs, reminding herself that of course he would know where she lives. He's her employer. Her address is in her file.

Luke opens the door. "You know, that breeze actually feels warm today," he says over his shoulder. "It's nice not to wear a heavy coat and gloves for a change. I'll see you tonight, Rose."

"See you tonight," she says, pushing aside her nagging doubt about just who left that package on her pillow, and why.

Isabel's cell phone rings as she's standing beside the driver's side door of her Mercedes, shaking Jason Hollander's hand.

"I'm sorry—I should answer that," she says.

"Of course you should." He releases her hand. "Thank you for everything. Why don't you call me when you have the appraisal ready?"

"I will," Isabel promises, sneaking a glance at her watch as she reaches into her pocket for her phone. It's five minutes to three. She'll only be a few minutes late meeting Mr. Gabriel and his wife if she hustles back to the office right now.

Watching Jason Hollander stride back up the well-shoveled stone steps into his house, she flips open her Motorola and lifts it to her ear. "Isabel Van Nuys."

"Isabel, it's Amy. That Mr. Gabriel just called. He said he and his wife are stuck in traffic and running a little late."

Relieved, she says, "So am I. I was just going to try to beat them back to the office, but I'll take my—"

"He said not to bother meeting him here," Amy cuts in. "He said they'll just meet you over at the Gilder Road address."

"Oh." Isabel frowns. "Did he leave a phone number? I'd rather meet him at the office."

"No, he didn't. I assumed you had it. I'm really sorry," Amy says nervously. Just this morning, Mary flew off the handle at her for failing to screen one of her calls. "If I'd known you didn't have the number I would have asked him for it. Maybe he'll call again—"

"It's all right, Amy," Isabel tells the anxious girl. "I guess it's fine if I meet him at the property."

Is it?

Just yesterday, she had herself convinced Mr. Gabriel is a serial killer.

Now, in the broad light of this sun-splashed afternoon, that seems ridiculous.

And anyway, he's bringing his wife with him, she reminds herself.

David's hand trembles as he dials the phone.

Why the hell are you doing this? he asks himself, but he doesn't stop dialing.

And when a woman answers, he finds himself saying, "Hello, may I please speak with Olivia McGlinchie?"

The voice on the other end of the line emits an odd sound, something that sounds like a gasp, then falls silent.

Mystified, David clears his throat. "Hello? Is anybody—"

"I'm Olivia's mother," the woman says quietly. "Olivia died last year."

Died?

The woman to whom Angela's precious eyes were given?

David doesn't know whether to be more shocked by the news, or by his own utterly unexpected reaction to it. His throat painfully tight with emotion, he says hoarsely, "I'm sorry to hear that. I . . . I don't know what to say."

"Who is this?"

Make up a name. Just make up something, a story about how you're an old friend who knew her years ago or something, and get off the phone. Don't go into the truth. Not now. There's no reason to tell her now.

David opens his mouth to speak, but nothing comes out.

"Hello? Who is this?" the woman asks again, and to his horror he realizes that Olivia's mother sounds as though she's crying.

"I'm sorry, Mrs. McGlinchie," he says, fighting off the threat of tears himself. It's almost as though Angela has died all over again. "I didn't mean to . . . to—"

"It's just hard," she says, sniffling. "Whenever I hear her name, I—"

She breaks off, and he can sense, somehow, that she's trying to get hold of herself. Her voice is stronger when she again asks, "Who is this?"

He takes a deep breath.

"My name is David Brookman, Mrs. McGlinchie. My wife Angela was Olivia's organ donor."

Still wearing her workout clothes beneath her yellow parka, Leslie hurries into Toddler Tyme, hoping she isn't late. In her mad scramble to get dressed after her last Yoga class, she forgot her watch in her locker at the gym. So much for total inner peace and relaxation.

She's taken only a few steps down the corridor inside the day-care center when a woman materializes in her path. Her dark hair is in a single long braid and she has on ballerina flats, a long denim skirt, and a bright blue sweater embroidered with yellow daisies. Green plastic shamrock earrings dangle from her ears—a bit early for Saint Patrick's Day, Leslie thinks.

"May I help you?" she asks Leslie.

"Yes, hi. I'm Leo Larrabee's aunt, and I'm supposed to be picking him up today. My sister-in-law has to work later than usual."

"Right. Rose called from the bookstore to say that her replacement hadn't arrived and you'd be here to get Leo instead. I'm Candy Adamski, the day-care center's director."

"Nice to meet you." Leslie reaches toward her, but the other woman shakes her head.

"I'd shake your hand, but the flu is going around. I'm sure you understand. I've been encouraging the children to wash their hands and we wipe down the toys with bleach water every night, but you can't contain every germ."

"No, you can't," Leslie murmurs, wishing this chatty Candy would just go find Leo. She's anxious to get home with him and see if there's any sign of Cupid. The puppy somehow disappeared overnight.

Rose seemed oddly stilted when she told Leslie about it on the phone this morning. It was almost as if she wasn't willing to reveal all the details. But maybe that was because Jenna and Leo were within earshot.

All Leslie knows is that when the three of them woke up this morning, Cupid was gone.

"It's a beautiful day out there, isn't it?" Candy Adamski chirps. "Still cold, but it's wonderful to see the sun at this time of year."

"Yes, it is." Leslie clears her throat. "Is Leo . . . ?"

"He's in the big playroom. You can come with me to get him, if you'd like. He's had a difficult day, poor little thing."

"Did he tell you about his puppy running away?"

"Yes, and on top of that, I'm afraid his favorite instructor is out sick today," Candy confides as she leads the way to a large, bright room filled with toys and children. She adds, in a low voice, "Mrs. Helfer, the substitute, is wonderful, but Leo has really bonded with Mr. Silva."

"Aunt Wes-wee!" Having spotted her, Leo comes bounding across the floor and throws his arms around her.

"Hi, sweetie." Leslie strokes his hair. "Are you ready to go home?"

"Yeah. Mist-o Gwegg wasn't my teacher today. He's got the fwu."

"I know. But I'm sure he'll be better soon."

"Yeah." Leo's lower lip trembles. "Did Mommy tell you about Cupid?"

She hugs him close. "Yes, she did, Leo. But we're going to go home and look for him. In fact, why don't we go for a walk and call him? Maybe he'll hear us and come running."

"Do you think so?"

No, she doesn't. Her intuition tells her the puppy is gone for good. But she can't bear to dash the hope on her nephew's face.

"Sure. Come on, sweetie. Let's go home."

There are fresh tire tracks in the snowy driveway at 27 Gilder Road.

Isabel heads slowly up the winding lane, wondering how Mr. Gabriel's wife feels about the prospect of living in such a secluded spot. Even with the leaves off the trees at this time of year, you can't see the house from the road. It's tucked behind a thick stand of evergreen trees and shrubs.

But some people really like their privacy. Mr. Gabriel certainly strikes her as somebody who would.

She pulls to a stop beside a small black sedan with New York rental plates, surprised to find it empty.

Maybe he took his wife around back to show her the property, Isabel concludes, turning off the ignition and opening her car door. After all, the sun is already low in the western sky, and he did say his wife was interested in the perennial gardens—which amount to little more than muddy patches filled with dried up stalks at this time of year.

Clutching her keys and Mr. Gabriel's black bag, Isabel steps out of the car, then hesitates. Should she leave his bag here? Yes. No reason to lug it around the house.

She tosses it back onto the seat and closes the door behind her. The slam seems to echo loudly.

This really is the middle of nowhere, she thinks. No woman in her right mind would want to live out here, especially in an ugly house like this.

She looks up at the deserted contemporary, its blind-covered windows making it seem especially desolate and forlorn in the long late-afternoon shadows.

Well, your job is to build the place up, not focus on its shortcomings, she reminds herself, her feet making a pleasant crunching noise in the snow as she walks around the side of the house. *If you sell it, you'll be able to—*

She cries out as a strong pair of hands grab her from behind, and a familiar voice ominously says, "You're late."

The late-afternoon sun is sinking rapidly in the western sky when Christine pulls into her driveway, the back of the station wagon filled with groceries. After driving out to a deserted beach and brooding for a few lonely hours, she found her way to a supermarket.

A different supermarket chain than the one in Laurel Bay. A store for which she doesn't have the bonus savings card Ben expects her to use at their regular place. Nor did she have her coupon pouch.

She bought all brand names, all at full price, loading a cart with every forbidden junk food she could find.

When all else fails, eat, she thinks grimly, turning off the ignition and opening the door. *Eat Hostess Twinkies and Breyer's Chocolate Chip Ice Cream and Lays Barbecue Potato Chips, real ones, not the fat-free kind.*

Eat, because you just got your period and you can blame it on PMS.

Eat, because your husband isn't the least bit interested in you, and even if he were, you can't seem to get pregnant anyway.

Eat, because gorging yourself on food might keep you from feeling so incredibly hollow . . .

As she steps out of the car, her feet promptly splash into a puddle leftover from yesterday's rain.

"Damn," she says softly. "Damn, damn, damn."

A lump rises in her throat as she stares down at her soggy leather flats, feeling more sorry for herself than ever, if that's possible.

You've done enough crying today.

She attempts to push the lump back down again. It refuses to budge. It only takes a few moments for her eyes to become as soggy as her shoes.

Crying freely, she pulls two bulging shopping bags from the back of the station wagon. The first thing she's going to do when she goes into the house, she decides, is turn up the heat. She'll turn it up to sixty-five. No, seventy. She'll turn the heat up to seventy and if Ben comes home and dares to—

"Umm . . . hello?"

Startled, Christine looks up to see a young woman peering at her over the hedge that separates the Kirkmayers' yard from the Larrabees'. She has a long brown ponytail and she's not wearing a coat over her navy hooded sweatshirt.

"Hi," Christine says warily, sniffling and balancing the bags in one arm so she can wipe her eyes on her sleeve.

"I'm Leslie Larrabee, Rose's sister-in-law."

Oh, no. After what happened yesterday with the children, Christine has no idea what to expect. For all she knows, Rose is about to hit her with a lawsuit.

"I just wanted to—are you okay?" Leslie breaks off to ask, as Christine juggles her packages and swipes at her eyes again.

"I'm fine," she says, just as a jumbo-sized package of Doritos tumbles out of one of the bags.

"Are you sure you're okay?"

"I'm fine," she repeats through clenched teeth.

Leslie doesn't look as though she believes her, but goes on, "Well, I just wanted to check with you . . . the kids' puppy is missing, and—"

"They think I took it?" Christine is incredulous. "I would never—"

"No! Nobody thinks you took it. He's just gone, and we think he must have run away last night, and the kids are really upset. I'm checking with all the neighbors to find out if anyone's seen him."

"I'm sorry, but I haven't."

"But if you do . . ."

"I'll bring him home."

"Thanks. Rose would appreciate it. She had to go to work and she's worried sick about the dog, and the kids, and . . . Well, she's going through a really bad time right now."

Christine contemplates that, then finds herself asking tentatively, "Will you give her my best? And tell her . . . tell her I'm really sorry. About the dog, and about yesterday. I didn't mean to scare her. I should have called before I brought the children out."

Leslie nods. "I'll tell her."

"Aunt Wes-wee!" Leo calls from the open back door of the house. "The toast popped up! Can I put the choco-wat on?"

"Coming, Leo." Rose's sister-in-law turns away.

Christine watches her give the little boy a hug, then bring him back inside.

Poor little guy, she thinks, as she carries the groceries toward the house. She'll have to ask Ben—when she decides to start speaking to him again—to keep an eye out for the missing puppy.

When at last David hangs up the telephone, he lets out a tremendous, shuddering sigh.

Olivia McGlinchie is dead.

Murdered, after disappearing during a snowstorm last winter. Her mother, distraught the entire time she was telling him about the case, mentioned that Olivia's body was found by hunters after the spring thaw somewhere upstate, in the mountains.

Could it be . . . ?

No. Absolutely not. That would be too bizarre a coincidence.

David's heart is pounding as he takes out his laptop computer and flips it open.

As he goes through the succession of steps required to log on to the Internet, he searches his memory, frustrated. He remembers reading about a murdered woman from the New York boroughs . . .

But it couldn't have been her. Of course it wasn't. Things like that happen all the time.

Swiftly launching a search engine, he types in Olivia McGlinchie.

He taps his fingers nervously on the arm of his chair as the computer hums and clicks, processing the name.

When the search results come up, there are dozens of them—mostly references to news stories.

He clicks on the first.

POLICE BELIEVE BODY THAT OF MISSING STATEN ISLAND WOMAN.

He squirms in his chair. The headline is vaguely familiar, but back when he read it the first time, he never connected it with the organ recipient from Staten Island. Why would he? He never even knew her name.

Olivia McGlinchie can't be the woman he remembers reading about. That simply would be too far-fetched a coincidence.

But as David scans the article, his blood turns to ice in his veins.

He struggles to wrap his mind around the impossible:

Olivia McGlinchie's body was found a mile from his cabin in the Catskills.

Before Isabel can cry out again, a gloved hand roughly clamps something over her mouth. Some kind of tape.

Duct tape.

"I knew you'd be late, Angela." The voice is chillingly guttural, yet recognizable.

Mr. Gabriel.

Dear God.

As she begins to struggle, the first dazed, coherent

thought she manages to form is that she was right about him all along. She should have listened to her instincts.

Her next thought: who on earth is Angela?

"Are you listening, Angela?" He remains behind her, unseen, a madman who clearly believes she's somebody else.

"Angela?" he barks, and she nods, whimpering behind the tape, still struggling, panting through her nose.

She can't get enough air. She feels light-headed and her knees have gone liquid, as though she's going to faint. But she can't. If she does, she knows, she'll never wake up.

"Now, listen. Here's what I want you to do," Mr. Gabriel says calmly, as though he were a kindergarten teacher about to teach a child how to tie her shoes. "First, I want you to stop fighting with me for a moment and stop trying to scream. You're wasting all that effort. There's nobody to hear you."

If you cooperate, he might let you go.

She forces herself to go utterly still and silent in his grasp, even as hysteria screeches through her.

"Good." His voice is laced with an eerie calm. "Now isn't that better? You really should listen to me, Angela. If you had listened to me in the first place, we wouldn't be here. We'd be together on a tropical island somewhere, living happily ever after. But you didn't want that. You chose *him* instead."

Isabel attempts to swallow the saliva welling in her throat, and chokes. Her body wracked with spasms, she begins to struggle again.

"No. Be still!" he barks. "You aren't doing what I want you to do."

I can't breathe. Oh, please, I can't breathe. I'm going to die.

Bile is rising in her chest.

"Breathe through your nose," he commands. "That's all you have to do. Take a long, deep breath through your nose."

She sucks in air through her nostrils.

"Good. Now hold it."

With one rapid movement, he raises something in front of her face, holding it high over her head.

A rock, she thinks frantically, *he's going to kill me with a rock or—*

But when he presses it against her, it's not a rock. It's soft.

"Did you savor that deep breath, Angela?" he asks. "Because it was the last one those lungs of yours are ever going to take."

A pillow.

He's clamping a pillow over her face, holding it fast, blocking out oxygen.

She falls to the frozen ground. He pins her there, flat on her back in the snow, smothering her with the pillow.

He's killing me.

Panic sets in.

"Just remember that the odds for survival are with you, Isabel."

Galvanized by Dr. Henry's long-ago words, she grapples with the steely arms above her, but they won't budge. She raises her knee sharply, hoping to make contact with his groin. He grunts in pain, but his death grasp doesn't flinch.

"There's an excellent chance you'll be around to dance at your daughters' weddings."

Her lungs are aching, violently straining for air.

No, Dr. Henry. You were wrong about that. I won't be around for my daughters' weddings or anything else. And they need me. My children need me.

Her strength waning, her lungs on fire as she slowly suffocates, Isabel's anguished last thought is that now she knows.

Jenny Cavilleri was wrong. It *does* hurt.

Death isn't falling off a cliff in slow motion.

It is hurtling through an icy black pit toward her doom, hitting bottom with an explosion of sheer agony.

Driving home from the bookstore, Rose does her best to prepare herself for the difficult evening ahead.

When she called Leslie earlier to check in, she learned that both Jenna and Leo have been crying on and off all afternoon about the missing puppy. Leslie even took the kids around the neighborhood to call his name, but there's been no sign of him.

"They keep accusing each other of having been the one who let him out last night or this morning, but they're both denying it, Rose. One of them must be lying, but I can't tell who it is."

Rose almost told Leslie her suspicions about Leo, but then she'd have to bring up the necklace. And if she brings up the necklace, Leslie is going to think Hitch is the one who left it there.

Of course it wasn't Hitch, Rose tells herself. *The necklace had somebody else's name on it.*

It had to be Leo. He stole the wrapped gift from someone who meant to give it to a woman named Angela, and then he lied about it.

Just as he lied about going outside, or at the very least, opening the door this morning.

Approaching the last intersection in town, she keeps a wary eye on the green light up ahead.

If it wasn't Leo . . .

That is, if somebody actually snuck into the house last night to leave the necklace . . .

Well, the puppy could have slipped out then.

Round and round her thoughts keep spinning, making her dizzy with confusion.

If you really think somebody broke in, why didn't you call the police first thing?

The light changes to yellow.

Because you can't bother them for another false alarm.

Her nerves on edge, she accelerates a bit to make it through the intersection. All she wants is to get home.

Do you really believe an intruder was in the house?

Of course not.

Fine. So now that that's settled . . .

She'll ask Leo again about the necklace.

And if he denies it . . .

Well, she'll have to ask around at Toddler Tyme to find out who this Angela could possibly—

A blaring horn shatters the thought.

Rose slams on the brakes.

Oh my God.

The light is red.

She was about to barrel right through it.

The Blazer screeches to a stop inches from the car that had the right of way. The driver, a woman Rose's age with children strapped in back, shakes her head and mouths something at Rose as she drives by.

Shaken, Rose doesn't blame her. She could have

caused a terrible accident. She could have killed those children, or their mother . . .

Or yourself.

Then Jenna and Leo would be orphaned.

Leaning forward, Rose touches her forehead to the steering wheel, shuddering at the thought of what her death would do to her poor babies.

They'd be traumatized.

Closing her eyes, Rose can't fathom how they could possibly get through the death of a parent for the second time in their short lives.

After the initial shock wore off, would they be okay, just as they eventually were after Sam's death? Would they go on without their mommy, just as they went on without their daddy?

If something happens to Rose, Leslie will be the children's legal guardian. Rose and Sam planned it that way when they wrote their will shortly after Leo's birth.

The will was their lawyer's idea, just in case something happened to them and Rose's father came out of the woodwork seeking custody of the kids or their meager assets. After all, he had suddenly popped up to unsuccessfully stake a claim in Rose's inheritance when his ex-wife died.

How lighthearted she and Sam were when they made their will. She remembers how they joked their way through the process. Sam said Leo was so colicky they should probably put in a special clause just in case Leslie tried to refuse to take him. And they both found it amusing that they had nothing to leave anyone but the kids, a fixer-upper Victorian on the unfashionable side of town, and a pile of bills.

"But that's okay, because we're not going anywhere for

a good sixty or seventy years," Sam said as they signed the papers.

"Yeah, just think . . . by then, maybe we'll actually have something to leave behind," Rose told him.

"But Leslie still gets the kids. I don't want them going into any nursing home," Sam quipped, and they laughed again.

Had either of them sensed what loomed before them, they would never have joked their way through—

Behind her, a car horn honks.

Rose bolts upright in the driver's seat, looking around wildly, relieved to discover that this time, the honk was merely because the light has turned green.

She isn't in danger. Not this time.

And anyway, nothing will happen to me, Rose reassures herself fiercely, pressing the gas pedal and steering cautiously toward home. *Nothing can possibly happen, because my children need me.*

It's that simple.

Yet morbid thoughts persist as she heads out onto the highway. Worse, she finds the anonymous caller's piano music floating through her head, over and over. Every time she thinks she's about to remember what the piece is called, the title darts out of her mind before she can grasp it.

I need music, she thinks, fumbling for the radio dial. *Regular music. Something to help me get that damn melody out of my head before I go crazy.*

She tunes in to WLIR, only to hear the meteorologist in the midst of his weather report.

". . . turning colder tomorrow with snow beginning late in the day. This could be a big one, folks. Because this is shaping up to be a coastal storm, those of you on the eastern end of the Island might see up to a foot of accumulation before it blows out of here Thursday morning."

A foot of snow? Rose grins. The kids will be thrilled. She'll be able to take them sledding at last. But she won't say anything to them. Not yet. The last time snow was predicted, it didn't happen.

This time, the forecaster had better be right, or the kids might have to put away their new sleds unused.

After all, Rose realizes, with March only days away, the promised storm could be the last chance this winter for snow.

Now comes the hard part, he thinks, gazing down at the body lying in the snow.

Unlike Angela, who landed facedown in the gutter after he struck her with the cab, Isabel Van Nuys lies faceup. Unlike Olivia, whose eyes sockets were charred black caverns by the time he finished with her, Isabel's eyes are open, staring in vacant horror at a fixed spot somewhere over his left shoulder.

But like both Angela and Olivia, Isabel lies in a pool of her own blood. Precisely at the moment he felt her go limp beneath his grasp, he slit her throat, a move that will undoubtedly make little sense to whoever examines the body, he thinks smugly. But it makes perfect sense to him.

Oh, how he's craved the intense satisfaction triggered by a glimpse of crimson blood on pure white snow. Twice before, the sight filled him with an exquisite sensation, and the knowledge that he'd won.

This third time is no disappointment. Triumphant power surges through his veins as he watches her blood pool beneath her head. Such a shame he has to move her.

She put up one hell of a fight. He rubs his bruised thigh where she kneed him.

So did Olivia. They fought like caged animals. It was so much more satisfying than it was that first time, with Angela.

I told you that you couldn't escape me, he silently tells the woman who started all of this. Her lungs may have ceased respiration in Isabel's body, but he still feels her presence, taunting him.

It's because she's still out there. As long as her heart is still beating in Rose Larrabee's rib cage, he'll have no peace.

But it won't be long now. In fact, if it really does snow tomorrow night, it will be all over.

He shivers with giddy anticipation, imagining the beautiful red blood that will stain the snow when he drives a blade through the heart that betrayed him.

But he mustn't get ahead of himself. First things first.

Isabel has to be moved.

With a sigh, he begins to spread the lavender vinyl shower curtain on the snow beside her corpse.

If only there were some way to leave her here, yet still accomplish his objective.

If only . . .

He breaks into a smile, realizing that there is a way, and it's very simple indeed.

Ten

Having lived his entire life in New York City, David has never set foot in the borough of Staten Island, ten miles across the bay from Manhattan.

He's driven through it, yes, on the expressway. And once in awhile, he and a couple of his friends used to ride the ferry round trip from the Battery to catch a bay breeze on hot spring days when they were supposed to be in school. But they never got off the boat. Why would they? As far as they were concerned, there was nothing on Staten Island but a bunch of houses.

Tonight, David has actually guided his Land Rover off the expressway, on a mission even he doesn't quite understand. He only knew, after reading about Olivia McGlinchie's disappearance and murder, that he must speak to her parents face-to-face.

That her body was found so close to his cabin might very well be a coincidence. But if there's the slightest chance that it isn't . . .

But how on earth could it not be? Nobody would ever link her to Angela—the donor information is confidential. And even if somebody did figure out the connection—what does that have to do with Olivia's death? And the cabin? Angela was rarely even there.

None of it makes any sense.

Yet David is here on Staten Island nonetheless, propelled by some inner urge he can neither comprehend nor deny.

He drives through a maze of residential streets, some better lit than others, and all of them dotted with old houses in various architectural styles: colonial, Victorian, and a smattering of fifties-style ranches.

Olivia McGlinchie's parents live in a well-preserved Queen Anne on a quiet side street, in the kind of neighborhood David never quite comprehended existed within the boundaries of New York City. Cozy lamplight spills from the windows of the houses on the block; there are station wagons and basketball hoops in the driveways; a woman is out in slippers and a housecoat walking her dog in the chilly evening air; commuters stride briskly home in overcoats with briefcases in hand.

This could be some small New Jersey town, David thinks, as he parks at the curb and presses the remote on his keychain to lock the doors. New Jersey, or Long Island, or upstate.

He feels a pang for Olivia McGlinchie, who grew up in this comfortable little world, only to be wrenched out of it by an unknown abductor and violently murdered on a remote mountainside miles from home.

David pauses at the curb to look up at the house, wondering what the hell he's doing here.

You should just go, he tells himself. *You have no business butting into these people's lives, and you sure as hell don't want them butting into yours.*

But it's too late.

A curtain flutters in a downstairs window at the

front of the house, and then the porch light clicks
on, flooding the spot where he's standing. The
front door opens and a lanky, balding man is there,
beckoning him.

"Is that you, Mr. Brookman?"

"Yes." He moves forward, squarely into the light,
up the porch steps.

"I'm Ralph McGlinchie. My wife told me you
called back around dinnertime to ask if you could
come over. I'm glad you did."

"Thank you."

David shakes the older man's bony hand and
feels it tremble in his grasp as the man says, "No,
thank you . . . for what you did. For Olivia."

There are tears in Ralph McGlinchie's eyes.

David has always been uncomfortable with un-
abashed emotion, yet he isn't now. There is a
connection between him and this stranger that
goes beyond the fact that he is the organ donor's
next of kin.

It's the grief, he realizes. *We both know what it is to
suffer an unexpected loss, a loss so immense you don't
know how you're going to make it through each day.*

"I'm so sorry about your daughter, Mr.
McGlinchie," he manages to say, his throat clogged
with sorrow.

"It's Ralph. And I'm so sorry about your wife.
Joanne and I—we never forgot for a second that a
young woman had to die so that our daughter
could see. But it wasn't until we lost Olivia that we
really understood your sacrifice."

Sacrifice?

No. It wasn't a sacrifice. The word makes it sound
as though David chose to give up Angela. And that
is something he never would have done. Ever. He

fought to keep her when he discovered her adultery, and he fought to keep her alive in the hospital long past the realization that there was no hope.

"Come in," Ralph says, holding the door wide open. "My wife wants to meet you. And I know you said you wanted to talk to us about Olivia."

"I would, if it's not—"

"It's fine. It's been almost a year, Mr. Brookman. We need to talk about her."

David nods, wondering if he'd feel the same way about Angela . . . if he had anyone with whom he could share the burden of grief. Her family grieved in their own way, but Angela severed her ties with them so long ago, it was as though they had already lost her. And the people she called "friends"—the socialites with whom she shopped and lunched, the gay men she met through her charity work—attended the funeral, sent flowers and platters of food, made charitable donations in her name, and quickly moved on, leaving David to mourn alone.

There is no one on earth who loved Angela the way he did.

No one, he thinks fiercely, pushing aside the nagging memory of his wife's anonymous lover as he follows Ralph McGlinchie into the house.

"I guess I should go. Peter's probably wondering where I am," Leslie says reluctantly, setting down her mug, drained of the herbal tea Rose brewed for both of them after a dinner of take-out pizza, Leslie's treat. Rose, she knows, is flat broke.

"Are you sure you don't want to borrow some money?" she asks Rose, pushing back her chair and looking around for her purse.

"No, Les, it's okay. But thanks anyway. You're sweet. Like I said, my boss is supposed to come over to bring me my paycheck, and I'll deposit it first thing in the morning. It'll be fine." Rose smiles, but her eyes are worried and rimmed by dark circles, as though she hasn't slept in a week.

"Do you want me to wait until he shows up, just to be sure?" Leslie offers, as they hear a clattering sound from the other room.

Leo's block tower toppling over again. He's trying to build it taller than he is, as Jenna coaches him from the coffee table, where she's coloring with markers. They're actually getting along this evening, for a change.

"No, you should go home before it gets late," Rose tells her. "I'm sure he'll be here. And if worse comes to worst and he forgets, I'll just get the check in the morning when the store opens and he'll have to let me go back out to the bank then. Anyway, you've already done enough today, Les."

"I just wish we'd found Cupid. I can't believe that even if he ran away, he wouldn't find his way back."

"Maybe he still will. That's what I keep telling the kids." Rose closes her eyes and rubs her temples, as though her head is aching.

"Why don't you let me stay and get them into bed while you go take a long hot bath or something?" Leslie suggests. "I can answer the door if your boss shows up."

Rose smiles. "Go home, Leslie. You have Peter there waiting for you, and you told him you'd leave right after we ate. That was two hours ago."

"Yeah, but notice he's not so worried he's calling to see if I've left yet," Leslie says wryly. "He's probably snoozing in my living room in front of some game, oblivious. Then when I get there and try to get him to come to bed with me, he'll say he's not tired and he'll stay up on the couch with the lights and TV on till all hours."

"Welcome to being somebody's wife, Les," Rose says with a grin, carrying both their mugs to the sink and turning on the water. "Sam used to do that all the time. It's a guy thing, just like dropping clothes on the floor in front of the hamper, and—"

She breaks off with a startled cry, her gaze focused on the window above the sink.

Leslie rushes over to her. "What's wrong?"

"Nothing, I . . . I thought I saw something, but . . ."

"Outside?"

Rose nods.

It's difficult to see out with the kitchen light casting a glare on the glass. Leslie hurriedly reaches for the nearby wall switch and flicks off the overhead fixture.

Now the yard is more visible, albeit dark. There's no moon tonight.

"Maybe it was Cupid," Leslie suggests, going toward the door. "I'll go see if he's out there."

Rose trails her to the door. "Be careful, Les."

"Cupid?" she calls as she steps outside, her breath frosty in the crisp night air. "Cupid, puppy, are you out here?"

No answer.

Nothing.

Leslie walks out into the yard, gazing at the dark, silent clumps of shrubs that border the property.

"Cupid?"

Her voice is slightly hoarse after an entire afternoon spent doing just this. She listens carefully for scampering in the bushes, or any sign that the puppy is lurking close by. There is nothing.

Leslie stands there for a few minutes, watching, listening.

She can't help but think about Sam. Her brother died a few yards from where she's standing, in the side yard, beneath the electric cables stretching to the street.

She shudders.

Convinced the yard is empty, she gives up and retreats to the house, where her sister-in-law is waiting anxiously in the back doorway.

"What did you think you saw?" she asks Rose as she closes and locks the door behind her. "Because there's definitely nothing there." *Unless the bogeyman is hiding in the bushes,* she almost adds, but catches her tongue. She doesn't even want to joke around about something like that. Rose is stressed out enough.

"I don't know . . . I thought I saw someone standing out there, looking in at me." Rose presses a hand against her chest. "It almost gave me a heart attack."

"Don't even kid about that, Rose." Leslie puts an arm around her sister-in-law and pulls her close. "I'm not going home. I'll stay. With the puppy missing and everything . . . you just shouldn't be alone tonight."

"Oh, Les, you don't have to—"

"I know. I want to."

Rose bows her head for a moment. When she raises it, her eyes are shiny with tears and gratitude. "Thank you. That would be . . . you have no idea how great that would be."

"Good. I'll call Peter and tell him." Leslie is already

walking toward the phone. As she dials her own number, she tells Rose, "Why don't you go take that bath now? I'll get the kids into their pajamas and put them to bed."

"You know what? I'm going to take you up on that. If my boss comes, just tell him I'm . . . I don't know. Just say I went out."

"Why?" Leslie asks as the phone rings on the other end of the line. "Don't you want him to picture you lounging naked in a tub full of bubbles?"

Rose doesn't return her suggestive smile. "Actually . . . no, I don't. He's been a little . . ."

Intrigued, Leslie asks, "A little what?"

"I don't know. Maybe it's just my imagination. It just seemed to me like maybe he might be . . ."

She trails off, but Leslie has read between the lines. "He's interested in you, Rose?"

"No! Not really. Just—"

"Flirting?" The phone rings again.

"God, no. He's not the type to flirt. It's just that he's been really nice to me lately, and now he's bringing my check over here. I guess I'm glad you're staying so that I don't have to—"

"Be alone with him?" The phone rings again. Where the hell is Peter?

"Everything sounds so much more sordid coming from you, Leslie," Rose says, shaking her head. "But yeah. I guess that's what I meant. Anyway . . . like I said, it's probably just me reading things into it that aren't there, so . . ."

Leslie hears a click in her ear, but it isn't Peter's voice that comes on the line. It's her own, on the answering machine's recording.

Frowning, she waits for the beep, then says, "Peter, if you're there, pick up. I'm going to stay at

Rose's tonight, so . . . can you pick up? Come on, it's me. Peter?"

No answer.

"Peter? Are you there?"

Apparently, he's not.

"Maybe he didn't hear the phone if he's sleeping," Rose suggests as Leslie hangs up.

"It's right next to the couch."

"Maybe he's in bed."

"He wouldn't go to bed this early. I guess he went out." She throws up her hands to make light of it. "Maybe I'm out of coffee grounds and he had to run to the store. Who knows? I'm sure he'll call when he gets back and realizes I'm not home yet."

"I'm sure he will. But if you want to go home and—"

"Are you kidding? This is girls' night. I'm putting the kids to bed. Go take your bath and when you come back down we'll find something to watch on TV. Anything but a basketball game."

Left alone in the kitchen, Leslie finishes washing the mugs, then turns out the lights. Before leaving the room, she crosses again to the window above the sink and peers out.

Nothing but an empty yard.

But she can't help feeling unsettled this time—as though there might be some unseen threat lurking in the shadows.

It's just because stupid Peter didn't answer the stupid phone, she thinks, turning away from the window. *Where could he possibly have gone at this hour on a week night—and why didn't he at least call to tell me he had to go out?*

* * *

Peering out from behind the trunk of an ancient maple tree, he notes that the kitchen window has gone dark once again.

He glimpses the figure of a woman standing there, and then she's gone, and he's alone again in the silent depths of the yard.

He wonders how long Leslie is going to stay tonight. Usually, when she visits, she's long gone by this hour.

Not that it matters.

He won't be venturing into the house again tonight.

Standing over her bed last night, watching her sleep for as long as he dared, should have been tantalizing enough to last him until tomorrow.

Tomorrow, when it snows.

But what if it doesn't? What if the forecasters are wrong again, or if this storm fizzles out before it reaches Long Island?

He can't wait any longer than twenty-four hours.

Rather than sating his blood lust, killing Isabel left him ravenous.

If it doesn't snow here tomorrow night as predicted, he'll just have to bring Rose with him.

There's plenty of snow on the ground in the Catskills. What's the difference if he brings her there alive? It might be nice to show her around David Brookman's cabin.

After all, he and Angela spent so many passionate hours there—when she wasn't feeling guilty, that is.

"If David ever found out I brought you up here . . ."

"Don't worry," he would say, kissing the worry lines on her forehead. *"He'll never know."*

They only used the cabin in January and February, when her husband was safely out of range, and relaxing at his condo and on the golf course in the Florida sunshine. Angela was supposed to spend the winter there with him, but she kept finding excuses to fly back to New York on weekends.

"I can't stay away from you," she would tell him, falling into his waiting arms at the airport.

"What did you tell him this time?"

"That I had to host a charity benefit. He'll barely notice I'm gone. He's too busy golfing with his father and all their rich buddies. You don't golf, do you?"

"Never," he lied, kissing her neck.

Of course he golfed. He golfed, and he sailed, and he skied—rich men's sports, all of them. It amazed him, sometimes, that he and David Brookman had traveled in the same circles all their lives, but never met. Of course, David is a good ten years older and went to MIT; he, on the other hand, went to Berkeley, drawn to the bohemian northern California lifestyle—and of course, the fact that Father didn't agree with his choice. Not that there was a damn thing he could do about it. Mother was paying. Mother was always willing to pay, just as long as he stayed out of her hair.

A light goes on in an upstairs window. It's the bathroom, he knows. The shade is down, but it's a lace one that isn't entirely opaque. The silhouette of a woman is visible there, and she's getting undressed.

His pulse quickens. He eyes the lattice against the side of the house. It stretches nearly to the second floor, ending just below the bathroom window. If he used it as a ladder and put his face right up to the window, he might be able to catch a glimpse of Rose through the shade.

He moves swiftly, mounting the lattice with the agility of an acrobat. The snarl of bare wisteria vines make it a tricky climb, and he winces when a splinter embeds itself into the tender palm of his hand, but he presses on. He's nearly reached the top when he hears a car coming down the quiet street, slowing just in front of the Larrabee home.

He freezes, clinging to the lattice.

The car turns into the driveway below, the glaring headlights illuminating his perch like the sweeping searchlight from a prison guard tower.

Don't move.

Don't breathe.

Maybe whoever it is didn't see you.

But the car door opens abruptly, and a male voice calls sharply, "Hey! What the hell are you doing up there?"

After testing the temperature of the brimming tub, Rose turns off the water. A little hot, but it will cool down quickly. She steps in gingerly and sinks gratefully into the rose-scented bubbles, leaning her head back against the edge of the tub.

It's still hot. Too hot.

Maybe if she—

What was that?

She distinctly heard a sharp thudding noise from somewhere outside.

She sits up quickly, the water sloshing around her, some of it splashing over the side and onto the mat beside the tub.

"Leslie?" she calls.

No answer.

Not surprising. Rose can hear her in Jenna's

room on the opposite end of the second floor. The three of them are giggling in there, singing silly nursery rhymes. It's good to hear Jenna and Leo sounding so happy after today's trauma with the lost puppy. Thank God for Leslie.

Everything is fine, Rose tells herself. *Just take your bath and stop being so paranoid.*

Hah. Paranoid.

On her way to the bathroom, she made a detour to her bedroom. Just to make sure Sam's gun was still in the night stand drawer. Just to make sure the bullets are still in the locked box in the top of the closet.

Both the gun and the bullets are just where Sam left them.

And you're not going to do a damned thing about it, Rose tells herself sternly. She simply can't take the chance of keeping a loaded weapon anywhere in this house. Not with Leo here, there and everywhere, getting into things.

And anyway, she has no idea how to load a gun, and would be afraid to try.

Hitch would probably show you, if you really wanted to know.

But she doesn't.

She doesn't want to know.

Smiling at the sound of her children's laughter wafting in from Jenna's room, Rose sits back in the water.

Ouch! It really is burning her skin.

Reaching for the cold tap, she turns it on to cool the tub down a little, disappointed when the loudly splashing water drowns out the laughing voices down the hall.

* * *

"And the police never had any clue who might have done it?" David asks Olivia McGlinchie's parents, who shake their heads sadly.

They're seated together on the old-fashioned sofa opposite David's wingback chair, the husband's arm protectively around his wife's frail shoulders. David can't help wondering whether Joanne McGlinchie was always this delicate wisp of a woman. Judging by the framed family photos on the table, she wasn't. He suspects overwhelming grief robbed her frame of a few dozen pounds and put the gray streaks in her dark hair.

"The detectives on the case never even pinpointed a single suspect." Ralph sighs. "When she disappeared, they treated the case as though she were a teenager who had run away. They looked at the situation—at this young woman who suddenly could see after a lifetime of disability—and they thought that she had probably gotten carried away with her new independence."

"We told them she would never do that," Joanne inserts, her voice unwavering, almost hardy, for the first time tonight. "Our daughter would never abandon her car in a parking lot and take off in the middle of a snowstorm. She would never leave us to worry for months on end, not knowing if she was alive, or—"

She breaks off, shaking her head. As her husband pats her shoulder, the dog at their feet stands and nuzzles his nose against the woman's leg, as though he senses her sorrow.

His name, the McGlinchies told David when he first arrived, is Buddy, and he was Olivia's Seeing Eye dog. When she regained her sight, she couldn't bear to part with him and kept him as her beloved pet. They found him hungry and distressed in their daughter's Port Richmond apartment after her disappearance.

David clears his throat, deciding now is as good a time as any to tell the McGlinchies that he owns a home close to the spot where their daughter's body was found. And that somebody opened and read the letter Olivia sent him through the donor agency.

But Ralph speaks first, resuming the account where his wife left off. "No, Olivia would never have put us through that hell. We knew something was wrong but there was nothing we could do about it."

"We tried," Joanne puts in. "Ralph bought a computer, and he learned how to use it. He sent Olivia's picture all over the Internet, asking if anyone had seen her."

"Nobody had, but I found out that there are far too many people like us out there, desperate parents with missing kids," Ralph says sadly. He takes a deep breath. "By the time our daughter was found, murdered, too many months had passed for the police to pick up anybody's trail. They tried, but—"

His wife snorts.

"They did try, I'm sure," he repeats, patting her shoulder again. "They came here several times to question us, wanting to know all about her life, and if there was anybody we thought was suspicious."

"And there wasn't?"

Ralph McGlinchie shakes his head. "She had so many new friends, once she regained her sight and got a place of her own, started driving. She went to the city sometimes, and she started dating."

"She had a boyfriend?" David asks.

"A few." Her mother smiles. "She said it was a whole new ball game, dating when you could see what the other person looked like, and they could see you. She spent a lot of time on her appearance, you know. She started shopping, and wearing makeup, and paying attention to fashion. She went through what most girls experience when they're adolescents. It was such fun to see her that way. And she looked so beautiful. I know that coffee will be ready in a moment, but first . . . would you like to see some pictures of her?"

"Sure." David nods politely.

In truth, he doesn't want the coffee his hostess insisted on brewing, nor does he want to see pictures. But it seems to be almost therapeutic for Olivia's mother to share her memories of her daughter.

Again, David wonders if his own grief for Angela might be tempered if he hadn't isolated himself in his lonely, sorrowful little world.

Joanne moves purposefully for the first time since David arrived, standing and crossing swiftly to the shelf beside the fireplace. She plucks a thick photo album from the end of a long row of them and carries it over to David.

"The first few pages show what she looked like before the surgery," she says, as he opens the album. He murmurs appropriate comments as he peruses the photographs of a plain-looking young woman whose eyes, when they aren't obscured by dark glasses, betray her blindness in a vacant upward stare.

"This is her right after the bandages came off," Ralph says, having come to flank David's chair with his wife. He turns on a floor lamp behind the chair, illuminating the page.

"She looks happy." David scrutinizes the young

woman's smiling face, telling himself that those are Angela's eyes twinkling up at him.

But they aren't. Not really. Olivia McGlinchie looks nothing like his late wife. Perhaps it would have been different to gaze into her eyes in person, but now, as he stares at the photo, David feels no connection to Angela; nothing other than sorrow for this poor girl's tragic death.

He flips through the pages as her parents describe various scenes: Olivia learning to drive, Olivia tossing a Frisbee at the Jersey Shore with Buddy, Olivia on the top of the Empire State Building with binoculars . . .

"This one was taken on her last birthday," Joanne says, pointing to the last photo in the album, a group snapshot. "One of her newer friends sent it to us in a Christmas card a few months ago. She said she had forgotten she even took the picture and came across it when she had an old roll of film developed. She thought we might like to have it."

The photo shows a collection of young men and women posing around Olivia, with a birthday cake in the foreground, covered in lit candles.

His hand poised to close the album, David says, "How nice. They must have thrown her a part—"

He stops short.

Shakes his head.

It can't be . . .

His heart pounding, he holds the album up to the light.

Panting, his veins still pumping with adrenaline and fury, he gives Luke Pfleuger's battered, bloody corpse one last kick before leaving it on the ground at the foot of the lattice.

He turns to stride away, then curses under his breath.

The car, he realizes, is still in the driveway, motor still running, headlights on.

Certain it's only a matter of moments before somebody in the house realizes it's there, he contemplates slipping into the driver's seat and moving it. If only he had on a pair of gloves . . . But his hands are bare, and he can't risk leaving fingerprints on the steering wheel. The car will have to stay there. But he can at least turn it off, so that it'll take a little longer before Rose or her sister-in-law spots it.

He can hardly believe they didn't hear the scuffle, or Luke's strangled, gurgling gasps as the life drained out of him.

He untucks his shirt from his jeans and leans in the open car door. After wrapping his shirttail around his fingers, he grasps the key and turns it.

The motor's hum ceases.

He glances up through the windshield.

Pfleuger's body, the throat slit from ear to ear, is illuminated in the headlights's glow, the spotlight act in a macabre theater.

His only regret is that he couldn't use the monogrammed letter opener he stole from David Brookman's study to do it. It served him well with Olivia, and again this afternoon. But he left it behind, carelessly tossed into a thatch of pachysandra not far from Isabel's body, where the crime scene detectives will be sure to find it and assume her assailant accidentally dropped it as he fled. It will be all the evidence they need to arrest David Brookman as a suspect.

Brilliant. It saved him having to lug her body all the way to David Brookman's cabin.

Brilliant, too, that he thought to arm himself with a kitchen knife before venturing over here this evening. It was just a hunch—he never dreamed he'd need to use it. Luck is certainly with him tonight. He takes that as a sign that accelerating his plan was the right thing to do.

Wincing, he uses his fabric-wrapped hand to turn off the lights. His palm is sore where the splinter went in, and his knuckles are bleeding.

He thinks he'd better get the hell out of here before somebody sees him. He doesn't want to risk getting caught. Not now, when completion is so close at hand.

After stepping out of the car, he turns to look at the house one last time. The light is still on in the bathroom window upstairs.

"Sweet dreams, Angela. I'll see you tomorrow," he whispers softly, before scurrying off into the night.

"Christine? I'm home," Ben's voice calls from downstairs.

Crouched on the bathroom floor in front of the toilet, she doesn't answer him.

"Christine?"

She waits, half-expecting to hear his footsteps coming up the steps, but instead they retreat to the back of the first floor. He knows she's here—her car is in the driveway. Yet he didn't even bother to come up and make sure she's all right.

She hears the pipes groan as water begins to run in the downstairs bathroom.

Ben is washing up at the sink, she knows. It's the first thing he does every night when he walks in the door, saying he has to get the city grime and newsprint off his hands.

Another wave of nausea grips her and she stares miserably into the vomit-filled toilet bowl. It's like the chemo all over again, she thinks bleakly, wondering what the hell is wrong with her.

It couldn't be all that crap you gorged on earlier, could it?

The thought of potato chips and Twinkies is enough to gag her, but she really didn't eat *that* much. Not enough to make her this sick.

If she didn't have her period, she might be able to convince herself that her body clock is screwed up and this is a bout of morning sickness, but it would be wishful thinking, of course. She no longer believes she'll ever get pregnant. They've been trying for months, to no avail.

Plop . . . plop . . . plop . . .

Damn that dripping tub faucet. She still hasn't called a plumber, and God knows she can't ask Rose Larrabee about the one she uses now.

"Christine?" Ben's footsteps are on the stairs at last.

Good. Let him find her here in all her misery. Let him feel sorry that he took his time coming home tonight, that he didn't come right up here to check on her first thing.

Yeah, right. Ben, she knows, is immune to guilt.

She coughs loudly, forcing a dry heave, wishing she could make herself retch right about now to show him exactly how miserable she is. But the urge seems to have passed, her empty stomach left merely queasy in the wake of the storm.

Ben knocks at the bathroom door. "Christine? You in there?"

"Yes." Her voice is wan.

"What are you doing?"

"I'm sick."

He opens the door and looks in. "What's wrong?"

"I don't know . . . I think I have that flu you had or something."

Ben takes a step backward. "Don't give it back to me. I can't afford to get sick at this time of year. I'd better sleep downstairs on the couch tonight."

She tries to tell herself that he's really not a selfish bastard. That she should know better than to expect tea and sympathy from him. That he's overworked and overtired, and he never was the nurturing type in the first place.

"Do you, uh, need anything?" he asks belatedly, as though he just realized he should at least pretend that he cares about her.

"Just to be left alone."

"Do you think you're going to be long?" Ben is still hovering in the doorway. "Because I want to take a shower before bed."

"Trust me, when I'm done vomiting, you'll be the first to know," she snaps, reaching out with her foot to kick the door closed in his face as she gags again, this time for real.

This time, when Leslie calls home, Peter answers the phone on the first ring.

"There you are!" Relieved, she smiles and nods at Rose, who has looked up expectantly from the field trip permission slip she's filling out for Jenna to take back to school in the morning.

"I had to run out and pick up a few things," he says, sounding a little breathless.

"Really? Like what?"

"Just some stuff . . . you know, from the drugstore."

"Guy stuff?"

"Yeah. Listen, what's up? Where are you? I thought you'd be home by now."

"Didn't you get my message?"

"No, I just walked back in the door."

"Oh. Well, I wanted to tell you I'm staying here with Rose tonight."

"You are?" He sounds disappointed. "If I had known that, I would've just gone home tonight instead of tomorrow."

"You're going home tomorrow night?"

"I have to. I haven't even gotten my mail in days, Les."

"But then I won't see you till Thursday."

"So come home tonight. I'm here now. And I've got a surprise for you."

"You do?"

"Yup. Just come home."

"I'd love to, but . . . ." She glances across the room at Rose, curled up on the couch leafing through her magazine. "I can't."

"Why not?"

"I'll tell you later. So . . . have a good night, Peter. Can I still get that surprise when I see you?"

"Definitely."

"Love you."

"You, too," he says. He never actually uses the word love, she realizes. Just echoes *you too* whenever she says it.

She hangs up the phone and sets it on the table beside her chair, frowning.

"What's wrong?" Rose asks.

"Did Sam ever say 'I love you'?"

"All the time. Why?"

"Peter doesn't."

"Ever?"

"No." She sighs, filled with doubt about Peter, their wedding, their future. "Sometimes I wonder . . ."

"What?"

She wants to tell Rose how lucky she was to have had Sam. For as long as they were together, there was never any doubt that he loved her.

But Rose already knows that.

And anyway, Peter isn't Sam, Leslie reminds herself for the second time today. *You can't compare. It isn't fair.*

Plus, Peter just said he has a surprise for you. He sounded so mysterious. Maybe it's—

"Leslie?" Rose prods, breaking into her thoughts. "Sometimes you wonder what?"

"Oh . . . never mind." She checks her watch. "Hey, what time did you say your boss was coming over?"

"I have no idea. It's getting late, isn't it? Maybe he for—"

"Why don't you call the store to remind him?"

"It's already closed."

"Do you have his home number?"

"No, and even if I did, I wouldn't use it. I guess if he doesn't show up, I'll have to get the check to-morrow." Rose reaches for the remote control. "Come on, let's find some sappy girl movie to watch on TV to take our minds off our troubles. Too bad I don't have a bag of chips in the cupboard. I could really go for—"

"Chips! Oh, Rose, I almost forgot. Your neighbor, Christine."

Rose glances at her, startled. "Christine? What about her?"

"I saw her today. She was taking groceries out of her car—she dropped a bag of chips, which is what made me think of her. So anyway, I asked her if she'd seen the puppy—she hasn't. But she said to tell you again how sorry she was for yesterday."

"She did?"

Leslie nods. "I felt kind of sorry for her. She seemed so . . . I don't know. There's just something about her that struck me as sort of pathetic. What's up with her marriage?"

"I never see her husband. He commutes, and he's always at—"

The phone rings suddenly, startling both of them. "Want me to get it?" Leslie asks, reaching for it on the table beside her chair.

"Would you?"

"Sure. Maybe it's your boss." She lifts the cordless receiver and presses Talk. "Hello?"

Silence.

Then a man says, "Uh, who is this?"

"Who is *this*?" she shoots back, though she recognizes the voice.

Scott Hitchcock.

"Uh, I was looking for Rose—"

"This is Leslie. Hang on a second." She raises an eyebrow at Rose as she passes her the phone. "It's Hitch."

"Hitch?" Rose looks surprised. Pleasantly so.

Leslie watches her carry the phone into the other room.

I knew it, she thinks, shaking her head, looking up at a framed photo on the mantel. *I just knew it.*

He's trying to take your place, Sam. And I hate to say it, but . . . I have a feeling she's going to let him.

"Who . . . do you know who this is?" David asks the McGlinchies when he manages to find his voice. He points at the smiling young man standing beside their daughter in the photo.

"No, I don't . . . do you, Joanne?"

She shakes her head, telling both her husband and David, "These are friends Olivia made that last summer, after she regained her sight. She met most of them in the city, I think."

"Do you mind if I take the photo out of the album so that I can take a closer look?" David is already slipping it, with trembling fingers, from its protective plastic pocket.

"What's the matter?" Ralph asks. "Are you all right?"

"I just . . ." David stares at the photo, incredulous. "I know I've seen that face before, and . . ."

And something is very, very wrong here.

Because the young man standing next to Olivia McGlinchie—the man whose baseball cap, scruffy beard and shaggy hair almost, but not quite, obscure his face—is the same person David saw coming out of the restaurant with Angela on St. Mark's Place on that warm spring night.

"So what's up, Hitch?" Rose asks, carrying the cordless phone into the kitchen, unwilling to sit there and talk to him with Leslie in earshot, just in case . . .

In case what? In case he's calling to pick up where he left off yesterday, in the kitchen?

"I just called to see how your day went," he says, and she realizes he sounds a little anxious. "I hope it was better than yesterday."

She gives a brittle laugh. "Well, the kids didn't disappear today, if that's what you mean. But Cupid did."

"Cupid . . ."

"Their puppy," she says, absently sponging the counter she already wiped down earlier. "He's missing."

"What happened? Did he run away?"

"He must have. I'm thinking Leo must have opened the door to check for snow—he's dying to use the sled you got him for Christmas—and the puppy probably got out."

"He'll probably find his way back. But the kids must be upset."

"They're devastated. Leslie's staying here tonight, and it took her forever to get them into bed. She must have read a dozen bedtime stories and sung a hundred nursery rhymes before they finally calmed down."

"Hopefully she didn't sing 'Where oh where has my little dog gone,'" Hitch says dryly.

Caught off guard by his dark humor, she forces a laugh. "I doubt that."

"I'm sorry. I didn't mean to joke about the puppy. I just—"

"It's okay," Rose assures him, tossing the sponge back into the sink. "Trust me, we can use some jokes around here these days. Actually, we can use a lot of things. Jokes . . . money . . . snow . . ."

"Well, you might be in luck there," Hitch says. "I

heard there's going to be a big storm tomorrow night. So the kids might get to use those sleds after all."

"My fingers are crossed," she says around a yawn.

"I'll cross mine, too," Hitch says. "You're tired, Rose. I'll let you go. And I've got an early day tomorrow. I'm driving into the Bronx to the plumbing supplier. Maybe I'll stop by on my way back."

"Do that. Goodnight, Hitch."

"Sweet dreams, Rose."

"May I see the photo for a second?" Joanne asks, and David hands it to her wordlessly, his mind racing. He doesn't know what any of this means, but as far as he's concerned, two coincidences linking Olivia McGlinchie to his world are two too many.

Joanne flips the photo over, then holds it up to the light. "That's what I thought. Olivia's friend wrote the names of the people in it on the back. That means this person's name would be . . . let's see, he's the one, two, three, fourth person from the left, so his name is Clarence."

Clarence?

Clarence . . .

"Is there a last name?" David asks.

Joanne shakes her head. "She only wrote first names."

"Do you know him?" Ralph is watching David carefully.

David looks from Ralph to his wife, noting their expectant expressions.

If I tell them what I suspect, it will only upset them, he realizes. *Because I'm not even sure what I suspect. I only know that something odd is going on here.*

Odd . . . and maybe dangerous.

"No," he tells Olivia's parents, rising abruptly and handing over the photo album. "I don't know him. I just . . . I thought I did. You know, I have to be going now."

Joanne protests, "But the coffee is ready, and—"

"I'm sorry. I just remembered something that I have to do right away."

Hopefully, it isn't too late.

Eleven

Rose awakens slowly, her senses gradually coming to life as she stretches her arms high above her head.

Hmmm. Sniffing the air, she smells toast. And when she opens her eyes, she sees gray light filtering through the shade.

It's actually morning?

She slept through an entire night? No Leo, no phone calls, no . . .

She turns her head quickly, darting a look at the empty pillow beside her.

Nope, no wee-hour visitors.

She even had sweet dreams, as Hitch instructed. In fact, he was in them.

Not just in them . . .

He had a starring role.

Rose closes her eyes, trying to grasp the fleeting remnants of her dreams. She can't quite remember what they were about, but she feels her cheeks grow warm and flushed as she recalls one particular detail.

Guilt surges through her and she opens her eyes, glancing again at Sam's empty pillow.

She can almost hear his voice, teasing her. *You're into my old pal Hitch, Rose. Come on . . . admit it.*

She shakes her head. She doesn't want to admit it, not to the imaginary ghost of Sam; not even to herself. It's too soon. It feels like a betrayal. Sam hasn't even been gone . . .

A year. He's been gone a year, Rose. Going on fourteen months, to be exact.

So what does that mean? That after a year, she's free to fall in love again?

Who said anything about falling in love?

All she wants is . . .

Well, it would be nice not to be alone all the time. Alone with the kids.

Having Leslie around last night made her remember how nice it is to relax and watch television with somebody who doesn't keep asking if it's almost time for *Blue's Clues* to come on.

And it would be nice to be kissed by someone who doesn't drool and smell of Fruity Pebbles . . .

Really kissed. The way she hasn't been since Sam died. The way Hitch kissed her just now, in her dream.

She quickly pushes that thought aside, climbs out of bed, and sticks her head out into the hall. Both the kids' bedroom doors are open, and she can hear voices downstairs and pans clattering in the kitchen. Heading toward the bathroom, she pauses at the top of the stairs to call, "Hey, what's going on down there?"

"Aunt Leslie's making chocolate toast!" Jenna shouts up.

"And I'm helping," Leo calls, followed by the sound of breaking glass.

"Leo! Mommy, Leo broke a dish!" Jenna bellows.

Rose sighs and starts down the stairs.

Leslie appears at the bottom, dustpan already in

hand. "Don't worry, Rose. I've got it all under control. Just go get ready for work. The kids are dressed for school, teeth brushed, and I'm making breakfast for them."

"I swear I'm going to recommend you for canonization, Leslie," Rose says gratefully. "Thank you."

She walks into the bathroom, closes the door, and catches a glimpse of her reflection in the mirrored medicine cabinet as she reaches for the day's first dose of pills.

Good Lord.

She might feel better today—more rested, more optimistic—but she looks like hell. There are dark circles under her eyes, the muscles around her mouth look tense, and her complexion is as pale and pasty as overcooked spaghetti.

Maybe it's just the lighting in here, she thinks, reaching for the cord to raise the lace window shade.

Not only does that do little to improve her appearance, but the sky outside is depressingly dark.

Well, it is supposed to snow. In fact, maybe it's started already.

Rose peers out the window, checking the ground for white flakes . . .

And lets out a bloodcurdling scream.

His stomach rumbling loudly, David sits back on his heels, wishing he hadn't included the cook when he fired the household staff yesterday. He hasn't had anything since yesterday's breakfast, unless he counts the countless cups of coffee he consumed throughout the sleepless night. All that caffeine has left him nauseous and jittery . . . or maybe that's not due to the caffeine at all.

He looks around at the piles of papers, stacks of books, and boxes of clothes surrounding him on the attic floor. He's spent the last ten hours rummaging through everything that ever belonged to Angela, and he hasn't come up with a single clue to her lover's identity. She covered her tracks well. Even her date book for the last year of her life contains only references to charity board meetings, Pilates classes, lunches with friends . . . but nothing about somebody named Clarence, or anybody else David doesn't recognize.

He rubs his sore, tired eyes, wearily calculating his next steps.

He could go to the police . . .

To tell them what?

That the woman who received his dead wife's organs might have been murdered by her lover?

It's nothing more than his own personal theory, really. In fact, if he were to go to the police, he would have no proof that Angela's lover even existed in the first place. He could show them the photo in Olivia's parents' album . . .

But what would that prove? The only place that face is linked to Angela is in my head. Besides, the Snow Angel has achieved legendary status in New York. Chances are, even the police wouldn't want to believe that she was an adulteress. And what if, considering where the body was found, they decide to investigate David for the murder?

What if they do? You have nothing to hide.

But the press would have a field day with a story like that. The Brookman name would be dragged through the mud. Every skeleton in the family closet—and David is sure there are many—would be examined.

He thinks of his father and stepmother, enjoying their retirement in Florida, and his mother, living in Paris with her fourth husband. They don't need this, and neither does he.

The press was bad enough when Angela died.

His parents never cared for their daughter-in-law. After trying unsuccessfully to talk him out of marrying her, they kept their distance after the wedding. Of course, they rushed to his side in the hospital after her accident, accompanied by their current spouses, and they stayed there until long after the funeral, making sure the world saw them as grieving in-laws.

Appearances are everything when you're a Brookman. It wouldn't do for people to discover that David's family couldn't stand his wife, and it sure as hell wouldn't do for David to be investigated for her murder, innocent or not.

He sighs.

If he can't go to the police, and he can't figure out who Clarence is—short of returning to the McGlinchies and getting in touch with their late daughter's photo-sending friend—then what can he do?

You can track down the other two women who have Angela's organs . . . and what? Warn them that a crazed killer named Clarence might be stalking them?

Yeah, sure.

He shakes his head.

His stomach growls again, more insistently than before.

Or you can forget the whole thing, David tells himself, *and you can go out and get something to eat.*

* * *

Christine has just finished vomiting—*again*—
when she hears the sirens.

Startled by how near they sound, she quickly
flushes the toilet and goes to the front bedroom to
peer out the window that overlooks the street.

A patrol car, red lights flashing and siren wailing,
has just screeched to a stop at the curb in front of
the house next door.

Christine briefly presses her hot, aching forehead against the cold glass, praying that nothing
has happened to Rose or one of the children.

Then she makes her way downstairs as quickly as
she can, clinging tightly to the bannister with a
clammy hand, wishing she were dressed so that she
could go next door to see what's going on.

You could get *dressed,* she reminds herself.

No, she can't. Right now, she doesn't have the
energy to do anything more than walk and breathe.

Chemotherapy—hell, even cancer—were nothing compared to this flu, if that's what she has.
She's much sicker than Ben was when he claimed
he had the flu.

Her doctor, when she called him first thing this
morning, said it sounds like the nasty strain that's
been going around. She's had a temperature of a
hundred and four since last night, accompanied by
vomiting and diarrhea, and it feels as though somebody is attacking her skull with a sledgehammer
and her throat with a blowtorch.

He offered to see her, but he's in Manhattan,
and she hasn't yet found a physician out here on
the Island. So there's nothing to do but tough it
out. And if it gets worse, she'll have to go to the
emergency room.

"Too bad we were so busy with the move that we

didn't get our flu shots," Ben declared. "Do you think it's too late for me to get one now?"

"Definitely," she couldn't resist saying, and felt a flicker of satisfaction when he shuddered.

"Well, I'm sure I already had what you've got. I was deathly ill."

Yeah, right.

Naturally, he slept on the couch. He did come up to check on her before he left for work this morning, and he brought her more Advil and a glass of water. He seemed concerned, and didn't scold her for having bought the brand name instead of generic ibuprofen. He even made her promise she'd call her doctor as soon as the office opened.

But he didn't offer to stay home with her.

Now, feeling dizzy, Christine stops at the bottom of the steps to steady herself against the bannister. But a fresh blast of sirens are screaming down the street, and she makes her way to the front door, her cold dread mounting with every shaky step she takes. Pulling the front door open, she shivers violently as the icy air hits her feverish body.

Three patrol cars and an EMS unit have arrived at 48 Shorewood Lane.

Christine sees the men swarming around something lying on the ground in the side yard.

No, not something.

Someone.

Living in the city, Christine was no stranger to violent death. How many times, while going about her daily business, did she stumble across telltale yellow crime-scene tape? The ring of uniformed officials hovering around a corpse—a dead bike messenger, a dead homeless man, a dead gang member who couldn't have been more than twelve . . .

She was never quite accustomed to it, yet in the city, you expected and accepted it, you moved on, you got over it.

But out here . . .

Here, it's shockingly *wrong* to confront death just beyond your doorstep on a gray winter weekday morning.

Please don't let it be one of those sweet children. Or their mother.

Trembling as much from icy dread as from the frigid, bay-scented wind, Christine closes her eyes and prays.

"I'm scared, Aunt Leslie." Jenna is sobbing. "Why did Mommy call the police to come again? What's going on?"

Leslie tries to hold her close, but her arms are already full of Leo. The little boy is squirming and doing his best to break away and escape the master bedroom, where Leslie herded both children at Rose's frantic order.

All Leslie knows is that there's a blood-covered figure lying on the ground below the bathroom window. She glimpsed the gory scene when she heard Rose's hysterical scream and rushed upstairs to the bathroom, the children on her tail. Thank God Rose had the presence of mind to stop them before they could look out.

But they know, of course, that something is terribly wrong. Sirens are wailing outside, and harried, muffled voices—Rose's and the detectives'—are floating up the stairs.

It has to be Rose's boss.

It has to be.

It can't possibly be Peter. Leslie spoke to him first thing this morning, when she called his cell phone. He was in his truck on his way to work. She kept pestering him about that surprise he mentioned, and he was amused, baiting her.

What if, after we hung up, he decided to swing by here and give me the surprise?

What if something happened to him out there, and he's the person lying dead on the ground out there?

Panic gnaws at her, yet she strains to maintain outer calm for the children.

Think only of the children. Don't think about Peter. He's probably fine. Of course he is.

"Why won't Mommy come up and tell us what's wrong, Aunt Leslie?" Jenna asks fearfully, sniffling and leaning her cheek against Leslie's shoulder.

"I'm sure she will, sweetie, as soon as she finishes talking to the nice policemen. Ouch, Leo, please sit still. You're hurting me."

"I . . . want . . . Mommy!"

"I know you do, and she'll be up in a few minutes."

"Don't hurt Aunt Leslie, Leo!" Applying seven-year-old reasoning, Jenna adds, "She loves you. She makes chocolate toast for you."

Chocolate toast.

How simple it is to be a child, to dwell in a world where love is proven by chocolate toast.

Leslie flinches as Leo's elbow lands below her rib.

"I didn't get to eat it. I want my toast!"

Clutching her writhing nephew, Leslie closes her eyes and tries to picture the body on the ground outside, even as she pushes aside images of another corpse lying there.

Her brother.

She never saw Sam after he died, but that doesn't mean she hasn't been tormented by thoughts of him lying facedown in the frozen grass, dead. Just like whoever is out there now.

It's a man . . . she could see that. A man in a long dark coat.

She's never seen Peter wear a coat like that in her life. Logically, she knows it isn't him based on that alone. She knows his wardrobe and his taste in clothes. In fact, she's done her share of criticizing both. An overcoat would be completely out of character.

But what if he bought a new coat?

What if that was his big surprise?

If she could muster a smile, she would. Peter buying an overcoat to surprise her? That is surely the most ridiculous notion that's ever entered her mind. She can't even picture him in dress clothes.

Peter is safely at work right now, where he belongs, wearing his worn jeans, work boots, flannel shirt and down vest, same as he does every day.

The poor dead man in the yard cannot possibly be Peter. Whoever he is, he isn't Peter.

"Why are you crying, Aunt Leslie?" Jenna asks, alarmed.

Even Leo stops wriggling and is looking up at her with a worried expression.

"I'm not crying."

Leo solemnly reaches out, touches a teardrop trickling down her cheek, and examines his fingertip. "Yes, you are."

She forces a smile. "Well, these are happy tears. I just thought of something happy."

Now, in the midst of chaos and tragedy and fear, she knows. At last, she knows.

He's the right person for me, because all I could think, when I thought for a moment that he was gone, was that life without him wouldn't be worth living.

How could I ever have questioned whether I love him enough to marry him?

The mere thought that something horrible could happen to Peter fills her with a hollow ache; yet she welcomes it, embraces it.

We really do belong together, Leslie tells herself firmly, casting her doubts aside once and for all.

And the next time she sees him, she's going to make him some chocolate toast.

You shouldn't be doing this, David scolds himself, sipping the last of his lukewarm coffee from a paper take-out cup as he spots the Saw Mill River Parkway exit for Woodbury Hills up ahead.

No, he shouldn't be driving on a slick, winding, high-speed highway on no sleep and an empty stomach.

And he shouldn't show up unannounced at 20 Colonial Drive.

But when he tried to phone Isabel Van Nuys, the answering machine picked up.

And when he tried, after leaving her a message, to convince himself that he had done his duty, his conscience refused to listen. He went to a coffee shop, stared blindly at a menu for about five minutes, and realized what he has to do.

Here he is, an hour later, steering the Land Rover along the exit. A light snow is just beginning to fall as he turns down a leafy Westchester County street, following the signs toward the village.

Moments later, he finds himself in the center of

a small suburban town with a quaint Victorian flavor. The businesses along the main road have mansard roofs and hand-painted signs; the lampposts look like gaslights; there are even a couple of black wrought-iron hitching posts beside the curb.

Angela wouldn't be caught dead living here, he finds himself thinking as he pulls into a diagonal spot marked TWENTY-MINUTE PARKING.

Caught dead living here?

He shakes his head at the bitter irony in the phrase as he steps out onto the uneven brick sidewalk.

Angela wasn't big on old-fashioned charm. She preferred the sleek and modern, and she loved the fast-paced city. He can just hear her voice in his head as he feeds a quarter into the parking meter. *If I had to live on, couldn't you at least have found me some organ recipients who don't live in the middle of nowhere, David? First Staten Island, now this.*

Oh, be quiet, Angela, he thinks, the corners of his lips curling upward despite his grim mission. *It could have been worse. It could have been Jersey.*

He scans the row of locally owned businesses, looking for a place to stop, get more coffee, and ask for directions to Colonial Drive.

There's a small deli in the middle of the block. A cloth banner depicting a steaming cup of coffee hangs from a flagpole beside the door. Perfect.

David steps in from the cold and is greeted by a blast of warm fragrant air: hazelnut coffee and eggs frying in butter.

His mouth waters.

There's a short line at the deli counter. The commuter crowd has no doubt long since boarded their Manhattan-bound trains. Two balding senior citi-

zens chat with one of the countermen as he pours
their coffee; behind them is a harried mother of
two toddlers who can't agree whether they want to
share a blueberry or banana muffin.

Waiting for them to decide, he half-listens to the
conversation among the men as he rehearses what
he's going to say to Isabel Van Nuys when he meets
her.

"I heard her daughters haven't even been told
yet." One of the retirees is shaking his head sadly.
"They're at two different colleges. I guess the ex-
husband wants to tell them both in person, so he's
got a lot of driving to do today."

"Well, he better drive fast if he wants to get to
them before they find out on their own." The counterman dumps two sugars into one of the coffees
and adds milk to the other without being told.
Clearly, the men are regulars. "Everyone who's
been in here this morning is talking about it."

"I'm not surprised it's all over town. Cripes, that
Mary she worked with at the real estate office is the
town crier."

"You got that right. I heard she called the *Daily
News* and offered them an exclusive interview. Are
you ready to order yet, Mrs. Hellerman?" the second counterman patiently asks the young mother
in front of David.

"Yes, we'll have a blueberry muffin and a bottle
of orange juice with an extra cup."

"No! Cranberry juice!" one of the kids screeches
so loudly that David winces.

"Ashley, I'm not buying two juices when you each
only take one sip as it is. Decide, girls. Orange or
cranberry?"

"Orange!"

"Cranberry!"

"You can go ahead," the woman tells David wearily, waving him past her children. "I have a feeling we're going to be awhile."

"Okay, sir, what'll it be?"

"A large coffee to go," David tells the counterman. Oh, what the hell? "And . . . an egg sandwich."

"Bread or roll, ham or cheese?"

"Bread. Ham. And cheese." If he's going to eat, he might as well *eat.*

"White, wheat or rye? Swiss, Muenster, or American?"

"Rye, Swiss, and would you mind giving me directions to Colonial Drive?"

The place goes silent, except for the whining toddlers.

David glances around to see everyone—the countermen, the senior citizens, and the mother—staring at him.

"You with the press?" one of the old men asks, eyeing him with interest.

"The press?" David frowns. "No. Why would—?"

"I've had reporters in here all morning, asking me how to get to Colonial Drive. Let me tell you before you go to too much trouble, the street is blocked off and there's cops all over the place."

The woman raises a salon-arched eyebrow. "Really? But I thought she was killed over on Gilder Road." On the word *killed* she lowers her voice and casts a protective glance at her oblivious children, who are happily poking holes in the wrapper of a loaf of bread on a nearby shelf.

"She *was* killed at that vacant place over on Gilder Road, but my nephew Tommy's a cop and my sister-in-law says they're looking for clues at her house. They don't need a bunch of reporters getting in the way," he adds with a meaningful glance at David.

"I have no idea you're talking about." Even as he speaks, David struggles to ignore the nagging inner voice telling him that he might very well have an idea.

"A woman who lives over on Colonial Drive was murdered yesterday," one of the countermen says, as the other flips the egg on the sizzling griddle. "Stuff like that doesn't happen in a town like this, so people are going nuts. She was a nice lady, too. Got really sick a couple of years ago and almost died. People were saying it was a miracle she got better after all that. Shame something like this has to go and happen to her now." He shakes his head and shakes some salt and pepper on the egg.

David no longer has an appetite; his stomach is suddenly churning.

"What is . . . what was her name?" he asks the counterman, and holds his breath for the reply, already certain what he's going to hear.

He shouldn't be caught off guard when he hears the name. But he is. It knocks the wind right out of him, and he can't decide whether suddenly everything—or nothing at all—makes sense.

"It was Isabel. Isabel Van Nuys."

"Good morning, Bayview Books."

"Bill?" At the sound of his chipper voice, she manages just that one word, his name, before her voice breaks. She's crying again. She's been crying for a few hours now, ever since she found the battered, bloody body of her murdered boss. The hysteria is subsiding but the shock, the sorrow, the fright are all more palpable now.

It isn't like before, seeing Sam lying there.

Sam wasn't bloody.

He was just . . .

Still.

Face down.

There was no blood.

And anyway, she went right into shock when she found her husband. She doesn't remember much about it.

This time, she isn't crippled by grief, yet she can't seem to block out the gory image.

"Rose?" Bill sounds alarmed. "Sweetie, what's wrong? Are you okay?"

"No. Bill . . ." She sinks into a chair at the kitchen table, where the children's toast has long since grown cold. "Luke is dead."

"What?"

"He's dead. He's here, at my house, and the police are here, and I found him this morning, a few hours ago, and he's—"

"Rose, slow down. You're not making any sense. How can Luke be dead? And what's he doing at your—"

"He was bringing me my paycheck last night. The police think he must have surprised a prowler, and . . ." She shudders, closing her eyes to block out the image of Luke's bloody, gaping neck wound.

"A prowler *killed* him?" Bill, incredulous, says, "Oh, my God." Then, again, "Oh, my God."

"I know. I'm sorry to tell you like this, I just— I realized I should call you. I thought you'd probably be wondering where I am . . ." She looks at the clock. Quarter past ten. It's only quarter past ten. It feels like an entire day has passed since she climbed out of bed.

"I was wondering. I just thought you were a few minutes late, so I didn't call. Sweetie, tell me, are you okay?"

"Not really. I can't even think straight. The police have been questioning me nonstop. I'm surprised they haven't been to the store yet."

"Oh, Rose . . . they don't think you did it, do they?"

"I don't think so . . ."

No. No, of course they don't think she did it.

Who would possibly think she could be a murderer?

But then, who would think there would be a murderer anywhere in Laurel Bay?

"I see a patrol car pulling up at the curb right now," Bill says anxiously. "What do you think I should do? Should I stay here? Should I close the store? Do you want me to come over there? You shouldn't be alone."

"I'm not alone. Leslie's here, and the kids. She's taking them to my in-laws' house. We're going to stay there for a few days . . . or maybe forever." She exhales sharply, unable to imagine ever coming back to this house.

"Your in-laws' house? The one here in town? You're not going to Florida, are you?"

"No! God, no," she says, vaguely noting that the top of her throat suddenly has that sore, pinchy feeling. "We just have to get out of here."

"So you're staying with your in-laws?"

"They're not there. The house is empty. And Leslie's place isn't big enough, so . . ."

"That's good, Rose. You should get out of there.

What if whoever killed Luke comes after you?" He gasps, as though realizing belatedly what he's said. "I'm sorry, Rose. Don't worry. I'm sure you're safe, but—"

"It's okay, Bill. I know."

It isn't as though she hasn't already considered the possibility that whoever was lurking outside of her house wasn't merely a neighborhood prowler turned violent.

It isn't as though she didn't tell the police detectives about the anonymous phone calls, and the valentines, and the necklace.

"Who is Angela?" asked Detective Molinari, the main one assigned to the case.

"I have no idea. It doesn't make any sense. That's why I thought my son must've stolen the necklace."

"Well, it sounds as though somebody may have been stalking you, Mrs. Larrabee." Detective Molinari proceeded to ask her whether she had recently broken off a relationship with anybody, or received unwanted attention from a stranger, or even a casual acquaintance.

She didn't tell them her hunch that Luke might have been interested. Why bother now?

Nor did she mention that she fleetingly thought Gregg Silva might have put the chocolates in her car. It would be downright embarrassing if they went to question her son's young, attractive teacher and mentioned that Rose thought he might have a crush on her.

And she certainly isn't going to tell them about Hitch. He was Sam's best friend. He's her friend. It was a stretch for her to envision him as her secret admirer, let alone to imagine him killing a man.

"You should be careful, Rose," Bill tells her.

"Don't tell anybody where you're going to be staying. Just in case . . ."

"Rose?" Leslie's voice calls from upstairs. "How many pairs of pajamas do you want me to pack for Jenna?"

How many pairs of pajamas?

It's such a simple question.

There should be a simple answer.

But she can't think what it might be. One pair? Four? All of them?

"Rose?" Leslie calls.

"Rose?" Bill asks gently in her ear.

Utterly numb, she tries to find her voice, to respond to him, and to Leslie . . .

But it's overwhelming, all of it. How can she possibly cope?

I need Sam, she thinks desolately. *I need big, strong, fearless Sam. He's the only one who can help me through this, and he's gone. I'm all alone.*

"Rose, I have to go," Bill is saying. "The police are here and they need to speak to me."

The police. Of course. They'll need to speak to Bill. Will they think he did it, too? He doesn't like Luke.

Didn't, she amends. Bill *didn't* like Luke. Luke is dead.

She swallows hard.

Her throat hurts.

And she's all alone.

You could call Hitch, a voice says, somewhere inside of her suddenly aching head. *He's big, strong, and fearless. And he really seems to care about you and the kids.*

She *should* call Hitch. He said he'd stop by on his way back from the city. If he comes and sees the police cars and the crime-scene tape . . .

He'll be worried.

Yes, she has to call him. Just . . .

Not yet.

A chill slithers over her.

Be careful, Rose. Don't tell anybody where you're going . . .

Maybe Bill is right. Maybe she shouldn't tell anybody else. Not until the police at least narrow down the suspects . . .

Not until she knows there isn't the slightest chance that Hitch might be among them.

Twelve

"Ben . . . where the hell are you?" Christine croaks into the phone when her husband's office voice mail picks up yet again. "Why aren't you calling me back? I need you. I've been trying to reach you all afternoon. And I need you to pick up more Advil for me on your way home."

She left several messages and he never returned any of her calls. Nor did he call to check in at lunchtime. And whenever she dials his cell phone, it clicks right into voice mail, which means it isn't even turned on.

Meanwhile, here she is, alone, burning up with fever, too sick to drive, and their neighbor's yard has turned into a bloody crime scene.

The victim was a middle-aged man, no relation to the Larrabees, according to the police officer she questioned—who then turned the tables and questioned her.

Right. As though she could possibly summon the strength to wield anything more deadly than a tissue at this point.

Her gaze falls on the fireplace poker propped against the coffee table within arm's reach. She put it there, just in case, when the police officer advised her to be cautious.

Apparently she had convinced him not only of her innocence, but that she didn't see or hear anything, because he beat a fairly hasty retreat back to the other side of the shrubbery. Or maybe he just doesn't want to catch this horrible flu.

Christine tosses the phone onto the coffee table and leans her head against the couch pillow again, gazing at the television with eyes that feel as though somebody boiled them.

She's anxious to find out more about the murder, but the first evening newscast is still more than an hour away. Without cable, they don't get the local Long Island station. The teasers the New York stations have aired throughout the afternoon have mentioned only the snow that is now falling over the entire metropolitan area. With a foot on the way, that's sure to be the top story, but they should at least mention the murder.

Ironic that Christine has no other way of gleaning information when she's a stone's throw from the scene of the crime. Every time she worked up her courage and dialed Rose's number, the line was busy. It's undoubtedly been taken off the hook.

From her living room, through a dense curtain of falling snow, Christine can see news trucks parked at the curb in front of the Larrabees' house, their camera crews and reporters held at bay by the police and a saw-horse barricade. A few times, they rang Christine's doorbell, but the police quickly put a stop to that.

Though the police presence is reassuring, she made sure all the windows and doors are locked. She even chained the front door from the inside, something she habitually did in the city. It always seemed unnecessary out here, but now . . .

When Christine pressed the police officer for details, such as the victim's name or relationship to Rose, the cop was frustratingly tight-lipped, saying he wasn't at liberty to discuss those details. All he would say was that the victim must have startled a prowler; there was a scuffle; the victim was stabbed.

She told the officer about the other night, when she thought she saw somebody lurking in the bushes. He took notes, then told her that the detective in charge of the case would want to speak at length with both her and her husband.

Terrific. Ben is going to love that.

Now, in the wake of the news that whoever she glimpsed lurking in the neighbors' yard that night might have been a cold-blooded killer, she sits here brooding, deathly ill, alone, becoming more furious with Ben by the minute.

Logically, she knows it isn't his fault that an armed prowler is terrorizing this charming neighborhood where Christine is supposed to feel so safe.

But other things are his fault.

That she has this lousy flu.

That she *doesn't* have cable television.

That she *doesn't* have a baby.

Well, technically, that might not be his fault. It might not be either of their faults. Maybe something is wrong. Maybe there's some physical reason they can't conceive.

But when she brought up the prospect of seeing a fertility specialist, Ben hit the ceiling. He said they haven't been trying long enough to resort to a specialist, and that the insurance won't cover it, and they can't afford it.

Money.

With him, it always comes back down to money.

She sighs, and tries to focus on the television.

A teaser for today's *Oprah* catches her attention. It is followed by another local news teaser, as a reporter surrounded by whirling snow says, "Coming up at five, the metropolitan area is bracing for a major winter storm. How much of this white stuff are we going to get before it's all over? Then, we'll take you to a peaceful suburban town, where residents are shocked by a brutal murder—and the killer is still on the loose."

There! There it is!

Christine sits up on the couch abruptly and watches intently as the scene shifts from the reporter to a long shot of a suburban house.

But it's the wrong house, modern and ugly and in a remote area, surrounded by thick woods. It's the wrong town. The wrong murder.

Christine leans back against the pillows, disheartened.

What a lousy world we live in. Lousy, and scary, and—

Suddenly, she hears a commotion at the front door.

She bolts upright again on the couch just in time to see the door thrown open, then halted abruptly by the chain.

With a trembling hand, Christine reaches for the fireplace poker and calls out, "Who's there?"

"I wish Mommy was here," Leo says, his little chin trembling as he looks around the living room.

"She'll be here soon, sweetie. She just has to finish talking to the nice policemen." Leslie goes around flipping switches, turning on every light in the room, but it still has an oddly murky feel.

It would be so different if Mom and Dad were here, where they belong, Leslie thinks angrily. *First Sam abandoned us, and then they did. It isn't fair that I'm the only one around to take care of Rose and the kids.*

She tried calling her parents several times from Rose's house, to tell them what's going on, but she got no answer. They're probably out playing bridge or hunting for early bird specials or whatever it is that's important enough to keep them a thousand miles away from home.

"I don't wike it here. Why can't I go to school to see Mist-o Gwegg?" Leo asks, as he has repeatedly all day.

"I told you, Leo, you can go to school tomorrow." At least, that's what she overheard Rose telling Candy Adamski when she called the director earlier. She quickly explained what happened, and then Candy seemed to be talking her ear off before she finally made an excuse and hung up.

"It's so cold in here, Aunt Leslie." Still wearing her red down jacket, Jenna shivers. Snowflakes cling to her hair and eyelashes. It's coming down hard out there.

Rose insisted that Leslie take her SUV to drive the children over here, and she's going to come later in Leslie's car. It's less than a mile, but she has to go out on the highway.

I should call Peter and tell him to go get her in the truck, she decides. He's coming over anyway, just as soon as he finishes working and goes home to check his mail. When she reached him on his cell phone to tell him about the murder at Rose's, he was shocked. She expected him to drop everything and come to her, but he called back to say that Arty wouldn't let him go. Peter and the other carpenters were racing against time to shore up the bungalow's roof beams, worried it might collapse under the weight of the coming snow.

"I'll be there as soon as I can, babe," he promised. "I'm just glad you're okay."

"And I'm glad you're okay."

"Me? Why me?"

"For a minute I was worried that it was you lying out there dead on the ground," she admitted.

"But I was at your place last night."

"I know you were. I'm just . . . I'm so relieved you're safe."

She wanted to tell him, right then and there, how much she loves him. How she no longer has a doubt in her mind about marrying him.

Then she realizes that he has no idea she was ever in doubt. As far as Peter knows, she's been enthusiastic about their coming marriage from the day he proposed.

"I'm freezing, Aunt Leslie," Jenna complains, sitting on the piano bench, her arms huddled miserably into her jacket.

"It's warming up in here already," Leslie tells her, hearing the telltale groan of the basement ductwork. "I turned the thermostat up to seventy. It just takes awhile."

"I want my Mommy," Leo says.

So do I, Leslie thinks, her gaze falling on a framed family portrait, one that was taken in her childhood. *I want my Mommy and my Daddy, and my big brother. I want somebody to make everything okay.*

When Peter comes, she'll feel better. She always feels safe with him nearby.

"I'll be back in a few seconds," she tells the kids, heading toward the kitchen, turning on more lights as she goes.

The first thing she'll do is put on some water so that Rose can have tea when she gets here. Then she'll call Peter and tell him to swing by and get her sister-in-law.

The instant Leslie steps over the threshold into the kitchen, somebody begins pounding on the piano's bass keys.

"Aunt Leslie!" Jenna shrieks. "Leo is giving me a headache!"

"Play gently, Leo," Leslie calls back, taking the empty tea kettle from its home on the stove's back burner.

"I *am* pwaying gentwee!" He continues to pound the keys in ear-shattering discord.

Not for the first time, she wonders how Rose manages to keep her sanity, alone with two small children all the time. It's not that they're bad kids, even, Leslie thinks, pressing the button to flip open the cap on the teakettle's spout.

They're just . . . noisy, she thinks, as the treble keys are added to the cacophony in the next room.

"Aunt Wes-wee! Jenna's ruining my song!" Leo bellows.

"No, she's not. It's a duet," Leslie calls back, peering into the tea kettle, then sniffing it. It smells clean, but she should probably wash it out before using it.

She picks up the phone on the way to the sink, dialing Peter's cell phone number. He picks up on the third ring, just as she's reaching for the hot water tap.

"Peter? It's me. Can you pick up Rose in your

truck? The roads are bad and I don't want her driving over here alone in my car."

"Yeah, but I'm not ready to leave yet."

"That's okay. I'll tell her to wait until you get
there. How long do you think it'll be?"

"I can't tell. We're still working on the roof. Tell
her I'll call when I'm leaving."

"Page her instead. She took the phone off the
hook because the press kept calling and bugging
her."

"What's her pager number?"

She gives it to him. "Be careful driving, Peter."

"I will. Are you okay over there with the kids,
Les?"

"We're fine . . . except, there's no water. Damn!"
She tries the cold water tap. Nothing. "The pipes
must be frozen."

"You'd better get a plumber over there right away
if Rose is going to be staying there with the kids.
She can't be there without water."

"I know. I'll tell her to call Hitch. Maybe he can
come tonight."

"Aunt Leslie!" Jenna yells. "He's hogging the
bench!"

Leslie sighs. "I've got to go, Peter. Love you."

"You too."

He hangs up.

Funny how the absence of the word *love* on
Peter's tongue doesn't bother her nearly as much
this afternoon as it did last night, she thinks, dialing Rose's pager.

The Land Rover's wipers beat a fast-paced
rhythm that seems entirely at odds with the creep-

ing traffic on the Long Island Expressway. David taps the steering wheel anxiously in time with the wipers, peering through the windshield at the string of red taillights dotting the sheet of swirling snow.

He should have headed south when he came off the Whitestone Bridge from Westchester. He could have taken the Southern State to Sunrise Highway, the way he and Angela used to do when they went out to visit friends in the Hamptons. He never takes the L.I.E. Why did he get on it today?

He's only at exit thirty. He's got over thirty more to go. At this rate, that's going to take hours.

But you might have days. Months, even.

After all, more than a year went by between Olivia McGlinchie's and Isabel Van Nuys' murders. There's no reason to assume that Rose Larrabee is in imminent danger.

For all David knows, Olivia's and Isabel's deaths were tragic coincidences.

No, he tells himself firmly, remembering the letters in his study. The letters that revealed the names of the organ recipients. The letters that somebody opened and read.

Olivia and Isabel's murders were connected, somehow. Connected to each other, and to Angela.

David is as certain of that as he is that Angela's mysterious lover has something to do with both deaths.

If only he had that picture of Clarence from the McGlinchies' photo album, so he could show it to Rose. He intended to make a detour to Staten Island to get it after he left Woodbury Hills, but by the time he reached New York the snow was coming down hard and traffic was a mess. He was afraid to go anywhere but straight to Rose Larrabee, driven by the urgent instinct to warn her.

So strong is his conviction that she's in danger that he even considered going to the police.

Yes, and they'll throw me in jail as a suspect the minute they figure out that I was up in Woodbury Hills this morning asking about Isabel Van Nuys, and that Olivia McGlinchie's body was found near my property, and both women have Angela's organs.

No, he can't go to the police. Not until he's sure. Not until he has concrete evidence linking the mysterious Clarence to both Isabel and Rose as well.

If only he had that damn picture.

Now he'll have to convince Rose to come with him back to Staten Island in a blizzard, probably in the middle of the night, he thinks, gazing up at the darkening sky.

He presses the brake and slows to a stop as the traffic in front of him stalls once again.

Dammit. This is maddening. He hasn't felt this helpless since . . .

Since you sat by Angela's bedside in the hospital.

No.

He doesn't want to go there now. This isn't about Angela. Not really.

Yes, it is. Of course it is.

Saving Rose Larrabee's life is David's last chance to keep a part of Angela alive.

Angela's heart beats in Rose's chest.

Her cheating *heart.*

Yes, but it's her heart, just the same.

All David knows now is that in the end, he loved Angela, no matter what she did.

And that Rose Larrabee isn't going to die.

She *can't* die. He won't let her.

Suddenly aware that the New Jersey radio station he was listening to has given way to static, David turns the dial until he finds WLIR, a local Long Island station.

"Coming up next, we'll have the latest on your rush-hour traffic and weather," the DJ promises as an old Elton John song comes to a close. "But first, these messages."

As the DJ's voice gives way to a jaunty jingle, David glances down at the cell phone lying on the console. He could try to call Rose again. But he should probably conserve the waning battery. And he has the feeling it would be futile, anyway. Her line has been busy for hours.

That can't be a good sign.

Maybe she just took it off the hook because one of her kids is taking a nap.

Or maybe she's using the Internet without a DSL line, so her phone is tied up.

The Internet!

Why didn't he think of it before?

Joan McGlinchie's voice drifts back to him.

Ralph bought a computer, and he learned how to use it. He sent Olivia's picture all over . . .

If Ralph sent Olivia's picture over the Internet, he can send Clarence's.

His heart racing, David reaches for his cell phone.

"Christine! Open up! It's me!"

"Ben?" Stunned, she rises from the couch and makes her way to the door, still carrying the fireplace poker. It sounds like her husband's voice, but why would he be home at this hour of the day?

She peeks through the crack in the door.

It's Ben, all right.

Maybe he couldn't stand being at work, knowing I'm so sick here. Or maybe he heard about the murder next door and he rushed home to make sure I'm okay.

She pulls the door closed enough to release the chain, then steps back to let him into the house. A gust of snow blows through the door with him.

"Christ, it's miserable out there. Why'd you put the chain on? Oh, hell, I think my shoes are ruined." Ben stomps his feet on the mat. She sees that he's wearing his black wing-tips, and resists the urge to ask him why he didn't think to wear boots when he left this morning.

Instead, she asks, "What are you doing home so early?"

"The office closed at noon because of the storm. Good thing, too. It took me four hours to get home. I couldn't get a cab over to Penn Station so I had to walk across town, and the trains were all running late when I got there."

Shivering in the fresh draft, she returns to the couch. So he didn't come home early merely because he was worried about her. She should have known better than to even entertain the ridiculous notion.

"Why didn't you call and tell me you were on your way?" she asks, pulling an afghan over herself and leaning her throbbing head against the pillow again.

"I didn't think of it. I left the office pretty fast. They wanted everyone out of there so the cleaning staff could do their thing and go home, too."

"I tried to call your cell phone. You didn't even have it turned on."

"I forgot to bring it with me. It's probably still on the dresser upstairs. Sleeping on the couch last night really threw me off," he says, almost in an accusatory tone.

She clenches her jaw, staring at the television, where Oprah is welcoming Dr. Phil.

"What's going on next door?" Ben asks, coming into the living room. He sits in a chair and bends to unlace his shoes. "There are cops and news vans all over the street."

"There was a murder."

He stops short, his hands frozen, clutching the ties. "A murder?"

She nods. "Remember that prowler? The one you told me was none of my business? Apparently, he came back and killed somebody."

"The woman next door?"

"No. A man. I don't know who he was. All I know is that the police haven't caught him yet, and they want to talk to both of us."

"Us? Why do they want to talk to us?"

"Because we live right next door, Ben. We're witnesses."

"I'm not a witness. I'm never even here. Did you tell them that I'm never even here?"

"They're not marriage counselors, Ben. They're cops."

"That's not what I . . ." He trails off, shaking his head, untying his shoes. As he removes them, along with his socks, he seems to be digesting the fact that somebody was killed right next door.

When he speaks again, his tone is kinder. "You must've been a wreck all day, Christine."

Tears well up in her eyes. "I was. And I feel so sick . . . and I'm out of Advil and my head is killing me."

"You're out of Advil?"

"I tried to call you at work to tell you to get me some on the way home," she says miserably, sniffling.

"I'll go get it for you. Just let me get changed, and warm up. Then I'll go to the store."

"You will?"

He nods. She's stunned.

"Is there anything else you need? Chicken soup?"

"No," she says quickly, her stomach churning at the mere thought of it.

"Jello? Ginger ale?"

"Ginger ale would be good," she tells him.

"Okay. Don't worry, Christine. You're going to be okay. Everything's going to be okay."

She nods, wishing she could believe that.

"Do you have a safe place to spend the night, Mrs. Larrabee?" asks the kind young policeman with the blond crewcut. Officer Shanley, his name is. "We're going to be patrolling the neighborhood, but—"

"Oh, I'm not staying here," she says with a shudder. "My sister-in-law already took the children over to—"

She breaks off, feeling a sudden vibration against her hip bone. Sam's pager is hooked to the belt loop of her jeans. Lifting it, she glances at the window, certain it's Leslie calling. For a moment, she's taken aback by the unfamiliar number. Then she recognizes that the call is coming from her in-laws' house.

"I have to get in touch with my sister-in-law, Officer," she tells the policeman, who has been at her side for the past half hour, showing her a series of local mug shots to see if she recognizes any of them.

Nobody, including Rose, was surprised when she didn't.

As she pointed out to the police, she never saw Luke Pleuger's assailant. Nor did she ever actually see a prowler lurking around her house, or have a run-in with anyone who might have been stalking her.

"Go ahead and make your call, Mrs. Larrabee," the officer says, standing and walking to the door. "And then you might want to get wherever it is that you're going. The roads are getting pretty bad out there."

"It isn't far," she tells him, managing a faint smile as she picks up the cordless phone. Remembering it was off the hook, she holds the Talk button down for a few minutes. As soon as she releases it and hears a dial tone, she punches in her in-laws' number.

As she waits for the call to go through, she presses the back of her hand to her forehead, as she does to the children when she's trying to figure out if they have a fever.

Her head feels warm, and it aches. And her throat is really starting to hurt. Candy Adamski told her earlier that Gregg Silva is still out with the flu, as are a number of the Toddler Tyme children. Rose wonders if she's coming down with it, too.

The phone rings twice before Leslie answers it.

Rose can hear a terrible racket in the background. "Les, is everything okay?"

"Jenna and Leo are playing the piano. I'm giving them a lesson. Maybe we can have a recital for you when you get here."

"I'm about to leave now, just as soon as I can throw some things into a bag." Rose carries the cordless phone up the stairs to her room.

"No, don't. Peter's coming for you in the truck, Rose."

"Why? He doesn't have to do that. I have your car, remember?" She opens her closet and pushes past the coats hanging there to find Sam's old duffel bag on a shelf in back.

"No, Rose, the roads are too slippery for you to be out in my car. Just wait there for him. He'll page you when he's coming. It won't be long."

"Okay," Rose says reluctantly, not wanting to stay in this house a moment longer than she has to.

If Peter takes too long, and the police leave . . . well, she'd rather take her chances on an icy road in Leslie's car than stay here alone after dark.

"Listen, Rose, I just tried to turn on the water and the pipes are—" Leslie breaks off, hearing a loud shriek in the background on the other end of the line.

"Leo! Cut it out!" Jenna screams. "Aunt Leslie!"

"Hang on a second, Rose." The phone clatters as Leslie hurriedly puts aside the receiver.

With the cordless phone propped between her cheek and shoulder, Rose goes into the bathroom. While retrieving her daily medication, she finds a half-full package of throat lozenges in the medicine cabinet. She pops one into her mouth and puts the package, along with the prescription bottles, into her duffel bag. Opening a dresser drawer, she counts out a few days' worth of underwear, then several pairs of socks. She carries it all over to the open duffel bag on the bed, listening as her sister-in-law soothes Jenna and Leo in the background. She can hear Leslie telling them something about teaching them piano again just as soon as she's done on the phone.

"We're going to work on that duet, guys," her sister-in-law is saying.

"How does my part go again, Aunt Wes-wee?" Leo asks.

"I'll play it in a minute."

"No, now!"

"Okay, but just quickly. Your mommy's waiting on the phone." Leslie begins playing the piano on the other end of the line.

After a few hauntingly familiar chords, Rose lets out a startled gasp.

"Mrs. McGlinchie? This is David Brookman. Thank goodness you're home."

"David! Where are you? The connection is—"

"I know. It's not great. I'm on my cell phone, driving on the L.I.E.," David says hurriedly, above the static. "Listen, Mrs. McGlinchie—"

"Joanne."

"Joanne," he obliges tightly, "I need your husband to do something for me."

"He's not home, David."

He deflates. "Do you know when he'll be back?"

"I hope it isn't long. He went to the supermarket to get bread and milk. We're all out, and we're afraid we're going to be snowbound if this weather keeps up. What's it like out there on the Island?"

David ignores her question. "Mrs. McGlinchie— *Joanne*—I need a favor, and it could be a matter of life and death."

The line crackles. His battery is low, and he doesn't have an adaptor in the car. Dammit.

"Did you say life and death?" Joanne McGlinchie asks.

"It might be. Does your husband have a photo scanner for his computer?"

"A scanner? I think that's what it's called."

"Tell him—"

The line buzzes with static.

"What, David?"

He shakes his head. "Tell him that I need him to scan the picture of Olivia's birthday party. The one we were looking at the other night. I need that picture of Clarence."

"How are you going to get it?"

"I'm going to give you my e-mail address, Mrs. McGlinchie. Do you have a pen?"

"I'll get one. Hang on a moment."

Hurry, he urges, his gaze fastened to the slow-moving stream of taillights ahead as the static grows louder in his ear. *Please hurry.*

"I've got a pen."

"Good! Write this down." He gives her his e-mail address. "Please have Mr. McGlinchie scan in the photo and e-mail it to me just as soon as he gets in."

"But why—"

Her question is lost in a loud, double beep as his phone's battery goes dead.

"Okay, now you guys practice that while I finish talking to Mommy," Leslie tells her niece and nephew, before leaving them on the piano bench and returning to the phone in the kitchen.

She has to smile, hearing the kids resume their disharmonious pounding on the keys.

"I hate to say it, Rose, but I don't think either of them is going to win a Juilliard Scholarsh—"

"What was that, Leslie?" Rose cuts in breathlessly.

"What was what?"

"That song? The one you were just playing?"

"Oh, that? It was the bass part of the duet I'm going to teach—"

"I know. I know the song, I used to play it with my father. And I tried to teach it to Sam, once."

"Sam? He was all thumbs on the pian—"

"Leslie, what is it called?" Rose interrupts again, her voice high-pitched. "I have to know."

"It's 'Heart and Soul.' Why?"

"Just . . . never mind. I have to go."

"Go where? You're supposed to wait for Peter to page you, Rose."

"I know. I will. I just need to talk to the police officer. I'll see you later."

Rose hangs up.

Leslie frowns. What was that all about?

Her gaze falls on the teapot, sitting in the dry sink.

The pipes.

Dammit. She forgot to ask Rose about calling Hitch to come over and take a look at them.

She'll have to page Rose again and—

Wait a minute. She doesn't have to wait for Rose. There's no reason why she can't just look up Hitch's phone number and call him herself.

"How does this sound, Aunt Wes-wee?" Leo calls over the din in the living room.

"It sounds great, sweetie," she calls back absently, taking the local directory from the shelf that holds her mother's cookbooks.

Sitting at the table with the phone in one hand,

Leslie flips to the yellow pages with the other. It doesn't take her long to find a large ad for Hitchcock and Son under Plumbers.

She dials the number and finds herself listening to a recording of Hitch's voice.

When the machine beeps, she says, "Hitch, this is Leslie Larrabee. I don't know if you've heard, but there was a . . . problem at Rose's last night." Not wanting to go into the details on a recorded message, she says, "She and the kids are fine, but they're going to be staying at my parents' house for a few days, and unfortunately, the pipes over here are frozen. If you could, would you come over as soon as possible to see what you can do? Thanks."

She hangs up, smiling.

With any luck, Hitch will access his messages from wherever he's working before he calls it quits for the night.

"Officer Shanley!" Rose calls, hurrying through the blowing snow wearing only her sneakers.

"Mrs. Larrabee! Is everything all right?" He turns away from the small knot of officers and detectives huddled near the wind-whipped yellow crime-scene tape surrounding the spot where Luke's body lay before he was taken to the morgue.

The weather is deteriorating so quickly that even the crowd of reporters and curious onlookers in the street has thinned to a hardy handful.

"Do you remember how I told you and Detective Molinari earlier that somebody has been calling me in the middle of the night, playing the same music every time?" Rose asks the young policeman.

"The prank caller? Yes, I remember."

"Well, I just found out that the song he kept playing is called 'Heart and Soul.'"

"Heart and Soul?" the cop echoes, looking blank.

"Hey, I know that tune," another officer says, and hums it.

"That's it," Rose tells him, tucking her already numb hands beneath the opposite arms to warm them.

"So what are you thinking? That it's a love song, so the stalker theory might be—"

"No, that it's a song about a heart. And the necklace was shaped like a heart, and so was the box of chocolates. And whoever broke in here and turned on the sound machine flipped it to the heartbeat setting."

"So you're thinking—"

"There's something I didn't tell the detectives earlier, Officer." She takes a deep breath. "I had a heart transplant almost two years ago. And I think that whoever killed Luke must know about it."

"But what does that have to do with . . . ?"

She shrugs. "I don't know what it means. I just think that it matters."

The cops exchange a glance.

"Who knows about your transplant?" one of them asks.

She shakes her head. "Just my family, and a couple of close friends. But it's a small town. The news might have gotten around."

The wind gusts, blowing wet snow into her face, stinging her eyes. She ducks her head, shivering.

"You shouldn't be out here without a coat," Officer Shanley tells her. "I'll talk to Detective Molinari about this and see what he thinks. Just be sure to give us a phone number for where you're going tonight in case he has more questions for you."

"I will," Rose promises and turns away, wading through several inches of snow already covering the ground.

What a shame. It would have been perfect weather for sledding, she thinks ruefully, as she makes her way toward the house.

Thirteen

The phone rings as Leslie rummages through her parents' cabinets, trying to find something she can possibly give the kids to eat. Only the dry macaroni is a possibility, but she can't cook it until Hitch gets here to fix the pipes.

Hoping to find him on the other end of the line, she hurries to answer the phone. But it's Peter's voice that greets her, and he sounds aggravated.

"Leslie? I can't get the damn truck started."

"You're kidding me. Where are you?"

"Where do you think I am? I'm standing on the street in Bellport, waiting for Triple A to come."

"What about Arty and the other guys? Can't they help you?"

"They offered me a ride, but I can't leave the truck here overnight, especially with the plows coming through. The town will have it towed away if I leave it."

"Oh, Peter . . . when is Triple A supposed to get there?"

"Who knows? They said they're really busy tonight because of the weather. I'll call you back when they show. Do me a favor and let Rose know I'm going to be late."

"I will. I love you."

"See you later," he says, and hangs up without even offering his customary *you, too.*

Frowning, Leslie crosses to the back door and reaches for the switch beside it. After flipping off the overhead kitchen light, she flips on the outside porch light. Now she can see that the snow is coming down so furiously that she can't even glimpse the chain-link fence at the back of the yard.

If Leslie pages Rose and tells her to wait for Peter, she'll insist on driving over here herself, and Leslie wouldn't blame her one bit. She wouldn't want to be alone in that house tonight for any length of time, either.

If only Rose had her SUV to drive, instead of Leslie's crummy old car.

She shakes her head, staring out at the storm.

The last thing she wants to do is take the kids out in it. But the Blazer has four-wheel drive, and they don't have far to go.

With a sigh, she heads for the living room, where Jenna and Leo are watching television.

"Come on, guys, let's get our coats on. We have to go get Mommy."

"What about supper?" Leo whines. "I'm hung-wee."

"We'll stop and get something on the way back. I can't cook anything here until Hitch comes to fix the water."

"Uncle Hitch is coming?" Jenna brightens.

Uncle.

Leslie nods and tells her, "Just to fix the pipes. Because he's a plumber."

Not to win your Mommy's heart, or anything like that.

"When is he coming?" Leo wants to know.

"Probably the second we leave," Leslie mutters, wondering what to do.

They'll only be out a few minutes.

Still, she'd better write a note and leave the front door unlocked so that Hitch can let himself in.

"I'm sorry to disturb you, Mrs. Larrabee," Officer Shanley says hurriedly when she answers his knock, "but I just wanted to let you know that we have to be going now. There was a bad accident—a big pileup out on Sunrise Highway just west of here. They need us over there."

Sunrise Highway? Rose hopes Peter isn't on it, trying to get here. Leslie said he'd page her first, but maybe he wanted to wait until he got close.

"Thank you, Officer." She can hear sirens in the distance. "Be careful driving over there."

"And you be careful, too. We'll be on patrol here tonight," he calls over his shoulder, already heading down the steps into the whirling snow illuminated by the porch light. Only one patrol car remains at the curb with Shanley's partner at the wheel. The motor is running and its red lights are already spinning.

"You're leaving soon, right?" Officer Shanley calls back from the curb.

She nods, thinking that she certainly hopes so. Even the media has abandoned her, undoubtedly chasing the police to the accident scene in hopes of capturing some grisly footage. Glancing over at the Kirkmayers' house next door, Rose sees that the lights are on. She can always go over there to wait for Peter . . .

No. After what happened, that would be too un-comfortable.

She watches the patrol car drive away, lights flash-ing, siren wailing.

With a shiver, she heads back inside, locking the door behind her.

The house is eerily silent.

Rose finds the keyring Leslie left her on the kitchen counter, then picks up the phone and dials her in-laws' number. She'll tell Leslie she's driving over. She'll be fine, as long as she takes it slowly.

The phone rings on the other end.

After all, Rose thinks, not counting the half-mile stretch of highway she'll have to drive, it's only a few blocks. Besides, why should Peter go out of his way to come get her? Leslie's parents' house is on the west side of town, not far from the Sunrise Highway exit. To pick up Rose, he'd have to come all the way through town and then circle back again. It doesn't make sense.

Nor, she realizes, does the fact that the phone is still ringing.

She counts ten rings. Eleven. Twelve . . .

No answer.

Feeling sick to her stomach, Rose bangs down the phone.

Maybe Leslie and the children are playing the piano so loud they can't hear the phone.

Maybe they're outside playing, making snow angels.

The image of Luke's bloody corpse fills her mind.

Or maybe . . .

No. Don't even think that.

Clutching Leslie's car keys, Rose races up the

stairs to the master bedroom, grabs her packed duffel bag, and opens the closet door to get her coat.

Listening to the rush-hour traffic report on the radio, David concludes that taking the Long Island Expressway was the best decision he's made all day. There's a nasty pileup down on Sunrise Highway east of Patchogue, not far from Laurel Bay. The road is closed due to multiple fatalities, and the backup stretches for miles. If David had chosen that route, he'd be stuck in that traffic . . .

Or worse.

There's nothing David can do for the poor people who were killed in that accident. But in less than two miles, he'll be at the Laurel Bay exit off the L.I.E., and racing to get to Rose Larrabee's house. This time, he isn't going to stop in town and ask directions. He bought a Suffolk County street atlas when he stopped for gas earlier, and he quickly pinpointed Shorewood Lane on it.

Now all he has to do is get there.

No, that's not all.

But it's a start.

When he comes face-to-face with Rose, he'll figure out what to say so that she won't decide he's a lunatic and slam the door in his face.

Slowing the car as he spots the green sign for the exit, he half-listens to a WLIR news report topped by coverage of the storm.

As he searches for the off ramp, he hears, " . . . murder in a quiet residential neighborhood has stunned the citizens of tranquil Laurel Bay on the south shore."

Uneasiness swoops over David. He quickly raises

the volume on the radio, listening intently as he steers cautiously off the highway, following the winding ramp to a sign that bears an arrow marked LAUREL BAY.

"Details are sketchy, and police are withholding the victim's name pending notification of next of kin. They do confirm the slaying took place outside a home on the east end of town not far from the water, and that the culprit is still at large. We'll bring you more on this story as information becomes available. The stock market took a tumble this afternoon as trading—"

Pulling up at a stop sign, David turns off the radio and presses the overhead light switch.

Grabbing the street atlas from the passenger's seat, he rapidly flips the pages until he comes to the one whose corner he folded down earlier.

Holding his breath, he scans the street map of Laurel Bay until he finds Shorewood Lane—and confirms that it is, indeed, on the east end of town not far from the water.

Leslie's heart sinks as she pulls up in front of 48 Shorewood Lane to find that her car is missing and the windows are dark.

"Where's Mommy?" Leo asks from the backseat.

"I have no idea. She must be on her way to Grandma and Grandpa's house." Peter must have paged her to tell her he wasn't coming.

"Is she going to be all right?" Jenna's tone is fearful.

"Of course she is." The kids don't know about the murder, but Jenna is old enough to be aware that something frightening is going on. "Come on, let's turn around and head back. I'll bet she'll be there waiting for us."

"But what about food?" Leo asks. "You said we could stop and get something on the way back."

"I know I did, Leo," she says wearily, "but nothing was open when we drove through town, remember? Everything is closed early because of the storm."

"But I'm hung-wee." He's starting to cry.

Fighting the urge to join him, Leslie says, "I know, baby. And as soon as we get to Grandma and Grandpa's we'll find something to eat."

"But you said there was nothing there," Jenna reminds her. "Can't we get some stuff from home?"

Leslie hesitates, eyeing the house. It would take her only a few seconds to run in and get some food from the kitchen . . .

"All right," she decides, turning off the Blazer's engine and debating whether to leave the kids here or drag them with her through the snow. That would take longer . . .

But after what happened here last night, she doesn't dare leave them outside, even locked in the car.

With a sigh, Leslie says, "Come on, guys, we're all going in. You can each choose two things from the fridge or the cupboards, and then we're outta here."

Stepping out of the cozy car, she gasps as the icy wind hits her. She hurries through the blowing snow to the curbside door and grapples with the straps on Leo's car seat, first with clumsy, gloved fingers, then with numb, bare ones.

"Hurry, Aunt Leslie," Jenna begs, shivering as she stands by, waiting in a snow drift.

"I'm trying!" The strap comes free, and Leo

scrambles out of his seat. She helps him out of the car, takes his hand and Jenna's, and together, the three of them trudge toward the front door.

Climbing the front steps, Leslie drops Jenna's hand to fumble with Rose's keyring as a car's headlights arc across the porch.

"Who's that?" Jenna asks, and Leslie realizes that the car has pulled into the driveway.

"Probably the pol—" Turning to see that it isn't a patrolling police car after all, she feels her heart skip a beat. She doesn't recognize the Land Rover in the driveway . . . or the stranger who quickly jumps out and strides toward her through the snow, calling, "Rose? Rose Larrabee?"

With a sinking feeling, Rose realizes that the driveway at her in-laws' house is empty. Judging by the barely snowed-over fresh tire tracks in the driveway, though, Leslie and the kids haven't been gone long. And they left all the lights on, as though they intended to come right back.

Maybe they just went out to get milk or something, Rose tries to reassure herself.

Slipping and sliding, still wearing her sneakers and clutching her heavy duffel bag, Rose makes her way up the snowed-over walk to the front door.

Turning the knob, she discovers that it's unlocked. She steps inside and sees a note taped to the mirror.

She's about to pick it up when she hears the door opening behind her.

With a startled cry, she spins around . . . then thumps her palm against her chest in relief when she sees the familiar face in the doorway.

"Oh, God, you scared the hell out of me," she says, trying to catch her breath and adding, "What are you doing here?"

"No, Rose isn't here," the young woman on the porch informs David as he mounts the steps two at a time. She places a protective hand on the children's shoulders and half-pushes them behind her, as though to shield them from him.

"I'm David Brookman," he says quickly, casting a glance at the wind-whipped yellow crime-scene tape stretching across the side yard. He spotted it the moment he pulled up in front of the house. Now, praying he isn't too late, he asks, "Is Rose . . ."

What?

Dead?

You can't just come out and ask that.

The young woman rescues him. "She's out." Relief courses through him as she adds, "I'm Rose's sister-in-law, Leslie. What did you say your name was?"

"David Brookman. You don't know me, but my wife . . ." He breaks off, casting a glance at the two small children staring up at him. Telling himself that he can't afford to waste time beating around the bush, he continues, "My wife was Rose's organ donor two years ago."

Leslie gasps. Before she can comment, David rushes on, "But that's not why I'm here. Is Rose . . . look, do you know for certain that she's safe?"

"Why?"

He shoots a meaningful look at the children, and then at the crime-scene tape.

The light dawns in Leslie's eyes. "Oh . . . you

heard about what happened last night? It was her boss, not Rose. She's fine. The police think he must have startled a prowler," she says cautiously, obviously not wanting to frighten the children, who are listening, wide-eyed.

David doesn't want to frighten them either. But somehow, he has to find out if the murderous prowler is the same person who killed Isabel and Olivia. "Did anyone see what the prowler looked like?"

"No." Leslie takes a wary step back, pulling the children more securely behind her. "Why?"

"Look, I have a picture of a man who just might be a suspect."

"Did you show it to the police?"

"No. First I'd rather show it to you, to see if you recognize him."

"All right. I'll look. But out here," she says, obviously not trusting him enough to allow him into the house.

"Unfortunately, I don't have the picture out here." Seeing the tide of doubt and fear wash over her, he adds quickly, "Look, I know it sounds bizarre, but I need a computer to access it. Is there one in the house?"

"No, there isn't. Mr. . . . Brookman, is it? I think you'd better go. I don't—"

"No, listen, all I need you to do is look at a photo. We can do it anywhere. Is there . . . is there a library around here with computer access, or one of those cyber cafes?" he suggests helplessly.

"In Laurel Bay? No. And even if there were, everything's closed because of the storm. Why don't you go talk to the police? Or come back when—"

"No, listen, there has to be a computer with Internet access somewhere around here," he says, desperately reaching for her arm.

Looking panicky now, she takes another step back, tripping over the little boy, who cries, "Ow! Aunt Leslie, you stepped on my foot!"

"I'm sorry, Leo."

"Christine has a computer," the little girl solemnly tells David.

"Who's Christine?" he and the aunt ask in unison.

"Christine. Our neighbor. She babysat me and Leo the other day, and she has a computer. She told me I can come over sometime and see the Powerpuff Girls website."

"She's your neighbor?" David seizes that, looking around at the other houses on the quiet block. "Where does she live?"

"Right over there," Jenna says, pointing to the brightly lit house next door.

"Good. Let's go." David is already on his way down the porch steps.

"We can't just go barging in there asking to use their computer," the children's aunt protests.

David pivots around to face her. "I can understand your hesitation, Leslie. Really, I can. But you've got to trust me. Your sister-in-law's life might be hanging in the balance."

"I told you earlier I'd stop over to check on you, Rose, remember?"

Her heart still pounding from the fright of seeing someone standing in the doorway behind her, she laughs shakily and tells Bill, "I forgot. But it's been a crazy day."

"I'm not surprised. Are you okay, Rose?" he asks, stepping inside, closing the door behind him, and stomping his boots on the mat.

"Other than the fact that my throat is killing me, I'm better than I was this morning." She takes off her coat and opens the closet, taking out a hanger for herself and handing one to Bill.

"Thanks." He unzips his navy parka, looking around. "Where are the kids?"

She quickly hangs her coat, then plucks the note from the mirror, reading it over.

Hitch—We'll be right back. Went to pick up Rose. Go ahead and start on the pipes. L.

"Oh, no." Her heart skips a beat.

"What's wrong?"

Hitch is coming here?

"The pipes must be frozen," she murmurs.

"Hmm?"

She looks up to see Bill watching her with a puzzled expression.

"Nothing, it's just . . . I have to try to call my sister-in-law at my house. She went over there to get me."

"Will she answer the phone there, though? She might not even go inside."

"I know, but I have to at least try to reach her. I don't want her to worry when she gets there and I'm not there. And I guess the pipes here must be frozen, because—"

"I'll take a look at them," he offers quickly, zipping his coat again. "That happens at my place all the time. Where's the basement?"

"Through the kitchen. Thanks, Bill. It's so sweet of you to come out in this nasty weather."

He grins. "What are friends for?"

In the kitchen, she points him in the right direction. "Be careful down there, Bill," she calls as he heads down the rickety stairs into the cobweb-draped depths of the basement.

"I'm always careful," he calls back up. "Don't worry about a thing."

She pops a lozenge in her mouth to soothe her aching throat, then begins dialing her home number.

Answer the phone, Leslie, she pleads silently. *I have to find out what you told Hitch and when he's supposed to get here. Or maybe he's already been here, and let himself in to fix the pipes.*

As the phone rings on the other end of the line, she crosses to the sink and quickly turns on the tap. It's dry.

So Hitch hasn't been here yet.

Or at least, he hasn't yet fixed the pipes, she thinks grimly.

"I made toast for Jenna and Leo," Christine says, rejoining Leslie and David Brookman in Ben's study.

Leslie flashes her a taut smile before returning her gaze to the screen. "Thank you. That was nice of you."

"It was no big deal," Christine lies. In truth, it was a big deal. She's dizzy from the exertion in the kitchen and the climb back up the stairs, and her head aches fiercely. Ben is taking an awfully long time to get back with her Advil, she thinks vaguely as she joins Leslie in looking over David's shoulder as he taps the computer keys.

"Did you access your e-mail account yet?" she

asks nervously, still trying to piece together exactly what it is that he's trying to do.

"Yes, and there's an e-mail from the person who was supposed to send the picture attachment," the man says. "We're just waiting for it to download. But it's taking an incredibly long time."

"That's because we don't have a DSL modem," Christine tells him apologetically. "My husband thinks the service is too expensive."

Nobody says anything. They just stare at the screen, watching the download meter go slowly from ninety-three percent complete to ninety-four . . . ninety-five . . .

Christine realizes she's holding her breath.

She doesn't know what she's going to see when the file is complete. She only knows that this man, this David Brookman, claims to have a photo of the murder suspect and he wants to show it to her and Leslie.

She probably wouldn't have even let these people into the house if the children hadn't been with them. One look at sweet, shivering Jenna and Leo standing on her snowy doorstep, and she opened the door wide.

Ben isn't going to be happy to come home to a houseful of strangers, though.

Hopefully, this won't take long. Then she can get back into bed and rest her head. It's killing her, and she's chilled from head to toe. Christine closes her eyes and rubs her hot forehead. She must be burning up with fever.

"Here it is," David says urgently. "It's coming up."

Christine opens her eyes to find Leslie peering at the screen, where a group photograph of somebody's birthday party has popped up.

"Which one is Clarence?" Leslie asks.

"He is. Do you recognize him? Take away the beard and the long hair . . ."

Leslie frowns, studying the photo. Christine leans in closer to see, trying to ignore the painful throbbing in her head.

As she zeroes in on the man in question, she lets out a startled gasp just as Leslie cries out, "Oh my God!"

"Everything okay down there, Bill?" Rose says from the top of the basement stairs.

"I'm working on it," comes the faint reply.

She paces across the kitchen floor to the phone to try calling Leslie again.

She jumps, startled when it rings just as she's lifting it to dial.

"Rose? Thank God you're there!" Leslie exclaims. "Are you okay?"

"I'm fine. I'm here with—"

"Rose, listen carefully. This is important. Your life is in danger."

Rose's blood runs cold. "Leslie, what are you—"

"Rose, please, just listen to me." Leslie's voice is high-pitched with hysteria. "We think we've figured out who killed Luke, and now he's after you. It's—"

The name is lost as the phone suddenly goes dead in her hand.

"What's wrong? What's going on?"

"The connection is broken!" Leslie wails, her fingers flying over the dial pad again. "I'm calling her back."

She holds her breath, waiting.

There's only a fast-paced busy signal, the kind that comes up when there's trouble on the line.

"Do you think something happened to her?" Leslie asks, hanging up and then dialing again.

David Brookman doesn't look very reassuring as he says, "It's probably just the heavy snow bringing the phone wires down. I'm sure she's fine."

Wires down . . .

Sam . . .

Gripped by a sudden sense of foreboding, Leslie looks from him to Christine. "But I didn't get to tell her. And she's not there alone. She started to say 'I'm with' and I cut her off. I just wanted to warn her about—"

"Oh, Lord. You don't think he's the one who's there with her?" Christine asks, sinking into the chair before the computer, her face flushed and eyes glassy.

"We've got to get over there." David is already striding toward the stairs.

"I'm coming with you." Leslie hurries after him, calling over her shoulder to Christine, "I'll leave the kids here with you. Can you call the police and tell them to get someone over to my parents' address right away?"

"What is it?"

Leslie rushes back to scribble it on a pad, along with the phone number. "Keep trying to get through to Rose, will you, Christine?"

"I will, but . . . you know, the day I babysat, she said she had a pager. Is there any chance she might have it on? You could send her the information that way."

"She probably does have it, but that doesn't help

us. It was my brother's, and it's the ancient numeric kind. You can't send letters or e-mail on it." Leaving Christine in the study dialing the phone, Leslie hurries back to the top of the stairs to catch up with David . . .

Then stops short.

"Christine!" she shrieks, rushing back to the phone. "The pager!"

Bill's feet come pounding up the basement stairs. "Rose? Are you okay?"

"I'm . . . I'm fine." She looks at the phone in her hand, then slowly raises her gaze to him. "The phone just went dead."

He turns his head toward the window, opaque with the glare of the kitchen light. "Must be the storm."

"Must be." She swallows hard. Winces. Her throat aches.

I'm coming down with the flu, she thinks vaguely, and then . . .

Leslie was about to tell me who killed Luke.

Rose can hear the scraping rumble of a plow truck passing in the street.

It's somebody I know. It has to be. The way she said it . . .

"Looks like you're going to need a plumber for those pipes, Rose." Bill's mundane words, his very presence, keep full-blown panic at bay. "But you're never going to get anybody over here tonight, in this weather."

Yes. Hitch, she thinks, dazed. *Hitch is supposed to be coming.*

"Listen, you can't stay here overnight without

running water. Why don't you and the kids come to my place for the night? I've got a pullout couch. It's kind of lumpy, but the kids won't mind, and you can have my bed."

"I can't . . . I can't take your bed, Bill," Rose protests, her mind gyrating with possibilities, one more dire than the next.

The door was unlocked when she arrived. Anyone could be here, hiding. Waiting. Listening . . .

She doesn't dare tell Bill what Leslie just said.

"It's just for one night," Bill tells her with a chuckle. "You can do the dishes to make up for it. I've got plenty of running water at my place."

She hesitates.

No.

No, you shouldn't go anywhere alone with him.

She doesn't dare trust anyone. Not Bill. Not Hitch. Not . . . not Peter. Or Christine, with whom she left her children.

Who is it? Who the hell is it?

"Come on, grab your bag and your coat, and I'll drive you over to your house to find your sister-in-law and the kids."

Torn, Rose wants more than anything to get out of here before Hitch arrives.

Bill's already on his way into the front hall.

But is she willing to take a chance?

Suddenly, she feels a vibration against her hip.

Her pager.

Quickly flipping it over, she frowns when she sees only four digits.

7718.

"Coming?" Bill calls from the hall.

"I'll be right there."

Rose gazes at the unrecognizable number.

Then it dawns on her.

Her panic now mounting unchecked, she unhooks the pager from her belt, turns it around . . . and stares at it in disbelief as the terrifying truth washes over her.

"Laurel Bay Police. Sergeant Reilly speaking."

"I need your help," Christine blurts, her voice scratchy and weakened from the flu. "My friend is in trouble. Somebody might be trying to kill her."

"Listen, you're going to have to speak a little louder. I can't hear you. First of all, give me your name and address."

Frustrated, Christine clears her throat, rasps, "Christine Kirkmayer. Fifty Shorewood Lane, Laurel Bay, and—"

"Shorewood Lane? That's where—"

"I know. The murder happened next door to me, and my friend who lives there is in trouble. Rose Larrabee. But she's not home, and I can't reach her where she is. Do you know if there are phone lines down because of the storm?"

"Where is she, ma'am?"

Lightheaded with fever, with fear, Christine desperately searches the desk for the address Leslie wrote down for her. "I'm looking for the address. I just found out that a friend of hers might be trying to kill her, and—"

"You just found out? How did you find out?"

"A man came to my door . . . look, I know it sounds crazy, but he said—"

"What is the man's name, Ma'am?"

"It's Brookline. No, Brook*man*," she remembers. "David Brookman."

There's a slight pause. Then, "Did you say David Brookman?"

"Yes."

"And you say he's trying to kill your friend?"

"No, he's trying to *save* her. He just went after her. He told me that somebody's trying to—"

"Ms. Kirkmayer, we have an A.P.B. on David Brookman. If you know where he is, you've got to tell us where to find him."

Dazed, Christine murmurs, "But he said—"

"You can't believe a word he said. The man is a suspect in three murders, including the one on Shorewood Lane."

Bill's boots make a squeaking sound as he steps out into the snow on the concrete porch in front of her in-laws' house.

Rose shudders.

"Careful, Rose. It's slippery." He grasps the black wrought-iron railing with one gloved hand and reaches for her with the other. "Here, let me help you."

Standing in the doorway, Rose pulls on her camel-colored dress coat, gazes out into the stormy night, and draws a shaky breath.

It's going to be okay.

Leslie knows where I am. The cops are probably already on their way.

"Rose?"

She blinks and looks at Bill Michaels. He's standing a yard away from her at most, his arm outstretched, leather-encased fingers ready to take hers.

Snow is falling hard, whirling all around him, already coating his hair and his eyebrows above his glasses.

Netta Bradley's voice drifts back to her.

"I've hired somebody new, Rose. He's starting next week, just in time to help us with the summer rush. He just moved to town and he's such a handsome young man. Single, too. He's a homosexual, though."

At the time, Rose had to fight back a smile at the elderly woman's discomfort with the word, and the topic of Bill's sexuality.

"Oh, really? What makes you think that, Netta?"

Looking even more uncomfortable, Netta confessed. *"I mentioned to him that he'd be working with a lovely young widow, and he became very nervous and finally admitted that he isn't interested in women."*

It was the first time Rose heard herself referred to as a widow.

As jarred by that bleak description as she was by the fact that Netta would even consider matchmaking just six months after Sam's death, Rose never thought twice about the fact that Bill came right out and told a potential employer that he was gay.

Why would he do such a thing? It certainly wasn't necessary.

He couldn't know, back then, that Netta was more tolerant than the conservative majority of senior citizens in this small town.

Nor could Netta—or Rose—know that the pleasant young man so eager for a minimum-wage job in the bookstore was really a cold-blooded killer.

"Rose?"

She looks into his eyes. Such unusual eyes, the palest blue-green color.

Why, Bill? Why?

It doesn't make sense.

Maybe she's wrong. Maybe the 7718 page was a fluke. Maybe she's jumping to conclusions, thinking that Leslie meant for her to turn it upside down, the way she did Jenna's calculator that afternoon more than a week ago.

7718.

If you read the numerals as letters . . .

They spell B-I-L-L.

But he's my friend. I can't believe he wants to hurt me. In fact, I won't believe it until . . .

"Are you all right? Angela?"

Angela.

The name again. The name on the necklace.

Leo didn't steal it.

Bill was in her bedroom in the dead of night while she was sleeping.

"No, I'm not okay, Bill." She slips her violently trembling hands into the deep pockets of her coat. "And my name isn't Angela."

Behind his wire-framed glasses, wrath flares in his gaze.

It's there only a moment, and then it's gone, his expression as benign as it was before.

But now she's certain.

He's the one.

And the phone didn't go dead just now because of the storm. Bill did something in the basement.

"Oops, sorry. I meant Rose. You'll feel better once we get out of here," Bill says smoothly, his breath puffing white in the snowy evening air.

Like a smoke-breathing dragon, Rose can't help thinking, gazing at him, wondering who he really is, and why he's doing this.

"I can't go with you, Bill."

His face is beginning to harden, yet his tone remains casual. "Why not?"

"Because. Because I know. About you."

She shrinks backward in dread as his familiar features are transformed by a mask of monstrous rage.

"Can't you drive any faster?" Leslie urges from the passenger seat.

David's eyes are focused on the blinding snow beyond the windshield. It's all he can do to keep the Land Rover between the white lines on the road.

"If we wind up in a ditch, we won't be able to help Rose," he mutters, checking the wiper switch to make sure they can't go any faster. They're working at top speed, but the snow is coming down hard and fast and it's impossible to see anything.

If what Leslie told him is true—that she knows Rose spoke to her coworker earlier on the phone and could very well have told him where to find her tonight—they may already be too late.

There isn't a doubt in David's mind that Bill Michaels and Clarence are the same man—Angela's lover—and that he killed Olivia, Isabel, and Rose's husband. That Rose is in grave danger is irrefutable. David only hopes—

"Listen!" Leslie turns in her seat, looking over her shoulder. "Do you hear sirens back there?"

He does. Glancing into the rearview mirror, David sees the red lights materialize in the haze of snow behind the Land Rover.

"Thank God," Leslie says. "Christine must have called them. Pull over and let them pass. They must be on their way to my parents' house."

David takes his foot off the gas and coasts onto

the shoulder. Touching the brake would mean risking a spin on the slick pavement.

The flashing lights and sirens don't pass them by. Instead, the police car follows the Land Rover onto the shoulder.

"What are they doing?" Leslie asks frantically, up on one knee, her body twisted around to see the car behind them. "Why aren't they going to help Rose?"

David is silent, jaw clenched, eyes on the rearview mirror. The squad car's door opens. A uniformed figure emerges in the swirling snow, gun drawn, aimed directly at David.

Speaking over a bullhorn, a voice bellows, "Step out of the car *now* with your hands over your head."

She's afraid.

Afraid of *him*.

Delicious power surges through him, electrifying his nerve endings.

"Of course you know about me," he says, taking a step toward her, giggling when she cowers back into the house. "Tell me, what exactly is it that you know? That I like women? That I was only pretending to be gay so that nosy old lady wouldn't get ideas in her head?"

Rose reaches out to push the door closed.

He easily stops it with his foot, his tone lethal as he warns her, "Don't you *ever* slam the door in my face, Angela. Do you understand?"

"I'm not Angela, Bill. I don't know who . . ."

"Enough, already." His words drip with disdain. "Stop calling me Bill. And stop pretending."

"Pretending . . . what?"

He leans toward her, so close he can smell the scent of her breath. Menthol.

He makes a fist, raises it, watches her cringe.

Grinning, he asks, "What's the matter? Did you think I was going to hit you, Angela? I wouldn't do that. I just wanted to show you something."

He palpitates the fist against his own chest, beating a slow rhythm.

Thump-thump. Thump-thump. Thump-thump.

"What does that sound like?"

"A heart." Her words are low, voice strained.

"Yes. *Your* heart. So you can stop pretending. I know." He reaches out and brushes her hair back from her eyes. "I don't like this style. You really should get it cut again, Angela. Cut and lightened. It looked so pretty when you did that for me the last time." He trails the backs of his fingers down the side of her face.

She says nothing. He can feel her tension, her muscles clenching as he brushes his fingers over her jaw.

"You lied to me, Angela. About Christmas. About everything."

"I never lied to you, Bill!" she protests. "I never even—"

"Stop it! Stop calling me Bill. We don't have to pretend anymore. You can say my name."

"But I don't . . ."

"Say it!"

"Bill. Bill Michaels."

"Michaels." He grins with renewed delight at his own clever pseudonym. "Before it's too late and I forget to ask . . . how do you like my little tribute to the Snow Angel?"

"I don't know what you're talking about."

"Michael. The angel."

She looks blank.

"Oh, come on, Angela. Don't tell me you didn't figure it out. *Michael.* Mr. *Gabriel. Clarence.* They're all angels . . . just like you. The snow angel."

"The snow angel?" She shakes her head, pretending to be baffled.

"And Clarence is the angel in *It's a Wonderful Life.*" He waits. She's still acting as though she's blank. Exasperated, he says, "Your favorite movie, did you forget? We watched it together. I chose the name Clarence for you. I chose all of them for you. I did everything for you. And you . . . you chose *him.*"

"I don't know what you're talking about."

"Him. Your husband."

Her voice is barely audible. *"Sam?"*

"Sam?" He bursts out laughing, dismissing the name with a wave of his hand. "Not *him.* I'm talking about David. Your husband."

"My husband's name is Sam," she says in a strangled whisper.

"Oh, I don't think Sam is anybody's husband anymore. Sam burned to a crisp that night, from the inside out." He is gleeful, remembering. "And I've got something even better planned for David. A fate worse than death, as far as the Brookmans are—what's the matter, Angela?" he asks, noticing her expression.

"How do you know about Sam?" She's gone motionless, staring at him as though the light has suddenly dawned.

"Oh, I guess you had to be there," he says glibly, remembering that stormy January night.

You had to be there . . . and he was.

The temperature was hovering just below freezing: cold enough for the rain that had fallen all day to freeze in a sheet of glare ice on the pavement and encase every tree, every shrub, every overhead wire with a thick, glassy coating.

Fresh from dumping Olivia McGlinchie's body in the northern woods, he meandered out to Laurel Bay, undeterred by the slick roads, eager to lay eyes on his next conquest.

Instead, as he crept around the perimeter of the house, looking for a glimpse of her through a window, he came face-to-face with her husband. The man was clutching a baseball bat, using it to knock ice crystals from an overhead wire.

He can still hear the outraged echo of Sam Larrabee's last words.

"Hey! What the hell do you think you're doing?"

"My husband died in a freak accident." Her voice is fraught with pain.

He shrugs. "If you say so."

Sometimes it still amazes him that he managed to pull it off. It happened before—something snapping inside of him, throwing into a rage. It happened with Dad, and with Angela. And it would happen again, with Luke Pflueger, under startlingly similar circumstances.

But he never made an actual decision to *kill* Sam Larrabee.

He simply reacted to the attack when Sam hurtled himself forward. They scuffled on the rock-hard, frozen ground. He managed to get hold of the bat, and then it was all over. One good swing to the back of Sam's head, and the other man went sprawling.

As he stood over his unconscious victim, panting, contemplating his next move, it happened.

The ice storm—and what he likes to consider divine providence—intervened.

That high-voltage cable coming down just yards away from Sam was as fortuitous as the abandoned taxicab, engine running, on all-but-deserted East 66th street.

He approached it cautiously as it lay sparking on the ground, thankful for his rubber-soled shoes and the wooden baseball bat so that he could safely—

"You killed him."

Angela. He almost forgot she was here. Startled, he looks up and is taken aback to see that the fear in her eyes has been replaced by a flinty glare.

Odd, considering that he's the one with the upper hand here.

"I killed him," he acknowledges. "What's the matter? Do you miss him?"

"You . . . *bastard.*" Tears have sprung to her eyes, yet any lingering vulnerability is rapidly giving way to palpable outrage.

"Don't worry, Angela. You're going to see Sam very soon, if you care that much. But I'm afraid you're going to have to wait for David. He's going to his own private hell, and I'd be willing to bet they give him twenty-five years to life. If he's lucky, he might get time off for good—"

He breaks off abruptly, finding himself staring into the barrel of a gun.

Through a haze of illness and fear, Christine can hear sirens piercing the night as she stands at the darkened window. She can see nothing but a curtain of blowing, drifting snow and the dim outline of the Larrabee house next door.

"Do you think there's a fire, Christine?"

She looks up to see Jenna and Leo standing behind her. They look smaller than usual, the little brother clinging solemnly to his big sister's hand.

Christine nods. "There might be a fire somewhere."

It isn't a lie, exactly. There's a fire in her swollen throat, and in her feverish, aching head.

But she knows what the sirens mean.

The police are racing against time to rescue Leslie from David Brookman.

He seemed so sincere, as though he only wanted to save Rose.

Showing Christine and Leslie that old photo of Bill Michaels, making them believe that he was the one threatening Rose's life . . .

"Christine? Where's Mommy?" Leo asks.

"Aunt Leslie said she'd be at our house, but she wasn't. Is she okay?" Jenna wants to know.

"I'm sure she's fine," Christine tells these two shaken children, who have already lost so much.

Then she gathers them into her arms.

The gun trembles in Rose's hands as she grasps it in front of her, elbows awkwardly bent in imitation of a pose she's seen in countless movies and television dramas.

For the first time tonight, Bill falters. She can see it in his twitching jaw, though his voice is even as he asks, "What are you doing, Angela?"

She is silent, glaring at him, swallowing audibly as she moves one thumb over the gun, wondering how to cock it, wondering if the sound will frighten him.

His eyes narrow. He is watching her intently.

Dammit. Does he know? Can he tell?

Oh, Sam. Why didn't I let you teach me how to shoot . . .

Or at least, how to make it look like I can?

Help me, Sam.

Jenna and Leo need me.

I need to see them grow up.

"You're not going to shoot me, Angela." He takes a step toward her.

She fights the waves of fear washing over her. "Yes, I will."

"I'll bet that gun isn't even loaded."

She swallows hard. "Are you willing to take a chance and find out?"

He shrugs, takes another step toward her. "What do you think?"

Her hands clench the gun.

Please don't let him come closer.

Please don't let him find out.

Her swollen throat constricted by apprehension, she manages to say, "I think you'd better stop where you are, or you'll be sorry."

"Oh, I won't be sorry, Angela. You're the one who will be sorry."

Don't let him move.

Please.

Bill raises a hand, reaching for the gun.

Please, Sam, help me.

"Give me the gun, Angela."

"My name is Rose."

"Give me the gun."

"Get back or I'll shoot."

"You can't shoot a weapon that isn't loaded."

His gloved fingers come closer.

She flinches.

Closes her eyes.

With a menacing laugh, Bill plucks the gun from her hand.

Rose steels herself for the inevitable . . .

And a shot rings out.

"Are you all right, Ms. Larrabee? Did he try to hurt you in any way?"

"No!" Leslie looks in desperation from Officer Shanley's concerned face to David Brookman's infuriated one.

"I wouldn't hurt her! I wouldn't hurt anyone!" David protests vehemently, as handcuffs are placed around his wrists by Shanley's partner. "For God's sake, I'm trying to save her sister-in-law from a killer."

Neither officer says anything.

Leslie's thoughts are spinning. If David is telling the truth, Rose is in danger. If he isn't, she is the one who was in danger . . . and she should be grateful to these lawmen for rescuing her just in time.

But there will be time to thank them later. When she knows for certain that Rose is out of harm's way.

"Is anybody checking my parents' house?" she asks urgently. "My sister-in-law is there."

"We'll send somebody over. There's been an accident out on Sunrise Highway and all of our officers are—"

"You've got to get somebody there right away," David interrupts emphatically. "If I'm telling the truth and I'm innocent, you'll have her blood—and a couple of orphaned kids—on your hands."

"You think we're going to let you walk away while we go chasing off to investigate based on your advice?" Officer Shanley flicks his gaze back to Leslie, shifts his tone to reassuring as he says, "Like I told you, we'll send somebody over. But I'm sure your sister-in-law is okay. There's no threat to her now that we've got him in custody."

Leslie exhales shakily, praying to God that the policeman is right . . . and that David Brookman is lying.

Rose opens her eyes just as the man who calls himself Bill Michaels falls to the floor at her feet.

Stunned, she can only gape at the blood pouring from a wound somewhere on his torso.

It doesn't make sense.

He's holding the gun.

But the bullets are still in a locked box on the top shelf of her closet.

Too frightened to even touch them, she didn't dare try to load the weapon.

She merely dropped it, unloaded, into the pocket of her coat.

Just in case.

In a stupor, she stares down at Bill, still clutching the useless gun in his hand . . .

And realizes that he's surrounded by broken glass . . . and that the blood is gushing from his back.

Even Leslie doesn't believe him.

David can plainly see the doubt in her expression as she stands frozen in the falling snow, staring at him.

And the cops . . .

He turns his head toward them and glimpses something far more potent than doubt in their eyes. Blatant malice bores into him, filling him with utter helplessness.

Rose Larrabee is destined to join Isabel and Olivia in death, and there's not a damned thing he can do about it.

Perhaps she's already dead.

Even if she isn't, she's already entered a doom-tainted limbo no different, really, than the condemned state in which Angela lingered for days.

Yes, and David's decision to pull onto the shoulder when he heard the screaming sirens was as lethal to Rose Larrabee as his decision to pull the plug was to Angela.

But Angela was already gone. No matter what you tried to tell yourself in the hospital, you knew she was gone the moment you saw her.

Rose might not be. Not yet.

But the clock is ticking.

And nobody's helping her.

David knew, when he saw the police car in the rearview mirror, that they were coming after him. He also knew that it would be futile—even deadly—to try to outrun them on the slick roads.

Thus, his own fate—and Rose Larrabee's—were sealed.

He lifts his resigned gaze to meet Leslie's tormented one. The wind gusts, sifting grainy snow into his face.

David is powerless to manage more than two futile words.

"I'm sorry."

Shrouded in silence, jaw clenched, she turns away.

* * *

With a curse and a blast of arctic air, Ben bursts in the door, looking like the abominable snowman.

He stops short, catching sight of Christine on the couch with the children on her lap. "What's going on? Babysitting again?"

"Yes," Christine says simply.

"You're sick. You shouldn't be—" He breaks off, shaking his head, and silently drapes his coat over the doorknob.

"Why is that man so mad at us, Cwistine?" Leo whispers loudly.

"He's not mad at you, sweetie."

"He's mad at Christine," Jenna explains.

Yes. Yes, he's mad at Christine.

Pointedly ignoring the comment, Ben holds up a bag. "I got your medicine. I had to drive all the way over to Patchogue to find a pharmacy that was open, but I knew you really needed it."

"Thanks."

She wants to tell him that it's too little, too late.

She wants to tell him what's going on with Rose, and Leslie.

She wants to tell him a lot of things.

But that will have to wait.

For now, she just holds Rose's children close and prays harder than she ever has before as her husband, oblivious, walks up the stairs.

Framed in the shattered storm door, his hair and lashes fringed in white, Scott Hitchcock breathlessly asks, "Rose, are you all right?"

She opens her mouth to reply, but all that escapes is a strangled sob. She looks down in time to see Bill's eyes roll grotesquely upward as he emits one last rattling breath.

Then Hitch is opening the door, pulling her out into the snow, clasping her tightly against his strong chest with the hand that isn't holding the gun.

"Hitch . . . where did you get the gun?"

"It's mine. I keep it in my truck so that—"

"But the roads are so bad. You don't drive the truck in bad weather."

"I drove it in to the Bronx this morning. I thought I'd be back long before the snow started. I called my voice mail from the road and got Leslie's message about the pipes, so I came straight here, and when I came up the walk I saw— Oh, hell, Rose, if I hadn't shown up when I did . . ." His voice is gruff, his cheek resting on her hair. "Who *is* he?"

"I worked with him. At the bookstore." She closes her eyes, not wanting to glimpse the bloodied body at their feet. "He thought I was Angela."

"*Who?*"

"Somebody named Angela," she murmurs, pressing a trembling hand over her heart. There it is; the familiar, rhythmic beat, faster than usual, but reassuring all the same.

Rose tilts her face skyward. She can see nothing but fat, swirling snowflakes drifting down from a black sky.

She closes her eyes, whispers softly to the heavens, "Thank you."

"You're welcome," Hitch replies, right here on earth.

Epilogue

"Mommy? I'm hung-wee."

Feeling a tug on her satin bridesmaid's gown, Rose glances down to see Leo, looking like a miniature version of Sam in his black tuxedo.

"I'm not surprised—you didn't eat your meal." She wets her thumb and wipes a lipstick smudge off his cheek. Who knew it would be so challenging to keep the ring bearer presentable until the photographer leaves the reception?

"I don't wike wob-sto."

"Everyone likes lobster, lion-boy."

"Not me," he says, scowling up at Hitch. "And my name isn't wion-boy. That's a dumb name."

"Leo," Rose says in a warning tone.

"I'm going to go see if the wedding cake is choco-wat," Leo says, and scurries across the dance floor.

Rose looks up at Hitch. "Sorry about that."

"No big deal. Someday he'll love me again. He's just jealous. He thinks I'm trying to steal his mommy away. And maybe he's right," Hitch says, and pulls her closer, whirling her around the dance floor as the orchestra plays "The Way You Look Tonight."

It's been six months now since the man Rose knew as Bill Michaels tried to murder her.

His true identity was Justin Everhard III, the scion of a West Coast billionaire who drowned when he fell from his yacht off the coast of Catalina Island. The irony is that Rose vaguely remembers reading the account in the newspapers back when she was in college, and feeling sorry for the man's teenaged son, who was the sole other passenger on board the yacht when the accident happened. The father's body was never found, but after a few years he was officially declared dead . . . just in time for Justin Everhard III to inherit a vast trust fund.

Nobody will ever know whether Justin Everhard II was murdered by his son . . . nor whether a similar fate befell Angela Brookman.

David Brookman is convinced that the jet-setting drifter was behind his wife's so-called hit-and-run accident. Given his confession to killing Sam, Rose believes David is right. There just isn't enough evidence for the police to reopen either investigation as a homicide. Nor is there a reason to.

Justin Everhard III currently resides in his family's mausoleum. Apparently, they don't believe he killed anyone. Or, as David explained it, they probably believe it . . . but he's still one of them. For the Everhards, like the Brookmans, appearances are everything.

"I just don't understand that," Rose told David.

"You can't possibly, Rose. You're from a different world. You're lucky."

She might be from a different world, but she and David Brookman have been on the same path these last six months. It has taken Rose a long time to come to terms with the fact that Sam's death wasn't accidental. Learning to accept the same thing about Angela, David was there to support her every step of the way.

One day, not long ago, he showed up on her doorstep with a gift-wrapped box, saying, *"It's something I thought you should have."*

Inside, Rose found a snow globe.

As she shook it, watching the fluffy white flakes whirl around the angel behind the glass, David told her, *"It was Angela's. I know she'd want you to have it."*

"Whenever I look at it, I'll think of her. And of you," Rose told David, touched by his warmth.

But it's Scott Hitchcock whose friendship has gradually, tentatively transformed into something deeper.

Leaning her head on his shoulder, Rose gazes over the crowded dance floor, smiling when she spots her new brother-in-law spinning a giggling Jenna. The layers of tulle in her pink organza flower-girl dress twirl prettily around her legs, and she looks astonishingly tall.

She's growing up, Sam, Rose silently tells her husband. *She's growing up, so is Leo, and I'm . . .*

Well, I'm growing up, too. And I'm going to be okay.

"Hi, Mommy!" Jenna cries out as Peter spins her past.

Rose has to admit, he cleans up nicely, dashing in his black tails. And he's obviously madly in love with Leslie. Rose will never forget the look on her sister-in-law's face when the Triple A tow truck deposited Peter on Shorewood Lane, holding a bouquet of limp, frostbitten flowers and a black velvet box.

"I told you I had a surprise for you," he said, and he sank down on one knee right there in the snow.

He'd had the emerald-cut diamond ring on layaway since Christmas. It was the reason he had been working so much overtime. When Leslie didn't come home the night before, he decided to dash over to the mall to pick it up and surprise her.

"Mommy! Look at me dancing!"

Rose laughs and waves at Jenna, noticing that Peter is keeping a watchful eye on his bride as she waltzes by with David, laughing at something he's saying.

Lithe, lovely Leslie could have stepped out of a fairy tale in a white silk gown and illusion veil. She was able to afford the dress of her dreams, thanks to David. He insisted on paying for the entire reception, insisted on lobster over chicken and roses over daisies in the bouquets and centerpieces.

"It's the least I can do," he kept saying, brandishing his checkbook, a gesture that wasn't lost on Christine Kirkmayer.

Searching the room for her neighbor, Rose spots Christine chatting amiably with Sam's parents. Newly slender and newly single, Christine has been a godsend for Rose and the children—and claims that they're the same for her, as she adjusts to life without Ben.

Christine doesn't like to talk about what went wrong in their marriage, confiding only that they didn't want the same things. She's become quite fond of saying *life is short, and I don't want to waste a minute of it.*

Neither do I, Rose thinks, content in Hitch's arms as the orchestra finishes the song and the bandleader takes the mike to call all the single women out to the dance floor.

"Go on," Leslie says, pushing Rose to join them, waving her bouquet above her head.

Rose groans, looks to Hitch for a reprieve, but he

merely laughs and raises his palms helplessly, shaking his head.

"Come on, Mommy!" Jenna pulls her out onto the floor to stand beside a giggling Christine.

There's a drum roll from the orchestra.

A grand flourish from Leslie, with her back to the crowd.

And then the bouquet sails over her head . . . right into Rose's reluctant hands.

Leslie turns, laughing, pointing at a mirror as she calls, "I cheated, Rose. I saw your reflection and I aimed right at you."

"Mommy!" Jenna squeals. "You won! If you're a bride, can I wear this dress again?"

"That's a healthy sign," Christine says low in Rose's ear, before David materializes at her side to ask, "How about a dance as a consolation prize?"

Rose watches them glide away. It would be wonderful if David and Christine wound up together. They're both lonely, and David would make such a wonderful father . . .

She feels a tug on her hem.

She looks down to see Leo standing there, accompanied by Hitch. His face is smeared with brown goo.

"I was wight," he says solemnly. "The cake was choco-wat, just like Aunt Wes-wee pwomised."

"Oh, Leo, let me take you and clean that off," Sam's mother says, hurrying over to take his hand. She smiles at Rose and Hitch. "Don't forget, the children are staying overnight with Poppy and Grandma, so you two can stay at the reception as late as you want."

Rose gives her a little hug, grateful they're back in town for the summer.

They couldn't bring themselves to go back to their house, after what happened. So they sold it and bought a small cottage right around the corner from 48 Shorewood Lane.

These days, Rose is never lonely, and rarely alone, unless she wants to be . . .

With Hitch.

She smiles as he lifts the bouquet she's holding, inhaling deeply. "Mmm. Roses always were my favorite."

"Is that so?"

He nods, grinning. "You know, Rose, they say if a person saves your life, you owe them the rest of it."

"Is that what they say?" She lets her eyes twinkle up at him.

"Something like that."

As he pulls her into his arms, she thinks of Sam, knowing this is what he'd want for her . . .

And of Angela, remembering a promise she made long ago, in her letter to David.

I said I'd take good care of this heart of ours. But there was a time when I thought it was irrevocably broken . . .

Rose sighs contentedly, knowing that a little piece of her heart will always belong to Sam . . . and that the rest of it is whole again at last.

Please turn the page for an
exciting sneak peek at
Wendy Corsi Staub's
next electrifying thriller

DEARLY BELOVED

coming in August 2003 from Pinnacle Books!

DEARLY BELOVED

For Sandy Cavelli, it begins on a frigid January day in Connecticut with a thrillingly romantic response to her personal ad. For ambitious New York editor Liza Danning, it takes the form of an inquiry from a best-selling author. For Jennie Towne, cashing in on her twin sister's winning sweepstakes prize, it's a chance to get away from Boston, and a troubled love affair. Now all three women have just arrived at a windswept island inn off the coast of Boston, unaware that they have something in common. It is the man who waits for them, his chillingly familiar face hidden behind white lace curtains, his unforgiving black heart consumed by one thing: *Revenge.*

Sandy Cavelli glances at her watch as she hurries up the icy steps of the red-brick post office. Four-fifty-nine. She has exactly one minute to retrieve today's mail before the place closes for the day.

She hurries over to the wall that is a grid of rectangular metal doors and eagerly turns her round key in the lock of post office box 129. Jammed, as it always is on Mondays. *Connecticut Singles* magazine comes out on Friday mornings, and Sandy is beginning to believe that every guy in the greater Hartford area who doesn't have a week-end date spends Friday and Saturday flipping through the classifieds in the back of the maga-zine, answering ads.

She removes the bundle of letters from the box and does a quick mental count. Nine—no, ten. Ten eligible single men have responded to her ad this week. So far. If everything goes according to the pattern that has established itself over the past month, only two or three more letters will trickle in over the next few days. Then, if she chooses to run the ad again—she has to decide by six o'clock Wednesday—there will be a new stack of letters waiting in the box next Monday.

Renting a post office box was definitely a good

idea, Sandy reminds herself, even if it has set her back over thirty dollars. This way, she doesn't have to deal with the questions her parents would undoubtedly have if she'd suddenly started getting a blizzard of mail at home every week. They would never go for the idea of their daughter's placing an ad to meet a man through the classifieds. Christ, they still wait up if she stays out past midnight!

Sandy walks slowly toward the double front doors, flipping through the envelopes as she goes. As usual, a few of them don't have return addresses; the ones that do are mostly from Hartford or the immediate area. . . .

But look at this one, from a post office box on Tide Island!

Intrigued, Sandy shoves the other letters into her oversized black shoulder bag, then slides a manicured nail under the flap of the envelope.

"Miss? We're closing," a uniformed postman says. He's jangling a ring of keys and waiting expectantly by the front door.

Sandy looks up. "Oh, sorry."

"No problem." He smiles. His teeth are white and straight, and his eyes crinkle pleasantly. "Pretty cold out there, huh?"

"Yup. It's supposed to snow again overnight."

She doesn't recognize him. He must be new. Almost every face in Greenbury is familiar; she has lived here all her life.

She isn't usually drawn to redheads. Still, he has a nice, strong jawline. And his hair is a burnished-auburn shade, and she likes the way it is cut—short on the sides, up over his ears, and slightly stubbly on top.

"More snow? Where was all this white stuff a few weeks ago, for Christmas?" he asks good-naturedly, reaching out to open the door for her.

"You got me." Sandy shrugs and glances automatically at the fourth finger of his left hand.

Married.

Oh, well.

"Thanks. Have a good night," she says, walking quickly through the door.

She pauses on the slippery top cement step to finish opening the letter she is still clutching.

A brisk wind whips along High Street, sending a chill through Sandy as she slits the envelope open the rest of the way. Her teeth are starting to chatter. It's too cold to read this letter out here, no matter how intrigued she is. She tucks it and the others into her purse and fumbles in her pockets for her gloves. Swiftly she puts them on and clings to the ice-coated metal railing as she picks her way down the four steps to the sidewalk.

Then she gingerly goes, slipping and sliding every few steps in her black-suede flats, along the nearly empty street to her car in the Greenbury municipal lot around the corner. Her footsteps sound lonely and hollow on the brittle frozen pavement.

Just a month ago, in the height of the holiday season, downtown Greenbury was strung with twinkling white lights and festive red bows bedecked the old-fashioned lampposts. Carols were piped into the frosty air from speakers at the redbrick town hall, and High Street bustled well past five o'clock on weeknights.

The picturesque, historic village is only fifteen

miles outside of Hartford. Even the lifelong residents are aware of the postcard beauty in its white-steepled churches, window-paned storefronts, and broad common dotted with statues and fountains. And as one of the few small towns in central Connecticut that still has a thriving downtown commerce area, Greenbury performs a feat that's becoming nearly impossible in America. It actually draws shoppers away from the malls and superstores that dot the suburban Hartford area.

But now that Christmas is over, the businesses along High close early and downtown is almost deserted in the frigid January twilight.

Sandy's car is one of the few left in the parking lot, which is really just a rutted, grassy area behind the town hall. She hurries toward the Chevy, stepping around patches of snow and absently noting the dirty chunks of ice that cling to the underside of the car just behind each wheel.

She doesn't bother knocking it off. The car is ugly enough anyway, with rust spots all over the body and a sheet of thick plastic covering the triangular opening in the back where a window is missing. She's come to loathe the old clunker; it belonged to her father, and she's long past being grateful to him for handing it down to her without making her buy it.

She's been saving for a new car—a new *used* car, of course—ever since she started working at the Greenbury Gal Boutique last spring. She blew a good chunk of her savings on community college tuition in August, and the spring semester bill will be due next week when she registers for classes. But that will still leave nearly four thousand dollars in her account. She socked away over five hundred dollars in December alone, when her commission checks were considerably higher than usual. Of course, that won't keep up. The store was dead all day today, and her hours have already been cut way back.

Sandy settles into the front seat, her breath puffing out in little white clouds. She whispers "brrr" and turns the key in the ignition. After a few tries, the engine turns over, and she adjusts the heat control to high. A blast of cold wind hits her in the face and she closes the black plastic vents. She'll probably be home before the hissing air actually becomes warm, but she leaves it on high anyway.

Eagerly, she reaches into her purse and retrieves the letter with the Tide Island return address. She takes out the single sheet of paper inside and notices that it's real stationery, creamy and heavy.

That's a first, she thinks, pulling off her right glove with her teeth and leaving it clamped in her mouth.

Most of the men who have responded to her ad so far have written on either yellow legal paper or their company letterhead.

The interior light of her car burned out long ago. Sandy tilts the paper so she can see better in the filtered glow from the street lamp a few feet away.

Dear Sandra:

I saw your ad in Connecticut Singles *and was struck by how similar our interests are. You sound like the kind of woman I've been waiting for my whole life. Like you, I never thought I'd resort to personal ads to*

*meet someone; but since I'm a medical doctor with a
thriving practice, my hectic lifestyle makes it hard to
meet anyone the traditional way. I've enclosed a photograph of myself. . . .*

Photograph? Sandy frowns and checks the envelope. Yes, she missed it. There's a picture tucked
inside. She grabs it and holds it up in the light.

He's gorgeous! is her immediate reaction.

He has rugged, outdoorsy good looks—and
what a bod! He's shirtless in the photograph,
which was taken on a sailboat as he hauled the
sheet in, or whatever people do on sailboats. Even
in the shadows, Sandy can make out his bronzed,
hairless chest and bulging arm muscles. He's grinning into the camera, revealing a face that she
instantly decides is honest, intelligent, and
friendly.

She anxiously turns back to the letter.

*. . . so that you'll recognize me when we meet—which,
I'm hoping, will be soon. However, I'm on call at the
hospital every weekend until mid-February. I've taken
the liberty of assuming you'll agree to spend a romantic weekend with me on Tide Island, where I have a
weekend house. Since I realize you may be hesitant
about staying with a stranger, I've arranged accommodations for you at the Bramble Rose Inn. Your
expenses will, of course, be paid entirely by me. I'm a
romantic at heart, and hope you'll agree that prolong-
ing our meeting until Valentine's Day weekend will
add to the enchantment of what may become a lasting
relationship. The innkeeper of the Bramble Rose, Jasper
Hammel, has agreed to act as our liaison. You can call*

*him at (508) 555-1493, to accept this invitation. I'll
look forward to our meeting, Sandra.*

Fondly,
Ethan Thoreau

Ethan Thoreau?
Sandy shakes her head and tosses the letter onto
the passenger's seat beside her.

This has to be a fake . . . some nut who gets his
jollies by answering ads and propositioning strange
women.

Grimly, she puts on her seat belt and shifts the
car into Drive. As she pulls out onto the street and
turns toward home, she mentally runs through his
letter again.

He sounds too good to be true, a gorgeous MD
with a name like Ethan Thoreau. Like a character
in one of those category romance novels Sandy
likes to read.

A romantic Valentine's Day weekend on an island.

Yeah, right.

Bramble Rose Inn—the place probably doesn't
even exist.

Call the innkeeper.

Sure. And find out that this whole thing is a stupid trick.

Well, she should have known that sooner or
later, some nut case was going to answer her ad.
Her friend Theresa, a veteran of the singles classifieds, warned her that would happen.

Still, what if there's a chance that this guy is for
real? After all, he did send a picture. . . .

A doctor.

A gorgeous, muscular doctor.

A gorgeous, muscular doctor with a thriving practice and a weekend house on Tide Island.

Sandy chews her lower lip thoughtfully as she rounds the corner from High onto Webster Street.

Well, what if he is for real?

Things like this happen, don't they? Sure they do. She recalls reading, a few years back, about some lonely bachelor who had rented a billboard, advertised for a wife, and proposed to one of the women who responded before they ever met in person.

This guy—this Ethan Thoreau—didn't propose. All he'd done was invite Sandy to meet him. He doesn't even expect her to stay with him.

The Bramble Rose Inn. Jasper Hammel.

Hmm.

Sandy slows the car as she approaches the two-story raised cape where she lives with her parents. The house is pale green, the color of iceberg lettuce, and it desperately needs a paint job.

A grime-covered, white panel truck bearing the name *Cavelli & Sons, Plumbing and Heating Contractors* sits in the short driveway. Sandy parks the Chevy behind it, inwardly groaning. Now that she's on break from college, she likes to beat her father home at night so that she doesn't have to get up early to move her car out of the way when he leaves in the mornings.

She grabs her purse from the seat beside her. Then she thoughtfully picks up Ethan Thoreau's letter and photograph.

"So what's the deal?" she asks, and sighs, her breath coming out in a milky puff of frost. "Are you real, or not?"

Sighing, she puts the letter into her purse with the rest of them. Then she steps out onto the slippery driveway and makes her way along the frozen walk to the house.

In the kitchen, Angie Cavelli is stirring a pot of sauce on the stove. The front of her yellow sweatshirt is splashed with greasy tomato-colored dots.

"Hi, Ma," Sandy says, closing the door behind her and stamping her feet on the faded welcome mat by the door.

"You're late," her mother observes, then takes a taste from the spoon. "I thought you got off at four-thirty."

"I did. I had to run an errand afterward." Sandy shrugs out of her coat and walks across the worn linoleum.

"Your father's already at the table. He wants to eat."

Sandy fights back the urge to say, *then let him eat.*

After twenty-five years of living in this house, she should know better than to consider questioning her father's rule. If you're living in his house, when it's five o'clock, you sit down at the dining room table and you eat. Everyone. Together.

Sandy walks toward the hallway off the kitchen, carrying her purse.

"Ah-ah-ah—where are you going?" her mother calls.

"I just want to change my clothes. I'll be right back down for supper, Ma. Two minutes."

"Two minutes," her mother echoes in a warning voice. She's already at the sink, dumping a steaming kettle of cooked pasta into the battered stainless steel strainer.

In her room, Sandy kicks off her shoes and takes the letter out of her purse again.

She stares at it.

If she doesn't call this Bramble Rose Inn place, she'll probably always wonder whether she passed up the chance to meet a handsome, wealthy doctor.

If she calls, she might find out that he actually has made paid reservations for her. That he really does exist.

Sandy pauses for another minute, thinking it over.

Then she takes the letter across the hall to her parents' room. Unlike the rest of the house— including her own room—which holds an accumulation of several decades of clutter, Angie and Tony's bedroom is spare. The walls are empty except for the crucifix hanging over the bed, and the only other furniture is a dresser and the wobbly bedside table. On that sits the upstairs telephone extension.

Sandy perches carefully on the edge of the old white chenille spread, lifts the receiver, and starts dialing.

Liza Danning hates Monday nights.

Especially rainy, slushy Monday nights in early January, when you can't get a cab and the only way of getting from the office on West Fortieth Street to your apartment on the Upper East Side is the subway. That, or a bus . . . and the glass shelters at the stops are so jammed that waiting for a bus that isn't overcrowded to finally roll by would mean standing in the rain. Which wouldn't be so bad if she had an umbrella.

And she doesn't.

She'd left for work this morning from Alex's place, where she'd spent the night. And since the sun had been shining brightly when they rolled out of bed, borrowing an umbrella from him, just in case, hadn't occurred to her. Besides, she'd been too busy dodging his efforts to pin her down for next weekend.

"I don't know, Alex," she'd said, avoiding his searching gaze as she slipped into her navy Burberry trench—a gift from Lawrence, an old lover—and tied the belt snugly around her waist. She'd checked her reflection in the floor-to-ceiling mirror in his foyer and tucked a few stray strands of silky blond hair back into the chignon at the back of her neck. "I think I have plans."

"What plans?"

She'd shrugged. "I'm not sure."

"You think you have plans, but you're not sure what they are," he'd said flatly.

So she'd told him. She'd had no choice. "Look—" She bent to pick up her burgundy Coach briefcase. "I like you. Last night was great. So was Saturday. And Friday. But I'm not ready for an every-weekend thing, okay?"

He'd stared at her, the blue eyes she'd found so captivating on Friday night now icy and hard. "Fine," he'd said, picking up his own Coach briefcase—black leather—and Burberry trench, also black.

Then they'd walked to the elevator, ridden the fifty-three stories down to the lobby in silence, and stepped out into the brisk Manhattan morning. Alex had asked the doorman to hail them separate cabs, even though his law office was just two blocks from the publishing house where she was an editor.

The doorman had blown his whistle and immediately flagged a passing cab. Alex stuffed some bills into his hand, then leaned over to again narrow that ice-blue gaze at Liza as she settled into the back seat.

"West Fortieth at Sixth," she'd said to the driver. Then, to Alex, "Call me."

"Right," he'd replied, and she knew he wouldn't.

She'd shrugged as the cab pulled away from the curb. So he'd expected more out of their little tryst than she had. He'd get over it.

She hesitates on the street in front of her office building, trying to talk herself into taking the subway. But it will mean walking the two and a half blocks to the station near the library on Forty-second Street. Then she'll have to take the Seven train one stop to Grand Central and wait for the uptown local. That will take forever.

She shakes her head decisively and checks the Movado on her left wrist. Six-fifteen. If she goes back upstairs and works until seven-thirty, she can take a company car home. The publishing house pays her peanuts and doesn't offer many perks besides free car service for employees who work late. But it's the least they can do. After all, most of the editors are females, and Manhattan's streets are increasingly dangerous after dark.

Liza walks briskly back into the lobby.

Carmine, the night guard, looks her over appre-ciatively, as he always does. At least this time, he doesn't tell her how much she resembles Sharon Stone, or ask her if she's ever considered becoming an actress.

"Forget something?" he asks, his eyes on her breasts even though she is bundled into her trench coat.

"Yes," she replies shortly, walking past him toward the elevator bank, conscious of the hollow, tapping noise her heels make on the tile floor.

An elevator is just arriving, and she steps aside to let the full load of passengers step off.

"Liza, what's up? I thought you'd left," says a petite brunette, emerging from the crowd.

Liza vaguely recognizes her as one of the new editorial assistants who started right before Christmas. The girl is one of those bubbly, fresh-from-the-Ivy-League types. The kind who can afford to take an entry-level job in publishing because her rich daddy pays the rent on her Upper East Side studio.

"I have to go back up. I forgot something," Liza tells her briefly.

"Oh, well, have a good night. See you tomorrow," the girl says cheerfully, fastening the top button of her soft wool coat.

Liza recognizes the expensive lines, rich coral color, and ornate gold buttons. She'd reached for that coat in Saks a few months ago. The price tag was over a thousand dollars.

She'd put it back.

"See you," she echoes, and strides onto the elevator. She rides alone up to the sixth floor and steps into the deserted reception area of Xavier House, Ltd.

She fishes in her pocket for her car key and flashes it in front of the electronic panel beside the double glass doors behind the receptionist's desk. There is a click, and she pushes the door open.

Liza walks swiftly down the dimly lit hall, past a janitor's cart parked in front of one of the offices. She can hear a cleaning lady running a vacuum in another part of the floor. She turns a corner and heads down the short corridor toward her own office. The other editors who share this area are either long gone or behind closed doors, probably catching up on manuscript reading after taking the holidays off.

Liza unlocks the door marked LIZA DANNING and steps inside. She slips her coat over the hanger waiting on a hook behind the door, then smooths her cashmere sweater and sighs. She isn't in the mood for reading, although she *should* try to make a dent in the pile of manuscripts that sit waiting on her credenza.

You could open the mail, she tells herself, glancing at the stack in her IN box. She hadn't gotten to it today. Or Friday either, for that matter.

She sits at her desk and reaches for the first manila envelope, slitting the flap with the jewel-handled letter opener that had been a gift from Douglas. Or was it Reed? She can't remember anymore. And it doesn't matter, anyway. He's long gone, whoever he was. Like the others.

She removes a sheaf of papers from the envelope and scans the top sheet. It's a painstaking cover letter, composed on an ancient typewriter whose vowels are filled in with smudges. Some anxious would-be writer, a midwestern housewife, describes the enclosed first chapter and outline of a historical romance novel about a pirate hero and an Indian princess heroine. The woman has spelled desire *d-e-z-i-r-e.*

Liza tosses the letter into the wastepaper basket and reaches into her top drawer for the packet of preprinted rejections letters she keeps there. She removes one and slips it under the paper clip holding the partial manuscript together. She tucks the whole stack into the self-addressed, stamped envelope the woman has included, seals it, and tosses it into her OUT basket. Then she reaches for the next envelope.

Fifteen minutes later, the stack in her IN box has dwindled and her OUT basket is overflowing. She has worked her way through all the large packages and is now starting on the letters in their white legal-sized envelopes.

She glances idly at the return address on this first one.

What she sees makes her sit up and do a double take.

D.M. Yates, P.O. Box 57, Tide Island, MA.

D.M. Yates—David Mitchell Yates, reclusive best-selling author? She recalls that the man has a home on some New England coastal island.

Liza grabs the letter opener and hurriedly slits the envelope open. She unfolds the single sheet of creamy white stationery and notices that a train ticket is attached to the top with a paper clip. Amtrak. Penn Station to Westwood, Rhode Island. First Class.

Intrigued, she skips past the formal heading to the body of the letter.

Dear Ms. Danning:

As you may or may not be aware, I am the author of several best-selling spy novels released by Best & Rawson, a New York City publishing house, over the past ten years. Since my editor, Henry Malcolm, retired last month, I have been searching for a new home for my novels. Would you be interested in meeting with me to discuss the possibilities of a deal with Xavier House, Ltd.? I have enclosed a round-trip train ticket to Westwood, Rhode Island, for the second weekend in February. You will be met by a limousine that will transport you to the dock in Crosswinds Bay, where you will board the ferry to Tide Island. I have arranged for you to stay at the Bramble Rose Inn. I will, of course, pay all expenses for your journey. I will be traveling abroad for the next several weeks. To confirm, please contact the innkeeper, Jasper Hammel, at (508) 555-1493. It is imperative that you keep this meeting confidential. I'll look forward to meeting with you.

Sincerely,
David Michael Yates

Liza is electrified.

David Michael Yates.

The man is gold.

He's also an eccentric recluse whose face has reportedly never been seen by the world at large. The jackets of his books bear no photograph; not even a biography. Over the years, it has been rumored that David Michael Yates is actually a pseudonym for a high-ranking government official; that he's really a woman; that he had his face blown off in Vietnam.

Just last week, the cover story in *Publisher's Weekly*

chronicled the retirement of Yates's longtime editor and the bitter contract battle that resulted in the severed deal between the author and Best & Rawson. According to the article, Yates was about to depart for Europe to research his newest novel and hadn't yet decided upon a publisher, although several of the most prestigious houses were courting him.

How on earth did he decide to approach me, of all people? Liza wonders.

True, she's been getting some PW press herself lately. She recently put together a well-publicized nonfiction deal with an elusive, scandal-ridden senator for a tell-all book. Of course, the powers-that-be at Xavier aren't aware of just how Liza had managed to persuade the man.

And she'll never tell.

Eagerly, she reaches for the phone and begins to dial the number for the Bramble Rose Inn.

Jennie Towne hears blasting music—an old Springsteen song—the moment she steps into the first-floor vestibule of the restored Back Bay town house. She rolls her eyes and hurries toward the closed white-painted door ahead, which bears a nailed-on, dark green *1*.

She transfers the stack of mail from her right hand to her left, then fits her key into the lock and turns it. It sticks a little, as always, and she tugs.

Finally the door opens, and she steps into the apartment. She stomps her snowy boots on the rug and deposits the mail on the small piecrust table that once sat beside her grandparents' front door in the old house in Quincy.

"Laura?" she calls, walking straight to the stereo on the wall unit across the living room. She lowers the volume to practically nothing and promptly hears a disgruntled "Hey!" from the other room.

"It was too loud," she tells her sister, who appears in the doorway within seconds.

"Oh, please." Laura tosses her head. Her ultra-short cap of glossy black hair doesn't even stir.

"Come on, Laura, do you want Mrs. Willensky down here again, threatening to call the landlord?"

Laura shrugs. She says, "Keegan called."

"What did he want?" Jennie looks up from tugging off her boots.

"What do you think? To talk to you. He said he'd tried you at the shop but you'd already left. He wants you to call him. He's on the overnight shift and he's leaving for the precinct at six-thirty."

Jennie just nods.

"You going to call him back?"

"No."

"Oh, come on, Jen, cut the guy a break. He sounded so pathetic. I mean, he didn't *say* anything specific, but I could tell the guy's going crazy without you."

She tries to ignore the pang that jabs into her at the thought of Keegan hurting. "Laura, I can't. I have to make a clean break. Otherwise we'll keep going back and forth forever."

"I see what you mean," her sister says dryly, folding her arms and fixing Jennie with a steady look. "You love him; he loves you; you both love kids and dogs and the Red Sox and antiques and the ocean. . . . It'll never work."

"Laura—"

"I mean, Jen, I know what your problem is, and you have to get over it. It's been three years since—"

"I don't want to talk about that," Jennie effectively cuts her off, fixing her with a resolute stare.

Laura sighs and transfers her gaze to the stack of mail Jennie dumped on the table by the door. "Anything good come for me?" she asks hopefully. "Like an airmail letter?"

Her new boyfriend, Shawn, is spending a month in Japan on business. She's been moping ever since he left right after New Year's.

Jennie shrugs. "I didn't look."

She unbuttons her winter coat and hangs it in the closet while Laura flips through the stack of mail.

Bill, bill, bill, b—hey, what's this?" she hears her sister say.

She glances up. Laura's holding an oblong white envelope.

"A letter from Shawn?" Jennie asks, running a hand over her own shiny black hair, exactly the same shade and texture as Laura's, except that her hangs well past her shoulders. And right now, it's full of static, annoying her.

I should just get it chopped off, like Laura did, she tells herself, even as she hears Keegan's voice echoing inside her head. *I love your hair long, Jen. Don't ever cut it.*

"No, this isn't from Shawn. The return address is

a post office box on Tide Island," Laura is saying with a frown. "I don't know anyone there."

"Well, open it."

"I'm afraid to."

Jennie knows what she's thinking. Laura's ex-husband, Brian, pursued her relentlessly after their marriage ended last spring. Her sister had finally been forced to get a restraining order against him. He'd dropped out of sight right after that, presumably returning to Cape Cod, where his parents still live.

Jennie's aware that her sister is still afraid he'll resurface and start bothering her again. Brian is a deceptively mild-mannered guy; but when he's drunk, he's a monster. Jennie witnessed his violent, alcohol-induced temper on more than one occasion and had suspected he was abusing Laura long before her sister ever admitted it.

"Don't worry," she tells Laura now, watching her carefully. "It's probably just some travel brochure, or a charity asking for money. And if it's not—if it *is* from Brian—you can take it straight to the police."

"I know." Laura, her face taut, opens the envelope carefully and withdraws a sheet of white paper.

Jennie watches her sister's features, identical to her own except for a small scar by her left eye— courtesy of her ex-husband—gradually relax over the next few seconds.

"What? What is it?" she asks, hurrying across the room and peering over Laura's shoulder at the letter.

"I can't believe it. I mean, I never win anything," Laura says, handing her the letter. "Read this."

Jennie takes it, noticing that the stationery is heavy and expensive. There is a delicate pen-and-ink drawing of a charming house on the top. The imprint on the stationery reads *Bramble Rose Inn, Box 57, Tide Island MA.* Jennie scans the bold type.

Dear Ms. Towne:

It is our pleasure to inform you that you have won the grand prize in the annual New England Children's Leukemia Society fund-raising sweepstakes. You are hereby entitled to an all-expenses-paid solo visit to Tide Island on the second weekend in February. The prize includes three-nights, four-days deluxe accommodations at the Bramble Rose Inn, all meals, and round-trip transportation on the Crosswinds Bay ferry. Please confirm with me at (508) 555-1493, upon receipt of this letter.

Sincerely,
Jasper Hammel
Innkeeper

Jennie lowers the letter and looks at Laura. "This sounds pretty good," she says cautiously.

"It *would* be, if it were any other weekend. Shawn's coming home that Saturday in time for Valentine's Day. I already arranged my hours at work so that I could take off and be with him. I can't go."

"Maybe you can switch to another weekend," Jennie suggests. "Then you and Shawn can both go."

Laura shakes her head. "See that small print on

the bottom? It says this offer is only good for that particular weekend. And I remember buying the sweepstakes ticket right before Christmas. The man who sold it to me said the prize was for *one* person, no guests. Sort of a pamper-yourself, get-away-from-it-all thing."

"I never heard of the New England Children's Leukemia Society," Jennie comments, scanning the small print.

"Neither did I. But he told me it's been around for a while. Actually, I think I've seen him before—he looked familiar. He's probably been collecting for charity before, and I'll bet I ducked him. If I hadn't just gotten paid and been feeling rich that day, I probably wouldn't even have bought the ticket from him. Although, I may have if I knew what it was for," she adds soberly.

Of course Laura would never refuse to contribute to that particular charity. Jennie wouldn't either. Their younger sister, Melanie, had died of leukemia fifteen years ago.

Jennie glances again at the letter. "Where'd you buy the sweepstakes ticket, Laura?"

"In the parking lot at Stop and Shop. Don't worry, Jen. It was legit."

"I didn't say it wasn't," Jennie says.

"But you're thinking that Brian might have something to do with this, aren't you? That it's some sort of set-up to lure me to this island so that he could convince me to give him another chance. Right?"

Jennie meets her sister's lilac-colored eyes guiltily. "The thought did cross my mind."

"Trust me. Brian's not this clever. Can you see

him going through all the effort of making up a fake charity, hiring some stranger to persuade me to buy a ticket, and then somehow getting his hands on the stationery for this Bramble Rose place and forging a letter from an innkeeper?"

Jennie grins. "You're right. He couldn't do that in a million years." She glances down at the drawing of the inn again. "Too bad you can't go. It looks really cozy."

"Why don't *you* go instead, Jen?" Laura asks suddenly.

"Didn't you read the rest of the small print? It says the prize can't be transferred."

"So? We're identical twins. When was the last time we switched places?" Laura asks with a grin.

Jennie smiles. "I thought we agreed never to do that again after that time in high school."

Her sister's boyfriend hadn't been very appreciative to discover that Laura had sent Jennie on a date with him while she went out with someone else. Of course, he probably wouldn't have figured it out if Jennie hadn't done such an unconvincing job of faking a sudden stomachache so she wouldn't have to have sex with him.

Laura had neglected to mention to her sister that they'd been sleeping together for over a year and he might expect it.

"Jen," Laura says, "this isn't high school. Take my driver's license as ID and go to the island. You can spend some time drawing and painting, or whatever. The place is really artsy. You know, that's why they call it Tie-Dye Land."

"Huh?"

"Tide Island—Tie-Dye Land. That's what everyone calls the place. Didn't you ever hear that before?"

"Nope."

"Figures. Sometimes, Jen, you're in a total fog," Laura says, shaking her head. "Anyway, a lot of artists hang out there in the summers. You know—long-haired types who wear grungy tie-dye outfits and sit around painting the scenery all day."

Hmm. The idea of bringing her art supplies to a picturesque island is tempting to Jennie. She's been too busy lately to spend any time on her hobby. Still . . .

"You have short hair in the picture on your license. Mine's long," she points out to Laura.

"So? I got it renewed over a year ago. I could have grown my hair out. Go ahead, Jen. You need to get away after all this craziness with Keegan."

Keegan. She winces.

Oh, God. Will she ever be able to hear his name and not react this way?

Jennie glances again at the drawing of the inn. It shows an old-fashioned, scallop-shingled house complete with plenty of gables and a picket fence with a kitten perched demurely on the gatepost. It appears to be a dreamy, quaint little place where you can curl up with a sketch pad and a mug of tea and forget about the painful end of a relationship.

"Maybe you're right," she tells Laura slowly.

"I *am* right." Her sister bounces the few short steps to the telephone on a nearby table. She picks up the receiver and dangles it from her fingers, looking expectantly at Jennie. "Read off the phone

number on the letter. I'll dial. And don't forget—
you're Laura."

Jennie sighs. "Right. I'm Laura." She looks down
at the letter and starts reading the number aloud.

The ferry isn't yet a far-off speck on the dusky horizon, but he knows it's there, cutting toward Tide Island through the choppy gray waters off the New England coast. Complete darkness will fall well before it docks at the landing down the road to release its load of weekend passengers.

In summer, the Friday-night ferry is always crowded with commuting husbands and vacationing families, college students who work as weekend waiters or lifeguards, couples in love, sticky-faced children.

But now, in the shortest month of the year, when winter is at its bleakest and the island offers nothing but silent, chilly isolation, there won't be many people on board. Just the few hardy nature-loving souls willing to brave the elements; perhaps some island-dwellers returning with groceries from the mainland; maybe a handful of summer house owners coming out to inspect the damage December's nor'easter inflicted upon their property.

That's about it.

Except for *them*.

He knows they're on board—all three of them. Still strangers to each other, but not to him.

He has been watching them for so long now.

Waiting.

A quiver of anticipation passes over him and he cautions himself to relax. He has to maintain control at all times. He can't afford to take any risks at this point, just when it's all coming together at last.

After all these years . . .

Soon enough, he assures himself. *It won't be long now.*

He casts his gaze back out over the water, giddy with excitement. He'd heard on the radio a little while ago that there's a growing likelihood this weekend might be stormy.

Wouldn't that be perfect?

Even at this moment, they're probably enjoying the brisk twilight ride. He pictures them scattered in different corners of the deck or cabin, lost in their own thoughts, thinking about the weekend ahead, filled with excited expectations.

They aren't the only ones who are looking forward to it.

His features twist with mirth, and he stifles a giggle.

Very, very soon.

He lets the filmy lace curtain drop back into place and turns away from the window.

He still has a lot to do before they arrive.

DISCARD